She surrendered to his kiss...

His hard mouth pressed to hers, and his body overpowered her. Though she tried to twist free she could not. Against her will, despite every effort to fight her own passion, the heat of his searing mouth and the impact of his hard body clamped against hers began to fuel her reaction. She tried to resist him, tried to quell her pounding heart and fluttering senses, but her will power drained with each passing second, and she felt herself swirling, dipping, dissolving into a whirlwind of heady desire. Of its own accord, her traitorous body sprang into response, straining against Stephen with shameless yearning. Her soft mouth gave way, welcoming him, as she whispered a moan of pleasure...

Moonlit Obsession

Jill Gregory

A JOVE BOOK

MOONLIT OBSESSION

A Jove Book/published by arrangement with
the author

PRINTING HISTORY
Jove trade paperback edition/May 1986

ISBN: 0-515-08585-5

Jove Books are published by The Berkley Publishing Group,
200 Madison Avenue, New York, N.Y. 10016.
The words "A JOVE BOOK" and the "J" with sunburst
are trademarks belonging to Jove Publications, Inc.

PRINTED IN THE UNITED STATES OF AMERICA

To my father, with love

MOONLIT OBSESSION

ONE

March
London, 1806

ANEMONE CARSTAIRS lifted the yellow crepe ball gown from the wardrobe and carried it carefully to the scantily clad girl before the dressing mirror. "Take care of the sequins," she warned, as she helped Cecilia Pelham slip into the exquisite gown. Layers of diaphanous material billowed about Cecilia's tall, statuesque figure as Anemone shook the gown into place. "There, my lady. It is quite splendid." She stood back a moment to enable the chestnut-haired girl to see the effect of the pale yellow ball gown adorned in glittering sequins as it hugged her voluptuous form. The gown was daringly low-cut, elegant, and delicate as lace. Cecilia, with her dark sable hair and fawn's eyes, looked particularly beautiful in it. But a crack of thunder from outside the window brought a groan to the girl's petulantly shaped lips.

"A storm? Oh, heavens, no, it cannot storm! This gown will be ruined by the mud puddles." Cecilia stamped her satin-slippered foot. "And anyway, I'm not at all certain that I like the way it fits. I prefer it to be a trifle more

1

snug here, in the waist. "Letty!" she snapped, her brown eyes narrow in the mirror. "Fetch the green satin one, the one with the pearl buttons and the velvet sash. Hurry, girl, I'm already late! Anthony will be in a rage. Well, let him rage, then." She tossed her head, sending the dark mane of hair flying about her narrow shoulders. "He'd much rather be off to his horrid gaming club, or a cock-fight, I daresay, but it is his duty to escort me to Almack's tonight. He's my brother, after all, and it will do him good to be in polite company for a change." She whirled in exasperation, her hands on her hips, making no effort to remove the crepe gown without her abigail's assistance. "Letty, do be quick! Find my pearls! And the green velvet reticule! I must get to Almack's before the doors close for the night!"

Anemone obeyed, hiding the impatience that chafed within her at these delays. She wanted Cecilia Pelham out of the house—quickly. But the damned girl kept changing her gown, changing her hair, debating endlessly which jewels to wear, which shawl to bring, whether or not her cheeks needed a tinge, just a tinge, of rouge to enhance their porcelain beauty. Anemone bore the green satin gown to her, encouraged her into admiring it, tied the velvet sash into an excellent bow. Quickly, she swept Cecilia's hair into a coif that left sausage curls dangling prettily about her somewhat narrow face, and she clasped the pearl necklace into place. At last, Cecilia stood before the mirror, her lower lip pushed outward in a pout.

"Welllll . . . ," she debated, but Anemone cut in before she could change her mind a final time.

"My lady, the hour is late. Is that not your brother calling you from the hall below?" Anemone smiled encouragingly as she draped the silken strings of the green reticule over Cecilia's wrist. "The company at Almack's will be atwitter over your looks this evening, miss. I have never seen you appear to better advantage."

"Oh, very well. I suppose you're right." Cecilia took

one last, speculative look in the ornate mirror, then turned with a flounce toward the door. "I expect to be quite late this evening, Letty," she called carelessly over her shoulder. "Wait up until my return. You can press my blue morning-dress, and mend the spangled shawl. And don't forget to sew the hem on my pelisse. I caught it on the carriage yesterday, and it looks simply dreadful! I'll want it for tomorrow, so mind you get it done!"

With these words, Cecilia swept out the door and shut it commandingly behind her. Anemone found herself alone in the room. The lamp-lit, rose pink bedroom was a shambles, with garments, jewels, and ribbons strewn upon the bed, the French marble dressing table littered with bottles and combs and gloves, the elegant carved chair draped by a discarded lace shawl, and the floor covered with an array of evening slippers Lady Pelham had abandoned with her changes of gown. Anemone gritted her teeth in disgust, wishing she could strangle her odious "mistress." When she had accepted this assignment, she had anticipated danger and the need for the utmost skill and caution, but she had never fully realized that she would have to put up with a spoiled and arrogant young woman's wholly self-centered demands. If this was any indication of the true life of an abigail, Anemone could only be thankful that her role of Letty Thane, ladies maid, was assumed, and for a most temporary length of time, at that. She could never have endured such an existence, especially under the selfish and despotic rule of a girl like Cecilia. Anemone herself, a soldier's daughter, had never known the luxuries of ladies maids, butlers, and cooks, but after sharing the servants' wing with the other employees of this fashionable London household, she found herself pitying those forced to eke out a living catering to the whims of the aristocracy. Personally, she much preferred a soldier's life, traveling from camp to camp, from battlefield to battlefield, answering the call of duty and valor rather than the call of a flighty young woman for her morning chocolate. She went to the window and peered around the pink silk curtains as the Pelham carriage clattered away across the cobblestones of Brook Street. At last, they were gone. Lord Pelham, Cecilia's father, had left hours ago to dine at his club and then, no doubt, spend the evening playing hazard. His son, Anthony, and Cecilia would be at Almack's well into the night. She was now free to keep her assignation, one which would not wait. It was already near nine o'clock, she realized, her stomach muscles tightening. Oliver would be pacing the floor, and tugging impatiently at the tips of his well-clipped mustache. She had better hurry.

She left Cecilia's bedroom in disarray, dreading the task of tidying it when she returned, and fairly flew down the dimly lit hall to the servants' wing of the house. It took her only a minute to fetch the blue wool cloak from her tiny bedroom at the top of the stairs and slip it on over the shoulders of her high-necked cambric dress. She put up the hood, hiding the little that showed of her fair hair, which was kept pinned in a demure knot at her nape. The cascading, waist-length ash blond curls which belonged to Anemone would not have been at all suitable for Letty Thane. Anemone smiled to herself as she ran lightly down the servants' stairway and let herself out the back door into the misty night. Her clear, gray eyes were alive with excitement and a sense of anticipation. Oliver would be pleased with her report. After three weeks of waiting and watching, she was all but certain that the Earl, Lord Edward Pelham, was indeed a paid informant to the French, a traitor to his country and his heritage.

With the assurance of one who has trod a particular path many times, Anemone threaded her way through the rain-spattered London streets, past the fashionable brick houses, past elegant Hyde Park, skirting the tree-lined squares, the rolling carriages, the lampposts whose light cast a silvery glow upon the wet gray mist of the

March night. At length she hailed a hackney and traveled in that manner to the heart of the city's business district. When she alighted and paid the driver, she glanced about to be certain no one had followed her. Then she set off at a brisk pace once more, hurrying the few remaining blocks to the harbor.

Her destination was a seedy, two-story brick tavern that faced onto the docks. A lettered sign hung from the roof proclaiming: *The Stone Bull—Where Good Cheer and Good Ale Meet.* She entered without hesitation, paying no heed to the shouting, drunken men clustered in the garishly lit gambling saloon. Walking straight to the narrow, uncarpeted stairway, she gave only a passing nod to the innkeeper behind the serving bar.

This stolid man caught her eye as she put her foot on the first step. He shook his head briefly, then jerked his thumb upward, in the direction of the landing above. Anemone frowned, nodded, and hurried up the stairs, wondering what was about. The innkeeper had signaled her that Oliver was not there, yet had urged her to go up. What was going on? She had a report to file, an important one. This was the designated time. Where was Oliver?

She left the tumult of the gambling den below for the relative peace of the upper hall and went without hesitation to the first door on her right. After knocking three short raps, she entered, not knowing quite what to expect. Oliver, as the innkeeper had indicated, was not there. Instead, a thin young man sat behind the scarred teakwood desk. His long fingers drummed upon the top of it. Spectacles sat upon his high-bridged nose; reddish hair was slicked down upon a pointed head; his ears protruded.

"Miss Carstairs? You're late." He had a high, peevish voice. His blue eyes snapped at her from behind the spectacles. "Come in, and close the door. I don't have all night."

Anemone surveyed him in her direct manner. "Who are you?" she asked coolly, as the door clicked shut behind her. "You are not . . . the gentleman I came to meet."

"Oliver was called away by the Foreign Minister," the young man explained impatiently. He stood and extended his hand. "I'm his assistant—Donald Bakersfield."

Anemone gripped his soft, white hand, and all the while her eyes never left his face. "Verification, please, Mr. Bakersfield."

"What?" The young man gaped at her. He looked like a skinny young banker in his dark, rumpled clothes and tightly knotted cravat. "What are you talking about?"

"We've never met," she explained calmly. "I don't know if you are indeed the person you claim to be. I am asking that you prove it."

"How the devil . . . ," he began explosively, but Anemone cut him off.

"The code, Mr. Bakersfield. The password, if you please."

"Oh." He ran a hand through his hair. "Of course." He spoke in a singsong tone. "Flutes and elephants—turbans, too. I fancy all can be seen in India, don't you? Though of course, in the matter of ports, I prefer Malta to Bombay."

They stared at one another for a moment after this absurd speech. Then Anemone nodded. "Very well, Mr. Bakersfield. Now, tell me, why on earth didn't Oliver warn me that he could not keep our assignation tonight? It is a ridiculous waste of my time."

Donald Bakersfield invited her to be seated, then he himself took his place again behind the battered old desk covered by sheafs of papers and inkpads and maps. He pinned his gaze to the slender young woman before him and was filled against his expectations with a grudging respect. He was a prim and most proper young man, and he saw no place whatsoever in the military branch of the government for a woman, yet he had to admit that Anemone Carstairs had surprised him. He had heard of her, of course. The daughter of Thomas Carstairs, one of England's master intelligence officers for well over thirty years. Keen as a whip, she was, or so Oliver had told him. But Donald wished he was dealing with her father instead. Too bad the old fellow was gone, killed on assignment in Spain some four months ago in an accident of some sort. The girl, a slip of a thing no more than twenty-one years old, had stepped right into his shoes. Oh, Oliver claimed she was perfectly suited for the job. Thomas Carstairs had trained her, hadn't he? She had traipsed all over the world with him from the time she was a child, when her mother had died of smallpox. They had followed the drum when Thomas had been an officer in the army, and she had frequently traveled with him on diplomatic missions which had actually involved some brilliant pieces of espionage. But now, to be working on her own, alone in the world of spies and informants? Donald Bakersfield thoroughly disapproved. A woman belonged in a parlor, pouring tea or playing the pianoforte. She had no place near a battlefield, or in the secret dens of enemy agents. Still, he had to acknowledge that Anemone Carstairs appeared eminently capable—for a woman. She had certainly been cautious where he was concerned just now. Obviously, she was intelligent. But how effective was she? Oliver had told him that her first few assignments had gone well, but this Pelham case was crucial. If they could establish that the Earl was truly selling secrets to French and American agents, they could take advantage of this knowledge by planting misleading information for him to pass on. It could be most useful in disrupting the all-too-efficient French intelligence system on which Napoleon relied. Bakersfield, an ambitious and patriotic young man, found himself suddenly eager for her report. If she indeed had found proof of Pelham's betrayal, it would be a coup for him to pass the information on to Oliver. He leaned forward. "Miss Carstairs, I regret that Oliver had no time to warn you he could not keep the assignation, but be assured that I am prepared to hear your report and pass it on to him when he returns. Your time has not been wasted. You may share your information with me in Oliver's stead."

Anemone pushed back her hood. "I'm afraid I cannot do that, Mr. Bakersfield." Her slim eyebrows rose questioningly. "Unless you have written instructions for me from Oliver that I should file my report with you?"

"Written instructions? No. But I am certain Oliver would have wanted you to tell me what you have discovered...."

"Did he tell you that? Did he instruct me to report to you?"

"No. No, he did not. But since I am taking his place in this office until his return four days hence, I assumed that..."

"Never make assumptions, Mr. Bakersfield." Anemone smiled at him as she stood and moved to the door. "One of the first things I learned from my father was that in the field of military and political intelligence, one must never violate a superior's orders unless those orders are specifically replaced by different ones. Oliver told me that I was to report only to him and to take orders only from him, unless he personally instructed me otherwise. I have no choice, you see, but to await his return. Do not fear, however. I can tell you that the situation with Lord Pelham is well under control, and by Oliver's return I will have in my possession additional details which can only add to my accounting."

Donald Bakersfield opened and closed his mouth several times, searching for a reply to this speech. At last, he stammered, "Well, yes, I suppose you're right. I expect you cannot violate orders, only ... well, dash it, I *am* his assistant, Miss Carstairs."

"Yes," Anemone responded with the utmost amiability. "And I am certain you are quite competent in that capacity. Oliver is certainly lucky to have you." She put up her hood again and opened the door. "Kindly tell Oliver I will see him on Monday, at our usual time. Good evening, Mr. Bakersfield."

She left him without a backward glance and made her way down the stairway and through the raucous tavern. It was a pity Oliver hadn't sent word canceling the meeting. She had been forced to give up a prime opportunity of searching through Lord Pelham's papers and belongings for evidence while the family was away, and in the end, it was all for nothing. She hadn't even been able to file her report, or to receive additional instructions. She sighed to herself, almost hearing the words her father would utter in this situation. *Blasted incompetents! How do they expect to win the war against Boney when the fools botch something as simple as this! I've seen it time and again, my girl. It's the small, daily mistakes and bunglings that add up to disaster. Organization, that's the key! Efficiency is the doorway to power!* She sidestepped a drunken lout who reeled into her path. *Oh, Papa,* she thought suddenly, achingly, and the sadness that filled her heart in that moment was almost unbearable. It went beyond grief, beyond even loneliness. She missed him with an intensity that stemmed from years of love, years of respect and companionship. *It was most inefficient of you to die before the war with France was won—before we had more time to work together, to spend together,* she thought accusingly. *How could you, of all people, allow such a thing to happen?* But there was no answer to her silent question, no balm for the pain of her loss. Anemone, reaching the door, pushed aside all thoughts of the past and braced herself for the chill, misty dampness of the night. Head bent against the streaming drizzle that now fell from a leaden sky, she hastened from the tavern out onto the wet cobblestones of the street.

Engrossed in her sorrow and the need to hurry back to the house on Brook Street, Anemone failed to perceive

the man rounding the corner as she rushed forward. The
streetlight had gone out. It was uncommonly dark, and
the rain splashing into the puddles concealed the sound
of approaching footsteps. She ran straight into the tall,
raven-haired man striding full upon her, and with a startled cry, she bore the brunt of the collision. It was like a
ship coming smack against a small boat. Anemone was
knocked backward upon the cobblestones, her breath
rushing from her body in a whistling gasp. The broad-
shouldered stranger stumbled and swore, then stared
down at the slight fallen figure before him.

"What the devil..." A deep, angry voice cracked the
night like a whip. Reaching down one long, hard-muscled
arm, the stranger hauled Anemone to her feet.

The girl was gasping for breath. She fought the pain
in her lungs, and in her backside, as she tried to collect
her reeling senses. She stared up into the dark, ruthlessly
handsome face of the stranger, as the rain pelted her
cheeks.

"Are you hurt? You ought to be!" the tall man said
harshly, his fingers enclosing her arm like steel bands.
"Didn't anyone ever teach you to watch where you're
going?"

"Let ... me go," Anemone managed to croak at last, as
the air returned to her lungs. Through the rain and the
shadows of the night she could make out only enough
of his features to see that he was angry. His devastatingly
blue eyes glinted coldly beneath the careless tumble of
black locks. He was very strong, she realized as she felt
the power of his hand on her arm. The many-caped greatcoat he wore across his wide shoulders obviously cloaked
a powerful physique. It infuriated her to realize that he
blamed her for this accident. *She* was the one who had
been knocked flat on her back. *She* was the one whose
cloak had been soaked by the puddles and splattered with
mud. *She* was the one who was owed an apology. She
shook free of his arm, and her small, gamine face came

alive with indignation. "If anyone should watch where he's going, it is you, you clumsy, dim-witted brute! How dare you speak to me so! You ought to beg my pardon, instead of adding your damned insults to the injury you've already inflicted! Now step aside so that I may be on my way without any further inconvenience."

To her dismay, the stranger suddenly threw back his head and laughed. He pulled her closer, up against the warmth of his heavy greatcoat. "So I ought to beg your pardon? More likely, I'll box your ears!" he grinned. "You're an impudent chit, aren't you?" He looked at her more closely. It was difficult to see much in the dim light, with the rain and the mist swirling all about them. The girl's hood hid most of her face and all of her hair, but he had an impression of youth and spirit and delicacy. This was no street harlot, despite her unladylike language. He'd rarely heard a female say "damn" before, and certainly not with such relish. Who the hell was she? "What is a child like you doing on the docks of London at this hour?" he mused, one hand reaching up as if to shift her hood in order to gain a better look at her face. "You ought to be home in bed."

Anemone struck aside his hand. "I would be in my bed, if some great clumsy oaf had not knocked me down on my way there!" she retorted. She wrenched free of his grasp, then gathered her sodden cloak about her with as much dignity as she could muster and started to move past the stranger. But again he grasped her arm, forcing her to stop before him.

Anemone felt a shudder of fear rush through her for the first time. Before, she had been merely annoyed by the mishap and the man's rudeness. Now, as she stared up into his hard, handsome face, a thrill of fear seized her. She caught her breath as his midnight blue eyes gleamed into her misty gray ones. She sensed something in him, something that made her nerve endings tauten. He was a dangerous man. He had a look about him, an aura. One of power, but also of recklessness. He was a man who did what he wished, and damned the consequences. Her heart began to pound in long, rapid beats. Her free hand fumbled in the pocket of her cloak for the pistol concealed there.

"I am sorry, brat." The words were a complete surprise. And so was the smile that suddenly curled his lips. Anemone's fingers went slack, and she forgot all about the pistol. He held her tightly against him, and the warmth of his tall, powerful frame penetrated her rain-soaked flesh. "I hope I didn't hurt you. And I'm sorry if I ruined your cloak. Here, take a silver coin for the purchase of a new one...."

"No. No, there's no need." Anemone shook herself, trying to clear the fog that had somehow penetrated her head. There was something powerfully magnetic about this man that made her want to stand here forever, his arm encircling her waist, his gaze holding hers. It was madness! She took a deep breath and dragged herself free of the moment's spell. "My cloak will be fine. Don't heed it. I...I'm sorry I snapped at you. Truly, the fault was mine. But now...I must go."

For a moment, he seemed about to say something more. Then, he released her abruptly. "Yes, go before I..." He chuckled suddenly. "Never mind. Go."

Anemone went. From behind her, in the darkness, she heard his deep, laughing voice. "Farewell, brat!" She grimaced and quickened her pace, nearly running toward the hackney standing beside a street lamp on the far side of the street. By the time she had given the driver her destination and settled herself in the dark, cramped coach, the tall, muscular stranger was gone. The street was deserted, save for the mist and the rain, and the lettered sign on the tavern which banged back and forth in the wind. A haunted feeling came over her, and for an instant she wondered if there really had been an encounter, if the handsome, blue-eyed rake had really existed. Then she laughed at herself. What silliness was this! Her cloak was wet and muddied, that was proof enough. And her backside ached from her fall. She withdrew her face from the window and tried to think about Oliver, and about her plans for learning more about Edward Pelham's treason. But the encounter with the stranger stayed in her mind. His image burned her brain, working strangely on the rhythm of her heartbeat. Anemone was amazed. She had never reacted so oddly to a meeting with any man. She knew men well, having grown up surrounded by soldiers. She was comfortable with them and accustomed to their ways. But this stranger had upset her equilibrium. She couldn't forget the way he had held her against him, the timbre of his deep voice, the glittering blue of his eyes which even the shadows of the fog could not dim. So engrossed was she in her reflections that she scarcely was aware of the drive or when the carriage halted. She paid the hackney driver absently and walked the rest of the distance to Brook Street without once glancing about to be certain she wasn't being followed. She didn't notice the man lurking in the shadow of the house on Brook Street until he jumped out at her as she reached the servants' door of the darkened mansion. Then it was too late. His thick hand covered her mouth, and a burly arm pulled her tight against him.

"Anemone Carstairs," he whispered hoarsely as she fought against his grip.

Anemone was astonished that he knew her name, but she didn't hesitate in her struggle to get free. She jabbed an elbow into her assailant's ribs and stamped down on his booted foot with all her might. She took advantage of his momentary pain and surprise by jumping free. Her hand dove inside her cloak for the pistol. She whirled to face him, and leveled the pistol at his brawny chest. He was a short though burly man, with a cap pulled low across his eyes. He had reddish brown side-whiskers and a pug nose. His woolen jacket was dark and ill-fitting.

He wore trousers and mud-splattered boots. She had never seen him before in her life.

"Who are you and what do you want with me?" she demanded in an imperious whisper that was only a little breathless. Her hands, holding the pistol, were quite steady.

The man in the cap stared at her a moment, then began to chuckle. "Aye, you're a fightin' one, ain't ye, miss?" he queried, vastly amused by something she failed to understand. "He warned me how it would be, but I didn't believe him. By the devil, he was right." He held up his hands before him in a gesture of innocence. "Now, miss, ye can just put away that pistol of yours because I've no mind to hurt ye. And I'm sorry if I scared ye a bit, but I meant no harm. I've a message for ye. An urgent one, and one ye'll be wantin' to receive."

"From whom is this message?" Anemone inquired quickly. She kept her voice lowered, and her eyes remained unwaveringly on the man's face. Despite his assurances, she made no move to put away the pistol.

"Aye, that ye'll see for yerself," he returned mysteriously. His hands slipped into the pocket of his woolen jacket and emerged with a sealed billet. "Here, miss. Take this, and I'll be off. My ship sails at dawn, and I've other business to tend to. Good luck to ye."

He pressed the billet into her hand, turned, and ambled off down the empty street, slipping like a ghost through the curtains of the mist until he disappeared in the direction of the park. Anemone watched him go, then glanced curiously at the missive in her hand. She turned it over, her fingers running lightly over the expensive stationery. She slipped the pistol back into her pocket and turned once more to the servants' door.

Alone in her tiny bedroom at the top of the stairway in the servants' wing, Anemone tossed off her wet cloak and sat down upon her cot. By the light of her bedside lamp, she broke open the seal of the billet and peered down at the single page of the letter. A series of numbers, letters, and odd symbols appeared in rows across the page. There were no words, no sentences. Just rows of letters, numbers, and symbols penned in flowing dark script upon the page.

Anemone stared in disbelief at the paper before her. She held it closer to the light and knelt before the lamp, studying it. Her hands began to shake. Her heart leaped, and she gave a gasp of pure, unbelieving joy.

The letter was written in a code she knew well, one which she had helped to invent. The system was one she had perfected with her father—their own secret, private code. It could mean only one thing.

Her father, Thomas Carstairs, was *alive*.

TWO

DAWN CREPT upon London with a cold, gray light. Anemone awoke to a gloomy sky and a faint, tapping rain still spattering her window. The shabby furnishings of her bedchamber, the patched curtains, the peeling green and yellow paper on the walls, the icy draft which circled the room and crept up through her woolen blanket to set her shivering in her cot all might have been expected to cast a pall over her spirits, but they did not. Her heart was light. Although she had slept little more than five hours, she felt refreshed and alive. She threw off her covers and got up from her bed with vigor, her mind already spinning with the various courses of action demanded of her.

The first thing she did, after wrapping the heavy wool blanket about her, was to seat herself in the single hard-backed chair the little room contained with the letter from her father in her hands. She read again the message she had decoded last night and felt once more the surge of joy, of wonder that had filled her then. A miracle had been granted her. Her father still lived. Last night, when she had sat alone in her room, the paper in her hands, she had hardly been able to take it in, to fully realize what it meant. She had simply stared at the coded message for a long time, tears of joy gathering in her eyes and slipping unheeded down her cheeks. At last, she had set the paper down, buried her face in her arms, and wept aloud, sobbing out all the pain and grief which had burdened her these past months. Wild elation had swept over her, and a deep, fervent gratitude, until at last her tears had turned to laughter. She wanted to see him, to hug him, to kiss that craggy face. And she wanted to throttle him for letting her think he was dead all this time! After a while, when she had gained control of herself once more, she had picked up the letter again. Where had he been all this time? Why, *why* had he let her think he was dead?

So then she had turned her mind to the symbols on the page and deciphered the message her father had sent her. *Emmy* it had begun, and the nickname Thomas Carstairs used for her had filled her with exultation. *You must come to the American city of New Orleans without delay. I need you. Tell no one—no one—of this message, or that I have contacted you. You are in danger, my dear, great danger. Come as quick as you may, for the urgency is great. I will explain all at the Hotel Bergeron. Ask for Mr. Dubois. Then we shall meet again. Until then, take the utmost care, my dear, delightful girl. As always, Papa.*

How like her father to avoid any reference to his supposed death, and to state simply what he wished her to do! Anemone had laughed aloud when she read the missive. The shackles of grief that she had borne in private for the past four months had slipped away from her with each word, leaving her light and weightless and filled with questions. If it hadn't been her father who was killed in that fire in Cartagena, then who had it been? The man had been burned beyond recognition, but her father's gold signet ring and pocket watch had been removed from the corpse and sent to her. There had been not the

slightest doubt from any quarter that Thomas Carstairs
had died in that fire. Anemone had realized that her
father, for reasons of his own, must have wanted it that
way. She had wasted no time lamenting that he might at
least have spared *her* from mourning him: no doubt it
had seemed to him the safest way. By truly believing he
was dead, she could not make any mistakes which might
betray the truth. She had turned her attention to the
matter at hand with the common sense that characterized
her. She would have to leave London quickly, to give
some excuse to her superiors, to book passage on a ship
to New Orleans. She had pondered all these matters on
her way to Cecilia's bedroom last night to attend to her
duties there. By the time Lady Pelham arrived home it
was nearly two o'clock in the morning, and by the time
she dismissed her maid for the night it was even later,
but by then Anemone had made all her plans.

This morning, as she scrubbed her face with the icy
water in the basin and shivered at the chill dampness of
her room, she reviewed her decisions with mounting excitement. She would report to Oliver in four days, giving
him all the information about Lord Pelham she could
garner in that time. Then she would tell him that she
needed an immediate leave of absence. Family obliga-
tions, she would explain, required her to attend a sick
relation, a cousin from Kent. It was urgent. She would
apologize, she would express regret, but she would insist
upon being let out of her assignment. Then she would
book passage on the next ship to New Orleans. Part of
her wanted to leave London this very day, to set out at
once to find her father and aid him in whatever skulduggery he was involved in, but the other part of her
insisted that she wait at least until Oliver's return. She
couldn't leave without filing her report. Thomas Carstairs
had taught her she must always honor her duty. *No*, she
told herself, when she had completed her toilette and
had donned her dove gray cambric gown, then paused

to brush her hair before the small oval mirror above her washstand. *I must wait until Oliver returns and I have given him my accounting. Then I may go with a clear conscience.*

In the mirror, Anemone's gray eyes suddenly clouded over. Parts of her father's letter baffled her, others filled her with concern. It was odd that she couldn't even confide in Oliver. Who was her father afraid of in his own intelligence organization? There must be a leak somewhere, a traitor within the upper echelons of the department. He had warned her of great danger close at hand. Anemone had the feeling that if she made one false move, danger would strike. It was unnerving not to know from where the peril came. She realized that she would have to be very careful. To reassure herself, she touched the tiny pocket hidden in the folds of her skirt. Her fingers felt the small vial of laudanum she had placed there when she dressed. Anemone had sewn a hidden pocket into all of her gowns and kept the vial with her at all times. One never knew when it would be necessary to render an adversary unconscious. It was impossible to detect, for it was concealed within the folds of her skirts, but it gave her a secure feeling, as did the pistol she kept within the pocket of her cloak.

She turned her attention to the cloud of pale hair that fell in shimmering waves to her waist as she looked at her reflection in the mirror once again. Her hands expertly twisted the cascading, ash blond curls into an elaborate knot at the nape of her neck. Over this, she secured a simple white lace cap. Now the transformation was complete. Regarding her reflection with critical eyes, she saw a slender young woman of medium height and plain demeanor. Her dove gray cambric gown, with its high, lace neckline and white cuffed sleeves could not conceal the soft, full curve of her breasts or the narrowness of her waist, but it was a simple, almost dowdy garment, and did not do justice to the slim grace of her figure. Her stockings were of simple black silk, her dark shoes un-

adorned by buckles or bows. She wore no jewels or ornaments and nothing in her hair, except the cap, which
almost completely hid her pale, plaited locks. Her face
could not be disguised, but it was not, she reflected, a
face that attracted much notice. It was a small, expressive
face, with a light dusting of freckles across the tiny nose,
and large gray eyes that could sparkle like silver when
she was in a mischievous mood or darken to charcoal
when rage overtook her. Her mouth, she had decided
long ago, was a fraction too wide. Small, bow-shaped
mouths like Cecilia's were all the rage. She had a fair,
delicately peach-tinted complexion and a long, graceful
neck that rose above slender shoulders. When her hair
was loose and flowing softly above that high-boned pixie
face, the effect, Anemone knew, could be rather appealing, but dressed like this, with her luxuriant, ash blond
locks imprisoned and concealed, she knew she looked
very much the prim and frumpish abigail, Letty Thane.
She laughed softly to herself, pleased with her ability to
blend into the role. Cecilia had never once seen beyond
the docile, unassuming ladies maid, and neither had Lord
Pelham, though Viscount Anthony Wickham, the son
and heir of the Earl, had once or twice tried to catch her
alone and steal a kiss. He was not above cornering the
parlor maids and pinching his sister's abigail, for he was
one of those young men who thought himself irresistible
to the female sex, and every woman fair game to his
attentions. Anemone had managed to avoid him for the
most part and certainly had done her best to reveal only
the facade that she had chosen to adopt in this house:
the demure, simple ladies maid, Letty Thane.

Satisfied by her appearance, Anemone folded the letter
from her father into a small square and set off for Cecilia's
bedchamber. She didn't know what Cecilia had planned
for her today, but she hoped to find an opportunity to
slip away from the house for an hour or two to inquire
at the harbor about passage to America.

Lady Pelham was still asleep when Anemone eased open the bedroom door. Moving quietly, the girl walked to the fireplace where a cozy blaze had burned all through the night, protecting the Earl's daughter from the March chill. Anemone knelt and tossed the letter from her father into the flames. She watched as the yellow-orange flames licked and swallowed the paper, leaving only a residue of ashes. Anemone smiled to herself as she rose, smoothing her gray skirt. Cecilia suddenly rolled over in her bed.

"Letty, is that you?" Cecilia yawned, stretching her arms high above her head. "What on earth is the hour? I've promised to pay a morning call on Lady Hetherton today. But oh, I'd love to stay abed. Did Mrs. Bimms bring my tray up yet?"

"No, my lady."

"Well, run down and fetch it from her, if you please. I'm famished for my roll and chocolate. And I'd like another pillow. Bring it before you go to the kitchen."

"Yes, my lady."

"And see what you can do about that fire. It's dreadfully cold in here today."

"Certainly, my lady." Anemone wondered what Oliver would say if he got word that Lady Pelham had died of strangulation at the hands of her abigail. A small giggle escaped her lips as she imagined his reaction to such news.

"What in heaven's name are you laughing about, girl?" Cecilia demanded, glaring at her from beneath a tousled mane of chestnut curls. "I'm waiting for my pillow!"

"Of course, my lady. I'll bring it at once. I do beg your pardon!"

By the time Cecilia managed to rise from her bed, it was too late an hour to pay the promised morning call, so she sent round a note of regret with a footman and prepared to sally forth on a shopping expedition instead. Attired in a gown of lavender muslin, with her sable curls adorned by a lavender chip hat tied under her chin with yellow silk ribbons, Lady Cecilia Pelham swept out in her dainty shawl, a silk reticule and parasol in her gloved hands. Her abigail trailed decorously behind her. The gloomy weather had lifted as the morning had progressed. A fair breeze ruffled Cecilia's curls, and a golden sun sparkled in an unusually clear silver-blue sky.

It was late in the afternoon when Cecilia's barouche finally pulled up before the house in Brook Street once more. The allure of Bond Street had attracted Cecilia to purchase five new gowns, a pair of yellow kid boots, a frothy turquoise confection of a hat, and two shawls of Brussels lace. Many of these purchases were to be sent to the house when the dressmaker had made the necessary adjustments to them, but Anemone emerged from the barouche carrying a square box containing the shawls, a smaller parcel containing the gloves, and a large round hatbox. She followed Cecilia into the house, almost pitying poor Lord Pelham, who, unbeknownst to his extravagant daughter, was hopelessly in debt and yet would be expected to pay for all of Cecilia's finery.

Late afternoon sun fell in an oblong across the blue and gold papered hall as the butler, an austere, high-browed beanpole of a man named Moffett, bowed to Lady Pelham. "Good afternoon, my lady. May I take your shawl?" he inquired with disinterested solicitation.

"Yes, Moffett, if you please." Cecilia untied the ribbons of her hat and tossed it onto the hall table. "And tell me, is my father at home?"

"Certainly, my lady. He is in the parlor with the Viscount, but..."

The butler had no chance to finish his sentence, for with an imperative, "Come, Letty!" Cecilia glided at once to the parlor's double doors of heavy oak and flung them wide.

"Father, you must look at the hat I bought today! It is simply the most beautiful...oh! I beg your pardon!"

Cecilia stopped short in the middle of the parlor as she realized that her father and brother were not alone in the room. Behind her, Anemone, her arms still laden with packages, saw the unexpected guest at the same moment.

Anemone could only stare in shock at the tall young man who had unfolded his long limbs from the Queen Anne chair and come to his feet upon Cecilia's entrance. Lord Pelham and Anthony also rose, but neither Anemone nor Cecilia even noticed them, for all their attention was riveted upon the stranger. Cecilia had never set eyes upon him before. But Anemone recognized him at once, and her heart began to pound. It was the man from last night, the one near the docks. The man who had knocked her down and called her "brat."

Gone today was the greatcoat, but there was no mistaking that it was the same man. Mist or no mist, coat or no coat, Anemone recognized the raven black hair, the tall, powerful physique, and most of all the midnight blue eyes set in that rugged, arrogant face. Today, in the lovely, sunlit parlor, attired in an elegant, close-fitting coat of dark blue superfine, buff breeches, and gold-tasseled Hessians upon his feet, the stranger looked every bit as handsome and as dangerous as he had last night. This afternoon, he had all the trappings of a gentleman: the magnificent clothing, which hugged his muscular frame to perfection, the exquisitely knotted white lawn cravat, the carefully brushed black locks, but there was nothing safe and respectable about him. He might have been a pirate, rigged out in the clothes of a gentleman. The glint in his eyes, and the hard set of his features betrayed him. He was every mother's nightmare of a rake: young, perhaps twenty-seven or twenty-eight years of age, devastatingly handsome, and subtly dangerous, with a cool, careless air which intrigued and frightened all at the same time. Anemone could only stare in amazement, wondering what he was doing here in this house. She struggled to hide the feelings she feared might show in her face. If he saw her, recognized her, she would be undone. How could she explain her presence on the docks last night? Frantically, she cast about in her mind for a plausible explanation, but found none. She could only pray, with fervent desperation, that he would not recognize her as she had him.

She realized almost immediately that there was little fear of that. He had not even glanced at her. He was looking at Cecilia, his eyes gleaming with appreciation as she stood, dark and lovely, before him. Her sable hair shone in the sunlight, and her statuesque figure was charmingly revealed by the clinging lavender muslin gown. The young stranger's cobalt eyes ran over her with undisguised interest. His lips curled upward in a lazy smile.

Lord Pelham broke the silence with his dry, weary voice. "Come in, my dear. It's quite all right. Allow me to introduce you to this gentleman."

Lord Pelham came forward and took his daughter's arm, drawing her into the elegantly appointed parlor. As Anemone followed Cecilia into the room, she managed to drag her gaze from the stranger to the Earl. He was a tall, thin man, with stooped shoulders and dark hair well peppered with gray. His face was lined and dissipated, making him appear older than his forty-one years. He had a high, aristocratic brow, and a beaked nose. His brown eyes were deep-set and lustreless as tiny prunes. She noted that he seemed even more haggard than usual this afternoon, and his gestures were quick and nervous. She wondered if this was due to some new, staggering loss at the gaming tables, or to the presence of this stranger, the man whose name she was about to learn.

"Cecilia, allow me to present your cousin from America," the Earl went on in a voice that shook just a bit, enough for Anemone to detect. "Mr. Stephen Burke. Uh, Stephen, my boy, this is my daughter, Cecilia."

Cecilia turned her wide, delighted smile upon him.

"What a pleasure this is, Mr. Burke! Are you truly my cousin? But how can this be? Father, I didn't know I had a cousin in America."

Lord Pelham coughed. "The relationship is a distant one, Cecilia. Stephen is, uh, the nephew of my Uncle Horace's first wife. He has just arrived in England on business. He will only stay a few days, I'm afraid."

"I will stay until my business is completed satisfactorily, Uncle," Stephen Burke spoke at last. His voice was hard as flint. Steel blue eyes flicked over the Earl briefly, and Anemone, watching, shivered at the coldness of his gaze. Her instincts told her that more was going on here than a mere visit by a relative. She edged her way to the back wall of the room, hoping no one would notice her and send her away.

"Aren't you going to invite our new cousin to dinner tonight, Cecilia?" Anthony spoke from the mantel, where he lounged with a half-filled glass of sherry in his hand. He was a fair, medium-built young man who favored his mother, whose portrait hung in gold-framed splendor over the fireplace. Lady Emily had died fifteen years earlier, while giving birth to a stillborn third offspring. Cecilia had been only three years old at the time; Anthony had been five. Anthony had her light hair and coloring, and his eyes, like hers, were a pale, milky blue. His features were neat, almost pretty, yet unlike the frail, gentle woman in the portrait, whose countenance was almost angelically demure, his face had a tendency to twist itself into a sneer, accentuating the impression of a spoiled, derisive young man accustomed to looking down upon the world at large. "Come, sister," he almost taunted Cecilia. "Where are your manners? Don't you suppose that after a horrid sea voyage our cousin stands in need of an excellent repast? Or has his sudden appearance in our midst robbed you of all propriety?"

Cecilia laughed, ignoring the mockery in her brother's tone. "But of course our cousin must stay to supper!"

She turned her face to Stephen Burke, gazing up at him with a fetching look of appeal which Anemone had seen her practice dozens of times before her mirror. "Oh, Mr. Burke, do say you will join us. Goodness—Mr. Burke. That does sound terribly formal, does it not? May I call you Stephen? After all, we are related, are we not?"

"Certainly we are." Stephen Burke's lips curled in a sardonic smile. As Cecilia seated herself on the blue damask sofa, he continued to stand, dominating the room with his height and the aura of reckless power that enveloped him. Lord Pelham and the Viscount faded into the background in the presence of Stephen Burke's powerful masculinity. "As for dinner," he went on in his cool way, "I would be delighted to stay. Your father has already gone a step further, as a matter of fact. He has invited me to make my stay with you while I'm in London."

"Oh, splendid!"

Only Anemone noted the Earl's startled look. Cecilia was obviously delighted by the prospect of Burke as their house guest, and Anthony accepted it readily enough. The Viscount strolled forward and spoke in his offhand manner. "Then you'll want to come about with me, old fellow, to the clubs and such. I'll be dining away from home tonight—previous engagement, and all that. But tomorrow I can put you in the way of things. We'll have a capital time!"

"Perhaps." Stephen glanced at the Earl. "I don't have a great deal of time to spend in London." His voice took on an edge. "I therefore hope my business will be settled quickly."

"Y . . . yes. Of course." The Earl glanced away from that hard, unwavering stare and sought out the sherry decanter. He poured himself another drink. "No need to worry, my boy. Not at all. I . . . I am certain you will get everything you came to London for."

Stephen Burke drained his sherry. "I had better, Uncle.

I am not a man to withstand disappointment. Any delay or failure brings out, I fear, the worst in my temperament. Those who know me well tend to quail when I turn my wrath in their direction."

Cecilia laughed, not noticing that her father had turned pale as he heard these words. "*I* shall certainly endeavor never to raise your ire, cousin," she teased in her pretty way. "Goodness, I should be positively terrified if you should turn your anger upon *me.*"

Anemone watched the American's eyes narrow as he regarded her. "Then, for your sake, cousin, I hope that I need never do so," he murmured.

Lord Pelham's hands shook as he set his glass down on the trestle table beside the sofa. "Cecilia, hadn't you best go upstairs and change for dinner? The hour is growing quite late, my dear."

Cecilia sent Stephen a sidelong smile before she rose gracefully from the sofa. "Yes, I suppose you're right, Father. I feel quite a mess, having spent the entire afternoon shopping in Bond Street. In fact, that's why I came into the parlor just now. I wanted Letty to show you ... oh! Letty!" She suddenly remembered her abigail's presence and turned to find the girl lurking in a corner of the parlor. Cecilia frowned.

Anemone's arms ached from holding the packages all this time, but she had not wanted to move or speak, at risk of drawing attention to herself. She had wanted to hear as much of the conversation as she could before being banished upstairs. But now, it seemed, that inevitable moment had come.

"Letty, run upstairs and put those things away. I'll be up presently." Cecilia dismissed her with a wave of her hand.

Anemone saw Stephen Burke's gaze shift briefly to her in her corner. Much as she tried, she could not keep her eyes averted. She met his glance, her heart thumping.

Would he recognize her? Expose her? She felt tiny stabbing pinpricks of fear all through her body. Stephen studied her for no more than five seconds. It was a look of indifference, as cold and unfeeling as the wind that blows in winter. There was no recognition in his eyes, no glimpse even of interest or curiosity. Certainly there was not the flicker of interest that had been sparked when he had first seen Cecilia. He turned away.

Anemone let out her breath and moved quickly to the door. She thanked heaven for the mist the night before, which had obscured her features. She was also grateful that she had chosen to wear a light shawl today, and not her cloak. Otherwise, who knew what might have happened? She was fortunate, she told herself, that Stephen Burke had not recognized her. Still, she could not help the small, disconsolate tug of her heart. She remembered the way he had held her last night on the docks. Then, he had been interested in her. Intrigued by her. Today, she was practically invisible to him, a nobody, a dowdy, faceless servant in the background. She shook herself free of these thoughts as she bore Cecilia's packages upstairs. What did it matter, after all? Why should she care if Stephen Burke noticed her or not? She ought to be crying out with joy that he had not! What was wrong with her?

By the time she reached Cecilia's bedroom, she had pushed aside all her ridiculous thoughts and feelings, and she had a plan for learning more about Stephen Burke's real purpose in this house. His veiled warnings to the Earl may have escaped Cecilia and Anthony, but she realized that he was no more their relative than she herself was. The suspicion had occurred to her that he was an American spy. If so, his business here could be crucial to her own assignment. She had to find out. Anemone realized that after dinner, when the men retired to the library for brandy and cigars, she would have her next opportunity to observe a private conversation between the Earl and Stephen Burke. Anthony, fortunately, would not be at home to hamper them from discussing their business together. There was only one thing for her to do. She would have to steal downstairs sometime during the family's dinner and conceal herself in the library. She would be hidden by the time the Earl and Stephen arrived. Such a scheme would enable her to hear everything that transpired between them, but it would also put her at great risk. If she was discovered, she would be exposed as a spy. She doubted whether either man would show her much mercy. Men like the Earl and Stephen Burke took desperate measures in desperate circumstances. She felt fairly certain they would kill her if they found her out. They couldn't let her go, and they wouldn't trust her enough even to try to buy her silence. No, they would kill her without delay, and probably never think twice about it. Her hands trembled as she folded Cecilia's shawls away in the bureau drawer. It was a risk she would simply have to take. After all, this entire assignment was a risk. There were no safeguards in this line of work. Still, hiding herself in the same room while they met was exceedingly bold—and dangerous. She steeled herself to be calm, to think clearly. Sometime between now and the dinner hour, she must figure out the best place to hide. It was a crucial decision, for in the end it might mean the difference between success and failure, and between life and death.

Anemone shuddered, despite the warmth of the late afternoon sun, which poured in through the sheer gauze curtains and made a gold-dappled pattern on the rose carpet. She saw again Stephen Burke's dark, rugged face and powerful physique. She remembered the immense strength in that muscular chest and those iron arms which had held her against him on the docks. The flash of anger in his eyes and the aura of ruthlessness which clung to him was vivid in her mind, and she knew without a doubt that he would make a brutal enemy. She only hoped, as she closed her eyes in order to shut out his virile, unsettling image, that he would never discover that she was his foe, that he would never have cause to pay the slightest heed to Cecilia Pelham's dull and mousy abigail.

THREE

NO SOUNDS came from the dining parlor as Anemone whisked down the stairway that led to the main hall. The double oak doors of the elegant, high-ceilinged dining room muted the laughter and voices of Lord Pelham, his daughter, and their American guest within, leaving the rest of the house strangely quiet. Alarmingly quiet. Anemone felt that every creak of the staircase beneath her slippered feet betrayed her presence, and she watched the doors leading to the dining parlor in apprehension, expecting that they would open at any moment and Lord Pelham would come striding out demanding to know what she was doing. But it was from the kitchen entrance beyond the stairway that trouble came. A touch at her elbow as she reached the hall startled her so much that she jumped as if someone had bitten her.

"Oh, Moffett! It's you!"

The butler frowned down at her. He wore his dignity as carefully as he did his starched, sober black garments. His wispy gray hair was combed neatly across his high, imposing brow and his brown, owlish eyes blinked at her. "Certainly it is," he sniffed.

Anemone allowed a hand to flutter to her throat. "Goodness, you shouldn't sneak up on people in that way. Where did you come from?"

He ignored this trivial query. "Miss Thane," he intoned, in the manner of a great personage addressing a peasant. "I hardly expected to see *you* down here at this hour. It is most unusual. Has Lady Pelham by chance sent for you?" His tone informed her that if not, she had no business straying from her duties in Lady Pelham's dressing chamber by roaming the house at will. Only Moffett had *that* privilege. During her assignment here, Anemone had come to understand that Moffett considered the house in Brook Street his exclusive domain, and he ran it as mercilessly as any ship's captain. Every servant, from the upstairs maids to the gardener's assistant to the liveried footmen in the Earl's employ, was stricken to mute silence merely by the sight of him. Now, his raised brows and pursed lips made it clear to Anemone that an explanation of her presence in the hall at this hour was required.

"No, Lady Pelham did not send for me. I have not seen her since she went down to dinner," she responded instantly. Her face was a study of innocence, and the gaze she directed to him was hopeful. "I am looking for my smelling salts. Have you by any chance seen them?"

"Smelling salts?" Again, Moffett blinked at her.

"Yes, my smelling salts. I was feeling a trifle faint earlier."

He regarded her trim form and flushed cheeks with skepticism. "You appear to have made a remarkable recovery, Miss Thane."

"Why, thank you, Moffett." She beamed up at him. "I am perfectly recovered now. But I was most distressed when I did need my smelling salts, and they weren't anywhere to be found. Of course, I do wish to have them

on hand should I need them on some other occasion."
She put a finger to her cheek, reflecting. "Perhaps I left
them in the kitchen. I shall check with Mrs. Bimms."

"If you must, do so at a later time," he ordered, flicking
a speck of imaginary dust from his black silk jacket. "His
lordship is still dining. The final course is about to begin,
and Mrs. Bimms has her hands full. She has no time for
you now."

"Oh, I see." Anemone bit her lip, and tried to look
apologetic. "You are quite right. I ought to have realized.
I will speak to her later." She turned and put a hand to
the polished oak railing. "Good evening, Mr. Moffett."

He didn't deign to answer her, but merely sent another
disdainful frown at her retreating back, straightened his
jacket lapels, and then went on his dignified way to the
dining room. He opened the door and stood back just as
two serving maids laden with silver trays marched from
the kitchen stairway directly through the opened doors.
The delectable aromas of fresh-baked strawberry tarts and
strong black coffee drifted tantalizingly up the stairway
as Anemone mounted the steps. She did not look back.
However, the instant the doors to the dining room closed
behind Moffett and the maids, she spun about and dashed
down the stairs once more, making a beeline for the library.

Once inside the dark-paneled room, with its heavy
door shut behind her, Anemone breathed more easily.
The fire had already been prepared for his lordship's comfort, and the lamps lit as well, so she had plenty of light
by which to survey her surroundings.

The library was a handsome room, furnished in dark
leathers and ornately carved woods, with heavy draperies
of gold-tasseled green velvet sheathing the multi-paned
windows of the southern wall. The other walls were taken
up by row after row of oak bookshelves filled with beautiful leather-bound volumes neatly arranged. Bracketed
brass wall lamps cast a soft glow upon the Turkish carpet.

Lord Pelham's mahogany desk and straight-backed chair were situated in the center of the room, facing the tall oak mantelpiece. Opposite them, two wide, carved armchairs upholstered in dull green leather were separated by a small trestle table bearing a brandy decanter with two glasses. The furnishings, originally purchased by the Earl's grandfather more than fifty years ago, were still beautiful, though showing some signs of age. The green leather cushions on the armchairs were worn and frayed, and the velvet draperies had lost some of their original sheen. The pattern on the carpet was faded almost to the point of being indiscernible. A better-endowed lord would certainly have replaced them, but the Earl of Pelham was in no position to undertake such refurbishings. For more than a year now, he had been struggling merely to retain possession of his lands, houses, and properties, all of which were threatened by the enormity of his gambling debts. It had been a difficult, agonizing struggle, one that had required him to sacrifice the one thing that could be bartered to save his worldly goods: his honor.

The Earl had always had a penchant for games of chance, and over the years had depleted his considerable fortune almost without realizing it. Still, all might have been well had he ceased his gaming habits when at last he became aware of the seriousness of his straitened circumstances. He had not. Instead, he became determined to rescue himself by winning back all that he had lost. In his later years, he played harder and more recklessly than ever before. His losses grew more staggering. His debts were on the brink of swallowing up the Earl and all he had ever possessed in the world. He had been desperate. Then, he had found a way to save himself. A way to collect vast sums of money to help him hold the creditors at bay. It meant betraying his country, passing on information he learned as a Member of Parliament and tidbits gleaned from his unsuspecting friends among the peerage. It meant becoming a traitor to England.

The Earl had made the bargain, and sold his country's secrets to her enemies in order to salvage his worldly goods. Or so Anemone and her superiors in the British intelligence service theorized. They had been watching the Earl for some time. Anemone, in the past weeks of working in his household, had gathered enough information to confirm the suspicions. She had taken careful note of the comings and goings in the Brook Street house and had more than once observed the Earl receiving a known agent of the French. From conversations she had overheard, and from some papers she had managed to find in his desk one afternoon when he had carelessly left it unlocked and unattended, she had enough evidence to prove his guilt. This meeting tonight with the American might well put the final touches upon her investigation. If Stephen Burke was indeed an American agent seeking to buy information from the Earl, what she overheard between them could be damnably incriminating for his lordship.

Anemone also suspected that Oliver would be interested in knowing what the Americans were after. Hostilities between the former colonies and England were increasing due to conflicts over America's trade policies. Both France and England had declared trade restrictions for all neutral countries against their own respective enemies, and America seemed inclined to honor none. England needed to damage the French in every manner possible, and trade was one area in which she sought to inflict harm. If America wouldn't cooperate in the blockade of French ports ordained by the British Orders in Council, the overall strategy of economic warfare was impaired. Too many adventurous American sea captains chose to ignore the British orders in exchange for the high profits of Continental trade. Their rebellion infuriated the British government. But that wasn't the only source of conflict between the two countries. England, Anemone well knew, had always claimed the right to stop neutral ships at sea in order to search them for British deserters who might have jumped ship at various ports of call. The British navy, the most powerful navy in the world, had need of every seaman it could find, and it reserved the right to impress deserters back into service. The Americans contended that their own citizens were often impressed, intentionally or not, and they objected fiercely to such search and seizure. Tension was high between the two nations, and Anemone wondered what Stephen Burke was up to, if he really was an American spy. Well, she decided, narrowing her gray eyes, she would soon find out.

She moved quickly toward the green velvet draperies and concealed herself in the far corner behind them. The only other hiding place in the room that would have concealed her fully was the small closet on the northern wall where his lordship stored some old paintings and books and an old, dusty globe on a carved wood stand. This she did not even consider. Ever since childhood she had had a fear of small, enclosed places, especially dark ones, and the very thought of huddling in the closet with the door shut tight and no glimmer of light made her inhale quickly as if desperate for breath. No, not the closet. The draperies. She would be cloaked by a mantle of velvet, not imprisoned by four hard walls. She positioned herself as comfortably as she could behind the heavy velvet and waited.

It was little more than a quarter of an hour later when she stiffened with excitement. She heard the latch click and the hinges groan as the heavy library doors swung open. The thump of boots on the oak floor announced that his lordship and Stephen Burke had entered.

It wasn't until the doors had thudded shut once more that either man spoke. From her hiding place, Anemone, tense as a tightly wound bowstring, heard Stephen Burke's voice break the silence.

"All right, Pelham. Your son is gone, and your daughter, too. Let's get on with it, shall we?"

"Yes, of course." The Earl sounded tired. Anemone could picture his haggard face. "I am ready to resume the conversation Anthony and Cecilia interrupted, but first, I desire a brandy. Would you care for one?"

The next sound was a violent eruption. Stephen Burke must have shoved a chair out of his way as he advanced upon the Earl. Anemone heard the breath hiss from between his teeth as he swore, and hardly daring to breathe, she edged her head to the corner of the draperies. She had to see what was happening. What she saw made her fingers clench the skirt of her gown. Stephen Burke had the Earl's ruffled shirt front in his two large fists. He was towering over the other man, shaking him, and glaring into his lordship's frightened face with an expression of murderous intensity.

"A brandy, Pelham? A *brandy*? I don't want your damned spirits, or your damned cigars, or your damned polite conversation! I want action! Do you hear me? I want to know exactly when you will have the information for me, and it had better be soon!"

The Earl tried to wrench himself free of the younger man's grasp, but Stephen Burke held him fast. "Damn you," the Earl rasped, his breath coming hard and indignation warring with alarm in his deep-set brown eyes. "Can't you . . . can't you even be civilized in your dirty dealings? You're a hotheaded scoundrel, Burke! Let me go, damn you!"

Stephen Burke gave him a shove that sent the Earl toppling into one of the wide armchairs. He glowered over him, a cold light glinting in his eyes.

"Try to understand, Pelham," Stephen growled in a voice every bit as menacing as the granite lines of his handsome face. He crossed his muscled arms, encased as they were in the elegant coat of black superfine that molded perfectly to his powerful physique. "I don't give a damn about the civilities. I only care about the information. Information you had better get for me quickly. I want to be on my ship, tracking down the *Belvidere* in two days time. Two days, do you hear? If you don't oblige me by then, you'll find out exactly how barbaric I can be."

"T—two days?" The Earl rose rather unsteadily to his feet. The fingers with which he tried to straighten his cravat were trembling. "How the devil do you expect me to come up with the information that quickly? Be reasonable, man! I told you this afternoon, I feel fairly certain I can find out the ship's destination, but..."

"Fairly certain?" Burke took a step closer to the Earl. His voice held a deadly quality, and the rippling, lethal power of the man seemed to fill the firelit library. "You'd better be more than fairly certain, your lordship. You'd better be damned sure you have the facts for me—and quickly. I'm not a patient fellow, and I won't sit around here kicking my heels while you flit around London in your own good time. *Two days.*"

The Earl stared into those glacial blue eyes. He shuddered, reading the cold determination and the very real anger in the young American's face. "Very... well," he whispered thickly. "You shall have it by then."

Upon hearing these words, Stephen turned on his heel and began pacing the room. The tip of Anemone's head ducked back behind the curtain. Her heart slammed against her chest. She felt the stirrings of sympathy for the Earl. Traitor or no, he was obviously terrified. Anemone herself felt cold with fear at the barely leashed violence of Stephen Burke. Charming fellow. Brutal and ruthless. What, she wondered, was so important about the whereabouts of a ship called the *Belvidere*? She could only hope that something said in further conversation would provide the clue.

The sound of liquid splashing into a glass told her that the Earl was finally pouring his drink. Scarcely daring to breathe, she peeked around the curtain once more. Lord Pelham was downing his brandy with a kind of fervent desperation. Stephen Burke stood by the mantelpiece. His hands were now shoved deep inside the pockets of his olive breeches. His black hair fell across his brow. The firelight flickering over his lean, rugged features enhanced the strong line of his jaw. His expression was dark, brooding, angry. Anemone found herself staring, trying to decipher what lay behind his scowling countenance. He looked very tough, very dangerous. She found it almost impossible to reconcile this ruthless stranger with the man who had held her almost protectively upon the dock.

"Er, now that we've settled when I will deliver the information, I'd like to know the exact terms." The Earl of Pelham seemed to have recovered a little of his self-assurance after the strengthening effects of the brandy. "My price, if you remember, Mr. Burke, was five thousand pounds."

"Done," Stephen said shortly.

The Earl gave a sigh of relief.

A moment later, Stephen crossed the room and poured himself a glass of the rich burgundy liquor. He raised it in a mock toast.

"To you, my lord. To all honorable men." His voice was filled with contempt.

There was a pause, during which Anemone heard only the crackling of the logs in the fireplace. Her fingers clenched and unclenched the fabric of her skirt.

"I'm aware of what you think of me, Mr. Burke." The Earl sounded weary, and there was more than a trace of bitterness in his voice. He sank heavily into the armchair Stephen had pushed him upon earlier. It creaked beneath his weight. "And I suppose I deserve your scorn. You—

you are young, idealistic, filled with patriotism for your country. Yet, you love your country no more than I care for England."

Stephen Burke's gaze narrowed on him. "You have an odd way of showing your loyalty, my lord," he mocked. "Selling secrets to the highest bidder?"

"I'm not proud of what I do." Lord Pelham drew a breath. "For the life of me, I don't believe anything I can do will truly harm England. She is strong enough to withstand Boney, to withstand your country and any others who would try to destroy her."

"My country has no wish to destroy her," Stephen returned evenly. "We want only fair treatment. We won't accept England's ruthless domination of the high seas much longer. We'll do what we must to protect our shipping rights and our sailing men."

The Earl ran a hand through his graying hair. "And I will do what I must to save myself," he almost whispered.

He groaned suddenly, and reached for the decanter. "I'm not an evil man, Burke," he said heavily. "I take no pleasure in my betrayal, you can believe that. If I hadn't gambled myself literally to the brink of debtor's prison, do you think I'd have resorted to this filthy business? Ah, damn it all to hell." He drank lustily, as if the brandy were to be his last. "I'm hanging onto my name, my reputation, and my fortune by the edge of my fingernails. I'd do almost anything to save my lands—and to save my children the humiliation of discovering that I've completely squandered away their inheritance. I'd make a deal with the Devil himself. Perhaps," he added bitterly, "that's what I've done."

"My contact told me you had gambled yourself to ruin. He said that for five thousand pounds you'd sell me your daughter's virtue, not to mention England's secrets."

Lord Pelham came to his feet, his fists clenched. His thin face blazed with fury. "I ought to run my sword through you, you bastardly scoundrel," he cried. "You leave my daughter out of this! Do you understand me? Leave Cecilia alone!"

Stephen Burke regarded him coldly. "Calm yourself, Pelham. I was speaking in jest. I have no interest in your daughter, lovely though she may be."

The Earl was still shaking. "I want you out of here," he raged. "You're an impudent rascal, and I won't have you in my house. I won't stand for it, do you hear?"

Slowly, Stephen Burke placed his glass on the trestle table and straightened to face the Earl. With his immense size, his black hair and glittery blue eyes, he looked as dangerous as any pirate plundering the high seas. The air of command he wore so easily about him, odd for one not yet thirty, allowed him to speak in a quiet but disturbingly perilous tone. "I will leave, Pelham. As soon as the information I need is in my hands. And not a moment sooner."

His gaze was riveted upon the other man. At last, the Earl dropped his head. "V...very well. But...I'm not accustomed to dealing with upstarts. Rude upstarts at that. I demand, that is, I *desire*, that you show some restraint and some respect. I have every intention of honoring our arrangement, of finding out what you wish to know about the *Belvidere*'s destination and schedule. There is no need for this...unpleasantness."

"Maybe not." Stephen Burke's tone was grim. "But this matter is very close to me—very close. I'll do whatever I need to do to settle it. Remember that, Pelham."

The Earl's jaw twitched. "You've made that very clear," he said stiffly.

Stephen Burke turned to leave the library and walked with long, pantherlike strides toward the door, but the Earl stopped him with a word.

"One moment, if you please, Mr. Burke."

"What is it?"

"I...there is something else which might be of interest to you—to your country."

"Oh?"

Now it was the Earl's turn to pace. He rose and moved nervously about the room. "I...I came into a bit of information the other day. It's not much. But I could find out more. And I think it would be quite worth your while. No doubt your President, Mr. Thomas Jefferson, would be interested in what's afoot in the territory of Louisiana."

Stephen Burke returned to the center of the room. "What about the territory of Louisiana?" he demanded.

Lord Pelham shook his head. "Not yet. First, I must know what you will pay to find out more."

"Five hundred pounds," Burke said impatiently.

"One thousand," returned the Earl.

Stephen eyed him piercingly a moment. From her hiding place, Anemone waited in breathless suspense.

"One thousand it is," said the American. "But it had better be worth it, my lord."

"Oh, it is. It is." There was the sound of brandy being poured once more; the Earl seemed relieved that the bargain was made and his price met. Anemone guessed that his debts must be closing in rather quickly upon him.

"All right, Pelham, I've agreed to your price. Now tell me what the devil this is all about."

"I don't know many of the details yet. But I can find out," he said quickly, as Stephen grimaced. "There is something going on at this very moment in the city of New Orleans. But you must wait to learn the details." He licked his lips. "When will you give me the money, Mr. Burke?"

"When you have told me everything—*everything*—I want to know." Stephen's tone was hard. "You won't get a shilling of it until you have told me all."

The Earl nodded. "In two days then we will complete both transactions. Is that agreeable?"

"The sooner the better," Stephen Burke growled. He leveled one long, penetrating look at the Earl before turning once more toward the door. "I'm going to my ship now to bring back the belongings I'll need for my stay. My very *brief* stay. Good night, Pelham."

He was gone with a thud of the door. Anemone waited in tingling excitement as the Earl drank yet another glass of brandy. Her mind was whirling. Louisiana—New Orleans. Lord Pelham knew of activities there of interest to United States intelligence. They *had* to be related to her father's mysterious doings. It would be entirely too coincidental were there no relationship. But what could it be? She had to find out before she left for America. What she learned might prove useful to her father when she found him in New Orleans. Her excitement mounted, and with it, her impatience. It seemed Lord Pelham would never leave the damned library. Her fingernails dug into her palms. The velvet draperies began tickling her nose. She was about to scream with frustration when at last she heard boots scrape the hardwood floor. She heard him, then, straighten the chair that had been overturned. She heard him sigh. Then she heard his footsteps approaching the door. It opened and closed. Then, there was silence, but for the sound of her own breathing and the crackle of logs upon the fire.

Slowly, Anemone peered around the draperies. The room was empty. She had to leave quickly. She knew Moffett would be in soon to bank the fire and turn down the oil lamps.

To her relief, no one was in the hall when she eased open the library door and slipped out. A swift glance in every direction reassured her, and she was at the steps in a flash. But once in her own room, with the door shut and the lamp glowing upon the neat, barren surroundings, restlessness seized her. She went over and over every aspect of the conversation between the two men, tantalized by what they had not said. She wished she knew why Stephen Burke sought the *Belvidere*, why he wanted to track it down at whatever port it was destined for. She wished even more fervently that Lord Pelham

had given a clue of what was afoot in New Orleans. *Oh,
Papa, what have you become involved in now?* she mused as
she paced her room with long, rapid strides. At last, she
paused before the window, her fingers tapping lightly at
the pane. It was a fine March night, clear and mild with
the promise of spring. Anemone, bursting with the heady
excitement that was the aftermath of spying, could no
longer bear the confinement of her room. She gave a
small, impatient cry and turned from the window.

Her destination was the gardens of the house on Brook
Street. The quiet, secluded grounds set well beyond the
street offered her cool, fresh air and peaceful solitude.
She needed that now. She needed to walk off the restlessness that gripped her, to think long and hard about
what she had heard. It would be good to breathe deeply
of the sharp night air, to clear her head, and steady her
senses. She wanted to let the darkness and the trees
envelop her, wrap about her in protective shrouds while
she worked off the excitement pounding in her blood.
She let herself down the servants' stair and out the back
door, threading her way to the gardens behind the main
parlor.

As she made her way through the shadows, heading
toward the small stone bench beside a stand of neatly
trimmed rose bushes, the French doors leading off the
parlor suddenly swung wide, and light from the room
streamed full upon her. Anemone stopped short, her
hands to her throat. She felt for all the world like a rabbit
cornered by a fox as she stood, caught, in the glare of
lamplight. Viscount Anthony Wickham was silhouetted
in the doorway. She could barely discern him as her eyes
sought to adjust to the sudden brightness, yet she saw
enough to know it was he. She swore very softly under
her breath, words she had learned from the battlefield.

"Well, if it isn't Miss Thane," Anthony drawled in his
familiar, sardonic way. He grinned, showing small white
teeth. In the light which flowed out from the parlor, his

pale face shone. He straightened his intricately tied cravat and sauntered forward. "How fortunate that you have come to relieve my boredom," he exclaimed. "My evening had turned quite sour. Do you know, I had planned to retire early after one glass of refreshment. But now..." Anthony strolled through the French doors and approached her where she stood, his milky blue eyes fixed upon her rigid countenance. "Now, it seems my luck has changed. How delighted I am to see you, my dear Letty."

He laughed and reached out an arm for her.

FOUR

BEFORE SHE could move, Anthony had her in his grasp, his smooth white hands pinching the flesh of her arms. His face was very close to hers, and his liquored breath was warm on her cheek. Anemone tried to shake off his hands, but his smug smile merely broadened, and his grip tightened as she twisted in vain.

"Let me go, my lord," she said, as crisply as she could under the circumstances. "This is unbecoming to both of us!"

Anthony gave a high-pitched laugh. He pulled her close against his dandyish, high-waisted yellow coat, and the small gold buttons pressed painfully against her breast. "Don't play coy with me, Letty!" he whispered, and pinched her chin between his fingers. "You're a pretty chit, and I just can't help wanting to kiss you. There's no harm in it, and I daresay you came out here hoping I'd find you. Come now, admit it!"

Anemone pushed against him with all her might, but though he was only of medium height and slim build, she could not free herself from him. "I want nothing to do with you!" she retorted breathlessly, trying to control the anger that flared within her. She knew that a strategically aimed kick would earn her release and send his lordship into agonized spasms, but such action would be uncharacteristic of Letty Thane, so she forced herself to squirm and argue in conventional fashion, wishing she could run a sword through this conceited viscount instead. Suddenly, her irritation turned to disgust as Anthony lowered his face to hers and planted damp lips against her protesting mouth. She struggled furiously, enduring a long, sucking kiss while his lordship squeezed her limbs in a crushing embrace. When he lifted his face from hers, she saw the sheen of desire on his pale countenance and read the smug pleasure which lit his milky blue eyes.

"Scoundrel, let me go!" she hissed, fighting anew for her freedom, but to her dismay, Anthony appeared even more aroused by her resistance.

"Ah, Letty, how sweet you taste," he whispered, and grinned down into her flushed face. One hand roamed up her rigid back, across her shoulders, to the slender column of her throat. He snickered as his hand descended to her breast. Anemone kicked at his ankle and cried out in furious protest. He kissed her again, one soft hand cupping her breast, oblivious to her indignation.

"No...no—stop..." Anemone's muffled cries fell against his lips, as she twisted futilely. He had positioned her in such a way that she could no longer kick or even move her arms and legs, and panic surged within her as she knew herself at his mercy. She shrank in revulsion from his marauding mouth and hands, but could not fling him from her.

Suddenly, though, Anthony *was* flung from her. She was free, standing gasping and disheveled as the Viscount was hurled against the stone bench in the garden. Unencumbered by his arms and legs and mouth, she felt as if she had emerged from a suffocating blackness. She gave a thankful cry, and turned to see who had rescued her.

It was Stephen Burke who stood there, his fists clenched beside her. He was watching Anthony with an expression of contempt on his face. Having thrown the Viscount against the bench, he was waiting to see if the young lord intended to continue the fracas.

"What . . . the devil do you mean by this, Burke?" Anthony staggered to his feet, staring incredulously at the American. "Damn you, man, what business have you attacking me in this manner?"

"The lady seemed in need of assistance."

"Lady?" Thoroughly confused, Anthony ran a hand through his fair, tousled hair. "You mean Letty?" His gaze fell on the girl who stood rooted to the spot, taking in every word and nuance of the scene. Twin scarlet blotches appeared on his cheeks as anger coursed through him. "It's none of your damned business what dealings I have with the chit, or with any other! Who in hell do you think you are, interfering with my affairs? I ought to call you out, you know! I really should!"

"Go ahead."

The amusement in Stephen Burke's tone set Anthony's teeth on edge. He shot the other man a seething glance, and opened his mouth to issue the threatened challenge, then clamped it shut again. Something about Stephen Burke made Anthony think better of a hot-headed reaction. Anthony was a notable shot, and he prided himself on it. He had fought duels twice before and bested, if not killed, his opponents. But this time, instinct warned him he would be dealing with a far more dangerous adversary. He glanced keenly at Stephen's broad shoulders and lean, well-muscled form as the man regarded him with those ice blue eyes. Stephen Burke was no ordinary opponent. He carried about him an aura which left no doubt in Anthony's mind that he would be quick and deadly with either a sword or a gun, and that he would show no hesitation in killing an adversary. Even now, the man stood there with cocky insolence, practically daring him to issue a challenge. *Where the hell did he get his confidence?* Anthony wondered uneasily. Though he wasn't blessed with a particularly superior intellect, Anthony sensed the answer: Stephen Burke's confidence came from knowledge of his own abilities. The man had no doubt of his ability to win. It was apparent in the cold gleam in his eyes, in the set of his firm mouth, in the way he stood, ready for a fight, yet relaxed, even enjoying himself. Anthony swore under his breath. He'd be a damned fool to fight Stephen Burke. Especially over something as trivial as his sister's abigail.

He shrugged his shoulders in a studied gesture and spoke in an offhand manner. "Out of respect for my father, I will refrain from fighting with a member of the family. Besides, it's not worth it." He turned his gaze away from Stephen Burke, focusing on the girl instead. "My, my, Letty, what a lot of trouble you've caused." His eyes were like small blue marbles. "Next time, don't put up such a fuss. My dear cousin thought you were truly in distress."

Anemone had been thinking swiftly while the two men squared off. Whatever her personal feelings, she couldn't afford to indulge them. It would be heavenly to slap Anthony Wickham's face, and treat him to a blistering account of her opinion of him, but Letty Thane would never behave so. She would be too cowed, too embarrassed, too fearful of losing her job. Anemone restrained her raging impulses. She still had work to do here, and she couldn't afford to indulge her personal feelings. She was too much of a professional to allow her temper to rule her judgment, so instead of snapping the stinging retort she longed to deliver, she ignored Anthony and turned to Stephen Burke instead.

"Thank you, sir," she said quietly, and raised her eyes

to his face. His gaze flickered over her. Her heart did a strange somersault as his piercing eyes touched her face. "I am grateful for your assistance."

He nodded and made no move to stop her as she slipped past him the way she had come, making for the servants' door. Moonlight showed her the path, and there was silence behind her in the garden. Then she heard a voice, Stephen Burke's voice, coming to her faintly through the cool, ruffling breeze.

"Next time find yourself more willing sport, my friend," he was advising in that deep, gritty voice that sent shivers down her spine. She heard him laugh, a cool, satiric sound in the echoing silence of the night. "Besides, the chit is hardly a raving beauty. Surely you can do better. . . ."

Anemone heard no more. She froze, every muscle coiled with outrage, every nerve end quivering with humiliation. She felt as she had last night when Stephen Burke had knocked the wind from her lungs. Gasping, breathless with indignation, and boiling with fury, she gathered her skirts in her hand and ran the rest of the way to the door. She let herself in and mounted the stairs in a flash, slamming the door to her own bedroom. She rushed to the window and threw it open, taking long, deep breaths of the cold March air in an effort to calm herself. Her hands were pressed to her burning cheeks, her eyes mirrored the storminess of her inner feelings. She wanted to scream, to throw something! She wanted to rake her nails across Stephen Burke's arrogant face! For several long moments, her emotions ran wild, and her breast heaved as she recalled the insult of his words, the sound of his satiric laughter. *Hardly a raving beauty*, indeed! She threw herself down upon her bed, pounding her fist against the pillow. Damn the man! Damn his arrogant, insolent, cocky superiority! What did she care what he thought of her? *Nothing!* He was despicable, the last man on earth she would want to admire her!

At length, the tumult within her subsided. She sat up, her delicate jaw jutting forward slightly. She would no longer give in to this madness. Stephen Burke could not upset or injure her in any way. She was too strong for such foolishness. After all, it was only her silly pride. His opinion was scarcely important, and in two days' time, he would be gone and she would be making plans to sail to New Orleans. How could she allow a man like that, one whom she scarcely knew, and who knew *her* not at all, to affect her so potently? It would not do and would only distract her from her mission. In one fluid motion she rose from the bed, and put Stephen Burke firmly out of her mind.

Anemone proceeded to undress and attend to her toilette, forcing herself to think about Oliver, about her father, about the tasks she must accomplish in the next few days. She wanted to think about anything except the tall, rugged American with the dangerous smile. Yet, when she stood before the oval mirror in her nightrail, hairbrush in hand, his image and his denigrating words returned.

She had turned down the lamp, and the small room was lit only by thin bars of moonlight. Her reflection looked pale and delicate to her own eyes. She turned this way and that before the mirror, gray eyes narrowed in self-appraisal. The sheer white nightrail clung to her slender form, revealing the full curves of her breasts and hips and flowing gracefully around her long, slim legs. Her hair fell in a bountiful, silvery veil to her tiny waist, each lustrous curl shimmering and shining in the glow of the moon. Now free and unrestricted by plait or cap, ash blond tendrils softly framed her high-boned, expressive face. She chewed her lips, studying each feature of her face, evaluating the merits and faults of each. Perhaps if Stephen Burke saw her like this, and not in that dowdy gray servant's gown and shoes and cap, he might think differently, she found herself musing. The sheer, clinging nightrail was certainly more becoming, more feminine than the cambric dress and plain, dark shoes. Especially with her hair loose and flowing softly against her skin. No doubt one of Cecilia's gowns, she decided with a lift of one slim brow, would appear equally flattering, something like the lavender muslin the girl had worn today, or the green satin ball gown of last evening. He might even think she looked *pretty* in such elegant confections. Then, she caught herself and anger overtook her. She didn't care what Stephen Burke thought. She didn't. She threw the hairbrush down upon the washstand and spun away from the mirror. *Damn him*. She compressed her lips and silently vowed not to think of him again.

Yet, when a faint, feminine flutter of laughter reached her ears from the opened window, she turned toward the sound with a sinking heart. It was followed by a rumble of masculine laughter. Something told her what she would discover when she peered down into the garden, and the suspicion sent a strange stabbing pain through her. She moved toward the window like a sleepwalker, her limbs heavy and rigid, her shoulders stiff.

The moon rode high in a sky so black and velvety one longed to touch it. Here and there stars glittered coldly, adding their white light to the gleaming luminosity cast down by the moon. The courtyard below, with its shade trees and ghostly statuary, was revealed in this silvery glow. Though the parlor was now darkened and the doors which had emitted lamplight earlier were closed, Anemone could see quite clearly. Too clearly. She sank down upon her knees by the window and clenched her hands beneath her chin. Her eyes stared fixedly at the couple in the garden below.

She had no idea where Anthony had gone—presumably he had retired to bed. Cecilia had obviously returned early from her card party at Lady Dunston's house this evening, for now only Cecilia and Stephen Burke occupied the moonlit garden. They were very close together, near the very spot by the stone bench where Anthony had accosted Anemone earlier. But Cecilia, unlike Anemone, seemed not at all chagrined by her situation. She stood in the circle of Stephen Burke's arms, her own twined about his neck, and slowly, as Anemone watched, she lifted her thin, beautiful face for his kiss.

Anemone stared. The kiss went on for a long time. When it ended, Cecilia appeared to have melted into the American's arms. He bent his head to her neck, and a low sound, half giggle, half moan, drifted upward to the tiny window high above. Stephen's hands began to slide over the girl's voluptuous body. Anemone heard the deep murmur of his voice, and then Cecilia said something so breathless and soft Anemone could not discern a word of it. Together they sank down upon the stone bench, and Stephen took her into his arms once more, holding her in a masterful way which made Anemone's heart flutter. She saw them kiss and embrace once more in the light of the moon, and then she withdrew from the window, shutting it, closing the curtains, and moving shakily toward her bed.

Cecilia looked very beautiful, she thought dully, turning back the sheets. And Stephen, well, Stephen Burke could take any woman's breath away. They were a good pair, she told herself as she settled her head on the pillow. They deserved each other. Certainly, it meant less than nothing to her.

Yet, why did she feel this dry, dull ache in her heart? Why did her head hurt, and her eyes sting? Why did she want to cry, even though no tears would come?

She didn't know the answer—didn't want to know the answer. She reminded herself of the need to sleep, to be alert for the following day. She thought of the importance of her assignment in the war against Napoleon and of her upcoming voyage to America. She thought of how lovely it would be to leave this house and everyone in it far behind, to sail to her father's aid. She lay stiff and miserable in her tiny bed, yearning for something she couldn't define, something that would banish the emptiness in her heart and make the hurt go away.

FIVE

THE EARL of Pelham was gone for most of the following day, but in the early afternoon, something occurred which arrested Anemone's full attention and drew her out of the lethargic mood that had gripped her all morning.

She had been disconsolate from the moment she awakened, unable to forget the previous night's events. Then, just after luncheon, the knocker sounded upon the door and Moffett opened it to a nervous little man named Mr. Sneed. Anemone knew him to be affiliated with the French agent, Henri Marceau. Sneed had called before, but on the past occasion, much to her chagrin, she hadn't been able to eavesdrop on his conversation with the Earl. This time, after Moffett informed him that the Earl was away, Sneed left a sealed message to be delivered to Lord Pelham when he returned. From her watchful position on the second floor landing, Anemone was amused by Mr. Sneed's nervous insistence that the letter *not* be left on the mahogany table in the hall, but that it be placed in the Earl's library. If the man had been the least bit competent, she knew, he would have hand-delivered it to the Earl instead of leaving it in Moffett's charge, but at least he made some effort to keep it away from prying eyes. Nevertheless, she meant to read it before the Earl's return and made up her mind to get into the library immediately. She waited until Moffett had closed the door upon the diminutive Mr. Sneed, and until he had taken the envelope into the library, leaving it, no doubt, upon the Earl's desk. When the butler emerged and closed the heavy doors behind him, he headed toward the kitchen, and Anemone slipped downstairs and across the hall.

She was not fearful of being caught today. Cecilia, after awakening in an unusually sunny mood, had sailed out on a round of morning calls and errands, blithely leaving her abigail behind. Anthony, too, had gone out early, and Stephen Burke, as far as Anemone could tell, was nowhere in the house. That was fortunate, for she had no desire to encounter him. It also meant she had only Moffet and the other servants to contend with, and they did not trouble her in the least.

Once inside the library, with the doors carefully shut, she darted over to the Earl's desk and picked up the sealed envelope. THE EARL OF PELHAM was written in a thick black scrawl upon the stationery. Anemone turned it over excitedly, wondering what it would reveal. Marceau was a clever fellow, aside from employing bumbling amateurs like Winston Sneed. She was eager to know just what he had to say to the Earl of Pelham. It occurred to her that the letter might be written in code, but this did not daunt her. Codes were her specialty. Thomas Carstairs had taught her to decipher them as a hobby, a game, the way some children work at puzzles. Quite aside from the one she had developed with her father, an intricate and highly effective piece of work, she had seen and studied some of the best. No, a code would not prevent her from learning what Marceau wanted with the Earl. She put her fingernail to the seal. But she never had the chance to break it. Without warning, the library doors burst open. Anemone whirled about just as Stephen Burke strode into the room.

Caught with the letter in her hand, Anemone felt a wave of panic rush over her. She fought it back, knowing that clear thinking would be the only way to extricate herself from this. But she couldn't help the color that suffused her cheeks, or the way her heart raced in her chest. With fingers that trembled despite her best efforts, she placed the letter back upon the Earl's desk.

Stephen Burke looked almost as shocked as she to find her in the room. He stopped in mid-stride. In the next instant, she guessed why. He had come to search the Earl's desk! He was as guilty as she and equally nonplused to be discovered in the library. This knowledge restored some of her confidence, and she knew what she had to do. She had to put Stephen Burke on the defensive—force *him* to explain *his* presence in Edward Pelham's library.

"Mr. Burke!" she exclaimed, before he could speak. "You frightened me! Why, whatever are you doing here at this hour?"

After that first startled moment, he recovered himself. His features lost their surprised expression and smoothed themselves into an impassive mask. He continued forward, moving toward her with a loose-limbed, easy grace. This morning his raven black hair glistened in the sunlight that streamed through the multi-paned windows. He looked, she realized, like a devilishly handsome young Samson, and as he paused before her, his almost overwhelming physical size and potent masculine appeal sent her senses reeling. She wondered what she would do if, in the next instant, he should seize her in his arms and kiss her? If he should embrace her the way he had embraced Cecilia last night, and hold her tightly in those powerful arms?

His next words drove all such dizzying possibilities

from her mind, as if someone had poured icy water upon her head. "More to the point, Miss Thane," Stephen Burke said in his hard, quiet way, "what are *you* doing here?"

Anemone fought to remain calm beneath his disconcertingly intense stare. Those piercing blue eyes unnerved her. They saw too much, and too well. She glanced down at her hands, so that he would not see the desperate workings of her mind as she searched for an acceptable explanation. But Stephen didn't allow her the luxury of avoiding his gaze. He put one strong hand under her chin and tilted her head up so that she was forced to meet his eyes.

She gasped. The touch of his hand upon her face sent a jolt of electricity through her body and increased the pounding of her heart tenfold. He was very close to her, and she could inhale the clean, musky scent of him. Magnetic sensuality captured her senses. In one brief instant, she was overwhelmingly aware of how lean and ruggedly handsome were his features. She saw the careless tumble of thick black hair over a scowling brow, the straight, chiseled nose and determined jaw, the mouth carved in lines of firm sensuality. Most of all, she saw his eyes, blue flames burning into hers with a searing impact that nearly caused her to sway upon her feet. Desperately, gropingly, she tried to think.

"Well, Miss Thane?"

For one frightening moment, her mind was blank. Then an idea leaped into her brain. "I am here on my mistress's business—private business," she said at last. She let her nervousness show, using it. "Please, sir, do not make the Earl aware of it! Lady Pelham would surely dismiss me if she knew that I had failed to carry out her scheme!"

"What scheme?" Stephen Burke released her chin, but continued to tower before her, making it impossible for her to move away from him, as she very much would have liked to do. The memory of his insufferable remarks last night served to awaken her anger, adding fuel to her

resourcefulness. She would not be caught by this man or
bested by him. She would give him an explanation that
would satisfy all of his suspicions. After all, he had no
reason whatever to suspect her real purpose. Thank heavens, Anemone thought fervently. She would not care to
see what he would do if he discovered she was a British
spy.

"Oh, sir, must I indeed tell you?" she queried, in a
quavering tone worthy of a stage actress. "Lady Pelham
will not like it, I am sure!"

"I suspect the Earl would not like it, either," Stephen
retorted, "if I find it necessary to tell him of this trespass."

"Oh, no!" Anemone clutched his sleeve, rather enjoying the farce now that she knew how to play it. "Don't
do that! I will ... I will tell you everything!"

He waited, not saying anything, so Anemone went on,
addressing him earnestly. "Well, sir, Lady Pelham was
concerned about a certain ... bill she received from the
dressmaker. It seems that she spent more than she should
have on a new ball gown for Miss Eliza Wentworth's
coming-out party, and the last time she overspent her
quarterly allowance, well, the Earl was most displeased!"
Anemone gazed up at him innocently, her hands clasped
before her in a supplicant's pose. "She sent me here to
fetch the dressmaker's bill before his lordship could see
it. If she can delay the woman a bit longer, Lady Pelham
will find a way to cover the debt before the Earl need
even know of it! And what harm will be done? Please,
sir, do not betray her to the Earl! Lady Pelham would
never forgive me—or you—I am certain! She would be
particularly mortified to learn that you know about this
... this scrape she finds herself enmeshed in. Oh, dear,
if only I could find that bill!"

She broke off here on a lamenting note, and made as
if to search the desk again, but Stephen Burke grinned
suddenly, and held her arm. "So, Cecilia fears the Earl's
wrath, is that it? That's what this is all about?"

"Yes, sir." Anemone hung her head. "If only you will not mention this..."

"Don't worry about that." He chuckled softly. "I'll keep Cecilia's secret, Letty—never fear. But I can't allow you to search through Lord Pelham's private papers. Run off now and tell your mistress the bill was nowhere to be seen. That should end the matter. Hurry, before the Earl comes in and catches you."

"Thank you, sir." She bestowed on him a small, grateful smile and turned toward the door. She was filled with relief and a surging sense of triumph at having outwitted him, but these emotions were short-lived as Stephen once again caught her arm, and spun her to face him.

"Letty," he said suddenly, staring down at her with an arrested expression. "Have we met before?"

Anemone's heart missed a beat. She felt the quick quiver of fear down her spine. "No, sir. Wh...why?"

He shook his head, midnight blue eyes searching the depths of hers. For the first time since his arrival at this house, Anemone felt he was truly looking at her, truly seeing her. It filled her with terror. If he were to recognize her now, it would raise a multitude of questions in his mind, and questions led to suspicions, suspicions often to truth. She held her breath, hoping that the icy fear running through her blood did not show in her face.

"I don't know, it's a feeling I had a moment ago." Stephen regarded her intently, from the tips of her plain black shoes to the prim black silk dress with its high collar and ugly, dark buttons. "Just now, when you thanked me, and began to move past, it reminded me of something. But..." He shrugged and released her. "Never mind. I'll think of it eventually. Off with you now."

She was only too glad to escape. She felt his eyes on her as she walked to the door. Apprehension coursed through her. She put a hand to the knob and spoke as calmly as she could. "Good day, sir." He didn't answer, and she left without daring to glance back. Every instinct warned her that she was in danger. Stephen Burke would remember. She knew he would remember. It was only a matter of time, now that he had turned his attention to her. *Damn Henri Marceau and his stupid message* she thought as she bolted up to her own quarters. Not only had she failed to see the letter, but it had brought her under the direct scrutiny of Stephen Burke. And that was a place, she reflected uneasily as she leaned with her back to her own closed door, in which it was most uncomfortable to be.

Stephen stood for a long moment staring at the library door after she had left. He wondered what it was about Letty Thane that had struck a chord of memory in him somewhere. She was a fetching little thing, now that he had had a close look at her. Not classically, dramatically beautiful like Cecilia, but her features were delicate and fine, like bone china. Her skin was flawless, the pale color of a fresh peach. He wondered briefly what she would look like with her hair down. Then he shook his head. Letty Thane probably never took her hair down. She probably slept with it all coiled up at the nape of her neck, wearing a buttoned-up woolen gown to boot. That young woman was as prim and straitlaced as they came, judging by the dreadful dark gowns she favored and her tightly knotted hair. Not exactly his style of female. Yet, there was something about her, something, perhaps, in her eyes, which belied her dowdy looks. They were an unusual color, Letty Thane's eyes. Gray, silver almost. Where had he seen eyes like that before?

The answer eluded him, much as he tried to grasp it. At last, he gave it up, knowing that it would come to him eventually. Probably in the middle of the night sometime, when he was sailing on the *Sea Lion*, following Johnny across the ocean to wherever the damned *Belvidere* had taken him.

Johnny. The thought of his lifelong friend creased his brow with a frown of concern. *Don't worry, Johnny. I'm coming after you*, he vowed silently. *Even if I have to choke the information out of Edward Pelham to do it.*

It had been nearly two months ago that he'd received the word about Johnny Tucker. Stephen would never forget that night. He had been home on leave after an assignment out west, holed up with a tavern wench named Bella. It had been a wild, tempestuous night, and far from over, when a messenger had dashed into the Crooked Tree tavern and demanded to know his where-abouts. At first angry at being interrupted upstairs in one of the tavern bedrooms, Stephen had quickly realized that something must be seriously wrong for his father to send men out in search of him. He had left the delectable Bella behind, ignoring her screeches of fury, and ridden home to his family's three-story red brick mansion in Philadel-phia as quickly as his mount could take him. There, in the elegant parlor of his parents' home, he had glanced at the faces of the four people gathered there and a savage fear had gripped his heart.

His mother, Elizabeth Burke, had come to him and drawn him gently into the room. Even at that moment, beset by worry and grief, her features held a beauty and serenity that years of love had given her. Oh, she had always been beautiful, with her abundant golden hair and eyes the color of violets. The years had not stolen her loveliness. If anything, they had softened her beauty, deepened it, giving her the added glow of a strong and proud and self-fulfilled woman. All his life, Stephen had adored her, and at that moment, when he looked into those breathtaking violet eyes and saw the pain in them, he had wanted to kill whoever or whatever had caused her unhappiness. He turned to his father and approached him, eyeing Alexander Burke with the cool, steady look so much like Alex's own.

"What is it, sir?" he had asked without preamble, shaken by the ravaged faces of Carrie and Ben Tucker. "What has happened? Is it Johnny?"

If anything, Alexander Burke had grown more hand-some, more rugged with the years. He was an older, calmer version of his son, but still every bit as strong and compellingly masculine. They had the same wide-shouldered, powerful build, the same thick, raven-black hair, though Alexander's now was peppered with gray. It gave the older man an air of distinction that matched his aura of power and influence. His frost gray eyes still missed nothing, and they could pierce a man's soul more deeply and coldly than any swordblade. They could also, Stephen knew, rest with great tenderness and pride and love upon the woman who had shared his life for the past thirty years. His father had taught him a great many things—he had guided Stephen in the path of courage and service to his country, shown him the ways of war, and taught him the value of peace. He knew his father was proud of his son's intelligence work for President Jefferson, proud of the way he handled himself in the tough and complex world of spies and diplomacy. The one thing Alexander wished for his son was a woman: one woman, a special woman who would unlock the searing love that Elizabeth had awakened in his own heart thirty years ago. Stephen had wooed and bedded many a girl, but his heart had never once been engaged. Alexander and Elizabeth, content in their own deep love, wanted the same happiness for their son. They hoped one day he would find it. Stephen was aware of their wish, but dismissed it with amusement. He was young, and as wild as Alexander had ever been. He was in no hurry to settle down. As for falling in love, well, he couldn't imagine that that particular fate would ever be-fall him.

That night, facing his father, he knew before Alex an-swered that it was Johnny who was in trouble. Alex had told him the story in crisp, concise words, explaining that Johnny Tucker's ship had returned to port from France without Stephen's boyhood friend aboard. Johnny, like

Stephen, worked for American intelligence and had just finished a mission in Paris. He had been on his way home to make his report when a British frigate called the *Belvidere* had stopped his vessel at sea. The crew reported that Johnny and two others had been impressed by the British ship during a search for "deserters." Johnny was gone. No one knew where the *Belvidere* was headed, but they all knew of the cruel treatment, the enforced slavery endured by impressed seamen. Men were usually imprisoned for life on the ships that captured them.

Stephen had turned in stunned silence to Carrie and Ben Tucker, Johnny's parents. Carrie and Ben were his parents' closest friends, just as Johnny was his. They were almost as dear to him as his own family, for he and Johnny had grown up together, and he had spent as much time in the Tucker home as in his own. The two boys had been inseparable since they'd been able to walk, and they had shared both childhood scrapes and dangerous government missions over the years. They would again, too, if Stephen had anything to say about it.

"Don't worry," he had told the weeping Carrie, putting his arms about her thin form and holding her tight. He couldn't bear to look at her face, to see the agony etched deeply there. Instead, he had met Ben Tucker's strong blue gaze. "I'll get him out. I'll bring Johnny home."

And that was exactly what he intended to do. Edward Pelham would shortly deliver to him the *Belvidere*'s itinerary, and he would track that ship to as many ports as necessary until he found Johnny Tucker and set him free.

Now, as he stood in the Earl's library, he forgot all about Letty Thane and Cecilia Pelham. Johnny was all that really mattered, and he turned his attention to the Earl's desk, wondering if his lordship had already learned what he needed to know and was holding back for his own reasons. A traitor to his own country, the Earl of Pelham could not be entirely trusted. Besides, Stephen guessed that he might find tidbits of information useful to the American government among the Earl's documents.

Stephen picked up the letter Letty had been holding when he entered, and scrutinized it. Then, he slit the seal and unfolded the paper. The message was written in code. His interest rising, he went to the writing desk. It didn't take long. After a brief episode with quill and paper, he had deciphered the contents of the letter. It was written in French but he translated easily. Then he sat back in the chair and expelled his breath.

"New Orleans," he muttered when he had read the whole. "De Vauban?" He frowned. "Damnation."

Upstairs, Anemone was kept busy the rest of the day tending to Cecilia's demands, and she had no further opportunity to seek out the letter from Henri Marceau. Cecilia had returned from her day's activities with plans to attend a play in the company of her brother and a group of young friends, chaperoned by her Aunt Augusta. She invited Stephen Burke to accompany the party. When he accepted, she flew into a mad frenzy of preparation, driving Anemone nearly to distraction by the many changes of her gowns and accessories. Anemone was filled with relief when everyone had departed for the evening, except for the Earl, who, as far as she could learn, had locked himself in his library straight after dinner and had not emerged since. Gnawed by an odd feeling of urgency, Anemone was determined to get into the library and read that mysterious letter. At ten o'clock, still attired in her sober black gown, she slipped down the stairs.

The house was dimly lit, cool, and silent. There was no one about. Anemone found the library doors closed, with a light showing beneath them. Astonishment filled her. The Earl was still there.

She cursed softly to herself and stared at the doors in frustration. She had never known the Earl to lock himself away for so long, and she wondered what he was up to. Chewing her lip, she hesitated. Then she heard it. A sound from within the library. A voice—shrill, high-pitched. Frightened? All her senses alert, she stepped closer.

She heard the voice again. It was the Earl. Then, another answered him. The words were indistinguishable. She quickly put her ear to the door, trying to make out the conversation. Suddenly, the Earl cried out.

"No . . . no . . . I swear I never saw it . . . I won't say a word about . . . *No!*"

The sound of a gunshot sent jagged slivers of horror through Anemone's body. She went rigid, frozen against the library doors. The blood pounded in her ears for that first wild instant as she recognized the explosive sound and realized what had happened. Then, like a flash, she reached forward and flung the double doors wide.

What she saw made her freeze on the spot, every drop of color draining from her face. The Earl of Pelham lay on his back in a puddle of blood upon the Turkey carpet.

He had been shot through the heart. Beside him hovered a thickset man in a black mask, a man who had just set a pistol upon the trestle table and stooped over the Earl as if to search him. But when Anemone burst through the door, the man straightened. For a moment he stared at her just as she stared at him. Then they both moved at once.

He was closer to the trestle table, but she was quicker. She dove for the table and knocked the pistol to the floor in a desperate and agile movement, before he could grab it. It skittered away toward the fireplace. Gasping, Anemone lunged after it. She was terrified he would reach it first or wrench it from her grasp, but instead, as she flew after the pistol, the assailant hesitated a fraction of a second, then wheeled in the opposite direction. He ran to the door and bolted through it just as Anemone came to her knees with the gun clenched in both hands.

She saw him disappear through the door, but had no time to fire. He was gone.

"Your lordship?" Anemone came shakily to her feet. Her breathing was rapid. Still holding the gun, she went to the Earl's side and knelt. She swallowed hard, trying to control the nausea that rose in her. She had seen dead men before, many times, but the sight never failed to sicken her. She reached out a cold hand and touched Lord Pelham's wrist. There was no warmth, no beat of life in his pulse. His chest was a horrible, gaping wound still gushing blood. The Earl was dead.

She remained a moment beside his body, trying to think. Everything had happened so swiftly that she could scarcely sort through the chaotic events. Her heart was thudding madly against her breast as she tried to catch her breath, tried to reason clearly in the aftermath of murder. One thing was certain. It was too late to help the Earl. Yet maybe there was something in his papers that could provide a clue as to who had killed him, and why. She rose to look upon the desk, but just then caught sight of something lying on the carpet not far from the Earl's lifeless hand. It was a paper, spattered with droplets of blood. Anemone picked it up.

The frigate Belvidere, the paper read. *Orders to patrol the New Brunswick coast. Charged to report to Commander Whiting in Saint John by the first of May.*

"The *Belvidere*." She didn't even realize she had spoken the words aloud. This was the information Stephen Burke had demanded of the Earl. The destination of the *Belvidere*. Right here in her hands.

"I'll take that, you murdering bitch."

A voice more deadly than any she had ever heard cut through the air, and she glanced up with a startled cry. She didn't know when or how he had approached without her knowledge, but Stephen Burke stood framed in the library door, black murder carved on his face.

"Hand it over, damn you!"

Without warning, he advanced on her, and Anemone did the first thing that came to mind. She whirled and hurled the paper into the blazing fire.

SIX

STEPHEN KNOCKED Anemone aside as though she were a wax doll. He jumped after the paper with single-minded determination, but he was too late. The fire snatched it with a tiny hiss, even as he reached into the flames. The paper crumbled to ash upon his outstretched fingertips, and fire singed the sleeve of his greatcoat before he snatched his arm back from the flames.

"Fool! Idiot!"

Anemone straightened up from the wall into which he had shoved her during his wild dive for the fireplace and swung to face him, forgetting everything else in this moment except Stephen Burke's rash action. Her role as meek Letty Thane, her assignment, even the Earl's corpse, all fled her mind when she saw him reach into the fire, and she lashed out at him in her own direct and scathing way, her cheeks flushed with anger at his recklessness.

"I never saw such madness in my life! Of all the crack-brained things! Are you trying to set yourself ablaze . . . ohhh!"

He rounded on her before she could finish the sentence. Involuntarily, she took a step backward.

His expression would have terrified a Philistine. His darkly handsome features blazed with wrath, a harsh and deadly wrath that set his cobalt eyes glinting and tautened his lean jaw so that he looked more than ever like a bloodthirsty pirate. He advanced, grasped her wrist, and twisted the pistol away before she even remembered she held it. Anemone tried to jerk free, but after he dropped the weapon into a pocket of his greatcoat, he seized her arms in a brutal grip.

"What did it say?" he demanded, giving her a shake that rattled her teeth. "You'd better answer me now before I throw *you* into the fire. *What did that paper say?*"

Anemone struggled against him, but he held her helpless, his fingers biting into her flesh. His hands might have been made of iron, so powerfully and cruelly did they crush the bones of her arms. For a wild, agonized moment she wondered if her bones would splinter beneath that fiendish grip. Through a dizzying pain, she tried to think. Any moment now, surely, Moffett or Mrs. Bimms or one of the other servants would come to investigate the gunshot. Any moment now Stephen Burke would have to let her go. Unless—her throat went dry as the thought occurred—unless the thickly paneled library walls had muffled the shot. Unless, snug and sleeping in their own wing of the great house, none of the servants had heard a thing. She drew a ragged breath, realizing that this was probably the case.

She was trapped alone here with Stephen Burke. Only she and a dead man stood within the blazing circle of Stephen's wrath. Only she could free herself from his ruthless hold upon her arms, a hold that forced her to fight back tears as he crunched her bones with merciless intent. Damn the man! Pain and a fury born of helplessness raced through her.

"The document," he said coldly, staring down at her. "What did it say?"

"Nothing . . . it said nothing!" she gasped through clenched teeth. "Damn you, let me go!"

Stephen Burke scowled, and shook her again, viciously, until she felt as though her head would snap from her neck.

"Answer me, you bitch! Tell me about the *Belvidere!*"

"I don't know what you're talking about . . . I never heard of the *Belvidere.*"

"Liar!" Stephen Burke yanked her up against his muscled form. His fingers nearly broke her arm. In spite of herself, Anemone cried out, no longer able to withstand the pain. Satisfaction showed in his face.

"I'll kill you if I must," he warned, staring down into her marble white countenance without a sign of pity. His eyes were as hard as agates. "I'll do whatever I must to get the truth from you. The fact that you're a woman won't save you." His mouth was a taut line and Anemone, staring up at him through a mist of pain, knew he meant every word. "If you're going to go around killing people and destroying valuable documents, you'd better be prepared to pay the price. You've just shot a man in cold blood. You're not exactly helpless or innocent. So don't plead for mercy, just talk. I'll let you go when you've told me who you're working for and what that document said about the *Belvidere.*"

Anemone could barely see him through the blur of tears that stung her eyes. She wanted to be free, oh, how she wanted to be free, but even through the crushing pain she knew it would be wrong to tell him. He was an American spy. He was an enemy. To tell him what he wished would be a betrayal of her honor and might put her country at risk.

"I didn't . . . kill the Earl," she managed to whisper after a moment, and then she swayed in his arms, her knees buckling beneath her.

Stephen swore savagely. He caught her against him, one hand releasing her only to snare itself in her coiled hair. He pulled her head back and spoke in a deceptively pleasant voice. "Still lying, I see. You must think I'm stupid. I found you with the gun still in your hand. I saw you snooping around in here this afternoon. I'm not a fool, Miss Thane. I..."

He stopped talking abruptly as the clatter of carriage wheels on cobblestones sounded outside the green-draped windows. For a moment neither he nor Anemone moved. Then, faintly, they heard the clank of steps being let down, and an instant later, Cecilia's high-pitched laughter was heard.

"They're back. Damn!" Stephen took a swift glance around the library, his gaze flickering over the Earl's body, the scattered papers, the bloodstained carpet, the trestle table that had been knocked on its side. "There's no help for it," he muttered. "Let's go."

"Go?" Anemone, barely able to move her head for the hold he had upon her, struggled anew in his grasp. Fresh alarm filled her at his words. "What do you mean? I'm not... going anywhere with you...."

"Shut up."

Stephen dragged her into the hall. Anemone felt panic rising in her. Anthony and Cecilia would be opening the door any moment. They would discover the Earl; the whole household would be in tumult within minutes. There would be hysteria, shouting, questions. The authorities would be summoned immediately. She couldn't afford to be involved in such upheaval. But to go with Stephen Burke, a man who had already hurt her and threatened her, who was forcing her to accompany him the devil knew where? She wanted to scream in frustration. Everything had gone terribly wrong in a matter of moments. She didn't know what to do, how to salvage herself or her mission.

But in the end she had no choice. She found herself

helplessly propelled to the rear of the house and out the servants' door in a matter of seconds. Chill air whipped at her as she was thrust outside into the darkness. She had no coat, only the meager protection of her dark silk gown. The night was far colder than the past evening had been; a wind reminiscent of February tore at her dress and hair. Stephen, still in his many-caped greatcoat, seemed not to notice. He pulled her along with him toward the street.

Anemone made one final effort to twist free. She kicked him, she dug an elbow into his ribs, and she opened her mouth to scream. But he had no trouble holding onto her with just one powerful arm, and his other hand clamped over her mouth. His grip was every bit as ruthless and overpowering as before. His voice in her ear was edged with mockery.

"Surely you don't wish to be left behind, Miss Thane. Do you know what they do to murderesses? Believe me, it's not a pretty sight. But perhaps you'd prefer that fate to the one I have in store for you. Too bad. I don't believe you have a choice in the matter."

His words drove new fear through her. Cold with terror, she felt herself being borne along the street at a headlong pace. Her arms ached. Her face hurt where his fingers clamped across her mouth. The sharp night air knifed right through her dress. Twice she stumbled, only to be dragged onward without a moment's pause. There was a hackney at the corner of Brook Street, and her captor hailed it with a shout. Anemone's heartbeat quickened. Surely the driver would come to her aid!

"The harbor! And be quick about it," Stephen ordered as the man perched before the coach leaned over to regard them in gaping astonishment.

Anemone fought with renewed desperation, her face turned in silent appeal toward the driver. Tightly held in Stephen Burke's arms, unable to move or speak, she begged with imploring gray eyes for his intervention.

"Hey, guv'nor, what's this all about?" the man demanded in a hoarse, suspicious tone. He eyed the slender, helplessly imprisoned girl with growing unease. It had not escaped his notice that the tall man who held her was dressed in the finest mode of fashion and appeared to be a gentleman of the *ton*. These gentry, he thought in disgust. Always kicking up a lark. Yet who was he to interfere with the pleasure of his betters? He licked his lips, glancing nervously from one to the other. "I don't want no trouble, sir," he began with caution, but Stephen cut him off.

"There won't be any trouble. Just a pound note for you, if you're quick and mind your own affairs."

Stephen held Anemone with one hand and used the other to fling open the coach door and to let down the steps. No sooner had he taken his hand from her lips than she shrieked at the driver.

"Help me! Please! Can't you see that this man is abducting me...ohhh!"

Stephen practically threw her up the steps and into the dark interior of the hackney. She fell against the leather seat with a thump. "Help me!" she screamed again, picking herself up and trying to bolt out the door, but this proved futile, for the tall American blocked her path and pushed her backward, then entered the coach himself.

She felt the hackney begin to roll away even before Stephen slammed the door shut upon them. By the time he settled opposite her on the leather seat, the carriage was swinging forward at a brisk pace, bouncing and jolting over the cobblestone streets. She realized in bitter despair that the driver had preferred the pound note to the prospect of aiding her. She gripped the seat of the coach so tightly that her nails scratched the leather.

"Where are you taking me?" she asked in a thin, hoarse voice she scarcely recognized as her own. Across from her, Stephen Burke lounged upon his seat, coolly at ease.

"To my ship. We have business to complete."

"No." Anemone swallowed. "We have no business. I have nothing to say to you."

"I disagree." He spoke almost softly. "It's merely a matter of persuasion, Miss Thane. That's all." His eyes glinted in the dark, like a panther's regarding their prey. "And believe me, Letty, or whoever you are, I am most adept at persuasion. If you're going to continue this pretense of innocence, you're going to endure a long and most uncomfortable night."

Anemone took a deep, rasping breath. She tried to stay calm. She wanted to fly at him, to tear that self-assured expression from his face. But she knew it would be useless. Her arms still ached from his grasp, and she knew she had no hope of overpowering him. Frantically, she tried to think, tried to figure a way out of this. All along, she had known that Stephen Burke would make a dangerous adversary, and now that he knew she had destroyed the information he wanted, he would be utterly ruthless. She swallowed, as the bile of fear rose in her throat. What would he do to force her to tell him the *Belvidere*'s destination? How much could she endure before she divulged what he wanted to know?

"This is all a mistake," she began, driven by a feeble hope that she still might win freedom. "I don't know what you want with me. I didn't kill the Earl—he was dead when I entered the library. I heard a shot and . . . "

"That's enough!" His voice whipped at her. Fury again darkened his lean features as Stephen Burke leaned toward her and gripped her shoulders. "One more lie, and I'll wring your neck," he warned, his breath warm upon her cheek. Anemone could only stare at him through wide, mist gray eyes.

"You'll tell me the destination of the *Belvidere*, and why you killed the Earl, and everything else I want to know before the night is gone, or I swear, woman or no, I will break every bone in your body and throw you overboard without a second thought! Think about that, Letty, until we reach my ship. Then you can begin to tell me your true identity, and whom you work for, and all those other details that interest me. But first, first and foremost, you will inform me of the contents of that paper you so foolishly destroyed. You will tell me exactly where the *Belvidere* is headed!"

"No!" Anemone broke free, throwing herself back against the seat. She straightened, and swung around again to face him. The streetlamps flashing by outside sent occasional stabs of golden light through the coach interior, enough for her to see the harshly frowning face of the man opposite her. He looked as dangerous, as deadly and formidably determined as anyone she had ever seen. He looked as though he would be quite willing to kill her.

But she knew what she was going to do and exactly what she was going to say. For Anemone, there was no other choice.

"No," she repeated, in a cool, even tone that reflected her own conviction. The shock of the Earl's death had begun to wear off, and she had at last regained her professional composure. It was patriotism that instructed her now, and there was not the slightest doubt in her mind that she was following the right course, the only course. She wrapped her arms about herself to ward off the chill, and lifted her head to meet Stephen Burke's hard stare. With her shoulders straight, her head high, and her gray eyes as dark as slate, she answered him. "I am not going to tell you one single thing. Not one." Her chin lifted. "Kill me if you wish, Mr. Burke, for you are obviously a man without scruples, and this is a dirty business. I am not afraid to die. But I will not answer your questions. Never! And nothing you can do will change my mind."

Their gazes locked and held for one long moment. Anemone was chilled by the coldness she read in his eyes, by the grim curl of his lip. She couldn't help the terror that washed through her. Still, she never faltered, never dropped her eyes, but instead met his icy stare with an expression of unrelenting determination.

"We will see, Miss Thane," Stephen said in response, leaning his shoulders back against the seat. He looked utterly assured, utterly calm, like a man without the slightest doubt of his own inevitable triumph. Anemone flinched, despite herself, at the sound of his harsh laugh. "Before the night is over, my pet, we will see."

SEVEN

A LONE ship slipped free of its moorings beneath the starless night sky. It glided from London harbor along the Thames with the swiftness and stealth of a great, prowling cat making its way through the shadows. Clouds the color of twilight twirled above, adding a ghostly quality to the night under which the *Sea Lion* sailed. On board, men worked and sweated with the rigging and the sails, but inside the captain's quarters, there was a stillness, a quietude, far removed from the grunting and groaning of the laboring seamen. Tension snapped in the air between the two people who faced each other in the lantern-lit cabin. As the *Sea Lion* swayed above the shifting currents of the river, with the uneven rocking motion common to all ships, Anemone clung to a nailed-down chair for support, her gaze never leaving the man who faced her.

They were sailing. *Sailing.* Anemone could not believe it. A short time ago she had been in the Earl's house, contemplating the end of her mission, planning her journey to New Orleans. Everything had been neat and orderly and under control. Now, events had gone astray beyond her wildest imaginings. The Earl was dead, and she... she was suspect in the murder and a prisoner on board this ship.

The cabin to which Stephen Burke had brought her after shouting orders to the ship's crew to cast off was a spacious and well-made chamber. It boasted several lanterns bracketed to the beamed walls, a small, square table flanked by chairs of carved mahogany, and a hefty bureau and wardrobe. There were also a handsome mahogany writing desk and a large bed against the near wall. The bed had brass posts and a fine silk coverlet of midnight blue interwoven with gold threads. It, like everything else in the cabin, was neat, masculine, and spotlessly clean. But Anemone derived no pleasure from the cabin's apparent comfort and the occasional elegant touches she noted here and there. The motion of the ship filled her with horror, for each movement sent her farther and farther from London.

Where were they headed? she wondered, trying to keep the panic from overtaking her. Her knees were shaking pitiably and she was grateful they were hidden under the folds of her gown. She stood gripping the back of the chair, fighting off her fear. But it rose in her like a tide that wouldn't be held back. She was alone in this cabin with Stephen Burke. She was trapped and virtually defenseless. She needed to be calm, to think clearly, yet terror broke over her in icy waves. She tried to guess what her father would do in such a circumstance. But all she could think of was what he had said when she had once asked him about getting caught. *Don't* had been Thomas Carstairs's sharp admonition, and from this she received no solace. She had already been caught. Snared like a rabbit by this implacable hunter. As far as Anemone could see, there was absolutely no way to escape.

He moved toward her then, the man who had brought

her here, who had hurt her and threatened her until every other emotion she may have once felt toward him was obliterated by her hate. Standing before him in her plain black gown, her coiled hair loosened somewhat from its tight chignon yet still pulled sharply back from her small-boned face, she found it incredible that only last night she had lamented his interest in Cecilia and wished that he might notice *her*. Well, he had noticed her at last, but she had discovered it would have been better to be noticed by a wild wolf than by this savage and ruthless man.

She would not be bested by Stephen Burke! She would not! But beneath her determination, the seeds of panic sprouted like ugly weeds, for in truth, she did not know how she would withstand him.

She flinched involuntarily at his approach, bracing herself for whatever he might do. "Are you frightened, Letty—or whoever you are?" He sounded almost amused. "You ought to be." He came forward slowly, with long, graceful strides, while one hand unknotted his cravat. He had shed his greatcoat upon a peg beside the cabin door, and now he faced her in his evening clothes, the ones he had worn to the play with Cecilia and Anthony. He looked superbly handsome. As she watched, he drew off his cravat and tossed it over a chair, then shrugged out of his fine black jacket and discarded this as well. He loomed above her in his white lawn shirt and elegant dark breeches, regarding her with a glinting light in his narrowed eyes. Anemone couldn't help but notice the way his muscles rippled beneath his shirt, or the way his breeches molded to his lean, powerful thighs. She was overwhelmingly aware of his strength and muscularity, of the raw male energy packed solidly into his elegant frame. As he towered over her, a grim smile curled his lip, as though he was enjoying the moment. Anemone wanted to strike him. This man held her fate in his hands. She, so accustomed to being her own mistress and making her own independent decisions, now was subject to *his* whims, *his* judgments. For Anemone, such circumstances were intolerable.

"Frightened? Why, no." She was pleased that her voice sounded cool and crisp, grateful that he couldn't hear the violent staccato of her heart. "I am angry though, Mr. Burke. I demand to be taken ashore immediately."

Apricot color flooded her cheeks as Stephen Burke gave a hearty laugh. "Oh, no," he said softly, one hand coming up to tilt her chin. "That's out of the question. You're going on a little journey."

"Where?"

"You tell me." His voice was deceptively silky. "Where is the *Belvidere*, Letty?"

"Do you mean... " Her eyes widened. "We're following it? The *Belvidere*?"

"Precisely. So you see why you had better tell me its destination. I need to chart our course." The silken tone had taken on an undercurrent of menace. "There's no more time for games, Letty. I need answers from you and I need them quickly. Before I lose my temper again. This time, I might not be able to restrain myself from breaking your lovely neck."

"What? No medieval torture?" Anemone pushed aside his arm so that he no longer held her chin. Sarcasm dripped from her voice. "I'm disappointed in you, Mr. Burke."

"Captain Burke. And I shall try not to disappoint you. If it's torture you want..."

She interrupted him with a note of derision. "Spare me the threats, *Captain*. They're beginning to bore me." Anemone put her hands on her hips and tossed back her head. She met Stephen Burke's piercing stare with a cool one of her own. Silently, she marveled at her own bravery, for knots of heated tension wound and rewound through her stomach, but she confronted Stephen with every appearance of ease. "I think I understand the situation, you see. Correct me if I'm mistaken. You're the captain of this ship, the one in command?"

"I am."

"And the crew will obey your every order, including the one to tip me overboard if I don't answer your questions?"

"They will."

"And you, Captain—you will not hesitate to inflict all the horrors of the Inquisition upon me if I defy you? Ah, yes, just as I thought." She laughed suddenly, a rich, rippling, mocking laugh. "My, what a charming party this is! Am I not fortunate to be in such company! Tell me, Captain, do you offer refreshments as well? And entertainment, surely there must be entertainment. Or is my torture and execution to be the sole diversion of this little soiree?"

He swore then between clenched teeth, with words that would have brought a blush to the cheek of any other woman. When he seized her shoulders, she could feel the electric tension vibrating through his body, as through coiled wires. His eyes flashed beneath their dark, slanting brows.

"You cold little bitch." His voice was gritty and rough as sandstone in her ear. "I almost admire your temerity. But don't push me. I will ask you one more time. Do you prefer to cooperate and ensure your health and safety, or do you really wish to find out exactly how entertaining this little party could be?"

Anemone's pulse pounded frantically at the undeniable savagery in his voice. His grip did not hurt her this time, but merely kept her immobile, staring helplessly up at him, and she could feel the power in his hands, power he didn't choose to exert—yet. The dangerous glint in his cobalt blue eyes made her want to run and hide. He looked enormous, very tough and thoroughly dangerous. She, on the other hand, had never felt more vulnerable. Her entire body quivered with the knowledge that she must battle and resist this man, and beneath the intensity of his hard stare, she was filled with despair. It seeped through her, chilling her blood. She felt her self-control slipping away, and with it, her bravado. Then an idea struck her, and she clutched at it with the eagerness of a lost soul glimpsing redemption.

There were more ways than one to triumph over an adversary. Hadn't her father illustrated that often enough with his anecdotes and stories? Physical intimidation was one method—Stephen Burke's method. In this respect, she was at an impossible disadvantage. But there were other ways to win a battle. She had to fight Stephen Burke on her own terms—with her wits as her arsenal. Her strength might be no match for his, but her brain certainly was. She reminded herself, gaining confidence from the thought, that she had already outwitted him once today. Surely she could do it again.

"I might be prepared to answer your questions," she said slowly, stiffly. She moved uncomfortably beneath his strong hands. Not meeting his eyes, she moistened her lower lip with her tongue. "But first... please... I don't feel very well. May I have something to drink?"

"You may have an entire bottle of my best sherry for all I care—after you've told me where the *Belvidere* can be found."

"Please..." she said in a broken voice, raising eyes of misery to his face. "I need a glass of brandy, ratafia... something. This—none of this—has been easy for me, you know."

To Anemone's chagrin, he appeared unaffected by her feigned distress. "You are a fine actress," he said ruthlessly, his hands tightening on her shoulders until she winced. "But this performance fails to move me. I have already observed that you are anything but a weak woman. I'll grant you courage, and resourcefulness, for those I've seen with my own eyes, but if you think to soften me with an appearance of fragility, I will quickly lose what little temper remains to me." Stephen's mouth twisted as he sneered down at her. "My terms are these: first answer my questions—all of them. Then you may have whatever refreshments you require, as well as a peaceful night's sleep."

"And if I choose not to answer them?" Anemone asked after a moment's pause.

"Then I will be forced to beat you until you comply," he responded coldly.

There was no mistaking the shudder that ran through her at his words. He must have felt it. He must have seen the sudden whitening of her cheeks. But there was no change in his countenance; he continued to regard her with that darkly determined expression that was even more frightening than his threats.

"All right! All right! I'll tell you, damn it. If you promise that I'll not be harmed when I'm done!" She glared at him. "Neither you, nor any of your men, will lay a finger on me. Swear to it. I want your word."

"Don't worry about that." Stephen Burke gave a short laugh. "If you think I plan to rape you, you can set your mind at rest. I'd sooner touch poison." There was such vivid contempt in his voice that Anemone was taken aback. "Go on," he said tersely. "Talk. You have my sworn word that no one will molest you once you've told the truth."

"Very well." She hung her head a moment and then broke away from him suddenly. He let her go, watching as she paced about the room. "The *Belvidere* . . . the *Belvidere* is headed for Spain," she said. "It is to dock in Barcelona the first week in April and . . . no! Stop it! What are you doing?"

She cried out as he seized her and spun her to face him, cutting off the rest of her words. "Barcelona?"

She nodded.

Stephen stared into her face. "You're lying."

"No, I . . ."

She broke off as fury like none she had ever seen blazed upon his handsome features. His voice flayed her like a whip. "Damn you, tell me the truth!"

"It is the truth! I swear it!" Anemone felt her blood turning cold. She was a good liar, an expert at deception. How did he know that her words were untrue? She had the sudden, terrifying suspicion that Stephen Burke could see right through her, that he could read her soul, and the idea that she couldn't deceive him shook her like a gale. In his eyes she saw hatred and loathing, and their brilliant blue fire filled her with dread.

"Let me go!" she demanded, fighting against him as she had earlier in the library, but he held her as relentlessly as he had before.

"I warned you, I'll have the truth!" he grated, and suddenly releasing her, his arm swung back and struck her full across the face.

Anemone felt the splinter of pain explode in her head. She heard the sharp crack as his hand struck her jaw, and then she was flying across the room, landing in a heap upon the hard, wooden floor, her vision filled with spinning light and then darkness, and all the while there was the pain, the jarring, agonizing pain.

He was standing over her. She was dimly aware of him as she lay where she had fallen, unable, unwilling to move. The floor was cold and hard against her cheek. Anemone closed her eyes. *He's going to kill me*, she thought dully. She opened them again, struggling to endure the sharp ache in her jaw. *He's going to kill me, and there's nothing I can do to stop him.*

She made no effort to get up.

Stephen looked down at her, his hands clenched at his sides. He hated this, hated what he was doing. He had never brutalized a woman in his life. But this one was different. She was a spy and a murderer, and he had to have the truth. Suddenly, as he gazed down at her on the floor, another image filled his mind for just a moment.

Another fallen figure. It was a girl. A waif alone in the darkened mist of the harbor, a waif with silver eyes and a muddied cloak. He swore under his breath. Letty Thane wore no cloak tonight, but as he stared at her slender figure, the chords of his memory stirred. Silver eyes. A lashing tongue. A gamine's face half-hidden by the mist. He knew then why she had seemed familiar this afternoon in the library; he understood his vague feeling that they had met before. Roughly, he reached down and yanked her to her feet.

"The dock! You're the brat I ran down on the dock!" He appeared stunned. He took her chin between his fingers and turned her head back and forth studying her face. With each movement, the pain in her jaw throbbed and Anemone gave a whimper which he seemed not to hear. "I wonder what skulduggery you were up to that night," he said suddenly, and his voice was harsh. "Were you spying on me? Was that little 'accident' between us staged, part of some plan? Or did I catch you fleeing another murder?" He shook her ever so slightly. "Perhaps not. Perhaps you merely had an assignation. Might it have been Marceau, Henri Marceau, you conferred with that night on the waterfront?"

"I never heard of . . . such a man," Anemone whispered, not even bothering to struggle in his arms.

Stephen's jaw tightened. "No, I suppose that's why I caught you snooping in the Earl's study. Trying to steal back Marceau's letter before the Earl could read it."

"I don't know what you're talking about." Anemone put a hand to her bruised jaw. "Please, I need to sit down. I can't think. . . . "

He caught her as her knees gave way beneath her. She seemed to crumple in his arms.

Murderess or no, the damned girl had been through a hell of a night, Stephen thought as he stared down at her. She looked like death. A few tendrils of pale hair wisped around a heart-shaped, pixie face that was white as a lily, except for the bruise on her jaw where he had struck her. Her gray eyes were dark with fatigue. She sagged against him, a soft, slender, pitiably light burden that suddenly weighed on his conscience far more than his strength. He reminded himself that she didn't deserve his pity. She had killed the Earl. She had destroyed the information he needed to free Johnny. She had lied to him over and over again. Now was the time to proceed, when she was too hurt and tired to go on. She would tell him everything if he pressed her now, if he forced her to talk. This was the moment to finish the whole nasty business.

He set her down upon a chair facing the table and went to pour her a drink.

Stephen removed the bottle of brandy he kept in the drawer of his writing desk, and watched the girl lay her head on the table and shut her eyes. He splashed brandy into a glass for her and did the same for himself. He studied her a moment in silent speculation, then carried the glasses over to the table. At that moment, a knock sounded on the cabin door.

Stephen's first mate peered at him as he opened the thick, wooden door. William Tuttle was a giant of a man, with a big, ruddy, weatherbeaten face and a red beard to match his hair. He had served on Stephen Burke's ship for more than seven years. He knew his young captain well, and there was little formality between them. Now, his bushy brows shot up in surprise as he took one glance into the cabin and saw the girl slumped over the table. He sent Stephen a sharply questioning glance.

"Captain, beggin' your pardon and all but—what the hell is going on? Why'd we cast off so quick—and who's this chit you dragged on board?" He leaned closer, fixing Stephen with a baffled expression. "And," he added after another quick glance at the girl's unmoving figure, "what did you do to her?"

"She'll come around soon enough," Stephen answered

him curtly. "Never mind that now." He ran a hand through his hair, feeling suddenly exhausted. "I suppose you also came to discover our destination. I'm damned if I know it yet. No, I'll explain it all tomorrow, William," he hurried on as the first mate started to speak. "I know you haven't a clue why we left London in such a damn-awful hurry, or what in hell's name is going on with this woman I've brought here, but take my word for it, I'm doing my best to find out where that damned ship has gone with Johnny. *She* knows, you see, and she's going to tell me. We'll be after him by dawn." He sighed, then straightened his shoulders. "I'll be able to chart our course in the morning. Until then, instruct the men to navigate to open seas and stay clear of any ships. Understand?"

"No," William Tuttle said frankly. "But I'll do as you say, Captain." He studied the younger man a moment. Stephen looked tired, but as determined as William had ever seen him, and William had no doubt as to who would be the victor in whatever kind of battle was going on in this cabin. He jerked his thumb toward the girl, watching Stephen's face. "What are you going to do with her once she talks? The men are all abuzz. Can't hardly concentrate on nothing. We ain't never had a woman on board afore now."

"Her fate," Stephen said grimly, "remains to be seen." His expression was unreadable. "Good night, William."

"And a good night to you, Captain." William grinned suddenly, his gaze traveling from Stephen to the pale-haired girl. He well knew his captain's reputation with women and felt certain this one, like so many others before her, would succumb to Burke's infamous charm before the night ended. "I'll be thinking of you, sir," he said warmly, rubbing his hands together. His meaning was unmistakable.

Stephen was scowling as he shut the door.

Anemone had heard the knock on the cabin door through a fog of pain. She lifted her head with an effort and saw the brandy goblets on the table before her. The germ of a desperate idea came to life, and she acted on it almost without thinking. Fumbling fingers reached for the vial of laudanum hidden in her black dress. Her fingers closed around the tiny vial. It was her last chance. Her final weapon. If this didn't work—she couldn't think of that. It had to work. At least it would render him unconscious for the remainder of the night and give her a chance to think. He couldn't hurt her while he was asleep, and by the time he woke from his drugged state, she may have come up with a plan. While the men talked in the doorway, she spilled several drops of the laudanum into the brandy Stephen had set on the table. She stirred it hurriedly with her finger just as he closed the cabin door. The vial went back into the hidden folds of her gown even as Stephen approached her.

Her breath came rapidly. Tension ran through her. She could feel his stare upon her and had to fight to keep from screaming, so sensitive were her nerves as she waited to see if her last, desperate ploy would work. His voice beside her made her jump.

"Let us drink, Letty," he said softly. "We will refresh ourselves. Then we can continue our talk."

She was aware of his eyes on her as she lifted her head from the table. Slowly, she reached for the glass nearest to her. She didn't look at him as her fingers touched the cool crystal. But before she could raise it to drink, his hand shot out and closed over her wrist.

"No, Letty, not that one. This one," he murmured, and nodded toward the other brandy. "I will drink from this glass," he said, and removed it from her hand.

Anemone knew the first stirrings of dread. "I . . . I beg your pardon?" was all she could manage to utter.

"Drink up," he said with a cold smile.

She swallowed and tilted her face up to his with a kind of awful foreboding. "What . . . what is this about, Captain? I don't understand."

"Humor me." The hardness was back in his voice. He picked up the glass she had left for him and brought it to her lips. "Drink this."

Anemone came to her feet, none too steadily. "This is ridiculous," she exclaimed. The pain in her jaw throbbed with each word she spoke. She began to stride about the room. "I am wholly confused. What kind of game are you playing, Captain Burke?"

He answered her with deadly calm. "You are the one playing the game. I know you have poisoned my drink. I saw you as I turned from the door. You're neither as quick nor as clever as you think. Now you will imbibe whatever potion was meant for me."

"You're mad!"

She backed away as he drained his brandy in one long swallow, set down the glass, and came toward her with the other in his hand.

"You will drink this, Letty. Make no mistake about it. I think it only fitting that you should suffer whatever wretched fate you had planned for me."

"No!"

She had come up against the wall, and there was nowhere else to move. Stephen Burke was closing in on her. "I'm not going to die, even if I drink the stupid brandy!" she cried. "It's only laudanum. A very little laudanum. I wanted to put you to sleep." She forced a laugh, but it sounded half-hysterical, even to her own ears. "Now, really, there's no *reason* ... "

"There's every reason."

Anemone tried to dodge away, but he jammed against her, his body pinning her arms to her side. He held her crushed against the wall, unable to move, and brought the brandy glass to her lips. "Drink it, Letty. Do it the easy way. Or else I'll be forced to pour it down your throat. You wouldn't like that at all, believe me."

She gazed into his eyes for one heart-pounding moment and knew he meant what he said. Frustration, rage, and despair all clamored within her. She drank. He didn't remove the glass until every drop of brandy was gone. Then he tossed the glass over his shoulder, his eyes never leaving her face.

"Now. What is the itinerary of the *Belvidere?*"

Anemone gave him a look of hate. She felt weary and defeated and sick to death of Stephen Burke and his damned questions. "Go to hell," she muttered.

He moved then, positioning his well-muscled frame so that he held her even more firmly against the cabin wall. Anemone could barely breathe and could not move at all. Her breath came in short, quick gasps, and she bit her lip against an outcry of frustration.

"Tell me, Letty." His voice pounded at her, relentless. "Tell me about the *Belvidere!*"

Suddenly, a mocking laugh half-tinged with hysteria bubbled from her lips. "I'm afraid you have ... outwitted yourself, Captain. In a very few moments, that laudanum you forced me to drink will put me soundly to sleep. You won't get any answers from me tonight. I cannot talk, cannot be tortured, when I am unconscious already. You have lost."

As if from a distance she heard his quick intake of breath. She felt the anger coursing through him as he held her pinned against the wall. She didn't care. There was little more he could do to her. All she wanted now was to sleep. The laudanum was taking effect—not surprisingly, considering the less than restful day she had already endured. Anemone felt her eyes closing. Stephen's voice came at her as if from a distance.

"Go to sleep without telling me and you'll wake up in the hold, my pet. I'll let you rot there until you're ready to cooperate."

Through her mist of exhaustion, Anemone stiffened. His words hammering at her somehow got through the gauzy layers of sleep already overtaking her. Her body went rigid. The hold! No, not the hold!

He felt her sudden tension and continued, pressing his point. "Have you ever seen a ship's hold, Letty? There are rats, I believe. It's quite dark and cold and the air is not pleasant. You won't like it, I assure you. You won't like it at all."

A cry of anguish sounded deep in her throat. Her eyes flew open, staring wide and unblinkingly into his. Stephen Burke saw terror and despair reflected in them where previously there had been only defiance. Nothing he had earlier done or said had elicited the kind of raw terror he now observed in her face. If her skin had gone white before, now it could only be described as ashen.

"No!" The word was a rasping, desperate breath. "No—not the hold! Please!"

"Then tell me, Letty. Tell me what I want to know."

"I ... can't." Tears fell then, as she shook her head helplessly from side to side. "Don't you ... see? I can't tell you. I can't betray... England..."

"Betray England? Is that what you're so worried about? Of all the idiotic—look, telling me about the *Belvidere* won't bring harm to England. It won't make you a traitor—Letty, are you listening? Damn it, girl, listen to me...."

But she was already sinking into the oblivion of laudanum-induced sleep, drooping in his arms until he found it necessary to scoop her up like a rag doll. He scowled and carried her over to his bed. Carefully, he laid her down upon the midnight blue coverlet. She looked utterly exhausted, sleeping there. And not terribly comfortable. The pins were sticking out at random from her still-coiled hair. One pressed against her neck. Almost without thinking, he tugged three or four of them free. To his astonishment, a shimmering cloud of ash blond curls tumbled loose, flowing in a silvery veil to her waist. Stephen caught his breath.

Who would have guessed she had hair like that? He had never seen such thick, luxuriant tresses, and of such a rich, silvery hue. They framed her high-boned, gamine face in a way that transformed her. She was striking, yet vulnerable, almost innocent. He noticed the rise and fall of her breasts beneath the ugly black gown. She was slender, yet temptingly curved. He sat beside her and his fingers worked at the plain, dark buttons of her dress until they were all unfastened. Then he slipped her arms free of the sleeves. When the dress stuck, and he could not free her from it, he tightened his jaw and simply tore the garment from her body. She lay at last before him in only a thin white chemise. Stephen took in her slim waist and full, rounded breasts, noting the lush curve of her hips and buttocks as she moved slightly in her sleep, curling on her side, with an arm tucked under her cheek. Her skin was fair and as smooth as the flesh of a peach. She looked delectable, as soft and appealing as a woman could be. He leaned close and ran his hand lightly over the lustrous silk of her hair. "Who are you?" he whispered, and then again, more insistently, in her ear, *Who are you?*"

In her sleep, she shifted and made a small, moaning noise. Her eyelids fluttered once. "Not ... the ... hold ..." she murmured, and then was still.

"Who are you?" Stephen Burke demanded yet again, his breath ruffling her hair as he leaned over to put his mouth beside her ear. "Tell me your real name."

To his surprise, her lips parted and she answered him as one answers in a dream. Her voice was faint and soft, but he heard the single word clearly for his face was very close to hers.

"Anemone," she murmured, and then turned her head away and was still.

Stephen rose. He stared down at her. Devilish little minx. She had indeed beaten him, for all that he had done to her. Despite everything, she hadn't told him where to find the *Belvidere*, or why she had killed the Earl. Dawn would find him still unsure of his own ship's destination. But he felt strangely victorious as he studied the girl asleep upon his bed. She had told him one thing. Her name. For some reason, he felt oddly euphoric. Then, he shook himself free of his odd, light-headed mood.

"Sleep well, Anemone," he said softly, running an eye over her lithe, nearly naked form. Several thoughts drummed in his head. Already he had another plan.

"Sleep well while you can."

EIGHT

ANEMONE AWOKE with great reluctance from the dark depths of sleep. Something terrible lurked at the edges of her mind—but what? As she felt the deep black cushions of sleep begin to lift, she sought to pull them back around herself, to sink once more into the shadowy oblivion of slumber. She wanted to escape the awful thing that awaited her when she awoke, but she didn't even know what it was. She clung to the shadows, but they fell away, and she came awake, lying with closed eyes and a heart full of fear, wondering what caused this strange and creeping dread in the corners of her mind.

Then she remembered. Panic gripped her, and her entire body stiffened. *The hold.* She would awaken in the hold. The familiar cold, black waves of fear washed over her, and with them, the nausea. She was afraid to open her eyes. Afraid to see that the darkness was real, that she was trapped, shut up in the confines of the ship's brig, enclosed like a mummy in a black and stifling tomb.

She started to tremble. Slowly, she forced her eyelids

apart. She braced herself for the overpowering rush of terror.

But it was light, not darkness, which greeted her. She was in Stephen Burke's cabin, alone—and she was lying in his bed.

She sat up so quickly that the blood pounded in her head, and it took a moment to steady herself. She felt weak with the aftereffects of the laudanum, and her jaw ached. She touched it gingerly and winced as her fingers found the swollen bruise. She gave herself another ten seconds, as the pain surged and then receded, before coming to her knees on the bed and taking stock of the room.

There was no sign of Stephen Burke. She let her breath out in a long sigh of gratitude. Dizzying relief filled her that she was not locked in the hold after all, and she felt also a sense of freedom at being alone. She had some space of time, at least, to gather her thoughts and prepare herself for the next barrage of Stephen's interrogation. She would need it, she thought wearily, if what was to come was anything like what he had put her through last night. She shivered, hugging her arms about herself. It was then that she realized her arms were bare. Her gaze swung downward, over her own body and the bedsheets in disarray about her. With a suddenness that stopped her heartbeat for a full three seconds, she realized that she was almost naked.

Her dress! What had happened to her dress? She stared in horror at the revealing white chemise that only partially concealed her breasts and ended well above her slim knees. In panic her eyes darted about the room, but there was no sign of her black gown. She went quickly back over the previous night's events without any recall of having shed her own garment. She had fallen asleep in Stephen Burke's arms while pinned against the wall, and she had still been wearing her damned dress! What had he done? What had that *bastard* done?

She turned and stared at the two pillows beneath the brass bedposts. There was a deep indentation in the one beside hers. She gave a cry of agonized pain mixed with raw, savage fury.

At that moment, the cabin door opened, and Stephen Burke strolled into the room. Anemone sprang from the bed and lunged toward him before he had turned back from shutting the heavy door.

"You abominable bastard!" she screamed, clawing for his face with her nails outstretched. "I'll kill you for this!"

He caught her wrists before she touched him, and he swung her around so that she was once again, as last night, pinned against the cabin wall.

"Let me go! I'll tear your eyes out!" She kicked and fought him with a maddened frenzy, but found herself unable to inflict any damage, for he held her almost totally immobile. "I'll kill you, you filthy, disgusting, despicable *cur!*"

"Cur? You *are* angry, aren't you?" He grinned, apparently undisturbed by her murderous attack. "Now I wonder what I did to cause such wrath," he mused, tightening his hold on her wrists as she renewed her struggles with a groan of fury. "I know. You're disappointed that I didn't lock you in the hold as I promised. Well, I can certainly oblige you, if that's what you want—Anemone."

Her mouth fell open. "How did you find out my name?"

His grin widened. "You told me. Don't you remember?"

"I don't remember any of it, you bastard! Thank heaven! I wouldn't want to remember the disgusting things you did while I was unconscious—and totally helpless! How . . . how *could* you take advantage of me in such a state?" Her breast heaved with the tight knot of fury inside her chest. Each breath was painful, and she felt the glitter of angry tears on her lashes. The agony in her face and in her voice came from the depths of her soul. "How does it feel to be a man without any trace of common decency, any scrap of moral character—a man so low as to drug a woman into a stupor and then m . . . molest her like a common wh . . . whore!"

She was crying, weeping like an idiot, like the kind of blathering, hartshorn and handkerchief ninny she had always detested, but she couldn't help herself. What he had done to her went beyond what she could bear. It had been the ultimate violence, the ultimate humiliation, and she hadn't even had the chance to fight back.

She heard him draw in his breath. Through the blur of tears she saw his face change and she heard the softening of his voice. "Is *that* what you think? That I molested you while you slept?" He stared unwaveringly into her tear-filled eyes. "Well, you're wrong," he said swiftly, releasing her wrists. She lowered her arms and gazed disbelievingly up at him. "I never touched you. I removed your gown, and I slept at your side, but you have my word—your virtue, Anemone, if indeed you possess such a thing, is still intact."

"How . . . how can I believe you?" Desperately, she wanted to believe it was true. She searched his face, trying to find the answer, hoping against hope that his words were to be trusted. Her face tilted up to his, studying the rugged planes of a countenance handsome enough to drive a woman to distraction, staring with frantic desperation into eyes that were so dark, so blue as to be almost black against the bronze of his skin. Her own eyes met his, held them in a long and painful gaze during which she sought to scour the hidden places of his mind, and at last, in the glinting, midnight blue depths of his eyes, she read the answer. She drew a long breath. Her body relaxed and the terrible gripping tension went out of her.

"I believe you." The words were soft, like a thankful prayer one says to oneself at the end of an ordeal. "I don't know why, but I do."

Stephen Burke nodded. "Good. I told you last night I

wasn't going to rape you. You ought to have believed me
then."

Her chin went up and she put her hands on her hips
in a stance of exasperation, all of a sudden oblivious of
her near nakedness before him. "After your behavior last
night, you could hardly expect me to believe anything
you might say, Captain Burke. You showed yourself to
be something less than a gentleman and I have numerous
bruises to prove it!"

Stephen laughed at her icy, challenging tone. She had
made a quick recovery from devastated maiden to coolly
professional spy. It amused him that this woman could
speak with such poise and acerbity while standing before
him in a thin cotton garment which showed a tempting
amount of delectable, silken flesh. Her breasts swelled
above the plunging, lace-edged décolletage of the chemise, and her long, lusciously shaped legs were bare to
his scrutiny. Scrutinize them he did, letting his gaze rake
over the entire length of her lush curves until the slow
apricot blush spread up from her rounded shoulders all
the way to her high-boned cheeks, and the large gray
eyes he found glaring into his were the stormy color of
a wind-tossed ocean.

"Get out of here!" Anemone cried in sudden wrath,
crossing her arms over her chest in an effort to hide herself from a gaze that made her cheeks burn. Her hair
swirled about her shoulders like a silvery veil. "But first
give me back my damned dress!"

"Your dress is gone," he replied with a chuckle. His
eyes narrowed. "It didn't suit you at all. You're not exactly
the abigail sort, Anemone. I saw that the moment I un-
pinned your hair. Not that I have any designs on you,"
he continued smoothly as she started to clench her hands
into fists, and the murderous glitter returned to her eyes.
"I believe I told you last night I'd sooner touch poison—
a fact you apparently have forgotten. No, my pet, my
only interest in you is professional, and that is something

we will take up again quite soon. But first, I suspect you'd like something to wear." He touched a strand of her hair, twining his fingers through it almost thoughtfully. "I happen to have something I believe you will like."

"Right now I'd settle for a shirt and breeches!" Anemone pushed his hand aside. "Stop staring at me, and give me some clothes before I slap your leering face!"

She stalked across the room before he could say another word and yanked the bedsheets up around her. She wrapped them about herself and then lifted her head to gaze at him. Today, he was attired in a handsome, elegantly cut coat of brilliant Prussian blue, worn over a shirt of fine white lawn. With a carelessly knotted cravat, tight-fitting buff breeches, and the inevitable gleaming Hessians upon his feet, he looked as dashing and formidable as ever. She felt ridiculous clad in a bedsheet, but at least she was clad!

"Kindly fetch me those clothes you spoke of, Captain Burke, and then get out of this cabin while I dress!" Anemone ordered.

Stephen Burke came toward her. His black hair was brushed in gleaming locks across his brow, and his devastatingly rakish aura was never more apparent than now. Anemone felt the power of the man flowing outward toward her. He was superbly fit and aggressively masculine. But it was more than his appearance that struck her. Never before had she felt such forcefulness of personality from a man. Anemone had met so many: soldiers, spies, diplomats. She was acquainted with great lords and cunning generals. None of them could match the vitality that surged through Stephen Burke. None of them had ever seemed capable of overwhelming her with his sheer power of being—as did this man now advancing on her. When he stopped before her and she tilted her head up to meet his stare, she had to fight to control the odd trembling in her limbs. Against her will, she found herself staring at the warm, sensual lines of his mouth, wondering how those firmly chiseled lips would feel upon hers. It was madness, she knew—especially after the way he had treated her last night. She ought to hate him. Instead, she felt a strange, irresistible pull, a surge of heat in her blood as he stood only inches away from her. She was intensely aware of her own near nakedness beneath the sheet. The pulse at her throat throbbed furiously with a sudden excitement. How could she, who had for years avoided all desire for any man, who had decided long ago to devote herself solely to her country, now feel such strong attraction for a man who was her enemy—and England's enemy, as well? She chastised herself. She reminded herself of what had happened the last time she gave her heart. Nevertheless, she felt herself staring as if transfixed at his mouth, and it was only with great effort that she dragged her gaze once more to his eyes. Yet here she found no relief from the potent vitality he emitted. His eyes were so blue, so electric, that the effect was like a lightning bolt striking her.

"In case you've forgotten, Anemone," he said very softly. "I am the captain of this ship, and I take orders from no one. Now, come along."

She jerked herself back to reality as he took her arm. "Where?"

"You'll see."

As he pushed her outside the cabin door, she started to protest her state of undress, but Stephen merely laughed and said, "Stop worrying about your virtue. Is that all you can think about? Do you imagine my crew and I have nothing more important to think of than ravishing you?"

"I insist on being told where you're taking me!" She tried to stop in the narrow corridor, but Stephen marched her firmly along. Suddenly, Anemone clutched his arm.

"Not . . . the hold! You're not taking me to the hold?"

"No." He glanced at her panic-stricken countenance. For a moment he seemed about to say something more, then, abruptly, he released her arm and pushed open a door behind her. "Here we are. Go in."

Anemone stepped into a cabin about the same size as her room at the Earl of Pelham's house. It was clean and tidy, though extremely plain, with none of the brass fixtures, ornate furnishings, or comfortable touches of Stephen's quarters. She appraised it in one swift glance, then turned questioningly to him.

"It's for your use," he acknowledged. "You'll find all you need here. Bathe and dress yourself. I want to talk to you in one hour. You'd best be ready."

He was gone before she could blink. Anemone turned slowly about, once more surveying her surroundings with a thoughtful eye.

The cabin had a bunk against one wall, neatly made up, with a pale blue woolen blanket folded at the foot. There was a tall, three-drawered bureau carved of pine, a single hard-backed chair nailed to the wooden floor, and a small wardrobe tucked in the corner. In the center of the room was a hip bath, filled with water. Hot water, she noted, as she stepped closer. A lovely little cloud of steam rose above the water, and Anemone moved toward it eagerly. She felt as rumpled and grimy as a soiled dishrag. She shed her bedsheet and chemise in a few quick movements and stepped into the tub without another thought.

As she sank as far down into the water as she could, she gave a small sigh of pleasure. Stephen Burke had provided her with a large cake of soap, and she lathered her skin and her hair with fragrant suds, delighted to find that the soap was scented with the perfume of roses. Now where did he come by this treasure? She didn't really care. All that mattered was that she felt wonderfully, deliciously clean when she at last rinsed the remainder of the suds from her streaming tresses and stepped from the tub.

There were towels in the bureau drawer, and, she discovered in amazement, undergarments. A woman's dainty lace-edged undergarments. An ivory-handled hairbrush and matching hand mirror, a toothbrush and toothpowder, and a basin of clear, cool water sat upon the top of the pine bureau. After rubbing her damp skin with a thick towel until her flesh tingled, Anemone tended to her toilette and soon found herself wearing the satin undergarments, with her hair curling in long silken tendrils to her waist. She felt wonderfully clean and refreshed, and would have been quite happy if not for the nagging anxiety in the pit of her stomach about what Stephen Burke intended to do with her today. She felt a bit like a pig being fattened for the slaughter. This feeling intensified when she peered into the wardrobe and saw the single gown awaiting her there.

The gown was a breathtakingly lovely day dress of rose pink crepe. Anemone couldn't remember when she had seen anything quite as beautiful. Cut low across the bodice and adorned by an Empire waist banded in rose velvet, a fetchingly frilled hemline, and dainty pink sleeves which came to a lace-edged point at her wrists, this pastel vision of femininity and elegance surpassed even the gowns of Cecilia Pelham. It was obviously Parisian in cut and style, and was lovely enough to make any woman gasp in pleasure. Anemone was no exception. She donned it with a sense of rare delight, reveling as the rich crepe slid over her skin and the softly flouncing skirt fell past her hips to the floor. Stephen Burke had thought of everything. There were even pink silk stockings to match the gown, and dainty white slippers tied with small velvet ribbons of the same rose shade as her velvet waistband. As she caressed the smooth material of her skirt, stepping this way and that about the cabin, Anemone wondered anew where her American captor had come up with such finery. But her questing mind soon moved on to more serious matters.

What did Stephen Burke plan to do with her today?

She still hadn't told him what he wanted to know. Did he intend to repeat the violent interrogation he had subjected her to last night? She felt sick with apprehension, remembering his determined brutality. Her hand moved gently to her bruised jaw. She didn't think she could risk lying to him again. Yet honor wouldn't allow her to divulge the truth.

She picked up the pearl-handled hairbrush in a hand that shook. As she began to brush her hair with long, thorough strokes, she fought off the trepidation that weighed on her heart. She had to be calm, to be strong. She thought of her father and his faith in her, and of Oliver, who had trusted her with her very first assignment. She couldn't let them down.

She had no sooner finished brushing her hair than a peremptory knock sounded on the door, and without waiting for an answer, Stephen Burke strode into the room. She set down the brush and swung to face him, her pale, luxuriant hair swirling about her shoulders as she did so.

"Feeling better, Anemone?" he inquired with a faint lift of his brows while he leisurely surveyed her from head to toe. At the gleam of appreciation that entered his eyes as he observed her temptingly curvacious form, Anemone felt a flush creep into her cheeks. "An admirable fit, isn't it? And most becoming. I far prefer you in this, my pet, than in that ugly servant's costume you forever wore in the Earl's household."

"I am delighted you are pleased," Anemone answered him coolly. "But if you think to buy my favor with pretty gowns and satin slippers you are mistaken! I accept this dress and these accessories because you owe them to me—having abducted me without benefit of a single item from my own toilette or wardrobe, and having confiscated the gown I had upon my back! But if you think I'm going to betray my country in exchange for such gifts, you are wrong. I am not the Earl of Pelham. My allegiance cannot be bought."

Stephen Burke threw back his head and laughed. He took a step nearer to her, towering over her with a grin of genuine amusement.

"You are by far the most suspicious woman I've ever met. First you think I want to rape you, and then you think that I want to buy your allegiance. If bribery was my intent, Anemone, I would offer far more than gowns and slippers."

"Five thousand pounds, perhaps?" she countered, and was pleased by the startled look that suddenly came over his face.

"How did you know about that?" The sharp edge was back in his voice. She suddenly regretted the impulse that had made her refer so knowledgeably to his bargain with Edward Pelham, but there was no retreating now.

"I know a great deal about you and your dealings with the Earl," she answered, her expression calm despite the quickened beating of her heart. "You are not quite as clever and as secretive as you may think, Captain Burke."

"So it seems." His brows knit in a frown as he regarded her. Anemone met his gaze with every appearance of serenity.

"I believe I underestimated you," he said slowly, after a moment. "I have seen that you are courageous and stubborn, and also that you possess a great deal of cunning. Now I know that you are also quite efficient at your work. I think we can be of use to each other, Anemone."

"Oh?"

"Come with me. You must be as hungry as I. We'll breakfast in my cabin, and then we will talk."

She made no protest as he took her arm to escort her to the doorway, but paused in the corridor to glance up at him. "I hope this is going to be a *civilized* discussion, Captain," she remarked carefully, hoping he would not detect her fear. "Violence does not always answer."

"Perhaps not." He chuckled softly. "But I have found it to be quite effective on a number of occasions." At her sudden intake of breath, he continued lightly, "Have no fear, my brave little warrior. I will not abuse you today."

She wasn't quite sure she believed him, but something inside of her relaxed, and she allowed herself to be drawn to his cabin without resistance. Stephen Burke, after all, held all the cards, and she was merely a player in his little game. She had no hope, at the moment, of winning, but if she was very careful and kept her wits about her, she just might live to finish the round.

He held the door for her with a faint smile, and she passed by him into the spacious room. Anemone kept her shoulders straight and her head high. There was no escaping him, so she might as well let the deadly little game begin.

NINE

BY THE time Stephen Burke had consumed a hearty breakfast and conversed pleasantly with Anemone about half
a dozen inconsequential subjects, she felt more than ready
to get to the crux of the matter. The suspense of her fate
and of what would happen today built with each passing
moment, and while Stephen gave every appearance of
enjoying his considerable repast, Anemone was only able
to nibble on a pear and to sip one cup of strong morning
tea. When a bony young seaman by the name of Ruggins
had left the cabin with the breakfast remains, she came
to her feet, nervously smoothing the rose folds of her
skirt. If Stephen Burke was in no hurry to get down to
business, she was. It was time to take the initiative and
end this nerve-rattling suspense.

"Captain, the moment has come to abandon all of this
polite and terribly inane chatter so that we can talk in
earnest," she began in a formal tone. "You seem to be in
a much more civilized mood today than you were last
night, and I am grateful for that." She inclined her head

graciously toward him. "I assume you have realized exactly how unpardonable your behavior was. You still have a chance to rectify it, however. Each moment that passes carries me farther from London. Now is the time to turn back and return me to English soil."

Stephen Burke came to his feet and approached her with long, easy strides. "A worthy try, Anemone, but a useless one," he murmured. "I told you yesterday. You are accompanying me on a journey to find the *Belvidere*. I haven't changed my mind about that. Now, the sooner you reveal that destination to me, the sooner we will reach it, and by that time, perhaps, I will be willing to free you to go your own way."

She spoke through clenched teeth. "I've already told you. Nothing will induce me to reveal that information to you."

"Nothing?" Stephen's voice was deceptively soft. "Not even a prolonged stay in the hold of this ship?"

Her quickly indrawn breath was followed by a rigid tensing of her spine. "Not even that," she managed to utter, though her voice was hoarse. Stephen studied her a moment in silence.

She was a breathtaking sight today. Gone was the last remnant of Letty Thane. Splendidly attired in the rose crepe gown which clung to her slender, voluptuous figure in a tantalizing way, with her fair hair cascading in lustrous waves to her waist, this most efficient and practical enemy spy looked utterly captivating. Now, her delicate, heart-shaped face with its light dusting of freckles and its elegantly carved features had taken on a slight pallor, and her lovely little mouth was tightly clenched, but Stephen knew the reason for that. He couldn't help wondering why his threats about the hold produced such terror in her. She had withstood his verbal and physical assaults last night with staunch courage and firm resolution, yet whenever he broached the prospect of physical confinement in the brig she cringed with unmistakable panic. This reaction was in curious contrast to the unshakable demeanor she generally presented. At this moment she was staring up at him with the expression of stony defiance she had maintained throughout last night, and yet he saw the glimmer of fear deep within her lovely gray eyes and knew she was terrified he would make good his threat.

"Don't worry, little one," he said suddenly, one hand coming up to brush her cheek. "I'm not going to lock you up." Her skin was like the silken petal of a flower beneath his strong hand. Though she flinched at his touch and tried to back away, he quickly grasped her arms and held her captive before him.

"What if I told you that in revealing the *Belvidere*'s destination you would be doing no harm to England?" he queried, watching her face. "What if I told you that my interest in the ship is personal, that my pursuit of it would in no way endanger your country or aid Bonaparte in his war against her?"

Anemone shot him a derisive smile. "I wouldn't believe you."

"Why not?"

"Because five thousand pounds is a vast sum of money, Captain Burke. You surely don't expect me to believe that you offered such a staggering amount on your own. It must have been put up by your government."

"You're wrong." Stephen grinned at her. "The money is my own."

"You must be quite wealthy," she mocked, and tried to break free of his hold, but his fingers tightened around her arms and held her still.

"I am," he conceded. "And I am willing to pay or do whatever is necessary to track down the *Belvidere*."

"Why?" she demanded swiftly, but he shook his head.

"Personal reasons," Stephen Burke said.

She regarded him coldly. "If you think that I will trust you as easily as that, Captain Burke, you are mistaken.

I must know all the details before I will even begin to discuss my information with you."

Suddenly, anger darkened his features. After what he had put her through last night, Stephen had decided to take a different tack this morning. Violence against women was not his usual method, and it had certainly gained him little against this particular female. In view of her courage, her stamina, and her obvious intelligence, he had planned to negotiate a bargain with her today and had come up with an offer he thought she would accept. But the damned vixen wasn't even giving him a chance to broach it. Instead of appearing subdued and intimidated, she insisted on attacking him at every turn, questioning his most basic statements. Who in hell did she think she was? He had been giving her an opportunity to save her skin, and she answered him as though *she* was the one conducting this interrogation.

"I believe I must relieve you of a misapprehension, my pet," he growled, and the next instant he picked her up and tossed her unceremoniously down upon his bed. She tried to spring up, but he pushed her back and straddled her, his lean, powerful body pinning her to the mattress. When she tried to hit him, he caught her wrists and held them over her head. Anemone gasped and struggled, but he held her prisoner with infuriating ease and gazed down with a satisfied expression into her furious face.

"You seem to have forgotten who is in command here," Stephen Burke said coolly, his handsome features wearing the most heartless expression Anemone had ever seen. "I am about to make you an offer which could save your pretty neck. You would do well to accept it and to remember that you are in a very, shall we say, *vulnerable* position here on my ship. From this point on, I expect you to bear that in mind. I am the one who must know all the details, and you are the one who will provide them. Do you understand?"

Anemone was panting breathlessly beneath him, still

trying to tear her wrists from that steel grip, to throw off the weight of his powerful frame. Helpless fury raged within her. "I understand only that you are a despicable scoundrel and I will never, ever cooperate with you!" she retorted wrathfully.

Stephen's blue eyes narrowed. "Oh, yes, you will." He waited as she exhausted herself fighting him. After several moments, her breath came in ragged gasps, and damp tendrils of hair curled around her temples. "Are you ready now?" he asked with exaggerated patience.

Anemone stared at him with a look of hatred. She could scarcely breathe from the exertion of twisting beneath him, yet her wild struggles had gained her nothing. Stephen Burke held her firmly beneath him, his muscular thighs pressed hard against her slender ones, his weight holding her helpless on the bed. His darkly handsome face leaned close to hers, revealing the faintly smiling lips, the mocking eyes which only added to her fury.

"Well?"

"I make no bargains with a man whose word cannot be trusted!"

One eyebrow lifted in sardonic amusement. "And what makes you think that my word cannot be trusted, my pet?"

"Because only an hour ago you assured me that you would not use force against me today!" she flashed. "And here you are, using your disgusting, superior male strength in a pathetic attempt to intimidate me! So much for your sense of honor, Captain Burke!"

Her words struck him like a slap in the face. He *had* promised not to abuse her today, damn it. Somehow or other, she had gotten under his skin and annoyed him enough for him to violate his own intentions.

"*Touché*, Anemone," he said coldly, then released her as abruptly as he had pounced upon her. He rolled off of her and walked to his writing desk, leaning his hip against it as he watched her rise unsteadily to a sitting position on the bed. She swung her legs to the ground, waited a moment as the ship gave a particularly violent lurch, and then came cautiously to her feet. Though she was disheveled and breathless and her color was high, she still held herself proudly as she turned to glare at him.

"You said you had an offer to make me. Go ahead and make it!" she challenged.

Suddenly, Stephen laughed. "You're one hell of a fighter, aren't you, little one? I'm damned if I ever met a woman combining so much courage with so much sense. So you are ready to listen to my proposition after all?"

"I'm listening." She bit off the words, watching him with the wary eyes of a cat who has been cornered by a hunting hound. For all his urbane air at the moment, she recognized that his barely controlled violence could erupt at any provocation. This knowledge made her nerve endings crackle with alarm, but she'd be damned if she'd show him how rattled she was. She tossed her hair over her shoulders and straightened her spine. The rose crepe gown rustled as she walked carefully forward until she stood directly before him. "I'm waiting," she said in an icy, level voice. "Let's hear your proposition."

For a moment, she thought she read admiration in his keen blue eyes, but then a mask shut down over his features, and she wondered if she'd imagined it.

"I will trade you safe passage to any destination you wish for information about the *Belvidere*'s itinerary. Of course, this passage will take place *after* we have located the frigate in question. You also have my word," and here he paused with a slight, sarcastic smile, "my solemn, sworn word, that my reasons for seeking out that ship are personal and will in no way harm your precious England." He moved off the writing desk, coming forward until he towered above her, locking his gaze with hers. "So there you have it, my lovely, deadly little spy. All you need to do is tell me what I wish to know, and you will be assured of eventual freedom. If you don't . . . " His voice trailed off regretfully. "I hate to even think about *that.*"

Anemone went cold at the undeniable threat in his words, but remained silent, weighing his offer. It was scarcely satisfactory to be forced into giving up the information, but when it came right down to it, what else could she do? Stephen Burke would not rest until he knew how to track down that damned ship. There was no escaping him. Besides, she thought with sudden inspiration, now that Lord Pelham was dead there was not much use for her in England, save for filing a final report with Oliver. She had wanted to go to New Orleans anyway—maybe this disaster could somehow be turned to her advantage.

"What will be my status on this ship if I answer your questions?" she asked slowly. "Prisoner?"

He shook his head. "Honored guest. You shall have your own quarters and receive every consideration from myself and my crew."

Anemone was silent. "And you will take me anywhere I wish to go, as soon as the *Belvidere* is found?"

"Yes."

She took a deep breath, then gave him a searching look. "I must have your assurance that this information will not be used against England!"

Stephen saw the determination in her face and something inside of him responded. Whatever else she might be—murderess, spy—she was loyal to her country. A patriot working on behalf of her land, just as he worked so tirelessly for America. "I promise you, little one. No harm will come to England as a result of our pact."

Slowly, Anemone turned away. She paced the length of the cabin and then returned to face him. "Very well." She bit her lip, then continued quietly. "I will agree to your terms."

"A wise choice," Stephen drawled, and then lifted her

slim hand in his strong one. Startled, her eyes flew to his face. He was smiling at her, coolly, mockingly. Without taking his eyes from hers, he brought her hand to his lips and pressed a kiss against her smooth white flesh. "To seal our bargain," he murmured, chuckling as she snatched her hand away.

The touch of his lips burned her skin. She felt a warm flush stealing up her neck and into her cheeks. "Need I remind you that this is strictly a business arrangement, Captain?" In an attempt to cover up the unexpectedly intense reaction his gesture had produced, she spoke with biting sharpness. "Simply because we will be traveling together for a time does not mean that any... friendship will spring up between us. I prefer to keep our relationship a strictly formal one."

"And so do I." He shouldered past her then and sauntered to his writing desk, opening a carved rosewood box and removing a cigar from it. As he lit it up, he regarded her with an infuriatingly offhand expression. Everything about him suggested a young man of arrogance and ease and supreme self-confidence. His assurance grated on her already frayed nerves, making her want to stamp down on his foot or box his ears, anything to wipe that suave expression from his face. "That reminds me." He blew a puff of smoke into the air. "Since we're going to keep this arrangement formal and professional for the length of the voyage, don't you think you'd best tell me your surname? I can hardly continue calling you 'Anemone,' now can I, Miss...?"

"Houghton," she supplied with only fractional hesitation.

"Very well, Miss... Houghton. Let's get down to business." Suddenly, his gaze sharpened on her, and she felt caught in the dark sphere of his icy blue eyes. "Where is the *Belvidere*?"

The bargain had been made. There was no point in delaying her own part in it. She faced him with chin proudly uplifted and answered the question that was so important to him. "The *Belvidere* has orders to patrol the coast of New Brunswick, and is charged with reporting to Commander Whiting in Saint John by the first of May." As she repeated the contents of the note she'd read in the Earl's study, she watched Stephen Burke's reaction closely. His eyes narrowed to deadly slits at her words.

"New Brunswick," he muttered, and paced about the writing desk. "By the first of May." Then he glanced up and bestowed a cool smile upon her. "Thank you, Miss Houghton."

Anemone nodded with all the friendliness of a dueling opponent. "We shall make it to New Brunswick by that time, shan't we, Captain?"

"You're damn right we will," Stephen said grimly.

"And then you will take me where I wish to go?"

"Yes. And where *do* you wish to go, Miss Houghton?"

"To New Orleans." She watched his reaction to this calmly.

At her words, Stephen Burke raised his dark brows and regarded her with a sudden intense scrutiny. She knew he was remembering the Earl's hints about the city, and a slight smile curled her lips as she turned gracefully about and moved toward the door of the cabin. "Now, if you'll excuse me, Captain Burke, I wish to take a stroll on the deck and enjoy the sea air. Good day."

"Just a moment." Stephen's voice flicked out, stopping her at the threshold, and she gazed back at him over her shoulder, her gray eyes the color of smoke.

"Yes?"

"Why do you wish to go to New Orleans, Miss Houghton?" he inquired in a thoughtful, deliberate tone.

Anemone's smile would have melted snow. "Personal reasons," she said sweetly, and then departed.

Stephen stared after her, caught between laughter and frustration. She was a damnable little minx. After what he had seen of her in the past day, he wondered how he

could ever have thought her plain. It was true, she hadn't
Cecilia Pelham's dark, classic beauty, but there was something intriguing about her. Hers was a fresh, unusual
kind of beauty. She was as graceful and fragile-looking
as a flower, and yet her backbone seemed made of solid
steel. It would have to be, he reflected with a grimace,
for her to murder Pelham in cold blood. He marveled
that she knew so many details about his bargain with the
Earl, realizing that she must have been hidden somewhere in the library during their conversation. She was
as daring as she was clever and she was remarkably efficient. She probably knew much more about this New
Orleans business than he did. But not everything, Stephen mused with satisfaction. Not the contents of Marceau's letter. With this thought, he went to his writing
desk and unlocked the ornately carved drawer. He lifted
out the parchment written in Henri Marceau's hand. The
curious message made little sense to him, but then neither
did this entire nasty business. Anemone Houghton could
no doubt shed some light on matters for him—if she only
would.

"It won't be easy," he thought, tapping the letter against
his palm. It had been difficult enough wringing the *Belvidere*'s destination out of her. Now that he knew exactly
where he had to sail to free Johnny, Stephen Burke turned
his attention to the doings afoot in New Orleans, doings
he was determined to uncover once his friend was free.
And if this cool-headed, wily English spy could help him
to do that, by the devil, she would!

There would be no violence this time, Stephen decided
as he sat down at his writing desk and began to assemble
the instruments he needed to chart the *Sea Lion*'s course
to New Brunswick. He knew a better way of dealing with
obstinate females. A way that had gained him admittance
into the boudoirs of a hundred women across the con-
tinents. Anemone Houghton (or whatever her name might
be) was a cunning spy, but beneath it all, she had the

same vulnerabilities, the same desires as the other ladies he had known. And Stephen was an expert at awakening those desires. Only this time it would not be for pleasure's sake that he courted and seduced. No, Anemone must fall under his spell and open not only her body, but her mind to him. By the time he was finished with her, by the time the *Sea Lion* reached New Brunswick, she would have told him all she knew about the New Orleans affair. She would be a most useful source, and he wouldn't have to harm a hair on her head in order to acquire the information he desired.

Stephen grinned to himself. He would have to watch his step with her. The cold-hearted little bitch had already murdered one man. It wouldn't do to turn his back on her. Still, he found himself eagerly anticipating the challenge of wooing her and stripping away that cool exterior. When it came to the sexual battlefield, he was a master strategist, and he intended to use every bit of his tactical knowledge against his fair opponent. All in the name of duty, of course.

A chuckle escaped him as he contemplated her defeat, before turning his attention to the maps before him. In this instance, the fulfillment of his duty would not be an altogether unpleasant task. In fact, he was rather looking forward to it.

TEN

THE NEXT five days passed more quickly than Anemone would have imagined. She found herself the recipient of a half dozen more gowns, which William Tuttle informed her had been purchased in France by the Captain himself. Though the first mate did not say so, she received the distinct impression that the ravishing garments of velvet, silk, and muslin, as well as the silken undergarments and the ivory-handled accessories she had already received, had been purchased as gifts for Stephen Burke's mistress. It gave her a perverse satisfaction to assume possession of the gowns, and she felt not the slightest guilt for doing so—after all, Stephen had forced her to come on this journey without a stitch of clothing. If sacrificing the gifts he had purchased for his mistress was his penance for that, so be it.

After countless voyages with her father, Anemone was an excellent sailor and never failed to feel a thrill of exhilaration when the fresh salt wind blew upon her face, and when she could stand at the rail for hours and gaze upon the vast, diamond blue ocean rolling endlessly into the distance.

The *Sea Lion* was a handsome, well-built ship, and the men who sailed her were a most capable and disciplined crew. Stephen Burke had apparently instructed them to treat her with polite respect, for no one disturbed her on her frequent wanderings about the ship, and when one of the seamen did speak to her, it was always with courtesy.

She saw little of Stephen himself those first five days. From time to time she glimpsed him striding about the quarter-deck, issuing orders or conferring with William Tuttle or one of the other crew members. He never gave her more than a passing nod. She dined alone each day in her own quarters, with only four beamed walls to gaze at, and no one at all with whom to converse.

On the sixth day following her pact with Stephen, Anemone stood at the rail watching the murky clouds swim overhead. The ocean whipped restlessly beneath the ship, its waters a deep, stormy blue as the cold Atlantic wind blew fiercely. Anemone shivered in her apricot silk dress with its flounced hemline and narrow lace sleeves. Though it was nearly April, the ocean air was chill and the salt spray splashed icy droplets on her upturned face.

She was engrossed in thoughts of England and the Pelham family when Stephen Burke came up behind her. Imagining the scene of pandemonium and grief that must have ensued after Cecilia and Anthony discovered their father's dead body in the library, Anemone didn't hear Stephen's approach. She was wondering, ruefully, what Oliver had made of the whole thing, especially her disappearance. England seemed far away to her now, another world, another life. Yet somewhere back in London, a murderer prowled with blood on his hands. The sense of unfinished business weighed on her. *Damn*, Anemone thought, gritting her teeth in frustration. Why had the

Earl been killed—and by whom? She wished it were in her power to discover the truth.

"Why don't you go below and keep warm and dry?"

The deep voice at her elbow made her jump, and she turned to find Stephen Burke beside her, an inquiring smile on his face. Seeing him brought her back to the present in a rush.

"I much prefer the fresh air." She shivered again. "I don't like being confined, Captain."

He put a hand on the rail beside her. For all that Anemone retained a cool demeanor, she was vividly aware of his tall, powerful form beside her, of the handsome features so close to hers. Against her will, she had thought of him constantly during the past days, and though many of her memories were angry ones, some were almost bittersweet. At night when she dined in her cabin, she sometimes reflected on the way he had intervened on her behalf against Anthony. Of course, fury would immediately set in when she recalled his deprecating words after that, when he thought she was out of earshot. His dismissal of her as an unattractive woman still smarted. And when she recalled how he had stood entwined with Cecilia Pelham, kissing her with such mastery, such *enjoyment*, her smoky gray eyes clouded over with a fine, damp mist. She was embarrassed to think she had ever wondered what it would be like to be held in his arms. *Lunatic musings*, she told herself contemptuously. But then, against her will, she would suddenly remember how his hands had felt about her waist when they had met on the docks, when she had been caught for that one magical moment in his mesmerizing spell. He had become strangely gentle then, and unexpectedly kind. Other memories came to her, disturbing her when she curled upon her bunk at night, tossed gently by the rolling sea. In the darkness of the tiny cabin, she would see his handsome, arrogant face, his vivid, gleaming blue eyes, and once again she would feel his arms around her, holding her tight and close against him. When this happened, she would shut her eyes and curse herself for a fool, then with the fierce determination that was so much a part of her, she would force him from her thoughts. Despite all her efforts, however, there were times when his image, his voice, his strong, vibrant touch would intrude upon the orderly workings of her mind and disturb her equanimity.

Now, as he stood beside her at the rail, she couldn't resist the urge to steal a glimpse of him. He looked magnificent in his brown buckskin breeches, open-necked yellow shirt, and polished leather boots. The wind ruffled his hair, and the grim, cloud-heavy day made a perfect backdrop for his rugged bronze features and splendid physique.

"Yes, Miss Houghton?" he murmured sardonically, lifting a brow at her thoughtful surveillance. Despite herself, Anemone blushed, mortified that she had been caught staring.

"Forgive my scrutiny, but I couldn't help it. You look like a pirate, Captain Burke!"

"And you look like a cold, bedraggled waif!" He chuckled, allowing himself to take in her dress blowing in the sharp breeze, the fine spray of mist upon her delicately sculpted features, and her hair, which had been caught by an apricot-colored velvet ribbon at the nape of her neck, only to be sent flying about her by the lash of the wind. "Come here, before you turn into an icicle," he added, grasping her arms and pulling her close against the warmth of his own body.

Anemone's first reaction was to pull away, but his arms about her were so warm, so comforting against the buffeting breeze that she remained, sheltered by his powerful frame and encircling arms, her head resting momentarily against one strong shoulder. "That's better, isn't it?" Stephen said softly. Snuggled against the hard wall of his chest, she nodded gratefully, then suddenly, through the dreamy contentment that had come over her, she recognized the intimacy of their position. She stiffened and disentangled herself from his arms.

"Thank you, Captain, but no. Perhaps next time when you abduct me for an unexpected voyage, you will think to provide a cloak." Her words were crisp, her gray eyes cool and direct upon his. "If you'll excuse me now, I think I *will* go below after all."

"By all means." He bowed in mocking amusement. His glinting blue gaze followed her as she turned and walked with light, graceful steps to the companionway. When she had disappeared from view, he grinned to himself and, whistling, took the stairs to the quarter-deck two at a time.

In her cabin, Anemone reviewed the meeting with anger, most of it directed at herself. How could she have actually allowed Stephen Burke to embrace her that way? What had she been thinking of? He was her enemy. He was ruthless, cold. But in the past few days, her feelings about him had undergone a subtle change. True, their countries were at odds, but they were not at war, at least not yet. True, he could be dangerous, relentless, and harsh, but she had only witnessed these traits when he was crossed. Mostly he was a determined and powerful man with the intelligence and strength to make a damned good spy. They were no longer working at cross-purposes. They had formed a truce. There was no longer the slightest reason to hate or fear him.

Anemone paced her tiny cabin, a rueful expression on her face. Maybe the fear she felt now was not one of physical violence. Maybe it was a fear of the intense physical attraction she had felt ever since their first meeting on the mist-shrouded dock. She, who had felt nothing for any man since Andrew Boynton had disillusioned her at the tender age of sixteen summers, now was dangerously drawn to another man totally unworthy of her trust!

It was ironic, Anemone reflected, sitting down upon

her bed and leaning back against the beamed wall behind her, with her legs stretched out in front. After the way Andrew had used her five years ago, she had sworn never to give her heart to any man, ever again! It still hurt her to think how blind, how innocent she had been. Andrew Boynton had been a dashing young captain in Lisbon when her father had been stationed there as liaison with General Wintersham. He had been charming, amusing, and handsome in a debonair, boyish way, with brown, wavy hair and smiling eyes. She had fallen under his spell like a lamb cajoled by the sweet pipe-playing of Pan himself and had believed herself totally, helplessly in love. Worst of all, and most painful, had been her conviction that he returned her ardor. He had assured her of that. He had laughed at her, teased her, and kissed her beneath a Portuguese moon, hinting at the life they were destined to share together. When her disillusionment had come, as it certainly had, it had devastated her. She discovered, quite through accident, that her adored Captain Boynton was also courting the daughter of the consulate general, and the niece of a Portuguese attaché. He was endeavoring through all of them to further his own career and advancement in the military ranks. When she realized that his primary wish was not to marry her but to curry favor with her father, her agony had shattered her. Anemone had wanted to die, or to kill him. The pain and betrayal had burst through her like cannon fire, ripping apart all the tender innocence of her sixteen years, destroying her girlish dreams in one shattering explosion. She had met him one final time after her discovery. Somehow she had managed to conceal her feelings while they strolled about the camp that sunlit afternoon, arm in arm. When they paused to speak to two of Andrew's fellow officers, Anemone had found the opportunity she'd been waiting for. Suddenly turning to him with a glittering smile, she had announced that she had a message which needed to be delivered and begged him to oblige her. In the presence of his colleagues, Andrew had bowed and gallantly offered his services, and then Anemone had told him the names of the two recipients of her message. He had paled at her words. The names she spoke, as well his fellow officers knew, belonged to the ladies with whom Andrew Boynton had intimate acquaintance.

"Tell these two, I am sure, charming ladies that they are more than welcome to you," Anemone had directed with a dangerously pleasant smile. Through the tightness in her heart, she had continued in a calm, bright manner, "I no longer have the slightest use for a spineless, lying, sniveling *toad* but they may not be as particular as I am in such matters. Please assure them that they have my most sincere felicitations for happiness with a man *I* don't consider good enough to lick my boots."

With these words, and her haughtiest smile, she had suddenly shoved him backward into the horse trough that stood directly behind the little group. In the midst of Andrew's outraged yelp, the officers' chuckles, and the stares of most of the nearby soldiers, Anemone had walked with her head held high and a disdainful expression on her face, back to her own quarters. There, in the privacy of her own surroundings, she had wept for the remainder of the afternoon, but no living person, even her father, ever knew it. From that moment on, whenever the name of Andrew Boynton was broached to her, Anemone showed a face of utter boredom and murmured merely, "Oh, *him?*" Yet deep inside, the pain had remained. She had made up her mind never to give her heart away again and had never been in the slightest danger of doing so. She enjoyed the company—the talk, the jokes, and the camaraderie—of many of the men of her acquaintance, but had never felt the spark of attraction to a single one of them. Until now. From the first moment she had encountered Stephen Burke he had triggered something long buried inside her.

This is madness, utter madness, Anemone told herself

angrily, driving her fist into the mattress of her bunk. *Stephen Burke is the last man in the world I should think of in this way. He's more dangerous than ten Andrew Boyntons!*

Anemone leapt from the bunk and paced the narrow confines of her cabin, berating herself for this unexplainable weakness. Surely she ought to be able to control these ridiculous emotions for a few short weeks, until the ship reached New Brunswick, and then New Orleans! She had only to avoid contact with Stephen until then. Once she set foot in America she would be free of his presence and no longer forced to gaze upon his powerful frame and rugged countenance. She wouldn't have to endure the bold stare of his vivid blue eyes or try to think when he was towering beside her. It wasn't fair that he had the advantage of distracting her with his mere presence. He seemed so calculatingly clear-headed every moment, and suffered none of the dizzying sensations that sometimes clouded her mind when he was near. She cursed her own stupid yearnings, painfully aware that *he* experienced nothing of the kind toward *her*. He had certainly shown little interest in her these past five days, and he had already declared her unworthy of even Anthony Wickham's attentions, much less his own. It was plain that she held no allure for him whatsoever. She stopped her pacing as she reflected suddenly on how he had drawn her into his arms a few moments ago, beside the railing. Her cheeks burned at the mere thought of it, for now it was obvious, humiliatingly obvious, that he had simply been amusing himself at her expense. Since there were no other more desirable females around, he had thrown out an advance in her direction. The man was no better than a satyr!

A knock on the cabin door interrupted her reflections. She composed her face before opening the door. She was surprised to discover Tom Ruggins, the steward who brought her meals, shuffling his feet outside the cabin.

"Yes?" Anemone smiled at the thin, shy young man

whose protruding ears and heavy spattering of freckles gave him a homely yet likable appearance. "What is it, Mr. Ruggins?"

"The Captain sent you this message, miss!" Blushing hotly, Ruggins thrust a sealed paper into her hands. "He said I should wait for your answer."

"Thank you." Turning away, Anemone tore open the seal. In bold, handsome black script, Stephen Burke had issued an invitation. Or was it a command? He wanted her to dine with him in his cabin that evening.

"No." Anemone took a deep breath, then spun to face Ruggins before she changed her mind. "Thank Captain Burke for his kind invitation, but tell him I . . . I have the headache, and will not be able to oblige." Something deep inside her longed for the company, for someone to talk to and laugh with over the evening meal, but every instinct screamed at her to avoid Stephen Burke like the plague. Dinner alone with him would be far too dangerous.

When Ruggins had departed, the cabin seemed emptier than ever. Loneliness settled over her. Her solitary supper had little taste or appeal, and her boredom increased with every minute that passed. An hour after dusk, with the supper tray cleared, and her spirit as restless as a caged bird's, Anemone could no longer bear the four walls of the cabin. She flung open the door and headed toward the companionway, intent on walking off her energy upon the deck.

Some few minutes later, she heard voices as she moved rapidly across the ship. The wind muffled them and for a moment drowned them out, but a moment later, she caught the sound of men laughing, not far from her, and she edged curiously in that direction.

It didn't take long for her to discover the source of the merriment. William Tuttle, Ruggins, and four of the other crewmen on the *Sea Lion* sat huddled amidst barrels and canvas and ropes in the forecastle, bent over a game of dice. A bracketed torch illuminated their play. Anemone watched them for a moment in silent amusement, unoffended by William Tuttle's muttered profanity when the "bones" turned against him. Suddenly, though, Patrick Simpson, the ship's purser, glanced up and saw her standing there. A dumbfounded expression came over his face as he beheld the slender, fair-haired girl, and he quickly scooped up the dice and thrust them into his pocket. The other men turned to follow his open-mouthed stare, and one by one they came to their feet. Their guilty expressions made Anemone laugh.

"Don't stop your game on my account," she begged. "I enjoy tossing the dice immensely myself. I won't tell your captain. Would you mind terribly if I joined you?" This last appeal was directed mostly at William Tuttle, who as second in command to Stephen Burke held a position of easy authority over the others. He stared at her in astonishment.

"Begging your pardon, miss, but what would a fine young lady like yourself be knowing about games of dice?" William demanded.

Anemone's rich, musical laugh rang out again. "I grew up following the drum, Mr. Tuttle. My father was a soldier. I'll wager I know more variations of such games than you do. Over the years, I've played with experts."

He weighed this surprising information, then a slow grin spread over his ruddy face. "Well, I don't have no objections, if none of you fellows do," he chuckled.

Tom Ruggins shook his head. Patrick Simpson hesitated a moment longer before shaking out a spare sheet of canvas for her to sit upon. The other men, after glancing uncomfortably at one another, shrugged their shoulders and squatted down once more. Anemone joined them, sitting with her legs tucked beneath her, her flounced silk skirts spread about her on the canvas Simpson had provided. Before long, all remaining formality between the crewmen and the young lady passenger had disappeared as the game heated up to an intense competition between Anemone and William Tuttle himself.

Tom Ruggins had pushed his pile of coins before her when she first began to play, insisting with touching gallantry that she use his winnings for her stake. Now he cheered Anemone on as she landed a successful throw of the dice, and William grunted in reluctant admiration before scooping up the "bones" in his own large, calloused hands. He swore under his breath when the numbers turned against him, then passed the dice to a black-bearded sailor called Nat. It wasn't long before Patrick Simpson noted Anemone shivering in the cold night air as she watched the play. He shrugged out of his brown woolen jacket. When he offered it gruffly to her, she threw him a quick, grateful smile as she slipped it onto her shoulders. Then they both returned their attention to the game. Nearly an hour passed. The bantering and the laughter grew louder. Engrossed in the play, no one heard the soft-booted approach of the Captain, who now stood silently in the shadows. For several moments, Stephen Burke watched the players in the flickering torchlight as they bent intently over their game.

Anemone gave a smothered cry of delight as the round ended in victory for her, and the men added glinting coins to her ever-growing pile.

"Well done—for a lady," William Tuttle muttered as the other men clapped her on the back and offered words of congratulation. Despite his effort to look grim, he couldn't help grinning at the mischievous smile on Anemone's delicate face.

"I'll offer you a rematch, William. Unless you're frightened you'll lose your whole stake, of course."

"Frightened?" It was nothing short of a bellow. William's face flamed, but his smile was good-natured. "I'll show you who's frightened, Miss Lucky Fingers!"

"Is everyone in again?" Anemone called gaily, but it was a new voice that answered her.

"The game is over, Miss Houghton."

Seven pairs of eyes flew upward at the cold voice that sliced the air. William Tuttle pocketed the dice in one swift motion and staggered to his feet. The others followed. Tom Ruggins helped Anemone to her feet. She was the only one to retain her composure under Stephen Burke's steely gaze.

"Captain?" She inclined her head at him with a frosty smile. "Is something amiss?"

Stephen drawled out his next words with a silken menace that made Anemone flinch. "I thought you had the headache, Miss Houghton. I'm happy to see how quickly you've recovered."

The men beside her shuffled their feet and stared at the wooden floorboards of the ship.

"Why, yes. I have." She had forgotten for the moment the excuse with which she had declined to dine with him; now she knew the reason for his anger. Her eyes narrowed. This arrogant, egotistical male was offended that she had chosen to play at dice with his crew rather then spend the evening in his cabin. His precious masculine vanity had been wounded. Poor man. Perverse satisfaction surged through her.

"As a matter of fact, Captain, my headache disappeared a short time ago, and I decided to seek out some fresh air." Her tone was pleasant, but matter-of-fact, as if she were making conversation with the most casual of acquaintances. She refused to explain how she had chanced upon the gamesters, how she had entered into the play. She was under no obligation to justify anything to Stephen Burke. Moreover, his attitude was insufferable. He had no right to demand any kind of explanation from her about anything she did. Under their agreement, she was his "honored guest," not his prisoner.

"Will there be anything else?" she continued with a little shrug of her shoulders. "If not, I believe we'd like to get on with our game."

"Your game is over." He took her firmly by the arm. Patrick Simpson's jacket slid from her shoulders. She started to protest, but then saw the grim determination on his face and changed her mind. She didn't want a scene here, in front of the crew. She tried to appear calm as he nodded at the silently watching men. "Thank you for providing Miss Houghton with your coat, Simpson. From now on, I'll see to it she is prepared for the sea weather. Ruggins, keep Miss Houghton's share of the winnings for yourself. She won't be needing the coin."

"But Captain," the young seaman started to protest, holding out a hatful of coins toward the slender, shivering girl, but Stephen snapped at him so sharply that the steward jumped.

"Keep it, I said!" He passed a withering stare over the circle of men. "Back to your posts. I'm going to forget this little incident ever happened. But the next man who strays from his duty to amuse himself over a pair of dice will receive twenty lashes for insubordination. Clear?"

Six grim faces nodded at him. "Dismissed!"

Ruggins, William Tuttle, and the others scattered like jack rabbits. Anemone found herself alone with Stephen Burke on the darkened deck of the ship. The torch light flickered nearby, yet not close enough for her to see his face. She was aware of the rapid, painful thumping of her heart. There was a long moment of silence during which she heard the waves slapping at the ship and felt the sharp sting of the night wind upon her cheek. She inhaled deeply of the salt air, trying to clear her head, for she needed all her wits when confronting this man. In the inky darkness, Stephen was a tall, formidable shadow outlined against a midnight sky.

"Well, Miss Houghton." His voice was soft, yet somehow mocking. "Since you're so enamored of games, I'm going to let you pit your skill against mine. Let's see just how adept you are."

"No, thank you!" she began furiously. "I don't wish to..."

He strode forward, dragging her with him. "Come along."

"Where are we going?"

"To my cabin. We're going to play a game of my choosing."

They reached the companionway. She was breathing hard after being forced to keep pace with his long-legged strides. "Oh, are we? And if I elect not to play?" she demanded, with an upward tilt of her chin.

Stephen laughed. "Oh, you'll play. I believe you'll like the stakes I offer."

With these words, he led her down the companionway.

ELEVEN

INSIDE STEPHEN'S cabin, Anemone watched uneasily as her host went to his writing desk and from a deep drawer removed a gold and ivory enameled box containing playing cards. He also set out a brandy decanter and goblets. "I've hidden away your vial of laudanum, so tonight we shall both be awake to finish the game," he remarked. "Brandy, Miss Houghton?"

"If you think I'm going to play your stupid little games, you're quite mistaken." Her face was pale with anger. Gold lantern light illuminated the elegant appointments of the cabin, touching Stephen's dark hair and lean, hard-featured countenance as he rested one hip against the writing desk and folded his arms across his chest. He cocked one dark brow amusedly as he regarded her.

"Don't tell me you're frightened of losing, Miss Houghton. You don't even know the name of the game yet."

"Whatever the game, I have no intention of playing it!"

"Remember the stakes," he urged. "I think you'll be interested in the stakes."

"I don't give a damn about the stakes!"

"No?" He rose and moved with pantherlike grace about the desk once more. This time it was a folded sheet of stationery he removed from the drawer. He walked leisurely toward her, the paper in his hand. He held it up for her to see.

Anemone's eyes widened. Stephen Burke held the letter from Henri Marceau! The one she had been trying to discover the night of the Earl's murder! She recognized the handwriting, the bold scrawl addressed to the Earl of Pelham. Her gaze flew to his face. "When did you . . ."

"After you left me in the library that afternoon—when I apprehended you in the midst of searching for this very same note, I wager. It was quite simple."

"But . . ." Anemone was trying to piece together the chain of events in light of this stunning revelation. "Then, the Earl never received it when he returned home that day? He never read the contents?"

"No. I had it all the time."

"I wonder . . ." Her voice trailed off. Her slim brows knit together as she thought back to that final day in the Pelham mansion.

"What do you wonder?"

"If the murderer might not have been after that letter."

"Very likely," he said in a dry tone.

She stared at him as the import of his deliberately spoken words struck her. "You think I killed him for it, don't you? Yes, you said as much the first night you brought me here."

"Didn't you?"

She ran a hand through her hair in anger and exasperation. "No! How many times must I deny it before you believe me? Oh, you are impossible! For a supposedly intelligent man, you are remarkably stupid!"

He studied her long and hard. She didn't appear to be lying now, but then he couldn't be certain. She had already shown her skill at deception. Still, she appeared just as mystified as he about the night of the Earl's death. And her curiosity about the letter seemed genuine enough—she could scarcely take her eyes off it. Surely, if she was working for whoever wanted the contents kept secret, she would already know what was inside. He considered the possibility that she might be innocent of the Pelham shooting. The thought cheered him for some reason he couldn't fathom.

"Why don't you tell me exactly what you know about the events of that night?" he suggested slowly. "Maybe together we can find the truth."

Anemone eyed the letter in his hand. She was itching to read it, but forced herself not to declare her eagerness. She had a feeling that Stephen wasn't ready to show it to her yet, not until she had shared her information with him.

Why not? Perhaps he was right. At this point, there was no harm in comparing notes about the matter. Quietly and succinctly, she related the events of that final day and night in London. She told him how she had seen Mr. Sneed deliver the letter, how she had guessed it was from the French agent, Henri Marceau. She went on to describe how, after Stephen himself had foiled her attempt to read the message, she had stolen downstairs in the evening hoping for an opportunity to get into the study.

"But the light showed beneath the door. The Earl was still there."

He frowned, watching her face while she talked. "Then what happened?"

"I heard voices. The Earl . . . and another man. The Earl was pleading. He sounded terrified. He said something about . . . never having seen *it*." Her gray eyes lit with

sudden excitement. "Yes, that's right. He yelled, *I swear
I never saw it—I won't say a word about....* Then I heard
the gunshot."

Stephen's gaze never wavered from her face. "What
did you do?"

"I bolted into the room. A man stood there, a thickset
man wearing a black mask across his face. He had just
set the pistol down upon the trestle table and was bending over the Earl—as if to search him—when I entered.
We struggled for the gun and I suppose he panicked. At
any rate, he fled. You came in a moment later, when I
had scarcely finished reading the information about the
Belvidere, which, I gather, the Earl had collected for you
that very day." She tapped a thoughtful finger against
her cheek. "It's entirely possible the killer came after Marceau's letter. Someone must have wanted very badly to
know the contents."

"Or to keep them from being passed on to anyone.
Unfortunately for the killer, he was too late." Stephen
frowned. He prowled the room, his mouth tightly set
and a thoughtful furrow in his brow. "Before I walked in
on you in the library that night, I had been to see Sneed.
And Marceau." She gave a cry of surprise and he turned,
smiling slightly at her startled expression. "You see, I had
read the letter already and wanted to question them about
it."

"You knew how to find Marceau? He's a most elusive
man."

"I knew." Stephen shrugged his shoulders. "I've been
doing this sort of thing for several years, Miss Houghton.
I have a number of useful contacts." He came to stand
before her again, meeting her questioning gaze. "At any
rate, I abandoned Cecilia and her insipid little party at
the last act of the play. I had a feeling of urgency about
the matter, something I couldn't put my finger on. So I
hurried down to find Sneed and Marceau. Moffett had

told me, when I questioned him that afternoon, that Sneed had been the only caller, with a message for the Earl. So I wanted to speak to both of them."

"And," Anemone prompted, impatient for the rest of the story. "What did they have to say?"

"Nothing." Stephen looked down at her intently. "They were dead."

"*Dead?*" Shock ran through her in tingling waves. She felt her pulse begin to race in mounting excitement. "*Both of them?*"

He nodded, his expression very hard and grim. "Murdered. Shot through the heart. You may imagine my feelings when I returned to Brook Street and found the Earl dead as well."

"I suppose you thought I killed all three!" she muttered darkly, but this made him shake his head and throw her an amused glance.

"No, actually, I didn't credit you with such energy. I guessed that whomever you were working for hired you, among others, to dispatch everyone connected with the letter."

Anemone drew herself up very straight and proud, meeting his gaze with flashing eyes. "For your information, Captain Burke, I work for the government of England, and they are not in the business of ordering murders, or assassinations, or anything of that nature! My assignment was to investigate allegations that the Earl was a traitor. That is what I did! I had no reason to want him dead!"

Stephen put a hand under her chin and tilted her head up toward him. "I think I believe you, my pet. Please accept my apologies for accusing you wrongly."

This was so unexpected, so out of character, that for a moment she could do nothing but gulp in astonishment. It was the gentleness in his voice that undid her. Staring into his keen blue eyes, his strong hand cupping her chin, Anemone felt breathless. She couldn't tear her gaze from his, could scarcely think. She was aware of the blood pounding in her veins, as she felt a curious, tingling warmth surging through her. She had an almost irresistible desire to melt against him, to feel his strong frame against hers. Wildly, dazedly, she fought all this, struggling to retain at least a show of calm.

"Th... thank you for that," she managed to utter in a weak imitation of her usual crisp style.

Stephen smiled down at her. She found herself drinking in his rugged features, the warmth of his smile, the glinting light in his eyes, and took a hasty step backward, out of his reach. She was dangerously near a precipice. She had to draw back, retreat, flee. In desperation, she forced her whirling thoughts back to the letter he held, realizing that her only safety lay in keeping strictly to the business at hand.

"Now that... that's settled, I... I think I'd best see that letter. Whatever information it contains must be the key to this entire matter," she commented, none too steadily.

"Ah, yes. The letter." He held it up once more, his grin deepening.

"May I see it?" Anemone held out her slender hand.

"No."

She stared at him as he removed it from her reach. His bold blue eyes laughed into hers. "If you'll remember, Miss Houghton, the letter is to be my stake. In the game, naturally."

She could only gaze at him in stupefaction. During their conversation she had forgotten all about his original purpose in bringing her here. Now it all came back, the entire stupid incident. He wanted her to play some game with him, and he intended to use that letter as bait!

"I insist that you hand the note over to me this minute," Anemone commanded, taking a determined step toward him. "I'm warning you, Captain Burke!"

"You terrify me," he said gravely, though the twinkle in his eyes mocked his words. "Now, Anemone, don't be foolish. You have no chance of wrestling this document from me, so you may as well accept my offer. I challenge you to a game of picquet."

"Picquet!"

He strolled to the writing desk and tossed the letter down upon it, then picked up the brandy decanter and poured the amber liquid into both goblets. "You do play picquet, don't you?"

"Of course."

"Well, then? You're not afraid to pit your skill against mine, are you?"

"Don't be ridiculous!" she snapped. Glaring at him, she decided not to tell him that she was an expert at the game, having twice beaten a renowned champion in Vienna only last year. "I fancy I can hold my own against you, Captain."

"Good." He walked forward, tall and elegant in the lantern light. He handed her a goblet of brandy. "To victory."

She sipped the warm, potent liquid that pleasantly burned her throat, and regarded Stephen over the rim of her glass. "You offer the letter as your stake in the game, Captain," she said suddenly. In a low, cautious tone she continued, "What am I to use for mine?"

Stephen took her arm and escorted her to the square table. He held out her chair. "That is not a problem, my pet."

"I am not your pet," she retorted with spirit. "And it certainly is a problem because you would not let me keep my winnings from the dice game, so I have no money to put up for a rubber of picquet."

"Three rubbers," he corrected, easing her down into the chair. He brought over the playing cards and the brandy decanter, then seated himself opposite her, very much the gentleman of leisure in his attitude and dress. "I challenge you to the best of three. Winner takes all."

"You still have not told me what I am to use as my

stake." Her tone was cold. She lifted her goblet and took another sip, then suddenly her eyes widened under his disconcertingly intense stare, and she choked on the brandy. "Not . . . not . . . you can't think . . ." Color flooded her cheeks as he lifted his brows at her in a mocking way. *"How dare you!"*

"Calm down, my sweet." He chuckled at her outraged fury. "I never meant you should offer your . . . virtue. All I had in mind was a kiss. One kiss."

"It's out of the question."

Anemone came to her feet and started for the cabin door, but he moved too quickly for her and blocked her path. He grasped her by the shoulders and gazed into her flushed, indignant face almost gently. "Don't forget the letter, Anemone. Isn't it worth risking one small kiss to gain possession of Marceau's letter?"

"This is outrageous. Let me go!"

"Are you so certain you'll lose and be forced to pay the forfeit? Perhaps your skill exceeds mine, and you will be the one to claim victory," he said softly.

Anemone was breathing hard. She stood very still beneath the gentle pressure of his hands. Their faces were only inches apart. She found herself thinking of his lips on hers, thinking of how his mouth would feel, taste. . . .

No! It was shameful. And dangerous. She could never make such a bargain. But then she remembered the letter. She wanted it. She needed to know what Marceau had written—what if it had something to do with the information about New Orleans, information her father would find useful when she joined him? She bit her lip and met Stephen Burke's piercing blue gaze with a wrathful look. Damn him. He had offered something she could not resist.

"Is there . . . nothing else you will accept as my stake in this ridiculous game?" she muttered.

"Nothing." His hands tightened on her shoulders.

She caught her breath, and then twisted away, returning to sit at the table once more. "Then, let's get on with it. I shall enjoy beating you very much."

"You are certainly free to try," he assured her, with an infuriating smile. He eased his tall frame into his chair with athletic grace. "Would you care to deal the cards?"

She took a long drink of her brandy before reaching for the pack.

TWELVE

IT WAS quiet in the cabin. Yet the atmosphere was charged. In the golden glow of the lantern light, the slender, pale-haired girl in the flowing silk dress and the darkly handsome young man in the open-necked shirt of fine white lawn bent their heads over the picquet cards in total concentration. The play moved swiftly at first. The opponents sized each other up as they moved through the intricacies of the game, analyzing and evaluating the other's perception and skill. Anemone lost the first rubber, but took Stephen to three lengthy games before doing so. She played her cards with cool precision and decisiveness, but observed with a twinge of unease that Stephen Burke played an equally shrewd game. To her chagrin, his strategy was faultless. He was given neither to impulse nor to distraction and seemed to keep track of the play with an icy precision and effortless nonchalance. As the play progressed into the second rubber, Anemone had the disquieting impression that he was toying with her. This sensation increased as he took the next hand.

"Well done!" she said lightly, though she was far from pleased with the outcome. She managed a confident smile, feeling that she'd rather bite off all her fingernails than let him see her dismay. "You are a hardened gamester, Captain. I see I must be on my toes in this contest."

Stephen picked up his cards. "You acquit yourself admirably, too, my pet. For a woman, your play is excellent."

His eyes gleamed as he said these words, and she had the distinct impression he was suppressing laughter.

"If you think to bait me with such inflammatory remarks in the hope of throwing me off my game, you will be disappointed!" she retorted, snatching up her own cards. "I never allow table talk to interfere with my concentration!"

"Neither do I." He grinned. "Your discard, Anemone."

Her play sharpened remarkably after that exchange, and she won the second rubber by a slim margin. When it had concluded and she had accepted Stephen Burke's congratulations, Anemone reached for her brandy glass and drank deeply, feeling somewhat spent.

"More brandy, Anemone?" Stephen lifted the decanter and refilled her goblet before she could decline.

Anemone knew she could handle a moderate amount of liquor without ill effects, but tonight in particular she wanted to be clear-headed. It seemed to her that Stephen Burke was issuing a challenge when he raised his glass in a silent toast to her and then tossed down the contents easily. He watched as she sipped carefully at her brandy, consuming only a few drops, and a roguish grin crept across his face.

"Not only won't you allow me to infuriate you into a blunder, but you won't even give me the satisfaction of plying you with liquor until you can't see straight," he complained.

Anemone couldn't help laughing. "You're incorrigible, Captain Burke. One would almost think you couldn't win on your own merits, resorting to trickery and diversion as you do."

"I fear my desperation has gotten the better of me," he said gravely. "I must beg your forgiveness. But with such high stakes at risk, I will go to almost any lengths to win."

Anemone met his glance with a slight flush. "I am just as determined as you are, Captain." Then, she bestowed on him a sweet and dazzling smile. "But, unlike you, I feel confident relying merely upon my abilities, without the aid of distractions."

"You don't need any other distractions to undo me, my pet. Just looking at you is distraction enough."

Sudden silence fell after these words. Anemone was startled. Surely he was jesting? But when she looked up at him, expecting to see mockery in his face, there was instead a warm and unsettling gleam in his blue eyes. Her heart skittered crazily in her chest. As she watched, his gaze traveled slowly from her sculpted features down the slender column of her neck and touched upon the swell of her breasts above the low-cut silk gown, then wandered upward again, meeting her eyes. She felt her gaze widen beneath the intensity of his look. A most becoming flush suddenly heated her cheeks.

"Let's get on with the game then, or we will never learn the outcome," she suggested, trying for the same light, bantering tone she had used before, but her voice sounded soft and breathless even to her own ears, and she was aware of his heightened tension across the table from her.

"As you wish," he agreed smoothly, and picked up the pack, but his eyes lingered on her face.

The third rubber began with intense concentration on Anemone's part and cool deliberation on Stephen Burke's. The luck, Anemone realized in growing dismay, seemed to be with him. Then she was forced to chide herself, for she was always honest to a fault. Though fortune did lean toward the tall American, it was not the only cause of his dominance in the game. His skill outmastered hers as well. This was something she was at last forced to concede. As the rubber progressed he was beating her brutally, and she saw her hopes of victory slipping further and further away. Though panic set in, she displayed a brave and calm front, trying desperately to salvage the match. Unfortunately, the effects of her second glass of brandy, which she had drained during the play, were now beginning to wear upon her. The burning liquid seemed to be having a potent effect on her; she felt deliciously warm, and her limbs felt weighted. She fought the drowsy, relaxed sensation that washed over her, frantically trying to clear her head. Stephen seemed not to notice her distress. His lean face was impassive, his posture relaxed, his play casually ruthless. He won the rubber in three prolonged games, and placed the last of his cards upon the table. He said nothing, waiting, watching her face.

Anemone stared in dismay at the small diamond he had discarded. She had lost. The match was over. She felt apprehension sliding over her, touching every limb, every pore in her body. Her breasts rose and fell with unwitting provocation as the tension spiraled suddenly inside her. Her own cards fell unnoticed from her hand. Slowly, reluctantly, she raised her eyes to meet Stephen Burke's gaze.

Watching her, Stephen felt myriad unexpected emotions. His pleasure at having secured her defeat was soon replaced by a kind of sympathy. She was not a young woman to whom defeat came easily. It grated on her; he had seen that in the proud, stiff way she had completed the match, never allowing her inner chagrin to show, except by the way she chewed mercilessly upon her lower lip, tormenting it between her lovely white teeth each time he had piqued, repiqued, and capotted her in the course of play. Now, knowing she would be forced to pay up her stake in the game, he saw the distress in her bent head, and her suddenly heaving breasts. He could understand her unhappiness. Yet a smile curled his lips as he beheld her agitation. You would think the girl was sentenced to a dungeon, instead of merely being required to offer up one little kiss to him. Amusement flooded through his muscular frame. Was it indeed such a terrible fate in her eyes, being obliged to kiss him? He wondered sardonically if she would feel the same revulsion after the kiss as before. He would certainly *try* to make it an enjoyable experience for her. After all, it was all part of his plan, wasn't it? If he couldn't soothe her fears and stir her passion with a kiss, his strategy for her seduction would be in deep trouble. Hell, he was the one who ought to be nervous. But he wasn't. He had wooed and bedded too many women not to know his own power over them. He had a kind of easy, masterful manner which had in the past gentled even the most cold-hearted of bitches, rendering them desperate and eager for his slightest caress. He never pondered this innate skill, never reflected much on it or took excessive pride in it; he simply knew it to be a fact, a very useful and generally pleasant fact. Now he had no reason to believe that his success with women would desert him when he kissed this particular female. Although he had to admit to himself, Anemone Houghton, or whoever the hell she was, was no ordinary female. She wasn't a bitch or a murderess, as he had first guessed when he brought her on this ship. No, he was convinced now that she was innocent of the Earl's murder, and not at all malicious or even evil-minded. But she was a spy, a very intelligent, clear-headed, and efficient spy, far different from the pampered, frivolous-minded girls or greedy, sophisticated courtesans he usually encountered. Still, Stephen reflected, with a glint of a smile, she was a woman. And therefore susceptible.

When Anemone at last lifted her head and met his

glance, a tremor of fear ran through her. He looked so splendid, so ruggedly, compellingly handsome, that she had to fight the urge to jump up and run from the cabin. How he would laugh to know the extent of her apprehension! She hadn't kissed any man in an intimate way since Andrew Boynton had caressed her beneath a midnight canopy of stars in Portugal, five years ago. Since then, she had avoided all romantic entanglements without much difficulty. No man since Andrew had awakened the dormant passion in her blood. But now, this man, Stephen Burke, who had from the first moment stirred something deep and powerful within her, was about to demand payment of her debt. Oh, how she wanted to run. But that would never do. No doubt he would stop her, and at any rate, it would be wholly dishonorable to renege on their bargain. Anemone's sense of honor bade her stay, even though her heart screamed at her to flee.

She couldn't speak, but her wide gray eyes stared desperately into his vivid blue ones. A long, heart-pounding moment passed during which she could not avert her gaze. He held her captive with his gleaming eyes; she felt herself being drawn, pulled toward him as if by the irresistible lure of a magnet, and at the same moment she was seared by the piercing blue fire of his gaze. When he spoke to her at last, in a soft, yet commanding tone, Anemone jumped as if someone had hit her.

"Come here, Anemone. You've nothing to fear." He smiled reassuringly.

Anemone didn't feel reassured, though. She felt a stab of terror. As she placed her trembling hands upon the table, she found the strength to speak, attempting to sound brisk and offhand.

"We agreed to one kiss," she reminded him. Her voice, even to her own ears, sounded as prim as a governess's. This seemed to cause him vast amusement. He chuckled, before nodding at her with mock solemnity.

"Just one, my poor condemned prisoner. Come along, your torture will all be over soon."

There was nothing to do but comply and get it over with as quickly as possible. She rose to her feet and came around the table, wondering uneasily why he too didn't stand. When she reached his side, he gripped her arm and tugged her down upon his lap, laughing quietly at her startled expression.

His arms slid about her as he settled comfortably upon the chair, leaning her slightly backward within the circle of his embrace. Anemone's slim body went stiff as a board, and despite the previous warming effects of the brandy, she was ice-cold in his arms. Though Stephen held her cradled in a most comfortable position, she knew acute panic as his face leaned above hers.

"It's time to pay your forfeit, my pet," he murmured, regarding her suddenly pale countenance with an intent look. "You needn't be so frightened, you know. I'm hardly a vampire about to suck your lifeblood."

Anemone swallowed. A defiant glimmer entered her lovely eyes, now a deep, smoky gray color as they stared up at her victorious opponent. "I'm...not frightened. Don't be...ridiculous. Let's just get it over with, shall we?"

"Your eagerness gratifies me," Stephen said dryly, and his eyes narrowed on her. "Very well. Suppose you bring your lips to mine."

"Very well." Absurdly she echoed his words. A mortified blush spread across her cheeks. This entire situation was ludicrous and humiliating! She was behaving like a prize idiot! With every intention of bestowing a quick, pecklike kiss upon him and being done with it, she lifted her head and stretched her neck upward. Softly, her lips touched his.

A shock wave ran through her, sending tremor after tremor rippling up and down her spine. Her lips felt afire as they came in contact with his warm, sensually chiseled mouth. Filled with pleasure and a heat that ran in a sizzling current throughout her body, she did not draw immediately away as she had intended to do. Her lips clung to his, even when she wanted to draw back in panic and alarm. Then it was too late. Stephen tightened his grip about her and lowered her in his arms so that he was bent over her while she lay in his lap. He extended the kiss, his lips playing upon hers, shaping her mouth to his and claiming it in a fierce yet tender way that sent delight surging through her like wildfire. Stunned, Anemone's soft lips parted, and he deepened the kiss still more. She felt intoxicated with a sweet, fiery pleasure that was far more potent than any brandy. She was kissing him back before she even realized it, her own mouth clinging to his, melting beneath his purposeful onslaught which sent her into a spiraling world of rapture and delight, far from the calm and rational spheres of thought in which Anemone usually moved. She actually ceased to think at all, for the world fell away, and they were alone in a universe of exquisite fire. She felt his arms tighten around her, felt herself held in a grip as strong as it was tender. Finally, she gave herself up to the delicious pleasure of being enveloped, enfolded, caressed, and kissed by this devastating man, who delighted all her senses and demolished the last of her defenses.

When Stephen's tongue slid into her mouth Anemone gave a moan of pure welcome. Her own tongue met his, and a thrill of excitement shot through her. The kiss deepened still more and she was whirling, spinning, clinging to him with every fiber of her being, her arms twined about his neck. As he caught her even closer to him and his mouth molded to hers, his tongue invading and tantalizing her with subtle expertise, her moans became breathless gasps of pleasure, and her slender, voluptuous body ignited into rapturous flames.

Stephen's hands moved over her in gentle exploration.

First his fingers slid through the silken cascade of her hair, stroking the shimmering curls, then caressed Anemone's delicate neck, and finally roamed downward to cup her breast. Anemone's breathing quickened and she strained against his fondling hands. Her nipples hardened, pressed against his palm through the sheer silk of her chemise and gown. He continued to kiss her, long, deep, dizzying kisses which drove her wild. Her body began to ache with pleasure, and she yearned for something, but she didn't even know what the something was.

Only when one strong hand slid to her thighs and began to hike up the flowing silken folds of her gown did reality come crashing back upon her. With a jolt she recalled who she was, where she was, and realized with horror what she had allowed to happen. She went cold in his arms. Every limb and bone in her body froze to rigidity. Then she wrenched her mouth from his and cried out in anger, at the same time attempting to sit up. When she shoved his hands away and tried to break free, she nearly tumbled from his lap. He grabbed her just in time, preventing her from falling. But when she jerked free again, he made no effort to restrain her. Anemone slid from his lap. Her knees wobbled beneath her silk gown when her feet touched the floor. She was shaking badly.

"You . . . you did that on purpose—k . . . kissing me that way!" she accused furiously, glaring at him through a mane of tousled blond curls. Her cheeks were flushed, her eyes glittering like silver daggers.

"Well, yes, I did." Stephen came slowly to his feet, regarding her in amusement. "And I greatly enjoyed it."

Her hand flew up to slap his cheek. He caught it just in time. As Anemone gasped, expecting to feel his fingers close in a brutal grip, he instead held her with firm gentleness. He lifted her small hand to his lips and kissed her open palm lightly. For a brief moment, his strong fingers caressed her dainty ones, then he released her.

She immediately clenched both hands into fists at her

sides and hissed at him. "You promised it would only be one kiss—and you deliberately lied to me! You are despicable!"

Stephen threw back his head and laughed. He looked remarkably calm and nonchalant in contrast to her obvious turmoil. "You seemed to be enjoying yourself every bit as much as I was, my sweet. You weren't exactly begging to be set free." His eyes rested on her adorably expressive face, considering the outrage reflected there. He looked thoughtful, considering, and at the same time, humorous. "You know, Anemone, I never thought our little game would be so enlightening. I've learned a great deal about you tonight."

Anemone's lips parted in astonishment. She could find no words to answer his casual remarks—remarks she found too insufferable and patronizing to bear. "I don't give a damn what you've discovered!" she cried, shoving past him in a beeline for the cabin door. "I'm not going to spend *another minute*, no, another *second* in your disgusting company!"

"Oh, yes, you are." He swung around so quickly it was like the agile movement of a tiger. He reached the cabin door first and leaned his massive shoulders against it, noting her dismay with a curling lip. He grasped her arm before she could leap out of his reach, and he pulled her to him. "You didn't think my company was disgusting a short while ago, did you, Anemone? You seemed quite fond of me—or do you always kiss men you find despicable in quite such an intimate manner?"

Again, she tried to slap him; again, he caught her arm. This time his grin deepened. "Oh, no, you don't." He shook his head musingly. "Anemone, you darling little brat, you may want me to think you're cold and indifferent, and too damned intelligent and professional to feel anything for a mere man, but you'll never convince me of that. Not after tonight. You may be a beginner in the matter of lovemaking, but your instincts are superb.

You're warm inside, like butter. You're so sweet to kiss. I could spend the whole night kissing you . . . and much more."

He was laughing, tightening his grip about her slim form as she fought to break free. "Let me go!" she demanded, straining against him with all her might. "Let me out of this room!"

In answer, Stephen gathered her to him, his arms like iron bars around her. He cupped her face in one hand and tilted her head up to his. The piercing blue of his eyes stabbed at her as he spoke in a deep, gritty voice that was surprisingly tender. "Not until I've kissed you again."

"No!"

"Yes."

He leaned closer. Anemone, for all her terror, felt an odd sinking sensation coming over her.

"Just tell me that you don't want me to, and I won't," he murmured, his face only inches from hers.

Anemone's lips parted. "I don't . . ."

Her voice faded as he leaned still closer. His mouth hovered just above her lips.

". . . want . . ."

It was a lie. She couldn't complete the phrase. He waited for a moment, smiled, and then buried his lips in hers. The instant he did so, her arms went around his neck and she pulled him closer. She felt herself caught tight against the magnificent length of him, felt all the rippling muscles of his body clamped to her soft, aching form. This time it was a long, deep, possessive kiss, one which left her shaking, wanting more. When he at last drew back and stared down at her, Anemone's fingers clung to his powerful shoulders.

"Stephen . . ."

"What is it, sweet?"

She gave him a dizzying smile.

"N . . . nothing. Just *Stephen*."

He laughed, and kissed the tip of her nose. "You are an innocent, aren't you, my pet?"

Anemone pinkened in embarrassment. "I . . . I am not! I have certainly kissed men before!"

"But not . . . like this?" he inquired softly, his grip tightening around her, one hand placed upon the curve of her spine.

"No . . . never like this," Anemone whispered, and it was the truth. Andrew Boynton had never kissed her with this powerful, arousing passion and, she recognized, this expertise. Andrew had been boyish and charming, his kisses light and awkward compared to the way Stephen Burke kissed her, held her, made her forget everything else. Good heavens, she must be insane, throwing all caution to the winds like this. But that was exactly what she was doing, and she didn't care! She lifted her face to him, showing a lovely countenance full of eagerness and desire, and said, "Kiss me again just so I can be certain I like it."

Stephen laughed, tracing her lips with his finger. "If you insist."

Those were the last words either of them spoke for a very long time. Much later, Stephen stood at the rail of the quarterdeck, staring out at the inky, rolling sea. There would be a storm before dawn, a bad one from the looks of it. Eerie black clouds filled the sky, obliterating all sign of moon and stars. The wind careened through the ship's sails and tore in whirlwind lashes across the Atlantic. Even now a drizzle of rain began to fall. There would be plenty of work to do in the coming hours, keeping the ship on course and free of injury. Stephen knew it would take every man on board to keep the *Sea Lion* safe.

Lost in thought, with the wind rushing all around him, he didn't hear the approach of booted feet upon the companionway. When he happened to glance to the side he saw William Tuttle approaching with his lumbering gait.

"So! You seem to have calmed down a spell!" William shouted so that he might he heard over the wind. He sent his captain a rueful grin and clapped him on the shoulder.

Stephen didn't reply.

"I just about split my gut, tryin' not to chortle when you lit into us for shaking those bones." A hearty laugh boomed from the first mate's massive chest. "Twenty lashes for insubordination! Never heard such rotted talk from you before—sir!"

His laughter was infectious, and Stephen found himself grinning back. "Pretty foul-tempered, wasn't I, William? I can't imagine what got into me."

"Can't you now?" William stroked his red beard. His eyes danced in the light of the wildly flickering torch that hung behind him. "I know exactly what it was. The girl. You didn't like seeing her keeping our company—instead of yours."

Stephen gave a shrug. He had to raise his voice to be heard above the wind. "The girl is unimportant!"

"Unimportant, is she?" William sent him a frankly skeptical look. As a crack of thunder sounded in the distance, Stephen wheeled away from the rail.

"Come below with me and have a drink! I want to talk to you before we begin our fight against this damned storm."

Only too happy to get out of the wind, William followed him down the companionway. They encountered several crewmen as they passed along the deck. The men were working frantically to secure the ship against the impending storm. Both Stephen and William Tuttle knew that soon every man on board would be working like the devil.

"I could do with some fortification," William muttered as they entered Stephen's cabin. "I've a feeling this night will be more like a night*mare.*"

When they each had a full goblet of brandy in hand,

Stephen leaned against his writing desk, regarding the other man thoughtfully.

William took a deep swallow of the burgundy liquid and then licked his lips. "Now, sir, what's this you say about the girl being unimportant? Since when has a woman ever been unimportant to *you*? Although I must say, Miss Anemone ain't at all in your usual style."

"Far from it," Stephen agreed shortly. "You misunderstood what happened on the deck."

There was a little silence. Stephen drained his glass and set it down beside him. Perhaps he wasn't being entirely honest with William, or with himself. It was true—an emotion amazingly like jealousy had gone through him when he saw Anemone so cozily in the company of his crew, when she had declined *his* invitation to dinner. He admitted with a hint of self-mockery that his vanity had suffered a blow. But only briefly. By the time he had brought her back to the cabin, he had himself in rein again, and after that, everything had proceeded according to plan. At the moment, he thought, remembering Anemone's enchanting little face lifted toward his a short while ago and the eager way she had kissed him, his strategy couldn't be proceeding more closely to plan.

William broke into his thoughts. "Tom Ruggins spotted you bringing her back to her quarters a while ago. Told me you two looked pretty right and tight," he chuckled.

"It's all a ruse, William." Stephen crossed his arms as he leaned against the writing desk. His face was hard. "She has some information I need—and I plan to extract it from her. It's a common enough method between men and women. I'm certain she's employed it herself a number of times. As of tonight, it's going quite well."

William frowned and stared fiercely at the tall young man whom he had served under for years. "A ruse? You mean you don't care two bits about her? You're just... courting her to find out what she knows?" He shook his shaggy red head. "That's not like you, Captain! You're not one to hurt a fine young woman like that. She's not like those common hussies that fling themselves at your feet."

Stephen turned his head slowly to meet the accusing eyes of his first mate. "You needn't look so angry about it, William," he replied coolly. "What's the girl to you? Or have you, and half the crew, been smitten by her charms?"

"Miss Anemone is a nice young lady." William set his goblet down on the square table so abruptly that some of the brandy splashed over the rim. He shoved his hands into the pockets of his woolen jacket. "I don't like it!" he announced with great decision.

Stephen sighed. "Keep in mind, William, that our beguiling young passenger is an enemy spy. She has already told me that after we rescue Johnny from that damned British frigate in Saint John, she wants to be taken to New Orleans. New Orleans, William! A place where I happen to know that a dangerous plot is underfoot at this moment—a plot that could propel America into war!"

"What's that you say? *War?*" William's bushy red brows shot up in alarm.

"Correct. Now do you suppose for one minute that it is purely a coincidence—her wishing to go there?" He ran a hand through his hair. "I intend to find out exactly what she knows about this matter, and what she hopes to accomplish in New Orleans. Then I'll send a message to President Jefferson for instructions as soon as we reach port in Louisiana." He straightened up from the desk and strode toward the first mate, who was still scowling. "Think about it, my friend. What is more important: the service of our country, or the feelings of one young woman, who will no doubt forget me thoroughly before a fortnight has passed?" He suddenly gripped the other man's shoulders. "Believe me, William, I've no wish to hurt her. But this situation in New Orleans could be crucial. You've aided me on missions before—you know that

you, Johnny, and I make a good team. I'm going to need
your help again on this one, if what I suspect will take
place in New Orleans is really about to take place."

"And what might that be?" William asked, fixing his
keen gaze on Stephen with avid curiosity.

"I'd rather not say just yet." Stephen shook his head.
He turned and paced restlessly across the cabin. "I don't
have the full picture—but I will soon, I hope."

The ship lurched violently then, and both men swore.

"Storm's breakin'," William muttered. He looked suddenly tired and old. "We'd best get above straight away—
this'll be a fierce one, all right."

"I'll be there shortly, William." Stephen was already
striding across the room, safely wrapping the brandy decanter and glasses in thick toweling before replacing them
in the drawer. The tossing of the ship in the throes of
the storm would break anything that wasn't tied down
or wrapped up. "William," he said abruptly, as the first
mate opened the cabin door.

Stephen straightened and met his gaze squarely. "You
understand, don't you? About the girl?"

William nodded. "But it's a dirty business, Captain,"
he said quietly. Then he was gone, slamming the door
behind him as a burst of icy air tore through the cabin.

Stephen stood a moment, a frown darkening his features. Anemone had said almost exactly those same words
to him the night he had abducted her in the carriage and
brought her to the ship. And they were true. It *was* a
dirty business. Somehow it had never disturbed him much
before.

He swore to himself then, a string of epithets that only
half described his frustration. He understood everything
he was doing as far as Anemone Houghton was concerned, and he knew it was all justified. Yet...

He hated it. He didn't want to hurt her. She was unusual and enchanting. He hadn't counted on caring about

her quite so much when he first devised this plan. Then
he had thought her a murderess. Now . . .

He couldn't forget the way she had kissed him. There
was hidden passion in her, and it ran deep. For all the
innocence of her pixie face, with its delicate features and
waiflike charm, she had a voluptuous body that had
sparked to life at his urging like a tindered match. He
wanted her, wanted to make love to her. And not just to
seduce information from her. Damn it, he thought. Cecilia
Pelham had throw herself at him, and he had felt only
the vaguest interest in her, for all her dark, alluring beauty.
Yet here he was, able to think of little besides Anemone.
She was a bewitching contrast. Intelligent and cunning
and strong-willed, yet oddly innocent when it came to
love. Her modesty had not been assumed. Her delightful
blushes had been completely natural, her protestations
sincere. The girl was a damned virgin. What he had in
mind would ruin her.

He realized suddenly that the reason he had explained
everything to William Tuttle in such detail was that he
was trying to justify his actions to himself. He was trying
to convince himself as much as William that he was doing
the right thing.

In that moment he wished she had indeed murdered
the Earl, that she was as cold-blooded and unscrupulous
as he had first suspected. It would then be a simple matter
to use her as he pleased. *This*, Stephen thought savagely,
as the ship rocked wildly again and he heard the pounding of feet above, *was anything but simple*.

He took one last glance about the cabin and then headed
for the door, throwing on his greatcoat as he ran. If he
didn't get that silver-haired minx out of his mind, the *Sea
Lion* might very well go down, and then where would
Anemone Houghton be? Maybe better off, he reflected
as he reached topside and felt the sleeting rain strike his
face in icy pellets. He was almost grateful for the intensity

of the storm, for as he raced along the rain-slicked deck, fighting the gale and the slashing rain, and peering through a lightning-illuminated sky at the huge tossing waves of the midnight sea, he had no time to think about the fair passenger below, no time to ponder what he intended to do to her in the name of duty and valor, no time to weigh the price of her well-being against the effort to preserve, in these tumultuous times, his country's fragile peace.

THIRTEEN

THE STORM would rage for two days and three nights. It awakened Anemone by tossing her from her bunk onto the floor shortly before dawn of the first day, resulting in a bruised elbow, but that was only the beginning of an ordeal that was to tax everyone on board the *Sea Lion* to the limits of their endurance. During the time that the storm lashed and shook the stalwart ship, the crew fought continuously to avert disaster. Anemone managed to drag herself up on deck that first morning when the sky was as dark as twilight although it was many hours since the sun should have risen. What she saw made her flinch in dismay. Icy waves broke in torrents over the bow of the ship, streaming over the floorboards in rivulets. High above, the wind tore in howling shrieks through tattered sails, while the ship itself dipped and rolled and shuddered, completely at the mercy of the heaving waves. Thunder crashed, sounding so close that Anemone started, and when a vivid streak of lightning bolted across the leaden sky, followed by a gigantic pitching of the ship, she was thrown to her knees. Men swarmed everywhere, drenched and shivering in their oilcloths as they worked to clear the decks, to repair rigging and sails and battered timbers of their besieged vessel. Somehow she managed to make her way up to the quarterdeck, clinging tenaciously to the handrail as chilling water crashed over her, and the ship groaned and swayed beneath her feet.

Stephen was there, as she had guessed he would be, issuing orders and overseeing everything, working side by side with the men who continually ran to him with reports of damage. As she reached the quarterdeck, he was striding toward the companionway, William Tuttle beside him. Both men's faces were grave, and they were soaked to the skin. When they saw Anemone at the top of the companionway, they stared at her in disbelief.

"I would have thought you had more sense!" Stephen greeted her, gripping her arm without further preamble and guiding her back down the stairs. "Stay in your cabin until this storm has passed—I've enough to do without worrying about you being swept overboard every time the..."

His words were interrupted by a violent pitching of the ship, which sent everyone sprawling. It was only Stephen's grip that kept Anemone from tumbling down the companionway. When they had regained their feet, he glanced grimly down at her. "You see?"

"I thought I might be able to help." Her teeth were chattering and she was drenched in water. Her gown clung to every inch of her skin. "I've sailed many times before; I've been through many storms. I am willing to do anything that will help...."

"Then stay in your cabin. That will help. It will give me *some* peace of mind, at least." He smiled at her at last, and Anemone, despite the slashing rain, the cold blast of the wind, and the horrid rocking of the ship, felt warm and solid and strong inside. The memory of last night's kiss flamed to life within her soul. It hadn't been a dream, after all. The proof was in Stephen Burke's face. The strong contours softened as he gazed down at her, and for a moment, in the midst of the horrendous turmoil all around them, a spark of something gentle and intimate flowed between them. "Go, Anemone," Stephen urged, putting her arm through William Tuttle's. "William, take her down and see that she gets to the cabin safely."

He didn't linger, but turned and strode off to where Tom Ruggins and three other men were working frantically at the ropes of the torn rigging. Anemone went below with William, knowing that in this situation there was little of value she could do.

The next few days were a nightmare. There was no rest, and very little food, and for Anemone, not much she could contribute to aid the efforts toward survival. She did insist on helping to distribute the dried fruits and salt pork and soggy bread to the exhausted men, allowing Anson Miller, the ship's cook, to lend his help in the battle to save the ship, but each time Stephen discovered her up on deck, he ordered her back to the cabin. She was worried about him. Strong as he was, he had not rested at all since the storm had hit, and every time she had glimpsed him he had been working feverishly on some aspect of the ship's repair, or issuing ceaseless orders to the men who rushed up to him constantly. The strain showed in his lean face and in his eyes, and Anemone wanted to put her arms around him and kiss away the tension and the weariness she knew must plague him. But she stayed out of his way, for instinct told her that Stephen would not admit his exhaustion and would only forbid her helping out in any manner at all. So she scurried around quietly, handing out food, tending to the sick and injured, and trying to keep up her own strength and stamina in the face of the seemingly endless violence of the storm.

Near midnight of the third night, Anemone was roused from her bunk by a rapping on her door. She had been dozing in her bed, wearing only her undergarments beneath the woolen blanket she had wrapped about herself. Her gown had been ruined while she was distributing the meager rations which constituted dinner, and she had shed it hours ago to huddle in her blanket, sick and weary. Now, she kept this covering about her as she hurried to open the door.

"William, what is it?" she asked fearfully as she saw the red-haired first mate's drawn face.

"The Captain's been injured, miss. A piece of the rigging fell; struck him in the chest. He was pinned beneath it for several minutes...."

"Where is he?"

"In his cabin. We've got to get back topside, miss. There's some signs the worst might be over, but there's much to do and..."

"I'll tend him. Go on."

With fear clawing at her heart, Anemone did not bother to don her clothes. Wrapped in her blanket, she darted down the hallway to Stephen's cabin and entered it without hesitation. He was lying on his bunk, bereft of his greatcoat, but with an open slash across his blood-spattered shirt which revealed an oozing chest wound. His eyes were opened, but they were dazed and bleary. Anemone ran to his side, the blanket falling away forgotten as she bent over him.

"Stephen? Dear heaven, Stephen!" She touched his icy forehead with her fingertips, smoothing away the damp black curls. The wound was deep, but not mortal. She ascertained that immediately, and a sigh of relief escaped her. She had seen many injuries upon the battlefield and had learned to distinguish between those which looked awful, and those which were truly fatal. This was a deep, ugly gash, but it could be mended, and mend it she would.

"Medical supplies, Stephen," she said urgently, kneeling beside him and grasping his hand. "I need medical supplies. Where are they?"

He focused with difficulty upon her face. "The desk."

She brushed her lips against his cold cheek as his voice trailed off and his eyes shut in an effort to withstand the pain. "I know, Stephen, I know. I'm going to help you as soon as you tell me—where is the key to the desk drawer?"

"My greatcoat pocket." He groaned then, and she saw the line of pain and exhaustion etched in his face.

Anemone glanced swiftly around the room and immediately saw the greatcoat which the men had tossed across a chair before setting Stephen on his bed. She dug in the pocket until she came up with the gold key she sought, and seconds later she had fitted it into the drawer of the writing desk. Frantically, she scrabbled through the contents of the drawer. She tossed aside the letter from Henri Marceau without a second glance, then gave a cry of thankfulness as she spied a large teakwood box at the bottom of the drawer. Lifting it out, she raised the carved lid. It was packed with rolls of bandages, ointments, and labeled vials, and Anemone even recognized her own distinctive glass vial of laudanum which Stephen had confiscated that first night on the ship. She gathered the box in her arm and carried it to the bed, then quickly began stripping away as much of Stephen's rent shirt as she could manage, along with his other sodden garments. He was shivering badly, and she drew the blanket over his chilled flesh. Then she turned her full attention to the wound. To her relief, she saw that Stephen had either fallen asleep or passed out. Either way, it was fortunate, for she could probably finish before he awoke, and he needn't feel the discomfort of her ministrations. Just in case, she kept the laudanum close by, so that she might relieve his suffering if he awoke in pain.

She worked quickly, though it was difficult, with the

pitching of the ship, to keep a steady hand. Nevertheless, before long she had succeeded in cleansing and drying the wound, applying ointment, and bandaging the jagged gash. Throughout it all, Stephen slept the heavy sleep of a drugged man, groaning only once, when she dabbed at the wound with a soapy cloth and fresh blood began to ooze again. By the time she had completed her ministrations and sat back exhausted upon the floor beside his bed, the rocking motion of the ship had eased considerably, and Anemone began to think that the storm may have been weathered and beaten at last.

She had time then to look at him, to touch his brow with gentle fingers. She had already covered him with the blanket she had brought with her into the cabin, as well as with his own, but not before noting, even in the rush of the emergency, the splendid contours of his muscular form. Naked muscles bulged beneath those blankets, and the bronzed and powerful length of him had made a vivid impression upon her mind. Now, as she smoothed the coverings across his shoulder, she remembered how beautiful and magnificent he truly was, and a thrill of pride swept through her that this man, this splendid man, had held her and kissed her as though she was the only woman he wanted in the world. She gloried in the knowledge that he had worried about her all through the savagery of the storm, that he had wanted to protect her from its ravages. She felt a fierce possessiveness, having nursed him and tended him, and seeing him like this, exhausted and injured, a new feeling of protectiveness swelled within her. She cupped his hand between both of hers and cradled it against her cheek.

"Stephen. *Stephen*," she whispered.

Tenderly, she sat by his side and watched him as he slept, reveling in the simple rise and fall of his chest as his breathing continued smooth and even throughout the night.

Sometime during the night, she must have fallen asleep,

for she awakened abruptly to discover that the ship no longer swayed and dipped and that there was silence outside the cabin. Stephen's pocket watch proclaimed the hour to be half past seven. Anemone sent up a prayer of thankfulness. It was morning, and the storm had passed. She moved stiffly from her position on the floor beside the bunk and discovered that she still held Stephen's hand in hers.

She released him and rose, bending over to glimpse him better by the light of the oil lamp. His color had improved; his breathing was regular. Carefully, she checked the bandage beneath his blanket and was relieved to see that the bleeding had apparently stopped, for no blood had soaked through.

Anemone stretched her aching limbs, suppressing a groan at their soreness. It was only then that she realized she was clad in nothing but her lace-edged undergarments. Smiling wryly, she pondered what to do. She hated to leave Stephen even for a moment, so she didn't wish to hurry back to her cabin to don a gown. Instead, another idea occurred to her and she went to his wardrobe. From inside, she selected one of his white silk shirts and a pair of clean black breeches. She managed a swift toilette and slipped into his oversized garments within a matter of moments. The breeches she rolled up and secured at the waist with a length of rope she found in a sea chest inside the wardrobe. Then she gathered up the ends of the silken shirt and tied them into a knot at her waist. Her feet felt ice-cold and she quickly pulled on a pair of dark woolen socks, but decided against even trying to fit her feet into Stephen's enormous boots. At last, she ran a comb through her tousled curls and then appraised herself in the mirror. She had to grin at the image she presented. Now who looked like a pirate? she wondered in growing amusement.

She checked her patient again, noting that he stirred slightly when she leaned over him. Yet he continued to sleep and she realized how truly exhausted he must be. She began to gather up all the medical supplies she had used during the night, and she replaced them carefully in the teakwood box. Then she carried the box to the desk and set it carefully inside the drawer.

It was then that she saw once more the letter from Henri Marceau. This time she picked it up, her attention fully arrested. She glanced once at Stephen still asleep upon the bed and chewed her lip contemplatively. It didn't take long to make up her mind. She felt only the slightest twinge of guilt for taking advantage of Stephen's indisposition; then she put aside such considerations, reasoning that she was entitled to the letter far more than he, since she had been the first to lay her hands on it at the Pelham house, and would have read it long ago had Stephen not walked in at that moment and prevented her. Moreover, Anemone told herself as she seated herself at the writing desk and eagerly unfolded the paper, if she had won the picquet game, Stephen would have been forced to surrender the letter to her anyway. He oughtn't to have risked it if he truly didn't want her to see it. Then she smiled to herself. What nonsense. She was going to read the letter because she needed to know what it said—and if Stephen didn't like it, that was too bad for him. She spread the single sheet upon the desk and turned her full attention upon it.

As she had suspected previously, the letter was in code. She studied it several moments in silence. Then she picked up a sheet of writing paper and Stephen's quill and began to experiment with the various symbols. Before long she began to glimpse the pattern. The familiar excitement filled her as she carefully transcribed the message onto the blank writing sheet, substituting letters for the coded symbols on Marceau's page. In a remarkably short period of time, she had broken the entire code, and had before her a flawless French transcription of the secret message. She read it through once and then again in growing concern, easily translating the French words into English as she scanned the page.

My dear Lord Pelham was the salutation Marceau used to greet the Earl. *I am writing to warn you against mentioning a single word to anyone of the plan I so foolishly spoke of to you in a careless moment. Forget that I ever did so! Having received your inquiry requesting more details about the New Orleans situation, I must advise you, my lord, in the strongest terms, to put all such thoughts of gain from this plot from your mind. L'Araignée, the Spider, is himself a part of this, and that makes it more dangerous, more secret than you or I can possibly imagine. It is better, my lord, better for us both, that we forget about this, since the consequences for your nation and mine, as well as for America, could be cataclysmic, and I shudder to think that we might, by word or deed, hasten the events De Vauban and L'Araignée plot to achieve. Let us hope for their failure, but let us not inquire too closely as to their intentions or their progress, for I, at least, have no desire to involve myself in such a scheme as this. If you have already broached the subject to anyone—anyone—my lord, do your best to undo your error. Deny all, forget all. If you do not wish the Spider himself to turn his black gaze on you and spin his web of death about you and your loved ones, forget my foolish words, put them far from your mind, and never allow so much as a hint of what De Vauban is plotting to escape your lips. And pray, my lord, that he fails, for elseways I foresee years of war and destruction for both of our nations, indeed, for all the world.*

It was signed simply *M.*

Anemone sat for several moments pondering the dire implications of Marceau's warning. The man sounded almost hysterical, and if she didn't know him better, she would think that he had panicked beyond reason. Yet she knew that Henri Marceau was a shrewd, competent agent, and such men did not frighten easily. There was also the fact that Marceau, Sneed, and the Earl him had all been murdered following this same letter's ery, and this circumstance gave Marceau's fears reality. Someone had killed three men over this letter and the plot it so vaguely described. Someone was very determined that the activities going on in New Orleans remain a very dark secret.

Anemone folded the transcribed message into a small square and stuffed it into the pocket of her breeches. *Papa,* she thought with a grim little shudder, *what kind of mayhem have you stumbled upon?* Then the deep timbres of Stephen's voice broke in upon her thoughts.

"Any idea who the Spider is?"

Her gaze flew to the bunk and she saw with mixed relief and dismay that her patient was sitting upright on his bed, leaning against the brass bedpost and watching her. She left the original letter on the desk and went to him, her cheeks flushed. "You're awake—I'm so glad! How is the wound this morning?"

The blanket had fallen away from Stephen's upper body when he had raised himself to a sitting position. He sat before her bare-chested but for the square white bandage she had so painstakingly applied. There was no sign of fever or weariness or pain about him today; he looked incredibly strong and fit as he sat there regarding her through those piercing, flame blue eyes. The dark bronze of his skin contrasted sharply with the whiteness of the bandage, and muscles rippled in his chest as he shifted slightly, one arm resting casually across his knee.

"I scarcely feel it," he remarked slowly, his eyes flicking over her face. "Did you bandage it for me?"

"Yes, and fortunately you did not awaken the entire time. Oh, Stephen!" She sat down on the edge of the bed and took his hand suddenly. "I am so glad you are all right! It was such a horrid accident! Of course, I knew that the wound was not fatal, yet one always has to beware of complications! And you were so exhausted—I had begun to fear that..."

"Anemone!" He cut her off and gripped both of her hands in his. "Stop babbling."

She stared at him a moment and then he continued in an amused tone.

"Relax, my pet. I'm not angry about the letter."

She didn't even bother to feign innocence. A rapturous smile dawned slowly on her face. "You're not?" She tilted her head to one side, studying him delightedly. She looked so adorable that Stephen couldn't help grinning as he pulled her against him on the bed.

"No, I'm not. I'd have done the same thing in your place. Quite a piece of work, isn't it? But," he continued, taking in the silk shirt and breeches worn upon her shapely form, "I'm not concerned about Marceau's literary efforts at the moment. What kind of costume is this?" He fingered the small silver buttons which closed the shirt over her breasts. "Not only do you steal my secret letters, but you take my clothing as well. I've the disturbing feeling that nothing is safe when you are around, my pet."

"Very true," she agreed, capturing his roving fingers between her own hands with a laugh. "That will teach you not to become incapacitated again. I'm likely to commit all sorts of fiendish deeds while you lie in a helpless stupor."

Stephen gave her a penetrating look. "Speaking of fiendish deeds, I noticed that someone has relieved me of my clothing while I was, as you say, incapacitated. Was that you, my prim little flower?"

A crimson blush swept over her cheekbones. Stephen threw back his head and roared with laughter.

"I didn't look!" Anemone protested, her cheeks flaming even brighter. "Well, not closely! Someone had to make you comfortable so that I might cleanse the wound and bandage it and William Tuttle was busy with the storm, and so were all the other ... Stephen!"

This last cry was stifled by his mouth clamping down upon hers, effectively silencing further explanations. He kissed her deeply, fiercely, as though he was branding her for his own, and Anemone's own passions sprang to life as he cradled her against him and his lips moved upon hers. Sweet, heady pleasure rushed through her. She gave herself up to the kiss, to him, sliding her arms around his neck. When at long last they drew apart, she remained in his arms with her eyes closed, her slender fingers curled about his neck. Only when she felt him slipping open the buttons of her shirt did she open her eyes.

Stephen began to slide the silken shirt over her shoulder, but Anemone caught his hand and sat up. "I see you're none the worse for your injury," she said softly, and a teasing smile flitted over her lips. "No, Stephen, you must rest," she protested, as he started to gather her to him once again. She squirmed free and slid her feet to the cabin floor.

Stephen slanted a purposeful look up at her. "I don't want to rest," he said with such deliberation that Anemone felt her heart begin to slam against her ribs. "Come here, Anemone."

She shook her head. Everything between them was happening too quickly for her cautious nature. She needed time to sort out the runaway emotions he sparked in her. There had been plenty of time during the storm, when she was confined to her cabin with nothing to do but think. During that time she had decided to proceed slowly, warily, to try to guard her heart. But now, with Stephen here, awake and vital and overpowering as ever, her resolutions were fading like the darkness before oncoming dawn. "No. I must go," she said hurriedly. "I can see that you're better now—you don't need me. There is work I can do above, now that the storm has passed. I must speak to William."

He leaned back and crossed his arms over his chest, wincing as he touched the bandaged area. "To hell with William. You can help me. I'm going to need a bath, and I'm not certain I can manage it alone. Stay."

"You expect me to help you with a *bath?*" Anemone

stared at him in shocked amazement, then quickly compressed her lips as she saw the glint of amusement in his eyes. He was laughing at her. "I'll send one of the crew down to assist you!" she retorted. She refastened the buttons of her shirt, keenly conscious of his gaze upon her. "Surely Tom Ruggins or Patrick Simpson, with their greater strength, will be of *far* more assistance to you than I."

"I doubt that," Stephen said dryly. He watched her walk toward the cabin door, enjoying the gentle sway of her hips in his breeches. The huge, masculine garments somehow made her appear even more lusciously alluring. Stephen was tempted to follow her and delay her departure, but realized that he was courting her too quickly. Anemone, for all her worldliness in matters of intrigue and danger, was artlessly innocent in matters of the flesh. Her shyness was a source of amusement for him, but he also found it oddly refreshing and even touching. He didn't want to frighten her.

"What about the letter?" he called after her when she reached the door.

"The letter?" Her tone was all innocence as she glanced over her shoulder.

"We need to discuss it. I assume you've broken the code?"

Anemone nodded.

"Then come here to dine with me tonight and we can go over it together. Seven o'clock. I'll be ascertaining the damage to the ship and supervising repairs until then."

"Nonsense." Anemone frowned at him, suddenly concerned. "You can't get up and about today. Stephen, you must give the wound time to heal, and your body time to regain its strength. Stay where you are, and I'll send William to report to you here."

Stephen patted the bunk beside him invitingly. "I'm perfectly fit, my sweet. Come here and I'll show you exactly how well I'm feeling."

"You needn't prove it to me," she shot back, opening the door. "But if you harm yourself by working above all day, we'll hardly be able to accomplish anything tonight at dinner."

"And just what do you plan to accomplish, Anemone?"

"Why, the note, of course. As you said, we need to analyze it."

"Ah, yes, the note." Stephen smiled lazily as she threw him a puzzled glance. "We'll certainly discuss the note."

Anemone met his cool, unfathomable stare for one moment, during which her heart began to race in swift, pounding beats. She knew that Stephen had much more in mind with this dinner tonight than merely discussing Marceau's letter, and she knew that she both yearned for and shied away from his advances. But there was no avoiding the evening now. She sent him a calm smile, which she hoped hid her inner trepidation, and began to close the door behind her, then suddenly poked her head back into the room. "I'll be here," she told him. "But there will be no more picquet! And no brandy."

With these words, and the echo of his laughter burning her ears, she made her way down the hall.

FOURTEEN

ANEMONE PACED restlessly the length of her tiny cabin. Then she retraced her steps. Again and again, she crossed the floor, her slim brows knit in a frown. It was nearly seven o'clock and Stephen would be expecting her. She knew all at once that no matter how long she delayed here, thinking and fretting, she would not find the answers she sought.

She stopped in the middle of the cabin and glanced down at her gown. It was lovely, that she knew, the finest of all those Stephen had provided her with at the start of this journey. Fashioned of velvet, with a square-cut neckline which displayed an almost indecent amount of creamy bosom, the gown fell in graceful aquamarine folds over her slender waist and shapely thighs. The sleeves were tight tubes that fell to lace-edged points at her wrist, and the high-waisted bodice molded provocatively to every curve of Anemone's voluptuous form. So well did it fit her slender and enticing figure that it almost seemed the gown had been made for her. Yet Anemone knew very well it had not been made for her at all.

Does he kiss *her*, his mistress, for whom this gown was an intended gift, with the same fierce passion that he kisses me? she wondered, with a sudden sting of pain. Her eyes darkened at the images conjured up by her imagination. Does he look at *her* in quite the same way, with that glinting light in his eyes that intimates both amusement and tenderness? Was all this common for him, a pleasant, if routine, pastime? For Anemone, what was happening between them was something wonderful and unique. She felt a wildness come over her when Stephen was there. She wanted to believe that he too felt the magical pull between them, that she meant more to him than a passing shipboard diversion. But he had neither said nor done anything to betray the depths of his feelings, and she was unable to hazard a guess.

"I think I love him," she thought suddenly, exulted by the thought. Then Andrew Boynton's image thrust itself into her mind. She had thought she loved Andrew, too. But that had been different. She had been only sixteen then, an infatuated girl, and what she felt now, for Stephen, was a thousand times stronger and deeper than what she had felt for Andrew. Stephen Burke, Anemone thought with a rush of wonder, was the epitome of what a man should be. And more. Beneath the reckless, handsome exterior, there was a strength of character and purpose, and a depth of intelligence which struck chords within her. Anemone, who rarely allowed her emotions to rule her, recognized that in Stephen Burke she had found a man of strong passions, a man often driven by his passions. He had a quicker, fiercer temper than she, yet he could keep his tensions under rigid control when he chose to do so. This leashed power emanated from him, filling her with a subtle excitement. He was everything that was vibrant and powerful in a man, yet he could be tender, humorous, and warm. The very thought of him sent pulsing drumbeats of desire through her veins, tormenting her with the newness of her emotions. Uncertainty battled with hope when she thought of what he might feel for her. She was treading in uncharted waters, testing the current as she swam. If she proceeded, she knew, she might be swept under—or she might discover paradise. This kind of exploration, Anemone noted with bitter astuteness, required a different kind of courage than she normally displayed. She was accustomed to risking her life, but never, since the day she had discovered Andrew Boynton's deceit, had she risked her heart.

It wasn't something she was certain she wanted to do. There was still time to retreat. Anemone, fearing her own weakness, debated canceling this dinner engagement. But that would only postpone matters.

I won't settle anything skulking here, she observed with a grimace. With her customary resolve, she turned toward the door. Even to herself, she couldn't admit her eagerness to go to Stephen tonight, to face him in this beautiful gown and see his expression when she entered his cabin. With a whisper of velvet skirts, she departed her own quarters, laying aside all her doubts and worries as anticipation rose to engulf her.

As Anemone lifted her hand to knock upon Stephen's door, a quivering excitement filled her. She waited in pounding suspense for the moment when the door would swing back and she saw him standing before her. She was surprised when, instead of answering her knock personally, he called curtly from inside the cabin.

"Come in!"

His tone was not very welcoming. Anemone pushed the door wide and entered the cabin, wondering at this brusque reception. Stephen was seated at his writing desk. He did not even look up when she walked into the room.

Dressed in formal black evening clothes, he was the

handsomest man she had ever seen. Yet his dark head was bent over maps and papers and he seemed oblivious to her newly arrived presence.

"Stephen?"

"Sit down. I'll be through in a moment."

All of her happy anticipation disintegrated. She went to a chair and lowered herself into it, her hands clenched tightly in her lap.

As she sat there, anger surfaced through her disappointment. *Overbearing ass!* she thought with a dangerous glitter sparking her eyes. *Insufferable, inconsiderate beast!*

"Forgive my intrusion!" she announced scathingly, and rose swiftly from the chair. "I can see that my presence isn't welcome. Don't trouble yourself on my account—I shan't darken your door again!"

He caught her as she yanked open the cabin door. Seizing her arm, he forced her back into the room. "Where the hell do you think you're going?" he demanded in irritation, his eyes narrowed upon hers. "Dinner will be here soon."

"Will it?" Anemone threw an icy look up at him. "Well, I certainly hope you enjoy your meal—and your own company!"

She tried to fling off his arm and leave again, but he swore and held onto her with infuriating ease. "Damn it, Anemone, what the hell is wrong? Ouch!" he winced as she inadvertently struck him in the chest while trying to twist free. She had forgotten about his wound, but instantly remembered as pain touched his face.

"I'm sorry! Forgive me!" Full of contrition, Anemone put a hand on his arm. Stephen lifted it to his lips, a wry grin replacing the discomfort that had flitted across his features. He pressed a quick kiss to her hand.

"No, my sweet, I'm afraid I'm the one to be forgiven," he said with an apologetic shake of his head. "I was so engrossed in those blasted maps—we've strayed damnably off course during the storm and ... never mind. All that can wait."

She bit her lip, feeling a fool for her anger and disappointment. What had she expected? Stephen was not the kind of man to sink to his knees at her entrance, to dote upon her with flowery phrases and foolish poems. And she had never been the kind of woman to wish for such nonsense. Somehow or other, he was having a startling effect on her good sense.

"Now that you've finally captured my attention, I feel it's only fair to warn you," he said with a slow, magnetic smile. "I'm not going to be able to take my eyes off you for the entire evening."

A slow flush dawned upon her cheeks. She felt suddenly, unaccountably warm. "I'm afraid I lost my temper for no good reason." She tried to appear calm and matter-of-fact. "Come, let's look at these maps and instruments. Perhaps I can help set us back on course for New Brunswick."

"A navigator, too?" Stephen made no move to return to the desk. Still holding her, he grinned down at her upturned face. "Not only do you decipher complicated enemy codes, and play admirably at dice and picquet, but now you can chart our course as well. Is there no end to your talents, Anemone Houghton?"

His teasing mood was infectious. "Oh, most certainly," she responded, and her eyes began to dance. "My talents are seriously limited. I can't play the pianoforte to save my life. Or," she continued after a moment's reflection, "embroider a handkerchief."

"Tsk, tsk." Stephen put a caressing hand beneath her chin. "How did a gently reared girl like you escape such essential accomplishments?"

"That's easy!" she responded with her rich, tinkling laugh. "I was not exactly gently reared!"

"Oh? How were you reared?"

"On the battlefield, practically. I followed the drum."

"Fascinating." Stephen's intent blue gaze dipped to her low-cut décolletage, drinking in the sight of her breasts swelled above the aquamarine velvet gown. His hands slid to her waist, then her hips, and finally her buttocks, lifting her and pressing her against him. "Later on, you must tell me more," he murmured, lowering his lips to hers. He kissed her slowly. His mouth moved with warm expertise over her soft lips, and when his tongue slid between her teeth, he felt her tremble in his arms.

They were interrupted by a sharp rapping at the door. "Damn," Stephen whispered, his mouth against hers. "That's Anson Miller with our meal."

By the time Stephen opened the door to admit the ship's cook, Anemone was seated demurely at the table, her waist-length silvery curls only slightly tousled, her lips alluringly reddened. Anson Miller nodded to her and gave his thanks for all her help during the storm, and then he proceeded to serve a quite creditable feast. Anemone felt deliriously happy. When Anson Miller had departed, leaving them alone with the heaped platters and dinnerware, Stephen noted her pleased expression.

"Hungry?" he inquired, as he bent down and kissed her on the neck.

"Starved."

Stephen chuckled and took his place opposite her. "Such a radiant smile all on account of some morsels of food? I'd no idea you had such a voracious appetite, little one."

The smile she gave him set her face aglow, and her eyes shone like polished silver. "A loaf of bread, a jug of wine, and thou," she quoted softly, then embarrassed by her own romantic fancies, she covered the moment by pouring a generous serving of the Madeira Anson Miller had brought into each of their glasses.

"I thought you said no brandy," Stephen commented.

"This isn't brandy. It's wine."

"Ah." His mock gravity elicited a laugh from her.

"Now don't worry. I won't get drunk and disgrace myself," she retorted. "Nor will I let you take advantage of me."

"Do you think I'd stoop to such measures?" Stephen's deep voice growled at her, sending her heartbeat into a violent staccato. "Admit it, brat, I've been a perfect gentleman."

"You've been a perfect rake!"

Anemone felt lighthearted all through that delicious meal. She felt as though she were in a runaway wheelbarrow, careening down a mountain, but she had not the slightest desire or ability to stop the mad rush, and she continued to flirt with Stephen, to tease him in that enchanting, feminine way, until she felt almost dizzy with the wild rush of emotions he stirred and jumbled within her. During the conversation, she learned that the ship had weathered the storm without any lasting damages, that Stephen's shoulder had not pained him overmuch during the day, and that he was not in the least fatigued. His sole concern seemed to be reaching New Brunswick with the utmost speed, and he appeared thoroughly annoyed to have strayed even slightly off course.

"Will you please tell me what is so terribly important about finding the *Belvidere?*" Anemone demanded at last. She put down her fork and regarded him across the table.

It was essential that he confide in her. If he didn't trust her with this information now, his feelings for her could not be other than shallow. She waited in tense silence as he took a sip of his wine then set the goblet aside.

Stephen met her gaze. "I have a friend imprisoned on that ship," he answered in his calm, purposeful way. "And I'm going to New Brunswick to free him."

Relief went through her as he told her then about Johnny Tucker and his impressment on board the British ship. Anemone, immeasurably pleased that he had shared this with her, could sympathize with his mission. No wonder he had been so furious when she had tossed the information he needed into the fire! He had seen his hopes of rescuing his friend go up in flames!

"I cannot defend the policies of impressment," she admitted, as Stephen drained the last of his wine. "But my government would not be forced to such unsavory methods of fortifying our Navy if Bonaparte were not such a damnable, continuous threat! If only we could bring an end to this interminable war!"

"Ah, yes, *le Petit Caporal*. I have no love of him myself."

"How do you propose to rescue your friend?" Anemone patted the corners of her mouth with her linen napkin and put it down beside her plate. "The *Belvidere* will be swarming with men—and New Brunswick is an English stronghold."

Stephen appeared unworried. "Once we reach port, I'll have a look around and size up the situation. Then we can come up with a plan."

"We?"

He grinned and pushed back his chair, coming around to take her hand. He helped her to rise and led her from the table. "In our short acquaintance, Anemone, I've come to admire the deviousness of your mind. It seems to me you'd have much to contribute to a plan requiring a great deal of thought and cunning." He raised his brows. "I assume you join in my goal to avoid any unnecessary loss of life—either English or American?"

"Of course!"

"Good. Then we'll work together to bring about Johnny's rescue with a minimum of bloodshed." He chuckled suddenly. "Of course, there's always the possibility he's managed to escape already. Johnny's a resourceful fellow." Then he shook his head. "But more likely, they've thwarted him and we'll discover him confined in the hold!"

Anemone shuddered. "I pity him, if that is true!"

Stephen turned toward her intently. She felt him studying her, searching her face. "Why does the hold conjure
up such terror for you, little one?" he asked at last. "I
saw how you reacted when I threatened to lock you up
that first night."

She lowered her eyes. "It's ... not the hold. It's any
kind of physical confinement."

Stephen perched his hip on the writing desk and drew
her into his arms. "Tell me why."

It had been a long time since Anemone had talked
about it. Though many years had passed, the terror she
had felt as a four-year-old had never ebbed.

"I was living in the countryside in Kent at the time.
My mother had only recently died in childbirth, and my
infant brother with her. Papa had to go on a special assignment to Brussels, and he had left me in the care of
his cousin, Amelia Crewe. She and her husband had
three sons, all several years older than I." Her voice had
grown softer as she related the story. Memories long set
aside came clearly into focus, and Anemone felt herself
slipping back to that time, to that dreadful afternoon. "I
suppose I made quite a nuisance of myself, trailing after
the boys day after day. I was only four, and a girl, and
they had no use for me. One cloudy noon, William, the
eldest, determined to play a trick on me. The boys had
wandered down to an abandoned cottage near the edge
of their father's property where they liked to play, and
they had discovered an old pine box filled with old clothing, books, linens, things like that. When they saw me
peeping in the window at them, they called me inside.
They had emptied the box, and before I knew what was
happening," she closed her eyes briefly at the memory,"
they had popped me inside, and shut the lid."

Stephen's gaze had grown hard. "The bloody little
bullies."

"I suppose they only meant to keep me there for a few

minutes—it was supposed to be a joke. But... they got to playing—outside the cottage, unable to hear my cries, and they forgot about me."

Stephen had grown very still and he was watching her face, noting how pale her skin had gone, and the slight quiver of her lip as the woman Anemone relived the child's terror.

"I cried for hours it seemed, and tried to push open the lid with all my strength, but they had latched it and it never budged. It was dark in there, and horribly musty, and I couldn't move—not my arms or my legs or even my head. I could scarcely even breathe, except that the box was not very well made and there were openings between some of the boards, letting in a bit of air. Otherwise, I am certain I would have suffocated."

"How long did they leave you there?"

"It was late afternoon before they remembered. They were at studies with their tutor when Cousin Amelia burst in, demanding to know if they had seen me. Then it all came back to them at once. They admitted it straight away, I must give that to them, and everyone raced down to the cottage to my rescue." Anemone took a deep breath. "The boys were punished, of course, quite fearfully. And Cousin Amelia, who was rather a flighty sort, felt horribly guilty about it and plied me with sweets and presents for days on end after that, trying to make amends for what she considered her laxness in looking after me." She gave a shaky laugh. "She was rather dear, in a scatterbrained way, and even her husband, Cuthbert, who normally had little use for children, patted me on the head at dinner each evening after that, and agreed to let me keep a candle burning by my bed all through the nights. But... I had nightmares for a long time. Terrible dreams reliving those hours—the darkness, the stifling lack of air—and I would wake ice-cold and screaming with terror in my bed."

Stephen's arms tightened around her. "And to think I

threatened to lock you up. No wonder you looked scared out of your wits."

Anemone shivered and leaned her head against his shoulder. "At least I don't have nightmares any more!" She tried to laugh. "But I can't abide the idea of being confined. Anywhere, or for any length of time. I think I would go mad if I had to endure something like that again."

"You're in a dangerous line of work, if that's how you feel," Stephen mused, his breath rustling her hair. "Don't you ever think about that, Anemone? About getting caught by the enemy? Spies are generally locked up if they're discovered in the wrong place at the wrong time."

"I've always made it my business never to get caught!" she returned lightly, snuggling deeper in his arms. "Until you came along, that is."

Stephen chuckled suddenly and stroked her hair. "You've nothing to fear from me, my sweet. I'd never hurt you."

Suddenly, she stiffened in his arms and drew back, looking up into his handsome face. "Wouldn't you, Stephen?" she asked almost wistfully.

"What do you think?"

Midnight blue eyes seared hers, compelling her to meet his gaze. She read a fierceness there that made her heartbeat jump. His hard features wore a look of such intensity, such challenge that she could not look away. How handsome he was. How dangerous and wild. She trembled at the splendor of him. "I am afraid," she whispered, and she saw the purposeful glint in his eyes darken to incredulity.

"Of me?" he demanded quietly.

She shook her head. "Of myself."

There was a long moment of silence while their gazes locked, and it seemed to Anemone that the sudden tenderness and understanding that flickered in his eyes then would warm her heart forever. Slowly, her arms glided

up and around his neck. She pressed closer to him and
heard his sharp intake of breath.

"Anemone, do you know—do you have any idea—
how beautiful...how desirable you are? How much I
want you—now, tonight?" His voice was a low, grating
whisper that sent prickling tingles up and down her spine.

She resisted the shivering sensations and somehow
found herself emitting a stifled laugh. "You said once that
I was hardly a raving beauty. You told Anthony he could
do better."

Her words jolted him visibly. "I *what?*" He frowned,
searching back through his memory. "Perhaps you're
right," he muttered in a wondering tone. "What the hell
was I thinking of?" Then his arms clamped around her
waist and she was gathered even closer against him, with
her breasts crushed against his chest. "I must have been
blind—or stupid beyond belief."

"You don't have to say that, Stephen." She smiled up
at him, feeling suddenly lightheaded and dizzy, as though
about to be swept upon some magical journey. Her heart
pounded against his chest, and the wild fire sprang to
life inside her body, flaming outward in shooting sparks.
"It doesn't matter. I don't mind that you don't think I'm
as beautiful as Cecilia or...or anyone else. It's how you
feel that matters."

"Not as beautiful as Cecilia?" He laughed, and swept
up a hand to cup her face. "My dear, she cannot hold a
candle to you."

"Oh, Stephen..."

"And as for how I feel..." A dark gleam lit his midnight blue eyes as he took in her fragile gamine's face
lifted so eagerly to his, her gray eyes shimmering silver
beneath their silky, fringed lashes. Her hair trailed like a
glistening veil to her waist, brushing his fingers as they
held her there. He felt intoxicated by her. He wanted to
drink his fill of her, to hold her and possess her and have

her as he had never had any other woman. "Let me show you how I feel," he said, and then his lips came down upon hers and he was kissing her fiercely, deeply, capturing her mouth and possessing it, sweeping her into an embrace as crushing and all-encompassing as the emotions surging within them both.

Anemone felt herself spun away upon the promised journey. She kissed him with love, she kissed him with fervor. Her soft lips parted, opening before him, welcoming him. Heated pleasure shot through her when his tongue darted between her teeth, and she answered his erotic thrusts with her own. Her tongue slipped inside his mouth, exploring and dancing and hotly teasing him, until he groaned and caught the back of her head between both hands, holding her still as their kisses grew more urgent, deeper and hungrier, and Anemone whirled into a fiery heaven, a golden-hot world filled with the lights and scents and heady textures of love.

An eternity passed and Anemone was vaguely aware of Stephen's fingers unclasping the dainty pearl buttons at the back of her aquamarine gown, of the heavy velvet gliding over her shoulders and down her arms. It floated past her hips to the floor in a rustling cloud. All the while, his lips never parted from hers. Her filmy chemise followed the dress, drifting over her silken flesh in a dreamy slow motion. She stood naked in Stephen's arms. Her delicate peach-tinted skin glowed in the lamplight and the rosy crests of her breasts drew first his hungry gaze and then the caress of his hands. Anemone moaned, craving his touch. Her fingertips worked at the buttons of his lawn shirt, and slid within to caress the dark mat of hair on his chest. They glided over his bandaged wound, slid across taut muscles, rested upon the place where his heart pounded. She felt it beating thunderously against the palm of her hand, and an ache more powerful and primitive than any pain she had ever known began deep inside her. Soon she and Stephen were both naked. He scooped her into his arms and carried her to the bunk, then lowered her gently upon the silk spread. Anemone watched him beneath the sweep of her lashes. He leaned over her, his bronzed body gleaming in the lamplight as he paused and gazed into her smoldering eyes.

"I want you, Anemone. I want you so much."

She drew him down to her and touched her lips to his. A fire burned within and between them.

"I want you, too, Stephen. I love you." Her words were an urgent whisper from the depths of her soul.

Stephen's body lowered over hers, pinning her to the bed, his hands tangled in the silver tresses that flowed like pale lace across his pillow. He kissed her deeply, roughly, intensifying the kiss as she pressed him closer and tighter against her. Then, he lifted his head and his lips burned a trail of fire across her breasts to her shoulder. He bit her flesh gently, nipping with his teeth. Anemone half-chuckled, half-moaned beneath him. Catching this new savage mood, she ran her fingernails down his back, scraping lightly over bulging muscles, delighting in the massive strength of him, in the fire of his need, in the passion that leaped from his body to hers every place their bodies touched. He muttered something low and indistinguishable deep in his throat, kissing her all the while, then began to part her thighs with his legs. Anemone stiffened suddenly, apprehension piercing her rising passion, but with tender reassurance now, Stephen's lips brushed her ear.

"Don't be afraid, Anemone. I'm going to love you, not hurt you. Don't be afraid."

His tongue circled the sensitive curve of her ear, and a shudder of desire shook her. Stephen felt it, yet still he continued his slow, delicious teasing. He licked her ear, then his tongue traveled leisurely to her throat and then scorched each breast with circles of fire. His hands cupped the firm mounds which strained against his fingers, and he tormented her nipples with his thumb until Anemone writhed and gasped beneath him. When he had driven her to a fevered excitement, her body tingling everywhere he touched, he kissed her mouth again as he gently entered her. The power of his desire for Anemone shook him, yet he controlled his movements, his passion, intent on not hurting her, on bringing her with him to the heights he knew they could reach. Feelings he had never known before had grown on him all through the evening. Tenderness and compassion mingled fiercely with physical lust, until all were changed and transformed into something utterly different, utterly new. He only recognized that she was like no other woman he had known before, and these feelings went beyond any he had ever felt. In the instant that he joined her as a man joins with a woman, he thrust aside every other thought and every other motive and knew only the need to make her his own.

She gave a cry, at first startled and hurt as he slid within her. His lips quieted her. Then the pain mingled with pleasure, and she was lost in the sweetness of it. She welcomed him, opening herself to receive him. She felt unexpectedly complete and whole. And at the same time, she felt on fire, burning and wanting and needing. As he thrust deeper and his movements quickened, a delicious excitement built within her and the passion bound for so long inside burst free at last. She matched his movements, as urgent and demanding as he, arching and giving herself to him and melding with him until they were one. She cried out, this time in a tormented ecstasy which reached its peak in an explosion which shook her to the depths of her being. *It is wonderful!* Anemone thought on the brink of that shattering pinnacle. *It is magnificent!*

And then she could not think at all, but only whirl and dip and spin and splinter. She and Stephen were one, and all the love poured out of her heart and she knew that she would love him forever. And when at long last their beautiful union was over and their bodies were spent, Stephen dropped his head to her shoulder and she touched her shaking fingers to his hair. She felt unfettered. Free and beautiful in a way she had never been before, and utterly, completely in love.

Much later, she stirred in his arms. Stephen raised himself up on an elbow and looked at her.

"What is it, my sweet?"

"Nothing, I just wanted to tell you."

"Tell me what?"

A tremulous smile quivered on her lips. "I love you."

Stephen bent over her, his gaze warm and serious. "I have never," he said deliberately, "loved any woman before. I never thought I would." He put a finger to her lips as she started to speak, and then he went on, his eyes taking in her lovely, disheveled beauty, lingering on her sweet and captivating face. "Until now."

She saw that he was just as surprised by his words as she was, and a joyous laugh sprang to her lips as she pulled him down to her. Then they made love again, in celebration, and it wasn't until some time in the small hours of the night that at last, exhausted and happy, they slept, still in each other's arms.

It was not yet dawn when Anemone awoke, cradled deep within Stephen's embrace. She shifted, and felt him stir beside her.

"Still awake, my love?"

"No, I just woke. There's something on my mind."

"What is that?"

"Never mind."

"Oh, no." Stephen turned her toward him very firmly and slid his hand across her thigh. "No secrets. Tell me."

Anemone disentangled herself and sat up with a sigh, drawing the sheet over her body as the cool night air wafted over her bare skin. "Very well, if you insist," she said softly. There was a pensive look in her eyes as she regarded him. "I just can't help wondering—we never did talk about it last night—who in the world is this De Vauban person Marceau wrote about in his note? I've never heard of him before."

Stephen gave a roar of laughter. "Only you, my pet, would think of something like that at a time like this." He, too, rose to a sitting position and reached out to capture a mass of her hair in each of his hands. He gently yet purposefully pulled her forward until she was up against his chest. "Is England and her safety never far from your mind?"

"Is America's well-being ever far from yours?"

He groaned. "What am I to do with you?"

Then, as she started to reply, he cut her off. "No, don't tell me. I'll show you." He caught her to him and kissed her fiercely, a long and savage kiss that stole away her breath and her senses. He didn't relinquish her until the breath was gone from her and she was clinging weakly to him, her hands on his chest. "Now, what were you saying about De Vauban, my darling?"

"Wh ... who?" Anemone whispered dazedly.

Stephen laughed. He released her with a nod of satisfaction, then swung his long legs to the floor and strode toward the desk. He appeared totally unembarrassed by his nudity, and Anemone watched in rapt admiration the rippling of his muscles with every movement of his tall, broad-shouldered frame.

"Wine or brandy?" he asked, picking up two goblets by their stems. She chose the wine. A moment later, after adjusting the oil lamp to a tiny beam of gold which left the room in near-black shadow, he was beside her in the bunk again and they were sipping a newly opened bottle of Madeira.

"Jean-Pierre De Vauban," he said, tracing a finger up

and down her slim arm, "is a brilliant, ruthless aristocrat fanatically loyal to Napoleon. I met him at the Coronation."

"Bonaparte's Coronation? You were there?" Anemone gazed at him in surprise.

"But of course." Stephen regarded her with mock disdain. "The best agents from all over the globe were in attendance. Who would have missed the opportunity to see Napoleon snatch the crown from the Pope's hands in the midst of Notre Dame Cathedral and place it upon his own head? Not I, surely."

She giggled. "How I would have loved to have seen that! And De Vauban? What did he think of the ceremony?"

A thoughtful look came over Stephen's features. He took a slow sip of the Madeira. "He delighted in every minute of it. The man positively idolizes Bonaparte."

Anemone, too, was lost in speculation. "And now he is engineering some scheme designed, no doubt, to benefit his idol. Is that what you make of all this?"

"Yes, unfortunately. De Vauban has a great deal of cunning and a vast fortune at his disposal. He is capable of carrying out all manner of schemes to further French domination, and particularly Bonaparte's empire. But what in hell's name can he be planning in New Orleans?"

"And how is the Spider involved?" Anemone pursed her lips. "I've heard of him, have you?"

"Of course." Stephen frowned. "A double, perhaps triple agent, working for several countries at once—suspected in nearly a dozen murders. Make that fifteen, if we can add Pelham, Marceau and Sneed to the list."

"The Spider is legend," Anemone said softly. "If we can discover and apprehend him..."

"You think on a grand scale, don't you, my pet?" Stephen teased. "Aren't you intimidated by his deadly reputation? They say he is utterly ruthless and has never yet failed in any of his machinations."

"Nonsense. No man is infallible." She sipped at her wine, and a slight smile played about the corners of her mouth. "What a coup to catch the Spider! My father would be very pleased."

"Your father?"

"Thomas Carstairs." She gave a shrug. "I'm afraid I lied about my surname, Stephen darling."

He was staring at her. "Thomas Carstairs? You're Thomas Carstairs' daughter?"

She nodded. "You've heard of him, I see."

"Every intelligence agent in the world has heard of him!" Stephen threw her a look of amazement. "They say he was the best—the master. He's regarded as the greatest code-maker and decipherer of our time. He has a reputation as a genius when it comes to embassy diplomacy and extracting the most delicate secrets from unlikely sources of information."

"That's nice." Anemone laughed. The wine felt warm and deliciously potent in her blood. She took another sip. "Yes, Papa has quite a reputation in the field."

Stephen shook his head. "Thomas Carstairs," he muttered wonderingly. "You say that the Spider is legend—well, Thomas Carstairs is his equal." His tone lowered to regret. "I'd have given a lot to have met him." He was looking at her closely. "I heard the reports that he died. In Spain, some months ago. I'm sorry, Anemone."

She lowered her eyelashes and regarded the rim of her wineglass, trying to hide a smile.

"Anemone?"

Stephen's voice forced her to look up at him, and this time, there was no hiding the sparkle in her eyes. She heard his indrawn breath. "So that's how it is," Stephen murmured, and a grin spread slowly across his darkly handsome features. "All right, brat. Where is the old wizard?"

"Where else?" Anemone tilted her head to one side and laughed at him. "In New Orleans."

Stephen very deliberately removed the empty wine goblet from her hand and put it, with his own, on the floor. Then he turned back to the girl regarding him with such rich amusement in his bed. He took her in his arms and pushed her firmly down upon the mattress.

"It seems, Anemone Carstairs," he said softly, "that there is a great deal about you I have yet to discover."

In the long look that passed between them, Thomas Carstairs was forgotten. There were only the two of them, the darkened cabin, and the gentle rocking motion of the ship. "My work is cut out for me," Stephen commented.

"There *is* a lot to learn," she agreed, cupping his face between her hands. Her voice was a throaty whisper. "Don't you think you'd better get started?"

"Immediately." He threw aside the tangled sheet, and leisurely surveyed her glowing nakedness. Anemone felt tiny stabs of anticipation as his now midnight eyes raked her. Then slowly, he leaned forward and planted a kiss upon her navel. She shivered. "It might take some time," Stephen remarked, as his mouth traveled upward to her breasts. "But I intend to be very thorough."

And he was, Anemone reflected dreamily, much later, when she could think again. He was.

FIFTEEN

SUNSET STAINED the sky over New Brunswick when the *Sea Lion* docked in the harbor at Saint John. Glorious banners of mauve and orange streamed across the sky, and a fiery light touched the tips of the white, gauzy clouds overhead. It was May and the air was filled with gulls and cranes, swooping for fish, squawking at the fishermen. There was charm and beauty in the scene. Anemone stared out at it all from the rail of the ship as the *Sea Lion* glided up the Bay of Fundy and cast anchor in the busy port. She was struck by the innocent and lovely vista of this coastal town. Forests of tall white pines and flat-topped hills rose in the distance beyond Saint John, and she could see the roofs of farmhouses and shops nestled beyond the harbor. There was certainly nothing sinister about the scene, nothing that bespoke danger or menace, yet the familiar tightening in her stomach began as she looked out at the tall sails of the ships bobbing in the water, at the bustling activity on the docks. She always felt this way when about to embark on a dangerous assignment. Her nerves tautened, and every muscle tingled with an odd, racing excitement.

"Ready?" Stephen's voice at her elbow made her turn her head quickly toward him. There was a crystalline sparkle in her wide-set gray eyes that gave him his answer.

The moment they sailed into the Bay of Fundy they had begun to make their plans, outlining how they would go ashore together posing as husband and wife, an American merchant captain and his bride. It was a beginning only. Once they had assembled what information they could about the *Belvidere* and its crew, they would begin to formulate a plan for the difficult part, the freeing of Johnny Tucker.

"Are any of the other men going ashore?" she asked as Stephen dropped an arm across her shoulders. Even though it was the third of May, the temperature here on the coast was chilly, especially with the descent of the sun. A light shiver ran across her shoulder blades beneath the gauzy green muslin of her gown, and Stephen felt it beneath his arm.

"No, I don't want to attract any more attention than is necessary," he replied curtly. "Although William will meet me on the docks at eight o'clock to get his orders, assuming we have any for him by then." There was something different about Stephen tonight also, Anemone noted. He looked grim and harsh, almost frightening, the way he had in England, and there was a cold quality to his voice she hadn't heard in a long time. He, too, felt the oncoming danger and knew the quickening of tension brought on by an imminent confrontation with unknown forces. She sensed his excitement, saw the glitter in his eyes. There was absolutely no fear in him about what was to come, only a kind of grim anticipation, a charged deadliness that communicated itself to her in the set of his jaw and in the keen way he scrutinized the long line of ships in the harbor. He thrived on this, just as she did.

Yet for him, what lay ahead tonight mattered, and deeply. Johnny Tucker was his best friend, and his pain was Stephen's pain. And Stephen's pain was hers. She was every bit as determined as he that Johnny Tucker should go free.

Stephen waited until they had watched the sun sink in a flaming yellow ball beneath the shimmering water. The sound of the waves surging against the wooden planks of the docks and the calls of the sailors on all the surrounding ships broke the quietude of the moment.

"It's time," Stephen said at last, and Anemone felt her heartbeat quicken.

"Wait a minute." Stephen turned and disappeared down the companionway in the direction of his cabin. A few moments later he returned with her shawl, the one he had given her some weeks ago, the morning after they had first made love. She had teased him about this too being a gift for his mistress back home and about how there was little left for the poor woman. Stephen had informed her, with that cool gleam in his eyes, that the shawl had been a gift for his mother. And most of her dresses, he had added, had been intended as gifts for his two sisters back in Philadelphia. The women in his family, however patriotic, craved French fashions and he didn't mind obliging them on his frequent sailings. "Fortunately for you," he had told her, tugging playfully at her pale, cascading curls. "Or else you would have found yourself like Lady Godiva, parading around this ship for weeks with only your bountiful tresses to clothe you from the eyes of the world."

He settled the shawl of heavy ivory lace about her shoulders. It complemented her long-sleeved gown of sea green muslin admirably. She had swept her hair into a chignon, deftly fastened by her hairpins, and her small, exquisitely sculptured face was now framed by only a few wispy tendrils. He chuckled suddenly, thinking of the razor-sharp mind behind that lovely, pixieish facade.

Heaven help anyone who underestimated this particular young woman. "Come on, my love, your hapless victims await you," he said cheerfully, and led her toward the gangplank of the ship.

A soft dusk was falling over Saint John as they walked along the planked docks of the harbor. The light mood fell away from Stephen as quickly as it had descended upon him. Both he and Anemone glanced casually at the names of each of the ships they passed and kept a discreet eye attuned to the sight of a British officer. Stephen inquired of a young sailor in a striped jersey where the nearest inn was to be found, and the thin-faced young man directed him through the center of the town. They walked in silence, Stephen's hand upon her elbow.

Anemone felt an odd kinship with the inhabitants of this tranquil city. They were, after all, English, like herself, and she could almost imagine herself back in the countryside in Kent as she and Stephen strolled through the quiet town not unlike the villages she had visited as a child. New Brunswick had been largely taken over thirty years ago by Loyalists fleeing the rebellious colonies in America, citizens wishing to remain bound to the crown of England. Many had left America rather than join the forces of revolt or have their safety, and that of their families, endangered by refusing to support the popular cause. They had settled in New Brunswick and prospered over the years, and they were loyal Englishmen to the core. Yet tonight, she knew, gazing out at the closed shops of the tree-lined street, as she and Stephen walked in silence, they were her enemies, just as they were Stephen's. She wished them no harm, and she would not lift a hand against them, but she knew that if she was apprehended aiding Stephen tonight, if they were captured and their purpose discovered, she would be considered a traitor, and no mercy would be shown.

Fishermen trudged past them, their day's catches in sacks and nets slung over their shoulders. A horse-drawn cart rumbled by and turned down a lane sheltered by tall white pines, the driver glancing over his shoulder at the tall young man in the impressive greatcoat and the slender, fair-haired young woman at his side. All about Anemone and Stephen came the sounds of people settling in for the night. One by one lamps sprang on in the houses ahead. They continued walking up the main street of the town, and as the sailor had promised, there was the inn at the easternmost corner. It was a sprawling white-washed structure with a clean and welcoming appearance and a wide set of steps leading up to a veranda. *The Foxhound Inn* proclaimed a bright red sign with white lettering above the huge double doors. Stephen guided her toward it even as the first stars beamed forth in the charcoal sky.

Stephen ordered dinner for them in a private parlor. The innkeeper, a portly, apple-cheeked man with keenly snapping blue eyes, took one glance at the tall, imposing stranger and his lady and knew that only the best would satisfy them. He personally escorted them into a comfortably appointed parlor that was snugly lit by a fire and furnished with a pair of satinwood sofas of crimson upholstery, several Hepplewhite chairs, and a footstool covered in crimson and blue embroidery. Blue and gold tasseled draperies of the same crimson silk as the sofa gracefully festooned tall windows overlooking the town square, and there was an oblong table in a separate alcove already draped with a fine white cloth. Timothy Nidd himself poured their brandy, and he promised that dinner would be forthcoming in a trice. In a very short time, he, his equally plump wife, and a serving girl paraded into the parlor bearing platters laden with a mouth-watering feast. Anemone, glad to be on land for the first time in weeks and thoroughly appreciating the cozy charm of her surroundings, greatly enjoyed each of the hearty courses set before her, particularly the lobster patties in their delicate cream sauce and Mrs. Nidd's specialty of steamed clams. By the time the serving girl brought in coffee and blackberry tarts, she felt fortified enough to take on an entire fleet of armed seamen without a qualm and told Stephen so the moment the girl had departed.

"You may have to," he remarked, lifting his coffee cup, "before this is over."

"What do we do first?" Anemone nibbled a bite of her tart. "Question the innkeeper?"

"Yes, we'll start with him. If we can't learn what we need to know, we'll be forced to take a room. While you go upstairs with Mrs. Nidd, you can question her and the servant who prepares the room. I'll remain in the taproom and make myself acquainted with the locals. One way or the other, we'll find someone who can tell us about the *Belvidere*."

"My money is on the innkeeper," she said suddenly. She pushed away the last bit of the tart. "He is just the type to know everything that goes on in the town and to be eager to discuss it."

"You may be right." Stephen pulled the bell rope. "Let's find out."

In answer to his summons, the serving girl came scurrying into the parlor. "Kindly send in Mr. Nidd," he requested as she began to gather up the dishes and forks and knives.

She cast a worried eye at him as he rose from the table and paced to the window. Anemone guessed that she feared he meant to complain about some aspect of her service.

"My husband wishes to compliment Mr. Nidd upon the excellence of his fare," Anemone told the girl, whose anxious face immediately brightened. "And so, of course, do I."

The girl murmured a pleased, "Thank you, ma'am," bobbed a curtsy, and left the room beneath her burden of plates and saucers. Stephen didn't bother to turn around. He drew back the heavy draperies to stare out at the ink black night. A handful of stars and a half-moon were the only illumination relieving the cloaking darkness of night and distant forest. He appeared lost in thought, but Anemone saw the tautness across his wide shoulders and sensed his tension..

Moments later, the innkeeper burst into the parlor, all wide smiles and obsequious enthusiasm.

"Ah, Captain Burke—and madam." He bowed toward Anemone. "I trust your meal was enjoyable? My wife is a fine cook—there is none better. I hope you found everything to your liking!"

"It was an excellent meal, and well served." Stephen had turned from the window at the man's appearance, and now he strolled leisurely forward, his superbly cut buff coat and tight-fitting black breeches conveying his wealth and breeding every bit as much as did his elegant demeanor. "I congratulate you, sir, upon your fine establishment."

Nidd bowed again and beamed at them. "Thank you, Captain. Thank you most heartily. We see a great deal of travelers here in Saint John, for it's a booming port, and growing all the time, and never have we received complaint upon the quality of our service. And if you and your lady, sir, would like to spend the night in one of our rooms upstairs, instead of on your ship, as I'm sure madam is happy to be on dry land for a bit, then you'll find that the sheets are well aired and the rooms as cozy as this very parlor. Me and the missus know what *the quality* like, sir, and we have got it—all you could ask for!"

"Have you rooms available then?" Anemone broke in, giving him one of her charming smiles. "The taproom looked quite full when we entered, and the harbor is certainly crowded with ships. I expected that you would not have a single room to spare."

"Oh, we have several. Most of the customers in our taproom are neighboring folk, though we do get some of the sailors, as well. But most of them spend the nights on their ships, madam. Especially the naval officers."

"Speaking of the naval officers," Anemone continued smoothly, "is Commander Whiting still here in Saint John?"

The innkeeper blinked at her in astonishment. "Well, right you are, Mrs. Burke! He is, he certainly is! His frigate, the *Zenith*, has been here nearly a month now, patrolling up and down the bay and clear over to the gulf. How, may I ask, madam, did you know about Commander Whiting?"

Stephen answered for her in his cool, nonchalant way. "My wife is an Englishwoman," he began. "Her brother is an officer on a frigate called the *Belvidere*. He had written to my wife some time ago telling her that his frigate had orders to report to Commander Whiting in May here in Saint John. My itinerary brought us to New Brunswick on our way to London, and we hoped to rendezvous with the *Belvidere* so that my wife and her brother might enjoy a brief visit."

"Well, well! Isn't that a wondrous thing that you should happen to be traveling through at the same time?" Nidd smiled happily from one to the other of them. "You're in luck, my lady! But only barely! The *Belvidere* docked a week ago, but will be casting anchor in the morning! If you're wishing to see your brother, ma'am, you'd best hurry and seek him out tonight!"

Anemone rose swiftly from the table, exchanging a startled look with Stephen. "Yes, I certainly will do that! Only think, my love," she said turning to Stephen with a smile, "if we had reached port one day later, we would have missed Philip completely. Oh, how fortunate that we have arrived in time!"

"Yes." Stephen put a hand on the innkeeper's stout arm and guided him toward the door. "We are indebted to you for your hospitality and your information, Mr.

Nidd!" Five gold sovereigns changed hands. "Now, if you will only tell us where we can find the *Belvidere*, we would be most grateful."

"A pleasure, sir, a pleasure!" Nidd pocketed the money in one quick motion. His sharp blue eyes lifted to regard Stephen's lean features. "The *Belvidere* is docked at the far end of the harbor, sir—beside the *Zenith!* All the way past the barrels on the dock. You can't miss them if you head north, sir, and keep walking 'til you reach the end."

Stephen nodded, the faintest glimmer of satisfaction showing in his face. "Thank you, Mr. Nidd."

"About that room, sir..." the innkeeper recalled as he passed out into the inn's hall, but Stephen shook his head.

"No, we won't be needing a room."

When the door closed behind him, Anemone came toward Stephen quickly, her face grave.

"We've got to move tonight, Stephen. Quickly. If Johnny Tucker is on that ship, he'll be gone by morning!"

"He'll be on the *Sea Lion* by morning," Stephen answered quietly. "Though how we're going to accomplish that I've yet to decide. Any ideas, my pet?"

Anemone took a seat on one of the Hepplewhite chairs. Her slim brows came together as she thought over the situation. "We'll need a diversion," she said at last.

"True. That way we won't have to fight the crew of two British ships docked side by side," Stephen agreed wryly. He walked over to the marble fireplace where the roaring blaze illuminated his dark features. "Impressed seamen are almost always confined in the hold when their ship is in port. Otherwise, they'd bolt at the first opportunity. And Johnny, no doubt, has tried escaping enough times that he's the first candidate to be thrown in the brig at the very sight of land."

"So that's where we'll no doubt find him." Anemone picked up where he had left off. "Someone will have to get onto the ship and unlock the hatch, then investigate the hold. Johnny and whoever else is down there with him could be in chains," she reflected.

"The crew will have to be kept occupied elsewhere during all this skulduggery." Stephen leaned his shoulders against the mantel. "Now what can we do to get their attention?" he mused.

His gaze settled on Anemone. Meeting his speculative glance, it was not difficult for her to guess the direction of his thoughts. "Exactly what did you have in mind?" she inquired with a laugh. "Must I seduce the entire crew at once—do some wild gypsy dance or something on the dock? Tell me at once and get it over with, I beg you."

"Nothing so elaborate, my love," he returned with that dangerous gleam of a smile. "But something irresistible to a man of chivalry."

Of course. Why hadn't she thought of it herself? "A lady in distress," she said slowly, and he nodded.

Anemone rose and took a quick turn about the parlor. "It might work," she remarked after giving the matter a swift analysis. "If the crew of the *Belvidere* and the *Zenith* are men of chivalry."

"Let us hope for all our sakes that they are," he said grimly.

Stephen crossed the room to her in two quick strides and caught her in his arms. He tilted her face upward and peered down into the delicate countenance set aglow by the flickering aura of the fire. "Are you absolutely sure you want a part in this, my love? If you're afraid, we can find another way. I could . . ."

"Shh." She stood on tiptoe and quieted him with a kiss. They gazed for a long moment into each other's eyes. Then she smoothed her fingers through his hair and smiled up at him, looking for all the world like a child about to receive a marvelous birthday present. "Just try to leave me out, my darling." Her laughter was soft and made his arms tighten around her. "I'd never forgive you. We're in this together, Stephen. From beginning to end. And besides, I doubt very much you could manage this little affair without me."

Stephen laughed before covering her lips with his and kissing her hard. "I'm beginning to wonder how I've managed anything at all without you," he said, and then kissed her again.

SIXTEEN

"HELP ME! For mercy's sake, someone help me, please!"

The woman raced down the dock toward the two frigates side by side at the end of the harbor. She was clutching her shawl about her shoulders as she ran through the inky night. A half-moon and a few brave stars sent down a slender thread of silver light upon the boardwalk and touched her face with a faint luminosity. Her expression was one of terror, and her voice rang through the peace of the night with the desperate clamor of cymbals clashing above a mellifluous string quartet. A dozen men on various ships ran to their vessels' railings to see what was causing the commotion.

"Help me! Help me!" Her shrill pleas rang even louder. "Commander Whiting! Captain Fredericks! I beg of you—save me!"

A man lunged toward her on the dock. He was quite tall and lean, with unusually wide shoulders. His clothes were finely cut, but rumpled, with the cravat askew, and his greatcoat was slung over one large shoulder. His appearance was in every way haphazard. "Come back here, you scheming little tramp!" he shouted. The man's face was twisted into a vicious mask. "I'll teach you to defy me!"

"Help! Please, *help* me, someone!"

Drawn by the woman's screams and the man's deep shouts, an increasing number of sailors abandoned their posts and their dice games to investigate the uproar. They stared at the woman running along the dock and the man pursuing her. Then the woman reached the end of the dock and paused before the *Belvidere*. She flung her arms up toward the men gaping down at her from the deck.

"The gangplank! Lower the gangplank, I beg of you! Hurry!"

The British sailors exchanged startled looks. "We can't lower it, miss! Not without the Captain's orders!" one stout, bewhiskered seaman in a too-tight uniform called out. He winced at the young woman's response: a cry of sheer anguish.

"What's going on here, miss?" He fingered his mustache uneasily.

"My husband! Oh, can't you see—no, Stephen, please, no!"

The man caught up with her at that moment and seized her arm. He swung her around and held her.

"Not so hard!" Anemone muttered under her breath, and Stephen's hold relaxed slightly.

"You dirty little tramp! I'll teach you to try to get away from me!" If she hadn't known better, she would have been truly frightened of him, for there was nothing but ruthlessness in his face. His deep voice filled the night with brutal resonance. "You're mine, Letty! Do you hear? Mine! And I'll do as I please with you!"

"Oh, Stephen, no! Don't beat me again! I can't bear it! I'd rather you just killed me and were done with it!"

Stephen swung his arm back and pretended to strike her. From the angle at which they stood to the ships, the blow looked real. Anemone fell to the boardwalk with a scream. Then hysterical weeping reached the ears of the ever-growing number of men hanging off the rails.

"What's going on here?"

A new voice broke into the chaos. Anemone's gaze flew up toward the man who now stood at the rail of the ship, the man for whom the others had made ample room.

"Captain?" She called to him in desperate entreaty. "Are you indeed the Captain? Oh, please, sir, take me aboard! I beg of you—protect me from this monster!"

"Lower the gangplank!" Captain Lucien Fredericks turned to the man at his right. The seaman jumped to obey his snapped command.

"Just a moment, sir!" the Captain ordered as Stephen dragged Anemone to her knees. "Don't lay a hand on that woman."

"Don't lay a hand on her?" Stephen bellowed. He cast a quick glance into the faintly glimmering water beyond the frigate for some sign of the smallboat containing William Tuttle and the two other men who had volunteered for the rescue attempt. He wondered if they had already hoisted the rope ladder aboard the opposite side of the *Belvidere*, if they were even now creeping across the far deck. "She's my wife! I'll do as I please with her."

"No! No!" Anemone wrenched free of him and rushed toward the tall, pale-haired man in the immaculate blue uniform and insignia of a British naval captain as he disembarked from the frigate. "Captain Fredericks? Oh, Captain, I beg of you, don't let him strike me again!"

Lucien Fredericks looked her over coldly. His natural aloofness and his long, battle-filled naval experience had given his rather gaunt face a harsh cast. It was thus a forbidding countenance. His blue-green eyes held no pity for the woman before him but merely engaged in a piercing appraisal. He was not a man who enjoyed being drawn into public displays, but with the woman screaming like a banshee beside his ship, what choice did he have other than to investigate the ruckus and dispense some form of justice in the matter? He studied her dispassionately, noting her well-cut gown and lace shawl and the elegant way she carried herself, even under these circumstances. The woman was attractive and well bred, with her fair hair and small-boned, sculptured features. Her eyes were wide and brilliant in the moonlight. Fredericks found his interest piqued despite himself. Her husband appeared to be a formidable fellow, big, mean, and more than a little drunk. The stench of liquor on him was obvious even at this distance. Fredericks wrinkled his aquiline nose and turned his attention back to the woman. He was conscious of the throng of men from both his ship and the *Zenith* leaning over the rail, watching the proceedings with eager curiosity, and he decided that it would be best to rid himself of them. "All hands back to your posts!" he ordered, and turned to address the woman, but her husband charged forward, roaring like an enraged lion.

"Nobody move! Not one of you men up there! Don't move!"

Something about the man's voice compelled the seamen to remain frozen on the deck. The enormous, black-haired stranger bore down on Captain Fredericks.

"I want witnesses! I want everyone to see what a filthy, no-good whore I have for a wife! You all can see that, can't you! She deserves it—every beating she gets! And you, Captain, I know what you're after! You want her for yourself! You think that just because she ran away from me, you can take her if you please!"

"You drunken scoundrel." Fredericks bit off the words in his most contemptuous manner. He glared at the man before him in cold hauteur. "You'd best cease these ridiculous outbursts at once or I'll be forced to order my men to..."

"I'm a citizen of America, you bloody bastard!" Stephen

gave the Captain a shove. "You can't lay a damned finger on me! Just because this bitch here calls herself an Englishwoman..."

"You're English?" Fredericks turned to Anemone with renewed interest.

"Oh, yes. Yes! That's why I thought, I *prayed*, you might help me." She clutched at the Captain's sleeve in a frantic way, raising desperate, pleading eyes to his. "Please, Captain. The innkeeper told me there were British officers in the town and where I might find you. I beg of you— take me away from this man, this ... monster! I can't bear to stay with him another night! I want to return to England...."

At this point, Stephen grabbed her by the arm and hauled her away from the Englishman. He yanked her up against his chest so that she faced the frigate's Captain, his arm across her throat. "Don't listen to the whore, Captain." He gave an ugly laugh. "All of you men up there!" He addressed the men who now lined the decks of both the *Belvidere* and the *Zenith*, all watching with a mixture of curiosity and amusement the little scene being played out on the dock. "What would you do with a wife who lies to you, throws her lures out to every man she meets, runs away from you every chance she gets? That's right—exactly what I'm going to do. Beat her, until she pays for what she's done, and the shame she's caused her rightful husband under the law. Is there a man among you who denies my right to do as I please with my own wife?"

A chorus of nays greeted him, and Anemone felt an inward shudder of disgust. Men! They loved to band together, didn't they, to keep their women in line! Stephen was playing on their basest instincts perfectly, holding them all in thrall, keeping them pasted against the railings despite their captain's orders to disperse. It was a brilliant ploy but, she reflected bitterly, one that made her thankful that this was all a charade and that her fate really didn't rest upon the aid of these men, all of whom obviously regarded women as little more than chattel. Then through the shouts and stirrings of the onlookers, she heard a new voice added to the discussion.

"Captain Fredericks—what goes on here?"

It was Commander Whiting who strode across the gangplank of the *Zenith* to join the little group on the dock. Captain Fredericks greeted him and directed a grimace of disdain at the scuffling pair.

"A marital disagreement, sir. This rogue has been abusing his wife. She is an Englishwoman and sought out our assistance."

Now it was Commander Whiting's turn to direct his attention to the couple. He was a short, rotund man with a round face and shrewd, coal black eyes. The aura of command about him offset his unprepossessing physical appearance. The buttons of his exquisitely cut coat gleamed in the faint moonlight, his gold-braided uniform was immaculately pressed, and there was a crispness and precision in every movement he made. Now his penetrating gaze fastened upon Anemone. "You are English?"

"Yes, oh, yes! Please, sir! Don't let him hurt me! I beg of you, allow me sanctuary on your ship! Take me back to England!"

"What is your name, ma'am?" he inquired in a patient tone.

Before Anemone could answer, a sound reached her ears. She recognized it, in horror, as the scraping of a rope ladder dragged against the side of a ship. Painfully loud, it drew the attention of several men on the *Belvidere*, she noted in alarm, as well as Captain Fredericks, who turned his head and said sharply, "What the devil was that?"

Still pressed against Stephen, she felt his sudden tension, and it matched her own. They had to do something quickly or the rescue party would be discovered.

Stephen released Anemone without warning and

sprang forward. He swung his fist into Captain Frederick's jaw.

There was a horrible crunching sound and the Captain of the *Belvidere* went down. Commander Whiting stared in shocked fury at the man before him.

"What in damnation are you doing, you scoundrel! I'll have you locked up for this! You can't..."

Stephen's fist slammed into his eye. There was a low roar as thirty men leaped simultaneously from the railings of their ships toward Stephen.

Anemone acted instantaneously. She had had a blinding image of what these sailors would do to Stephen for assaulting their commanding officers, and it was a horrible picture. There was only one way to save him and at the same time prolong their diversion. She lunged at him with all of her might and together they toppled off the dock and into the dark waters of the bay.

Frigid water rushed over her head as she and Stephen went under together. They came up gasping and drenched, their flesh and senses nearly numbed by the shock of the icy water. Anemone's shawl disappeared into the dark depths of the bay, and her hair came loose to swirl like a wet, clinging net in her face. She was shivering so badly she could barely stay afloat, but Stephen held her shoulders firmly above the water's chill surface. Icy droplets streamed into his face as he bore her through the numbing waters to the edge of the dock.

By now the astonished sailors had almost forgotten their vanquished commanders. Captain Fredericks and Commander Whiting were climbing unsteadily to their feet while the seamen crowded around the dock gaping at the pair in the water.

"Assist them!" Commander Whiting barked, as his first mate helped him to stand. "Get the woman a blanket!"

Captain Fredericks was in considerably more pain. His jaw was swollen and discolored and it took great effort for him to speak. As Anemone and Stephen were pulled

from the bay, he flashed Stephen a wrathful glance. "I
want this man brought on my ship and locked in the brig.
In the morning he'll receive twenty lashes at the post."

Two burly seamen grabbed Stephen and twisted his
arms behind him. Anemone felt someone put a blanket
across her shoulders. She blinked the water from her
eyes. Through the shock and the coldness, which seemed
to have turned her blood to ice, she tried to think what
to do next. She would have to put an end to this quickly.
If these men took Stephen to the hold of the *Belvidere*,
they would be certain to find that Johnny Tucker was
gone. Then they would start a search of every ship in the
harbor and every house in Saint John. There would be
an uproar. *Damn*, Anemone thought, huddling in her
blanket and trying to think despite her chilled, soaking
state. *If only the signal would come from the rescue party that
they were safely back on board the* Sea Lion. The sign they
had arranged earlier with William Tuttle was a lowering
of one of the *Sea Lion*'s sails. That would indicate that all
had gone well and the party had returned safely with
Johnny. So far, as she gazed down the moonlit dock, none
of the sails of the distant ships even fluttered in the still
night air.

"Let me go." Stephen grimaced at the two men who
held him. He had abandoned the drunken bellow he had
assumed before and now spoke through clenched teeth.
"Damn you, I'm not drunk anymore." Through the water
dripping down his face, his eyes blazed. "The bay washed
the liquor out of me. Let me go."

Commander Whiting frowned at him and approached
the tall, drenched figure. The Englishman's eye was already showing signs of swelling and would be black and
blue within a matter of hours. "So you're ready to be
sensible." His mouth was a grim line. "It's a bit late, I'm
afraid. My friend, I believe we must teach you a certain
lesson. It is bad enough to beat your wife, however much
she might deserve it. It is quite another matter to attack

not one, but two officers of the Royal Navy." He studied Stephen's powerful form slowly, taking in every aspect of the man before him. "I believe Captain Fredericks's judgment shall stand. A night in the hold and a hearty whipping are certainly in order."

"Wait." Anemone stepped forward and put a hand on Commander Whiting's arm as he began to turn away. "I beg of you, sir, let my husband go."

Captain Fredericks gaped at her in disbelief. "My dear madam, are you mad? You begged us to save you from him, and now you wish us to release him so that he might abuse you again? Or do you still expect us to take you, a lone woman, on board one of England's royal fighting ships?" He gave a short, exasperated laugh and his blue-green eyes hardened. "Lord preserve me from fools and women."

Anemone ignored him. She moved to stand before Commander Whiting, sensing that his was the fairer, keener mind and that he was more likely than Fredericks to act out of mercy. Her quick summation of his character suggested that he was a thoroughly professional, dispassionate, and seasoned officer whose pride would not influence him in his decisions as it would with the more egotistical Captain of the *Belvidere*. She was counting on that. It was their only chance. "Commander," she said quietly. "I am no longer in any danger from my husband. Neither are you. Only when he is drunk does he become a different man—violent and unreasonable. You see?" She gestured toward Stephen, who stood silently now between his two guards. He hung his head as if in shame while the talk went on about him. "He is no longer a threat to me, now that the effects of the liquor are gone. That dunking in the bay cleared his head and calmed him better than any beating could have."

"The fact remains," the English officer said curtly, "he must be punished for his unruly behavior tonight."

"I promise, sir, it won't happen again." Stephen's voice

was little more than a mumble. He lifted his head to meet the Commander's stern gaze, then dropped it quickly. "I'm sorry I struck you, sir. And the other Captain. But Letty here is right. I don't do that sort of thing, except when the liquor gets into me."

"Then I suggest you don't let it get into you again!" Commander Fredericks glared at him, his fists clenched as though he would like to strike the other man where he stood, constricted by his guards. He took a step forward as if about to do so, then suddenly became aware once more of all the men still watching and listening to the exchange. The last thin remnants of his temper unraveled. "Back to your posts!" he commanded with a sweeping movement of his arm that encompassed the entire length of the *Belvidere*. "Or you'll all be disciplined by the whip come dawn!"

The men dispersed rapidly, and those on the *Zenith* followed suit before their commander had opportunity to admonish them. There was a moment of tense silence on the dock, broken only by the lapping of the water against the anchored ships.

Anemone glanced down the harbor. Still there was no movement of the sails where the *Sea Lion* was docked. She felt a cord of anxiety tightening in her chest as she wondered if something had gone terribly wrong. But there was no help for it now. She and Stephen had stretched out this little charade to its very end, and there was nothing they could do to prolong it further.

"Commander Whiting." She broke the silence to speak in a soft tone. "I ask again that you allow my husband to return with me to the inn. We are leaving Saint John tomorrow. There won't be any more trouble." She put everything she had into the beseeching look directed at the British commander. "I love him, for all his faults. I beg you to spare him and release him in my charge."

Captain Fredericks stiffened as he saw the indecision cross his superior's face. His voice was tight with anger.

"May I respectfully suggest, sir, that we follow our original intentions and teach this scoundrel a lesson?" A muscle throbbed in his neck. "We have been publicly struck down before all our men. They must see that our retribution is swift and severe. It should also be public. Twenty lashes will demonstrate that no one can assault an officer of the British fleet with impunity. They must be administered! Otherwise..."

"President Jefferson might not look kindly upon your actions against a citizen of America—particularly a citizen of his close acquaintance," Anemone interrupted.

Both Englishmen wheeled to stare at her. "Your husband is acquainted with President Jefferson?" Commander Whiting demanded.

"Yes. They are related by marriage."

"Is this true?" Fredericks stalked in front of Stephen and jabbed him in the ribs. Stephen's head came up slowly, but Anemone caught the dangerous flicker behind his eyes.

"Yes." There was no bravado in the captured man's voice. His shoulders sagging, his soaked clothes sticking to his muscular form, and nothing but blank defeat in his face, he presented a most unthreatening picture. "I have dined at Monticello many times." Suddenly, he appeared to gain animation. "Yes, that's right. Letty, damned if you're not right. I've dined at Monticello. I know the President—related to him in fact. He'll hear about this. If you bastards don't let me go, I'll shout my bloody head off about mistreatment at the hands of the English! There's already a big fuss about impressment of our sailors on your damned ships—just wait until the newspapers and our Congress and Tom Jefferson himself hear about how you locked up an ordinary citizen and had him horse-whipped—a man with a wife, a business, a respectable citizen of..."

"Yes, yes, a citizen of America." Commander Whiting

threw him a look of disgust. "The devil take you! Let him go."

Anemone ran to Stephen the moment the guards had released his arms. "Take me back to the inn, dear," she begged. "I'm near frozen—and I don't feel decent."

Neither Captain Fredericks nor Commander Whiting had failed to notice how her wet gown was clinging provocatively to the curves of her body or how her hair had fallen free of the pins during her dip in the bay to swirl sensuously around her lithe form. Now they eyed her with a kind of terse regret as Stephen put an arm across her shoulders and led her down the dock.

"There, Letty, it's all right now!" he said in a bracing tone. "A cup of tea and a spell before the fire and you'll be good as new. Then I'll apologize properly for all I've done." His voice faded as the couple advanced along the boardwalk. Anemone pulled the blanket more tightly about her, trying to control her chattering teeth.

"Are you all right?" she whispered at last as they moved with measured steps further and further from the watching officers. "You're going to catch the devil of a cold!"

Stephen was peering ahead, his expression grim. "Where the hell are William and Johnny?" he grated in a lowered tone. "They ought to have reached the *Sea Lion* by now. What the hell could have gone wrong?"

"I don't know." She was equally uneasy. "Stephen, suppose they're still on the ship. Suppose someone discovered William and the others and overpowered them, and now they're all prisoners."

"In that case, our friends Commander Whiting and Captain Fredericks will deduce quickly enough that our little charade was a diversion. They'll be after us within minutes."

"What are were going to . . . oh. Stephen, look!"

He saw it at the same time. Far ahead, one sail swooped downward amidst the forest of proud white banners. For

Anemone and Stephen, it was a welcome and beautiful
sight.

"They're safe!" Relief blazed in Stephen's voice. Anemone felt his arms tighten about her frozen shoulders.

Still, they were not yet out of danger. Anemone could
almost feel the stabbing gazes of the two English naval
officers at her back as she and Stephen continued their
measured retreat. They were supposed to turn toward
the inn at the path leading away from the harbor. They
were almost there. Stephen paused as they reached it.
He drew Anemone around and into his arms. While he
kissed her, he scanned the boardwalk they had just tra-
versed. "They're gone," he said, his mouth against her
lips. "We're home free, my love."

She glanced back and saw that the dock was indeed
empty. She felt suddenly as light and carefree as a summer leaf. "Come on. Let's go!" she cried excitedly.

But Stephen yanked her back into his arms. Beneath
the glow of the stars, he kissed her again. His mouth
pressed against hers, his hands tangled roughly in her
hair. It was a hard kiss, and it seemed to melt the ice
right out of her blood and to turn her bones to jelly.
Anemone felt herself sinking against him, dissolving, forgetting everything but the feel of his hard, exciting mouth
on hers. Then it was over, and he was holding her at
arm's length, laughing.

"Come on." He grabbed her hand. "I'll race you to the
ship."

Next he was running, dragging her along with him
toward the *Sea Lion* at a breakneck pace.

Relief and exhilaration at the success of their mission
made them giddy. Their feet pounded the wooden boardwalk and the blanket slipped forgotten from her shoulders as they clambered up the gangplank onto the ship.
Tom Ruggins greeted them as they set foot upon the deck,
and Anemone noted the heavy pistol in his hand.

"Johnny?"

"Below, sir. William's with him. He's in bad shape, but tickled to be back. The other two men taken with Johnny are aboard, too."

"Very good. We sail immediately, Ruggins. You're in charge."

Stephen was already at the steps of the companionway, pulling Anemone with him. Tom Ruggins's expression froze to one of shock, and he called out weakly. "Me, sir? I'm in charge of casting off?"

"See to it quickly, Ruggins, or we'll have a pack of howling-mad British sailors overrunning our decks!" Stephen shouted over his shoulder, and then he had turned down the hallway toward Anemone's cabin.

"Johnny is in here? In my cabin?" She threw him a startled look as he reached for the doorknob.

"It was always his cabin when we sailed together on the *Sea Lion*. I had William move your things into my quarters when we left tonight for the inn." Stephen swung open the door and pushed her into the room. "It will be much more convenient this way, my love," he added with a grin, and then he turned from her to stare at the ragged and filthy man who lay upon the freshly made-up bunk.

Johnny Tucker looked more like a corpse than a human being. Dried blood matted his hair, which once might have been a sandy color, but now was dark with dirt and blood. There was blood on his clothes, too, the tattered, stained garments which seemed too big for his gaunt frame. Staring at him as he lay upon the bed, her bed, she realized that beneath all the bruises and blood and dirt was a young and pleasantly handsome man, with fair hair and strong features and faded brown eyes that squinted up at the pair who approached the bunk.

"It... took you long enough, old friend," he rasped, and his hand groped upward for Stephen's.

Stephen grasped it and held it tightly. Their eyes met and held for a long time. "You haven't changed a bit, have you, Johnny? You still get your knees scraped and your elbow broken every time I'm not around to keep an eye on you, just like when we were kids."

A slow grin spread across Johnny's bruised features. "I always thought I was the one who kept an eye on you," the young man in the bunk whispered, and then began to cough.

Watching them, and listening to their quiet ribbing, Anemone sensed exactly how deep and enduring this friendship truly was. For a moment, she envied Johnny Tucker. He had known Stephen for so many years, had been with him all through their childhoods, and had seen the rambunctious boy grow to a strong, keen-witted, thoughtful man. How much these two must have shared together, how many escapades and travails and triumphs. She felt like an outsider. The understanding that passed between them as Stephen questioned Johnny about his confinement on the *Belvidere* was palpable. William Tuttle had stepped back when Stephen entered the cabin, and now he was pouring brandy into a glass, waiting for a break in the conversation. When Stephen asked about the two men who had been captured with him and impressed on the British ship, it was William who answered.

"We brought them both on board, as you ordered. They're in much better shape than Johnny here. There were others in the hold, too, men impressed from other ships, and we let them go as well, but didn't bring them on the smallboat. We told them they could slip through the water along the dock and into the town to make their way as best they could into the countryside. With any luck, they'll be able to hide out when the British start searching. Ah," he said, glancing up as the ship leaned leeward suddenly and began a rough movement through the water. "We're sailing, I see. Another dead of night escape." His grin encompassed Anemone, as he referred to the midnight sailing from London when she had first been forced aboard.

"I imagine that after all these nighttime departures,

your crew could manage the *Sea Lion* blindfolded," she remarked with a smile at Stephen. He seemed to recall her presence for the first time since they'd entered the cabin. His gaze fell upon her wet, shivering form and bedraggled hair, and he instantly released Johnny's hand and turned toward her, frowning. "My apologies, my love. You're nearly frozen." His own similar condition didn't seem to bother him. He pulled a spare blanket from the foot of the bed and draped it around her shoulders to replace the one she had lost on the dock. "Johnny," he continued, guiding Anemone forward with one arm around her waist. "Meet Anemone—the lady who made possible your rescue tonight. We owe her a great deal."

Johnny Tucker fixed his weary eyes upon the slender, soaked figure of the girl before him. The way she stood, within the shelter of Stephen's arm, was oddly intimate and assured. She was different from Stephen's usual brand of woman. Something about her, about the confident, straightforward way she smiled at him, signaled to him that this girl was not at all like the others. "Thank you for your help." It was an effort to speak, but she didn't seem to mind that his voice emerged as a tortured wheeze. Her smile widened and she leaned forward.

"I've been waiting to meet you. Allow me to apologize for the lack of hospitality among my countrymen. I'm afraid you were roughly treated at their hands."

"Countrymen?" Johnny's limp body stiffened. He tried to push himself to a sitting position as angry color suffused his face. *"You're English?* Stephen, get her away from me! What the hell are you doing with a damned Englishwoman?"

Taken aback, Anemone's eyes widened in dismay. She realized too late that it had been a mistake to mention her origins. She wondered what to say to appease him, for Johnny Tucker's agitation was obvious and the look he shot at her from his bunk could only be described as murderous.

"Hold on, Johnny." William Tuttle eased him back against a propped-up pillow and lowered the glass of brandy to his lips. "Here, drink some of this. It'll calm you down." He glanced at Stephen, who had tightened his arm around Anemone reassuringly. "I put salve on his wounds," William remarked softly. "And Anson is bringing him some stew. He'll feel better after he's got a decent meal in him and a night's rest."

Stephen nodded. "You had a rough time of it, my friend," he said quietly, as Johnny glared up at him over the rim of his brandy glass. He watched as the exhausted man gulped the liquid thirstily, then pushed the empty glass into William's waiting hand. "We'll talk in the morning after you've had a chance to rest."

"Get this English bitch off the ship." Johnny's tone was no less furious for the fact that it was low and rasping. "I won't sail with her. I'll get off myself before we leave New Brunswick!"

"Stop being an ass." Stephen kept his voice level with an effort. He glanced at Anemone, standing silent beside him. "I've got to get Anemone warm and dry—I've delayed too long already. In the morning, we'll talk again."

"Stephen..."

But Stephen had already turned away, drawing Anemone along with him to the door. As they passed through into the hallway, she glanced back. William Tuttle had moved beside Johnny.

"Easy, mate, easy," William said gruffly. "The girl's all right, you know. She's right as they come. You'll feel different about her in the morning."

"The hell I will." Johnny's eyes stabbed at her, and the hatred in them reached her as she stood beyond the doorway. She recoiled under his furious gaze, and a dull coldness that went deeper than the chill from the bay penetrated her body. Then Stephen shut the door and they were alone in the corridor of the gently swaying ship, with only the image of Johnny's hostility between them. Stephen put a hand on her arm, and in silence they made their way to the Captain's quarters.

Neither of them spoke again until much later, after they had soaked together in a tub of steaming water and then crawled beneath several layers of thick blankets on the bunk, curling against each other in an attempt to get warm. A few glasses of brandy had helped to banish the numbness, but Anemone's blood still felt icy, and her shoulders trembled as Stephen drew her against his hard chest. All of the exhilaration they'd felt after the success of the rescue had evaporated with Johnny's stinging words, and a cloud of gloom seemed to have descended on both of them.

"Don't worry about it. Johnny will be reasonable by morning," Stephen whispered into her hair, nuzzling against the soft, delicately curling tendrils. "Fredericks was pretty rough on him because he tried to escape at every port. He's bitter. But he'll get over it."

"I know." Anemone couldn't forget the surge of fury that had ignited in Johnny's eyes when she told him her nationality. "I suppose it was stupid of me to have told him I was English right at the start. I'm sorry."

Suddenly, Stephen pushed himself up on an elbow and leaned over her, his lean face filled with tenderness. "You saved Johnny Tucker's hide today. And mine. So no more talk about stupidity. If you hadn't shoved me in the bay when you did, those sailors would have broken every bone in my body."

"I wouldn't have liked that a bit," she murmured, running a hand lightly across the bulging muscles in his upper arms. "I saved you for my own selfish reasons."

His blue eyes darkened to indigo as he bent over her. "And I'm keeping you aboard the *Sea Lion* for mine," he told her.

"Despite Johnny's feelings?" A smile glimmered in her eyes. "You mean you're not going to toss me overboard in my sleep?"

"That depends." He ran his tongue lightly about her lips.

"Depends on what?" Already she was beginning to forget her tension, her coldness, everything but the delicious heat building inside her as Stephen's hands cupped her breasts.

"On how well you please me tonight." Only the faintest glint in his eyes revealed he was teasing her. His expression was intent and purposeful as he raked her glistening flesh with keen, narrowed eyes.

"Oh, I will certainly try to please," she breathed, drawing his head down to hers and gazing with mock solemnity into his rugged face. "I don't ever want to swim in that icy, dark bay again."

"Clever girl." Stephen chuckled suddenly, and his mouth lowered to hers. He captured her lips in a long and sensuous kiss that ensnared Anemone in ribbons of silken fire. "Keep it up and I'll let you stay aboard until we get to New Orleans," he urged in her ear, and then he proceeded to kiss her eyelids, the tip of her nose, and the curve of her delicate jaw.

"Oh, thank you, kind sir, I'm so grateful," she murmured, and then, without warning, leaned forward and nipped his shoulder with her small white teeth.

She fell back laughing at his surprised grunt, only to writhe in delightful torment as he began to tickle her while pinning her beneath him. But soon their play turned to passion and their bodies clung together.

"Anemone," Stephen whispered huskily, and she reveled at the effects his gritty voice had on her nerve endings. "Don't even think of leaving me. I'll never let you go."

She stared into his beautiful, glinting blue eyes, and smoothed the raven hair back from his brow. A smile of great tenderness curved her soft lips. "I'll never want to," she whispered.

The night enfolded them in darkness, and they thought

of nothing and no one but each other. They were alone in a world of their own making until the pale banners of dawn unfurled against the morning sky, and the new day broke over the distant horizon.

SEVENTEEN

ANEMONE WOULD have thought that by the time the *Sea Lion* reached port at New Orleans, Johnny Tucker would have overcome his aversion to her and they would have become friends. It did not happen. During the weeks that they sailed the Atlantic and finally glided through the Gulf of Mexico to join the Mississippi River, and then wound their way toward the site of New Orleans, Johnny maintained a stony silence whenever she was present, and he confined himself mostly to his own cabin. This was due in part to the time it required for him to recover his health, for he had suffered beatings and starvation at the hands of his captors, incurred because he so persistently refused to accept his impressment into British service. It was, therefore, many days before he was well enough to take a turn unassisted about the deck. But Johnny also seemed to prefer to isolate himself in his cabin rather than to face the sight of Anemone roaming the ship and joking with the crew, or standing at the quarterdeck beside Stephen. His resentment of her lent an air of tension to the voyage, though nothing could completely dispel the joy Anemone felt at being with Stephen and basking in his love.

She grew increasingly eager to see her father as the days passed. De Vauban's plot, whatever it might be, consumed much of her thoughts, and she knew that Stephen shared her concern as to what the Frenchman might be planning. On the morning that the *Sea Lion* sailed into the port of New Orleans, she could scarcely contain her excitement. Soon she and Stephen would disembark and go together to the Hotel Bergeron. Then, with her father's aid, they would sort out this puzzle once and for all and take whatever steps were necessary to foil De Vauban's machinations.

It was quite early in the morning, but the heat was already stifling. The month of June on the Mississippi, Anemone had discovered, meant sweltering heat and merciless humidity. Only the river breezes made this combination of conditions bearable. She had dressed this morning, the day of their arrival in the city, in a thin, gauzy gown of palest blue muslin trimmed with wisps of satin, and her thick, ash blond tresses had been elaborately coifed atop her head to enable the summer breeze to tickle her neck. She had no jewels or ornaments other than the hairpins she had worn on the ship that first night Stephen had abducted her, yet her simple, appealing beauty shone through without the added adornment of superfluous trinkets. As she passed along the corridor toward the companionway, intending to watch the securing of the ship in port and to enjoy her first view of the bustling city, she noticed that the door to Johnny Tucker's cabin stood open, an uncommon occurrence. Glancing in, she saw Johnny pulling on his boots as he sat upon the bunk. He looked up as she paused before the door, and his brown eyes darkened with the familiar expression of anger.

"Good morning," she offered, her tone cool yet pleasant. "It's good to be in port, isn't it?" She could hardly pass on without speaking to him, yet she was hesitant to force her company on him when he obviously detested it. Thus, she was surprised when Johnny got to his feet and unexpectedly invited her into the cabin.

"I want to talk to you." He gestured to the chair in the center of the room. "Sit, if you'd like."

"Thank you, but I prefer to stand." Anemone was torn between wariness and compassion. Part of her wanted to win Johnny Tucker over and befriend him because he was Stephen's friend and an important part of his life. Another part of her resented his unfair attitude toward her from the very beginning and balked at the idea of lowering herself to seek out his approval. She was willing to be cordial, willing to give him a chance, but she was under no circumstances going to fuss and flutter about him, begging him to accept her. She waited in silence as he gave her a long, appraising stare and wondered what on earth he was going to say next.

"I *am* glad we're in port," he said at last. He moved about the room, limping a little from an injury to his leg, yet this in no way impeded his boyishly handsome appeal, nor the air of determination with which he spoke and moved. He was as tall as Stephen, a strapping, blond young man with a square jaw and straight nose and slanting brown brows above very long-lashed dark eyes. "Stephen's told me about this business with De Vauban. It is something that merits looking into."

"Yes." Anemone was glad they could agree on something at least. "Whatever De Vauban and the Spider have planned, it must be stopped. I am certain it bodes no good for either of our countries."

Johnny's lips tightened. He swung toward Anemone. "I wouldn't care if Napoleon overran all of England. To hell with England! It's America I'm worried about."

"I'm certain you are," she responded coolly, steeling herself to keep her temper in check.

"You know," Johnny said suddenly, taking a step nearer her, looming above her in the confined cabin, "Stephen's mother was English. She's a very beautiful lady, a great lady—and my own mother's best friend. Did you know that?"

"Stephen has told me about his family and yours. Your father and his sailed together years ago, when they were privateers during the war against England."

"Yes. And Aunt Elizabeth—that's what I call Stephen's mother—was kidnaped by Alex Burke, seized from a British merchantman and brought on board his privateer ship. They fell in love. It's a wonderful tale; I've heard it countless times over the years. And Aunt Elizabeth, for all that she was born in England, and was a great heiress as well, gave up everything to become an American. Yes, she aided us during the revolution against British tyranny. She foiled a Loyalist plot, exposed a traitor, and saved Alex's life."

"How admirable." Anemone was enjoying this discussion less and less. Johnny's effort to put Stephen's mother on a pedestal was only too obviously an attempt to highlight her own shortcomings in his eyes. "Is there a point to all this, or are you simply fond of reminiscing about the past?" she inquired with a cold smile.

Johnny laughed, an unpleasant sound. His features twisted into a malicious expression. "There's a point. I want you to know that you're nothing compared to Elizabeth Burke, to Stephen's mother. She is a great lady, a beauty and a patriot. You're just a damned little English spy who got in the way."

Anemone had to fight to control the fury mounting inside her. Johnny's words were so far from the truth they would be laughable if they weren't so cruel. "Stephen loves me, Johnny, and I him. We're working together for the benefit of England and America, and if it weren't for me, Stephen wouldn't know where to start investigating this New Orleans business. And if it weren't for me, you might very well be stuck in the hold of the *Belvidere* at this moment, or dead at the hands of Captain Fredericks. Why don't you accept the fact that Stephen has found a woman whom he loves? Why can't you be happy for him?"

"A woman whom he loves?" This time his laughter rang out even more insultingly. He raked the length of her with a contemptuous sneer. "You're a bigger fool than I first thought."

Anemone resisted the urge to slap the smile from his face. "There's no point in continuing this discussion." Her gray eyes flickered with pent-up anger, but she managed to keep her voice curt and steady. "I'm leaving. But if you really are Stephen's friend, you won't cause him pain by sniping at me. If he knew of this conversation, I'm certain he'd be most upset."

"And I suppose you plan to run to him and tell him the whole thing?"

"I have no such notion. You needn't worry about that. What you've said today isn't important enough to trouble Stephen over."

She started to turn away from him, but he quickly grasped her arm and held her still. His face was flushed now, his dark eyes glittering with some emotion between rage and triumph.

"Not so quickly, Miss Carstairs. I think you ought to know how Stephen Burke really feels about you."

"I know that already, Johnny. Let me go."

He continued to hold her, giving her arm a shake. "No, you're wrong. You think he loves you, although how you imagine Stephen could love a woman like you, I really don't know." He chuckled then, showing white, even teeth. "Women go mad over Stephen. They follow him around. I don't mean just common women, the harlots or courtesans. I mean all women. The most beautiful, accomplished, intriguing women you can imagine hurl themselves at him, and he has his pick of them. He has for years. Why in hell would he choose to throw in with someone like you?"

"That's enough!" She gasped at his audacity. She had known that he disliked her, that both her English birth and her intimacy with Stephen rankled with him, but she had never expected that his antagonism went this deep, that he could abandon all pretense of civility and attack her in this manner. She was shaken by it, and she tried in earnest to jerk her arm free. "I can understand your anger against me and your bitterness against England, and believe me, I've tried to be patient, for Stephen's sake, but you go too far, Johnny! Watch your temper, or I promise you, you'll be sorry!"

He shoved her away from him so suddenly that she fell backward against the cabin wall. She straightened up slowly, sickened by the peal of his hard, contemptuous laugh. "Who is going to make me sorry, Miss Carstairs?" Johnny Tucker taunted. "You? You don't have the muscle or the brains to do that! You don't even have the sense to know that Stephen's been using you all this time."

"That's ridiculous—" she began, but he interrupted her when he strode across the room and grabbed her shoulders, giving her a shake.

"It's the truth. William Tuttle told me all about it. It seems," said Johnny, biting off each word with distinctive relish, "that Stephen confided in him some time ago that he planned to seduce you to find out what you knew about this New Orleans business—that he wanted to use you to learn more about De Vauban's little plot."

"No! I don't believe you!" Anemone felt that the floor was slipping away beneath her feet, that she was grasping for balance and order in a world tilting dangerously askew. Johnny Tucker nodded down into her suddenly ashen face.

"It is true, you little fool. Stephen never loved you. He just wanted to discover what you knew about this New Orleans affair—and any other little secrets you might let slip. He as much as told William that you weren't important, that the only thing he was concerned about was keeping America out of a war."

Anemone felt as if the wind had been knocked from her. She couldn't breathe, could barely see Johnny Tucker's triumphant face before her. This was a lie. All of it, a lie!

Wasn't it?

A memory came to her then. Stephen's words the night he had interrupted Anthony's advances. "The chit is hardly a raving beauty. Surely you can do better." He had never thought her pretty. He had never so much as given her a second glance—until he knew who she was. Until he had found out she was a spy.

No! No. Desperately, she clung to the memories of his lovemaking, his caresses, those scorching, dizzying kisses, the tender, intimate words. He could not have used her that way—not Stephen!

"I don't believe you," she said again, but this time Johnny saw the uncertainty in her face.

"Yes, you do. You know how badly Stephen wanted to find out about the New Orleans affair. You know he's very dedicated and very clever."

"He would never do that...."

His scornful laughter cut off her words and made her choke on them. She stared at him, trying desperately to see past the mist of pain that blurred her vision. She searched his eyes for the answer she sought, the only answer that mattered. And when she had finished studying him, noting every line and angle of his boyishly handsome countenance, every glimmer in his brown, long-lashed eyes, she knew that the words he spoke were the truth, that as much as he hated her, he had not invented them on the spot.

"You believe me, I see." He released her now, almost gently, and stepped back, watching her face.

Anemone couldn't answer. She felt like a bit of driftwood washed up on shore after a typhoon. Battered and scarred and dead inside. All the joy and excitement she had felt earlier was gone. Numbly, she turned and walked from the room. She moved blindly, tears slipping from her eyes. She went straight to the companionway and, like someone in a trance, mounted the steps to the deck of the ship.

No one saw her leave the *Sea Lion*. The ship had just dropped anchor and the seamen were too busy securing the lines and adjusting the sails to notice the slender figure that marched down the gangplank to melt into the teeming throngs on the New Orleans dock. She never looked back, but simply walked as one walks in sleep, one foot before the other, her face blank and empty of emotion. Only her eyes betrayed her pain, for they welled with tears, a continuous flood of tears that caused many who passed her on the levee to turn their heads and wonder what had caused the poor young lady such terrible grief. But they merely shook their heads and walked on, and Anemone did the same.

EIGHTEEN

THE HOTEL Bergeron was a charming establishment in the Vieux Carre, not far from the levee. Anemone had no problem in reaching it due to the precise instructions of a young Creole gentleman who provided her with detailed instructions and even offered to accompany her to her destination. This offer Anemone refused. She thanked him and hurried on, relieved that her ridiculous tears had finally ceased to flow and that she no longer drew curious stares from every person she passed on the street. When she drew up in front of the hotel, which was a two-story structure built of brick and covered with stucco that had been painted a pearly shade of gray, she paused for a moment before passing through the ornamental wrought-iron portals. Pain squeezed through every fiber of her body. Her head ached, her chest throbbed with tight convulsions, and her throat felt as though she had swallowed a barrel of scorching sand. She had to gain control of herself before she entered this place, for she would need her wits about her. There was no telling what she would be walking into here, whether those inside would prove to be friends or the most deadly of enemies. Her father had taught her to enter unknown situations with extreme caution and the clearest of heads. Unfortunately, her own mind was murky with doubt, self-recrimination, and the bitterest kind of sorrow. She prayed she would have the fortitude to get through the next few moments, to handle whatever arose with aplomb and the kind of incisive thinking she was trained to employ. But first, she waited a moment beneath the molten New Orleans sun, her shoulders sagging and her heart as heavy as an anchor dragging at its chain.

Stephen had used her. The knowledge hit her as wrenchingly now as it had when she first was confronted with it, but she forced herself to go on, to think beyond that. She continued her train of thought, deliberately accustoming herself to the magnitude of his betrayal and of her own despicable stupidity. Brilliantly, ruthlessly, he had used her, she acknowledged, admitting with more than a touch of self-reproach that she had allowed herself to fall victim to his ploy. He had succeeded in sweeping her along on a tide of passion that had gained him everything he wanted and left her with nothing but shame. Like Andrew Boynton, he had courted her for his own purposes. Unlike Andrew, she thought with terrible bitterness, he had succeeded in seducing her to gain the information he sought. Despair swept through her when she thought back on how completely she had been taken in. She had given herself to him body and soul, and he had been laughing at her all the time. Those beautiful nights at sea, when Stephen had awakened her passion with effortless ease and kindled the flames of her love, he had been secretly triumphing over her, congratulating himself on his cleverness and her naiveté. Fool that she was, she had offered herself to him with utter abandon, and all the time he had been playing a charade. Dizzy and sick with anger, self-recrimination, and a pain keener than the thrust of a rapier, Anemone now stood before the hotel trying to master her grief. The tears had gone, but she felt as weary and broken as someone who has been beaten and left to lie in the street. She closed her eyes against the fine haze of the sunlight reflecting off the stucco facade. All about her wafted the heady perfume of magnolia blossoms intermingled with the fresh odors of fruits and vegetables being sold at the market levee down the street. The noises of New Orleans crowded in around her; faint shouts from the flatboats inching up the river, the cries of vendors hawking their wares of coffee beans and spices, the low babble of people bustling all around her. Taking a deep, steadying breath, she tried to immerse herself in these pungent smells and sounds, tried to blot out the pain of her memories. She had to go on. Johnny Tucker had done her a favor, she told herself through the numbing pain. She ought to be grateful. Instead she hated him. Almost as much as she hated Stephen Burke.

Enough of the past. Anemone opened her eyes, blinking in the sunlight. She had to find her father. She had told Stephen that she was to seek him out at the Hotel Bergeron, inquiring for Monsieur DuBois. As soon as Stephen discovered she was gone, this was the first place he would come. Whatever else happened, Anemone meant to find her father and leave with him before Stephen arrived.

Inside the hotel, she was struck by the elegant beauty of the interior, which contrasted markedly with the plain stucco facade. High ceilings and a graceful curving staircase added depth and a luxurious aura to the rose carpeted salon in which she found herself. Louis XVI furniture, gilt-framed paintings adorning the rose and cream papered walls, and numerous objets d'art brought the room alive with glittering color and exquisite French flair. Anemone approached the impeccable little man seated behind the gold lacquered desk which faced a grouping of rosewood and satinwood furnishings. He was riffling through a stack of papers, quill in hand, but he looked up at her approach.

"Mademoiselle, may I help you?"

"I hope so." Anemone responded in flawless French. This was, after all, the Creole section of town, where the aristocratic Old World families of both French and Spanish extraction held court. The man before her, a slim, diminutive figure in a neat black mustache and very light, almost luminous brown eyes, had an elegant air about him which she instinctively matched in her response. If he thought her French rather than English, so much the better. "I am looking for Monsieur DuBois. Is he here at present?"

"Monsieur DuBois! Most certainly he is here!" The Creole's dark brows rose. "I am Eugene Lamore, concierge of the Hotel Bergeron. Monsieur DuBois is in our employ. He is at this very moment at work upon the accounts."

"May I see him?" Anemone decided it would be wiser to avoid offering any explanations until she knew exactly what role her father was playing and what kind of part he wished her to assume in his little plan. She smiled at Eugene Lamore, hoping she looked cool and aristocratic. She felt awful. Catching sight of her reflection in the large, gilt-framed mirror hanging on the wall beyond the desk, she saw that she was pale and her coiffure had wilted pitiably in the growing heat of the day. The woman who gazed back at her from the glass looked thin and wan and beaten, with wisps of pale hair curling at her temples and sunken, dark-shadowed eyes. Eugene Lamore must have taken pity on her, for he pushed back his chair, came to his feet with great ceremony, and bade her to follow him.

"I will bring Monsieur DuBois to you in the *petit* salon," he said crisply. "May I offer you a lemonade while you wait, mademoiselle?"

"Nothing, thank you." She preceded him into a small, charming room beyond the main salon. It was as exquisitely appointed as the other, but the colors were different, yellows and blues and orchids, and Anemone felt as if a cool, refreshing breeze touched her when she entered this springlike haven. There was an Oriental carpet upon the teak floor, and fresh flowers in crystal vases were set upon the mantel and the white marble sofa-table. Wide French doors opened onto the inner courtyard of the hotel, which was hidden from the street. She saw a fountain in the exact center of the flagstone court, and there were pecan trees and magnolia bushes and roses to delight the eye. When Monsieur Lamore had bowed himself out and left her alone, she sank down upon the yellow damask sofa in the center of the room and her head dropped into her hands.

She felt again the sting of tears behind her eyes. Despite herself, her thoughts returned to Stephen Burke. *Stephen. How could you have done this to me?* she wondered in silent misery, and the pain swelled anew within her chest. But she wouldn't cry. She wouldn't cry again for him.

A door opened and closed. She tore her fingers from her face and glanced up. "Papa." The single word scraped from her throat, and then she was flying into his arms and the silly tears were slipping down her cheeks.

Thomas Carstairs enfolded her in his arms. His gray eyes moistened as he held the daughter who had never before clung to him in such a desperate manner.

"Emmy, Emmy," he murmured, smiling through his own unsteady emotions. "There, my girl, it's all right. What's all this, Emmy? Such tears! Not for me, I'm certain. What is it that has you in such a state?"

At forty-nine years, Thomas Carstairs was as modestly handsome as ever. He was a dignified-looking man of medium height and trim build, neither overly thin nor portly. His brown hair fell in neat locks over his forehead, and his nose had a decidedly aristocratic slant. Like Anemmone's, Thomas Carstairs's eyes were a clear, piercing gray, set deep within the sockets, and framed by thin, sloping brows that drew together when he was deep in thought. Anemone stared at him, drinking in the dear, comforting features of his thin, craggy face, her hands tightly gripping the lapels of his jacket. "Oh, Papa," was all she could manage to say for a moment, and he burst into familiar, hearty laughter.

"Well, that's the first time I've ever heard you come up speechless, my girl! Aren't you going to upbraid me for deceiving you like I did—letting you think I was dead all those months? I was certain you'd give me a tongue-lashing like none I've ever heard before! Emmy, Emmy, what is it?" The note of concern in his voice deepened suddenly as he held her at arm's length, looking down into her face. She had burst into fresh tears at his words, and it was so unlike her to be so overcome that he wondered with real worry what could be wrong.

"Papa, I'm sorry to be such a ... such a goose," she finished, for lack of a better word. She clutched the hand-kerchief he handed her and pressed it to her damp cheeks. The sight of him had affected her more powerfully than she had anticipated. He was the one person in the world who truly loved her and always had, and seeing him now, after the shattering discovery of this morning, brought home to her just how precious his love was. She had fallen into his arms, feeling a little girl again, the same little girl who had always run to him with her hurts. Only this time her injury went deeper than a skinned knee or a bruised elbow. Even then, Anemone remembered, she had never sobbed like this over such an injury, but had borne it and the accompanying salve, however much it stung, with only a slightly trembling lower lip. Well, now the pain went deeper than those other trifling hurts, but she must try to bear it as bravely. Her father was regarding her in genuine dismay, and it was time to reassure him.

"Papa, I'm all right, truly I am." She gazed tenderly through her tears at his dear, handsome face. Those penetrating eyes were studying her closely, searching beneath her words for the true cause of her distress. That was something she didn't wish him to discover—at least, not yet.

"It is just that I am so glad to see you," she said swiftly, smiling at him as she wiped away the last of the tears from her cheeks, and handed him back his handkerchief. "Although, as you say, I ought to give you a tongue-lashing and box your ears for letting me believe you were dead! But, I suppose you had good reason for doing so."

"The best of reasons," Thomas assured her. Then his face sobered. "You've come just in time, Emmy. I have reason to believe that a plot of assassination is about to take place, and if we don't act immediately, the most terrible consequences will occur."

It was just like him to plunge directly into the matter without even inquiring about her journey or Oliver or anything else. She hugged him to her again. "Oh, Papa, it is so *good* to be with you. And you must tell me everything. But we mustn't talk here. We must leave this place at once. There is a man who knows we are meeting at this hotel, and I have no doubt that he'll arrive here at any moment!"

"What man? Who is he?" Thomas's voice sharpened.

"I can't explain now." Anemone grasped his arm and began to steer him toward the door of the small salon. "When we're away from this place I'll tell you all about it. We must..."

She broke off as the ivory doorknob twisted suddenly, an ominous sound in that charming room. Her fingers clenched on her father's arm, for she knew who was there before she even saw him. Frozen, Anemone stared as the door swung open very slowly.

Stephen Burke walked into the room.

Anemone gave a cry at the sight of him. Thomas Carstairs stepped briskly forward, placing himself between her and the newcomer.

"Monsieur," he began formally, but broke off as his gaze settled upon the tall, imposing figure that had unceremoniously invaded the salon. His lips curved into a smile. "Why, it is Stephen!" he exclaimed, and there was no mistaking the surprised pleasure in his voice. "Damn me to blazes, it is Stephen Burke!"

Stephen, towering before them in tightly controlled fury, looked thunderstruck. Then the murderous gleam faded from his eyes. He shook his head incredulously at the trim, beaming man before him. "Wilcox?" he asked, as if scarcely able to believe his eyes.

Suddenly, Thomas chuckled and moved forward to clasp his hand. "Yes, it's me, Stephen, only the truth of it is, my name is actually Carstairs. Thomas Carstairs." Pumping Stephen's hand vigorously, he grinned at the younger man's bewilderment. "What a stroke of luck that you should be here at this time, my boy! We can use you, Emmy and me."

Anemone gazed from one to the other of them in mounting disbelief. They knew each other? It was impossible. She felt her head reeling. The sight of Stephen had nearly undone her and she had come the closest in her life to fainting. How handsome he looked in his pearl gray shirt and deeper charcoal waistcoat with buttons of glittering jet. His deep gray breeches were molded to his powerful legs and tucked into his gleaming top boots. The rugged, arrogant set of his shoulders and the unruly black hair she had so often run her fingers through struck a chord of pain in her so deep that she had to gasp to keep from crying out. She jammed her hands into fists so that he could not see her fingers trembling. His shocked gaze moved from her father's smiling face to her tense one, and the anger that had first been stamped on his face when he entered the room returned.

"So this is your father," he said, and his voice was harsh and cold, sending a thread of fear through her blood. "How unfortunate you did not wait to introduce me properly."

Anemone could not answer. Thomas glanced from one to the other of them. "You are acquainted with my daughter?" His brows came together swiftly. "Emmy, is this the man you were frightened of? Was he following you? Well, no need to fret, my dear." He smiled, a devilish light in his eyes. "I've worked with this young fellow before and I can tell you, he can be trusted. In fact, we'll need his help if we're to prevent a heinous crime."

"No!" Anemone couldn't help her sharp exclamation. Both men turned to stare at her.

She felt as though a knife were twisting inside her as she met Stephen's icy eyes. "How do you know this man, Papa?" she demanded desperately, coming forward to touch her father's sleeve. "You've never mentioned his name. And you," she whirled on Stephen, a tremor entering her voice. "You might have mentioned having met my father when I told you who I really was."

Stephen took a step closer to her. She drew back, and his expression hardened. "I never knew him as Thomas Carstairs. We worked together four years ago in India on an assignment of joint benefit to both of our countries. He told me his name was Harold Wilcox." An edge entered his voice. "It seems both you and your father have a penchant for using assumed names."

Thomas chuckled. "I taught her that. One can never be too careful, you know."

A reluctant grin spread across Stephen's features as he responded to Thomas Carstairs's droll smile. "I suppose

tomorrow I'll discover you're really the Duke of Wellington," he remarked.

Anemone couldn't bear their light-hearted camaraderie
a moment longer. Spinning on her heel, she fled to the
French doors that led to the courtyard and stared unseeingly out at the crystal spray of the fountain. "We don't
need him, Papa." She bit off the words, her hands twisting before her. "In fact, I won't work with him. Whatever
plot is underway, we can handle it alone."

Stephen's midnight blue eyes darkened. He stared at
her back. "I would like a few moments alone with your
daughter, Carstairs."

"No!" Anemone whirled around, panic in her face.
"No, I will not be alone with you!"

Thomas looked from Anemone's bone white countenance to Stephen Burke's harsh features. Beneath his jovial facade lay a mind that was keen as a blade, and he
had missed none of the tension flashing between the two
ever since Stephen Burke had walked into the room. They
had something to settle between them, that much was
obvious. But this wasn't the time to do it. If the plan he
had devised in the last thirty seconds was accepted by
them both and put into action, they would have plenty
of opportunity to discuss personal matters. In the meantime, a man's life came first. Besides, he thought Anemone seemed truly distraught by the prospect of being
alone with him right now, and Thomas guessed she could
use a bit of time to prepare herself for whatever confrontation was brewing. He moved forward with sudden decision, rubbing his hands together.

"There's no time for private discussions," Thomas declared. "Come, Anemone, sit beside me on the sofa. We've
much to discuss and not much time. Monsieur Lamore
will expect me to return to my accounting duties momentarily."

Anemone came forward obediently and seated herself

beside him, conscious of Stephen's frowning gaze upon her. She avoided looking at him. "What... whatever are you doing here working on the hotel accounts, Papa?" She tried to return her mind to the matter at hand. "And what is this terrible plot you referred to? We—Mr. Burke and I—already know about the Spider and Jean-Pierre De Vauban."

"Do you now?" Thomas Carstairs raised his brows. "It seems there is much we have to learn from each other. But we'd best do it quickly, my girl, or all will be for naught."

He then proceeded to tell them swiftly how he had stumbled upon news of a far-reaching plot while on an assignment in Spain, and how an attempt made on his life had forced him to pretend his own death all those months ago. Over a period of time, he had made his way to the port of New Orleans and taken on a new identity, that of Julien DuBois.

"A Frenchman, of all things!" Anemone shook her head in amazement.

"How better to slip in and out among these Creoles, Emmy? By securing a job keeping the accounts in this hotel, I was able to keep an eye upon the owner of this establishment, a Monsieur Bergeron, who is one of De Vauban's chief accomplices."

"Accomplices in what?" Stephen came to stand directly before the sofa. "What in hell is this damned plot De Vauban is hatching?"

Thomas Carstairs stared him straight in the eye. He spoke softly yet clearly. "De Vauban is going to butcher Lord Melvin Bromford and send the dismembered parts of his body to King George courtesy of the American people."

Both Anemone and Stephen stared at him mutely, stunned by his words. "But... why? How?" Anemone managed at last. Stephen gave a groan and raked his fingers through his hair. He strode quickly to the French doors, then the fireplace, then returned to the center of the room as Thomas replied.

"It is meant, of course, to disgrace America and to heighten the animosity between her and England. The real goal is to plunge the two countries into war. De Vauban intends for a small, anonymous band of both Creoles and other American citizens to take open credit for this crime—blatantly seeking to antagonize England into drastic reprisals. The devil knows, there's already enough trouble brewing between the two countries, what with all this impressment business and the trade blockades. Something like this would touch off the kinds of sparks that could easily ignite into full-scale war. That would no doubt ally America with France and weaken England still further in her struggle against Napoleon. De Vauban obviously believes, and he's probably correct, that a war on two fronts would be impossible for England to sustain for long."

Stephen was standing very still. "When is this barbarism supposed to take place?" he inquired grimly. "And who, precisely, is involved?"

Thomas Carstairs got to his feet heavily. "I'm damned if I know," he admitted with a sigh.

"Is Lord Bromford here in New Orleans now?" Anemone asked. The shocking plan had almost made her forget her own heartache. This plot took precedence over everything and everyone else. She could scarcely brood over a shattered heart when all of England was at stake. Yet she avoided looking at Stephen as her father answered their rapid-fire questions as best he could.

"He arrived yesterday. He's a guest of Governor Claiborne. The blasted murder could be taking place this very moment for all I know."

"No. De Vauban is a man of high drama. He'll choose his moment carefully." With an absent-minded air, Stephen paced to the mantel once more and ran a hand over the smooth white marble. "Is there a ball to be given in Bromford's honor?" he mused.

"Yes, as a matter of fact." Thomas's face lit with sudden speculation. "Stephen, you're as acute as ever. He's to be the guest of honor at a grand affair this Saturday. There are numerous festivities planned before then, of course, but the main fete is then."

"It's quite possible that's when De Vauban will put his plan—whatever it might be—into action. On the other hand," and here Stephen turned from the mantel to regard the other two with a narrow-eyed look, "we don't want to make too many assumptions. De Vauban could well choose an earlier moment. I'm not certain I want to gamble Bromford's life on my theories, however plausible they might be."

"I think we should warn Lord Bromford." Anemone had been thinking very quickly throughout all the talk. Now she sat up straight. Lord Melvin Bromford was arguably England's best-loved statesman of the time. He had close ties with the Duke of Wellington and was a favorite of the King. His death—no, murder—would devastate the country. Morale would topple, and the clamor for revenge would echo throughout the land. It seemed inevitable that war would follow, if not immediately, then within a preciously short space of time. Such an event, while Napoleon was still on the loose, would bode ill for the survival of England. "We must tell him what is afoot and get him on a ship bound for England at the earliest moment. Today, if that is possible."

Thomas Carstairs took a turn about the room. "I have considered that option, Emmy, many times in the past days. Yet I am reluctant to use it." He stopped and shook his fist in the air in a gesture of frustration. "I have no idea how many are involved in this conspiracy—or who they all are. The Spider must be masterminding this thing, for information is as hard to come by as rubies in a peasant's hovel. I've been working with a few trusted men for months, and still we have no proof of anything, few names, and very little that is specific. De Vauban is a respected man in New Orleans. So is Bergeron. If we whisk away their target from beneath their noses this time, they will simply plan another similar attack upon someone else. The next one might be even more disastrous—and we may not be fortunate enough to get wind of it in time. No, damn it. We've got to break this conspiracy. We have to come up with enough evidence, enough names of those involved, that Stephen here and the government of America can arrest them and end their threat to both of our nations permanently."

"I agree." Stephen nodded, his blue eyes glinting with determination. "We can't afford to frighten them off and give them a chance to reorganize and strike again." She knew that tone of Stephen's. His mind was made up.

"You are risking a man's life." For the first time since he'd come into the room, she voluntarily met Stephen's eyes. Her heart twisted painfully, but she managed to keep her gaze steady, despite the agony that filled her soul. "I cannot sanction keeping him uninformed, using him as unsuspecting bait to apprehend these conspirators. It's odious—and a terrible gamble. If we make a mistake—"

"We won't," Stephen cut her off abruptly. He spoke so coldly to her that each word sent icy pinpricks through her flesh. It was obvious to her that he was furious because she had run off before he had quite finished with her. He had wanted her to lead him straight to her father, to play the role of the docile, brainless lamb straight to the end. A kind of thin satisfaction filled her because he hadn't had it all his way. Whatever happened, she decided, bolstered by the last vestiges of pride she possessed, she would never let him know how grievously he had hurt her. She would never let him see her cry. She returned his steely gaze, lifting her chin with stubborn determination. Only inside did she quiver like jelly, wishing she was anywhere but under his deadly, cold scrutiny.

"I say we warn him," she returned, bracing herself to do battle.

Thomas Carstairs broke in hurriedly. "There's no time to fuss over such matters now. Let's settle it this way." He glanced between Stephen and Anemone as he spoke, appraising their reactions to his proposal. "The ball is not until Saturday. That gives us four days. If we make no progress in two days' time, we warn Bromford and put him on a ship for London. If we are close to uncovering the details of the plot, we delay a bit longer. We'll have to make a judgment each day that passes, based on whatever information we have or have not unearthed. In the meantime, perhaps we can add another man or two to the team I already have protecting his lordship."

"Oh, you have him covered already?" Stephen clapped him on the shoulder. "I was going to suggest that very thing. As always, you've beaten me to it."

"Lord Bromford, of course, has no idea of their purpose. They're doing their best to remain inconspicuous."

"An excellent idea." Stephen lowered his tall frame into one of the Directoire chairs flanking the sofa. "I can recommend two men on the spot who can serve as discreet guards for Lord Bromford. Their names are William Tuttle and Johnny Tucker."

At the mention of Johnny's name, Anemone flinched involuntarily. To cover the movement, she rose and paced once more to the French doors. She stared out at the lovely courtyard, with the fountain and the brilliant flowers and the pecan tree near a stone bench. She tried to find some tranquility in the scene, hoping to contain the torturous emotions battling inside her. She was tired and abominably on edge. Her nerve endings were frayed, ragged. "And what am I to do?" she asked in a strained voice. Behind her, the men were silent. Her fingers

clenched and unclenched the fabric of her skirt. "I did
not travel all the way to New Orleans merely to listen to
the two of you outline your strategy. Papa, you must
have sent for me for a reason. What role am I to play in
De Vauban's downfall?"

"A most crucial one," her father responded, and she
could hear the pride and excitement in his voice. She
turned slowly to face him, her eyes wide and alert in her
white, drawn face.

"You, Emmy," said Thomas Carstairs with great relish,
"will be De Vauban's undoing, his bane. You will be the
one to deliver him directly into our hands."

NINETEEN

FOR A moment no one spoke. Then Anemone flew forward quick as a bee. She was conscious of an odd tingling all through her body. "I?" she asked, her young face suddenly eager and alive. "Papa, I am to bring down De Vauban and his band of scoundrels?"

Thomas nodded. "Unless you have any qualms about tangling with such despicable adversaries. I wouldn't blame you if you did, Emmy. These men, De Vauban, the Spider—whoever he is, and I have my own suspicions about that—and their cutthroat accomplices from Tchoupitoulas Street are vicious criminals, as bad as or worse than any of the agents I've run across in all my years spying for the King. This is dangerous work. They'd cut your heart out in a trice if they discover what you're up to, I wouldn't blame you, dear girl, if you choose to pass this one by."

"Not a chance," Anemone exclaimed scornfully, and then hugged him, her eyes shining with excitement. "Oh, Papa, *thank* you. When do we begin?"

"It's out of the question."

Stephen Burke's voice sliced through their discussion. They turned together to look at him. He had been sitting in one of the Directoire chairs, but now he came slowly to his feet.

"What is out of the question?" Thomas demanded, with an uneasy glance at the door. "We haven't much time, Stephen, so let us not argue about details."

"This is no detail. I won't have Anemone as the centerpiece of whatever scheme you've concocted."

Thomas sent him a baffled glance. "And why not? Surely you're not envious because you are not the crucial figure in my plan?"

"Of course not." Stephen made an impatient gesture. "But I cannot agree that Anemone should be the one to take on this central role. She's far too young and inexperienced."

"How dare you." Anemone's cheeks whitened. Anger surged through her and her hands clenched at her sides. Slowly, she came forward to stand before him. "I am fully capable of carrying out this assignment and any other," she said in a low, furious tone. "And you know it."

"Of course she is," Thomas put in, coming to stand between them, for by the expression on his daughter's face, he feared she might strike the American at any moment. "Stephen, I've trained this girl myself. She may be young, but she is topnotch. I guarantee it."

"Your guarantee aside, we can't risk it." Stephen's mouth was set in a thin, harsh line. "This affair is too important."

Anemone felt as though she was going to explode. Stephen Burke may have robbed her of her happiness, he may have used her and tricked her and violated her love, but he wasn't going to deny her this as well. "My skills as an agent are equal to, if not better than yours, Mr. Stephen Burke," she cried, meeting his indigo gaze with eyes of flashing silver. "You cannot in truth tell me

that I haven't proven my abilities in both England and
New Brunswick. If, that is, you know the truth when
you meet it."

"What is that remark supposed to mean?" he demanded, but Thomas intervened.

"Shh. The door..."

There was a quick rap, and then the door to the salon
slid open. Monsieur Lamore whisked apologetically into
the room. "Forgive the disturbance," he murmured, with
a typically Gallic shrug, "but Madame Clampetre is to
take luncheon in this salon with a group of guests." His
gaze flickered about the occupants of the room, yet if he
was curious about the three, he did not show it but for
the slight lifting of his brows. His glance rested with some
interest upon Stephen. "Ah, Monsieur, I see you have
found the lady you inquired about, as well as Monsieur
DuBois."

"Yes, Monsieur Lamore, of course he has found us,"
Thomas exclaimed, and moved forward to draw the concierge into the salon with a jovial air. "Monsieur Burke
is the husband of this lady, my niece," he explained, and
proceeded to make introductions with exactly the right
note of pride and indulgence. "They have only just arrived in New Orleans, you see, and became accidentally
separated upon the levee. They both knew, though, to
seek me out immediately, and here they are, reunited
again."

"Ah." Eugene Lamore did not notice the sudden stiff-
ening of the lady at these words, or the startled look that
crossed the tall gentleman's face. By the time he turned
to them, their expressions were blank and polite.

"I apologize, madame, for referring to you as 'mademoiselle' when you first arrived. I did not know you had
a husband, and you made no mention of it." The concierge was carefully bland, but Anemone detected the
faintest note of curiosity in his voice.

"Oh, *did* you refer to me as 'mademoiselle'?" Anemone

turned wide, surprised eyes upon him. *"Mon Dieu*, I did not even realize it. The journey, you see, has been so tiring...."

"My wife has not been well." Stephen strolled forward then and took Anemone's arm in a solicitous fashion. "We shall require a suite of rooms, Monsieur. My wife has her heart set upon a lengthy stay in your excellent establishment—so convenient to her uncle. Can you accommodate us?"

"But of course." Here Monsieur Lamore unbent noticeably, going so far as to beam at them. At least the pair had not monopolized his salon and then waltzed off to stay at some common inn along the ramparts. From the looks of the man, he had money, even if he was an American. Though every inch a Creole, and fastidiously snobbish in his view of the "Kaintocks," as the Creoles called the vulgar native-born citizens of America, Monsieur Lamore had a healthy respect for wealth. And he could see by the splendid cut and styling of his garments, and the carelessly elegant way in which he wore them, that Monsieur Burke was not only wealthy but far more well-bred than one of those dreadful flatboatmen or merchants who had buinesses mushrooming all over the territory ever since New Orleans had returned to American hands. His wife, the concierge noted, the fair Madame, was a Frenchwoman of quite unusual charm, despite her pallor and the smudges beneath her eyes. Her beauty was *extraordinaire*, not at all in the common style. The lady truly did look exhausted, he thought as his gaze touched her. Something about her stirred his compassion, and with true French gallantry he made her a bow. "It will be my pleasure to have such a lovely guest in our modest hotel," he murmured. "If you would care to follow me...."

Anemone responded with an uneasy smile. "Uncle Julien," she said, suddenly panicked at the realization that she and Stephen were about to register in this hotel as husband and wife and to share quarters accordingly.

"Perhaps you would care to accompany us to our rooms and we could continue our visit?" she suggested in desperation. "It has been so long since we have seen one another...."

"No, no, I would not dream of it, *petite*." Thomas patted her hand. He then strolled to the door beside Monsieur Lamore, leaving Anemone and Stephen no choice but to follow. "I must return to my accounts—Monsieur Lamore has been only too understanding already. And you, *petite*, must rest. Stephen, later we shall have a cognac together. *Adieu*, children. Welcome to New·Orleans."

He was gone with a quick kiss of Anemone's hand and a cheery wave. Anemone remained rooted to the spot. She felt as though the world were spinning crazily all around her. She did *not* want to go upstairs alone with Stephen. She did not want to have to face him or talk to him or think about the way he had maimed her. He would question her about why she had run off without him this morning, and she didn't want to have to tell him that she knew the truth. It was too humiliating. Would he pity her or laugh at her? She didn't want to find out. She wanted to turn and run and lose herself in this colorful, overflowing bouillabaisse of a city.

Stephen took her arm. "I believe Monsieur Lamore will take us to our rooms now." Beneath the veneer of solicitude she heard the edge in his voice. "As your uncle said, my pet, you need to rest."

A feeling of unreality overtook her, and the ascent up that gracefully curving staircase was like a slow-moving dream. Down the corridor, past a row of mahogany doors, until with a flourish, the concierge flung open a pair of intricately carved doors at the end of the long hall. Anemone stepped into a gold and white room that was by far the most beautiful she had ever envisioned. It was a spacious, striking room, much larger and more lovely than any of the bedroom suites in the Pelham house on Brook

Street. It was far different also from the cabins on the *Sea Lion* or her aunt's country home in Kent or the accommodations provided by the British military when she was growing up and following the drum. She had never seen anything as beautiful, or luxurious, or inviting. A sea of gold carpeting, a small, mirror-topped table flanked by delicate Louis XVI chairs, and a white silk settee were arranged in pleasing formation near the wide-paned windows. Billowy white curtains floated in the breeze as the painted shutters were thrown back by Monsieur Lamore to reveal a magnificent view of the public square and parade grounds, known in the days of French rule as the Place d'Armes. French doors led to a wide balcony of lacy wrought iron. The room seemed to glow in the luminous New Orleans light, glimmering with cut crystal here, gilt lacquer there, everything shining with a luster and sparkle to rival the jewels in a crown. Anemone, dazzled, allowed Stephen to guide her across the thickly carpeted floor of the salon to a doorway which led to the spacious bedchamber and adjoining dressing rooms. A canopied bed with a spread of snow-white satin and small, gold-embroidered pillows was the dramatic centerpiece of the bedroom, but there were also a gilt dressing table and ivory-framed mirror, a many-tiered chandelier of winking crystal, a screen which partially hid a brass hip bath in the corner, and still another set of French doors and an accompanying balcony, this one overlooking the flagstone court of the hotel. She went to one of the crystal vases bountiful with fresh blooms and inhaled the perfume of jasmine, while Stephen saw Monsieur Lamore to the door, assuring him with smooth civility that all was satisfactory.

Seconds ticked by after she heard the concierge leave and the door to the suite click shut behind him. The dream was coming to an end. She waited, dreading the sound of Stephen's approach across the room. She touched the white petals of the flowers and lifted one long branch from the vase. As she waited for Stephen, she unconsciously crushed the petals between her fingers. Sweet fragrance wisped about her. Still Stephen did not come. No longer able to bear the suspense, she turned and glanced toward the outer salon. She was unable to see Stephen, and her heart gave a lurch. Where was he? What was he doing? Her palms grew damp with perspiration, and she felt trickles of sweat on the back of her neck, despite the cooling breezes from the balcony. Finally, she set the branch back within the vase, not even seeing the scattered remnants of the petals. With growing unease, she moved toward the salon.

Stephen was lounging against the door of the suite, his broad shoulders resting against the frame. His arms were folded across his chest, and he was watching Anemone with the kind of expression a panther employs when a rabbit dashes into its path.

"Going someplace, my pet?" he drawled.

She stopped dead, every muscle freezing. A cord of fear twisted up her spine at the ugly gleam in his eyes. She knew that look. He had not looked at her that way since the first night aboard the *Sea Lion*. Something wild and frightened flitted across her face as she felt herself caught, held, and examined, without his ever moving a finger.

"I have no desire to talk to you." She tossed off the remark with all the air of dismissal she could muster. She continued walking, making her way to a carved rosewood chair and sinking into it with lithe grace. "I want a bath and a rest before I seek out my father and learn what it is I am to do. You may leave whenever you wish, for I have no intention of sharing these quarters with you. Apart from that, there is really nothing to say."

An ominous silence met her statements. With a quickening of fear, Anemone fixed her gaze on the china figurine up on the table in front of her and studied it as if her life depended on it. Then she heard quick footsteps in the soft carpet, and there was a whoosh of movement. Before she could escape, Stephen yanked her from the chair and held her in front of him, his fingers closing around her wrists.

"Nothing to say? How interesting that you feel that way, Anemone." He spit out the words as if they were acid. "Last night you lay in my arms. This morning you said you loved me. The next thing I know, you've walked off my ship without a word and disappeared into this damned city. I think there is a great deal to say, my pet, and neither one of us is leaving this room until it's been said!"

"Let me go." She gritted her teeth against the pain of his grip. "You're hurting me, Stephen!"

His hold relaxed slightly. "My apologies. But don't expect me to release you until I've heard an explanation."

Her lips compressed. "There is a simple explanation. The ship docked. I wanted to find my father. I left."

She heard nothing but the sound of his tight, controlled breathing for the next full minute. Caught by his powerful hands, she was forced to stand there, staring at the shirt pleats on his chest, for she refused to meet his eyes. She could feel the rigid tension in his body and knew that his fury was barely under control. She told herself she wasn't afraid of him. He had already hurt her and deceived her in the cruelest way a man can deceive a woman. After that, what more could he do? What more could she possibly have to fear? Yet the raw power of his superbly muscled body and his coiled fury combined to stir the embers of fear deep within her.

"You little bitch."

His words were no less vicious for the fact that they were quietly uttered. He jerked her up against his chest and stared down at her face with undisguised wrath. "You never intended that we go ashore together, did you? You never intended to share this assignment with me once I brought you to New Orleans."

It took her a minute to realize just what he was saying. His assumption was so ludicrous that she could only stare at him. He was accusing her of the same kind of deceit he had committed against her! He thought that she had pretended all along to love him, that everything she felt was as false as his own emotions! Hysterical bubbles rose in her throat to escape as high-pitched laughter. His hands tautened around her wrists. "You never were anything but a scheming little liar," he snarled. "Right? Answer me, damn you!"

Suddenly, she gave a shuddering gasp, filled with blinding, white-hot fury. That was what he thought, after she had given him everything in her power to give, after she had shared every drop of love in her heart! He was not a man, Anemone decided, shaking with rage. He was a worm. A worm who thought everyone else was as base and low as himself. She peered at him through her haze of pain, and her eyes grew narrow and cold. Why not? Why not hurt him as he had hurt her? Why not shatter that egotistical pride and wipe the self-satisfaction from his arrogant soul?

Her face had grown, if possible, even whiter than before, and she was every bit as pale as the silk settee beside them. Her eyes blazed into his like huge embers of glinting charcoal.

"Let me go," she hissed, and the menacing fury in her voice echoed through the white and gold room.

To her surprise, he released her. He stepped back and stared at her, an expression of such astonished shock upon his features that Anemone was once again spurred to laughter.

"Do you find it so incredible that a woman should walk away from you, Stephen, *my pet*?" She gave a scornful laugh. Inside, she was dying, but it felt good to wound him, to hide her own pain with a shield of lies. "I needed you to bring me to New Orleans, Stephen," she continued. "I wanted to know the information you possessed about Henri Marceau and this whole vile business. You obliged me on both counts." The faintest sneer curved her soft lips. She laughed again. "Do you understand, Stephen?" she drawled. "I used you. It was all a pretense, from beginning to end—every single moment of it. But I don't need you anymore. And I don't wish to see you or speak to you or work with you. Is that clear? I'm bored with you. And I want nothing more to do with you."

For a moment, she thought she had gone too far and he was going to strike her. The most terrible fury closed over his face, and his body went rigid, every muscle straining with the effort of self-control. Involuntarily, she took a step backward for she had never seen him look as dangerous, but his hands shot out and grabbed her before she had gone two paces away. This time she winced at the cruelty of his grip, but he did not loosen it in the slightest.

"You damned, cold-blooded, filthy slut."

The words were an icy draft down her spine. She forced herself to smile, but her lips felt horridly dry. "And you are a complete fool. You really thought I was in love with you!"

His hands were crushing the bones of her arms. She blinked back tears. Suddenly, he flung her away so abruptly that she fell into one of the chairs. Stephen turned on his heel and strode to the fireplace, and his fist slammed against the white marble, shattering a glass figurine.

Wild, raging wrath tore through him, blacker than any storm. He had never come so close to committing murder, had never felt such overpowering hatred for anyone in his life. An urge to take Anemone's slender throat between his fingers and squeeze the life from her body gripped him, and he took hold of the mantel with both hands to release the violent energy. To think that he had been worried about her! To think that he had had his men search the entire ship for her, that he had paced and wondered and agonized about her disappearance, unable to conceive that she might have simply walked off the *Sea Lion* without a word to anyone. At first, he had been puzzled when there was no sign of her after the ship was secured in port. Then his bafflement had deepened to concern. Finally, after a thorough search of the ship during which he had suffered rising waves of anxiety and questioned every man on board, a kind of disbelieving anger had come to him. It had occurred to him that perhaps she had gone to meet her father without him, that perhaps she had deliberately slipped away without a trace. But this he couldn't believe. They had made their plans. They were to go to the hotel together. Anemone would have had no reason to depart alone, and there was no possibility of a misunderstanding. He had paced his cabin and downed two glasses of brandy, wondering where in hell she could be. Then he had come to the hotel because it was the only place left to look for her, but still he had not expected to find her there. When he first heard from the concierge that yes, a lady had come in search of Monsieur DuBois, and yes, they were meeting in the *petit* salon, tremendous relief had flooded through him. Then he had stopped stock-still and taken in the fact that Anemone had gone ashore without him. That was when the first real stirrings of anger had hit him. In the few seconds it took for Monsieur Lamore to point out the small salon and for him to stride to the door, anger had grown to rage. The dreadful suspicions stabbed at him, piercing him with bloody daggers of doubt. He could scarcely contemplate, much less believe, that this was a true effort to elude him, but ... what else was there to believe? And her expression when he had walked into the salon, her involuntary cry, had torn through him like a rifle shot. She could not have appeared more dismayed.

The entire time Thomas Carstairs had regaled them with De Vauban's filthy plot and the steps they could take to counter it, he had been waiting for a chance to get Anemone alone, to question her and get the answers he sought. Now he had them. All his suspicions, those ugly, unbelievable suspicions, were true. She was a far better actress than he had ever given her credit for, and the most despicable bitch alive. All those months at sea, when she had charmed and delighted him, had been a lie. All those nights when they had drunk of each other's kisses and had laid entwined upon his bed, she had deceived him. The knowledge that he had once formulated the same plan with the same intentions did not assuage the fire of his fury. For he had cast aside his plan the first night he had made love to her. He had forgotten everything but the woman and had simply wanted to love her and make her his own. And how he had loved her. He would have given his life for her. But she had never been his. She had been a phantom, a woman of imaginary virtues, a specter to tantalize and betray. How had he ever thought her an innocent?

"You play a dirty game, my pet," he remarked at last, when he had sufficient control of his voice to speak. He turned to confront her where she still sat in the chair. Her face had turned ashen, and her hands trembled slightly on the arms of the chair, but her demeanor was as cold and remote as that of an ice princess. Stephen straightened and came toward her slowly. His eyes were like shards of steel. He had begun their journey to New Brunswick with the intention of using her, only he had abandoned his plan when he fell victim to her false charms. But she needn't know that, he thought through the roiling fury and pain within him. He could still save his pride, if nothing else. It was a small thing, but it was all he had left.

"I, too, played a game during our journey," he continued in a hard, mocking voice which slashed through her like jagged needles. "Amusing, isn't it, that we both hit upon the same scheme?" He thought she made a small noise, a choking sound or a cry, but when he paused to regard her intently, she said nothing, sitting as still as death upon her chair. He went on. "Only I was under a misapprehension. I thought you were a lady—a young, innocent, vulnerable lady. So I planned to distance myself from you slowly, to protect you from unnecessary hurt." His laugh was curt and unpleasant in that beautiful, elegant room filled with flowers and crystal and broken dreams. "Now I see that was hardly necessary. You have no more sensitivity than a crayfish, and," he added with a small, cruel smile, "very little more appeal. I am relieved that our little farce is finally at an end. Neither of us must pretend any longer."

Anemone willed herself not to cry in front of him, knowing she would always hate herself if she did. She wanted to speak, to ask him to leave this room and never return, but she didn't trust her voice enough to try.

"Of course we must continue the charade before the eyes of the world, or at least, New Orleans society," Stephen continued in that same taut, hard voice. He drew forth a cigar from his jacket pocket and proceeded to light it with maddening coolness. "Your father's plan obviously calls for us to pose as a married couple, and it seems impossible to change that now. We're stuck with one another for a little longer, until this job is finished."

"No! I want you out of here!" Anemone cried, getting to her feet rather unsteadily. Stephen loomed before her, shaking his head in a mocking way.

"Anemone, Anemone," he chided, and exhaled a puff of smoke. "Your father assured me you were topnotch, but this is the behavior of an amateur. We have to play this one out until the end, my pet, whether it suits you or not."

"I won't share quarters with you! And I won't sleep in the same bed with you!"

"You are welcome to the settee." He turned away, bored, and moved with quick strides toward the door. "I'm going to have a look around and see if your father is free for that cognac. Obviously that's when he intends to tell me the rest of his plan."

She said nothing, merely staring after him in sick dismay. He glanced back at her critically from the door.

"I'd get some rest, if I were you," he advised. The coldness in his eyes seemed to pierce right through her flesh as he took in her drawn, pale appearance. "It might be a long evening. We'll have to make some form of contact with De Vauban tonight, for there's no time to waste. And we can't afford any mistakes."

"I don't make mistakes." Anemone spoke through numbed lips.

He ignored her. "In case I never mentioned it," he added, "De Vauban has an eye for women. His taste is quite particular." His smile was brutal, and it successfully hid the agony he was undergoing within. "I've a hunch your father's plan will somehow call upon you to attract him. But if you don't perk up a bit, my pet, the man won't give you a second glance."

The door slammed shut behind him. Anemone sank back into the chair. She started to shake, and then the tears came. With her head thrown back in anguish, she thought of all those times when Stephen's arms had come around her, holding her, warming her, comforting her. She needed him now to enfold her and soothe away the pain, but that was impossible. He was the cause of it. He would never again kiss her in that tender way that sent warm pulse beats shooting through her blood, or smooth her hair, or whisper loving words. He hated her. He thought she was as deceitful as he, and while before he had merely used her and pitied her, now he despised her. And she ought to despise him. But she couldn't. She could only feel pain and emptiness and a terrible, unbearable loss.

TWENTY

DUSK HAD long ago fallen over New Orleans. Anemone stood upon the balcony of the bedroom suite, staring down into the darkened, empty courtyard of the Hotel Bergeron.

It had been hours since Stephen had returned with a report from her father. During his absence, she had eaten listlessly from a luncheon tray sent up by Monsieur La-more, then bathed and rested until Stephen's return had demanded her full attention. Then she had sat stiffly in one chair and he in another. Like formal strangers they had spoken in polite, unemotional tones, discussing the strategy they would employ to trap the assassins. He had outlined the full plan for her in cool, businesslike tones, and she had responded with questions and statements that explored every angle of the approach they were to take. Anemone crisply approved the plan set forth by her father, but Stephen, she could see, had reservations. For some reason she could not understand, since her abilities were proven, he objected to her central role in the affair.

But why? He had no logical reason to do so. As she had pointed out, he had already seen evidence of her skills as a spy. He had even acknowledged them. Why then this strong dislike of her being placed in the thick of things, pitted directly against the murderers in their bloody machinations? It was exactly where she wanted to be.

No sooner had they reached the end of their discussion than the first stage of the plan had begun. Stephen, before returning to the suite, had visited a number of local merchants, explaining that he was in need of items for both himself and his wife, since many of their belongings had been damaged or lost during a storm at sea. He made all the arrangements and many purchases. Anemone soon found herself opening the salon door to a successive army of merchants, led by the formidable Madame Celeste, who had marched in with her crew of seamstresses bearing box after box of gowns and fabrics and sequins and pins. Anemone had stood and turned and twisted and stared at countless dresses draped over her slender form and whooshed over her shoulders to flow down from her waist. Then had come a milliner and a jeweler and a number of other people she was at last too weary to remember. She only knew that when she finished with them all, or more appropriately, they with her, she had found herself in possession of a dozen new gowns with matching shoes, hats, jewels, stockings, reticules, and shawls. It was almost overwhelming, and she knew the cost to be shocking. She wondered which of the governments involved would foot the bill for all this finery. Yet she knew it to be necessary. She and Stephen had to create the right impression if their mission was to succeed. In the next few days she must involve herself in banquets, theater, strolls along the public square, and all manner of entertainments which would throw her together with Jean-Pierre De Vauban. The condition of most of the gowns she had worn during the voyage rendered them inadequate for New Orleans society. She had to be appropriately gowned and groomed, for Creole society was lavish and elite, and she had to enter it without a whisper of doubt from anyone. It would help that Stephen was acquainted, however slightly, with De Vauban. From the moment she was introduced to him, however, the rest would be up to her.

Most of the new and delectable gowns were whisked back by Madame Celeste to her shop on Royal Street for precise alterations, but that very afternoon, she and her assistants had fitted Anemone for the gown she was wearing tonight. This was a white gauze creation, spangled by silver rosettes and bows. It had a high waist bound by a white satin sash, a frilled hemline, and a daringly low-cut bodice which clung provocatively to Anemone's full breasts. The silvery gown shimmered with every step she took. It displayed to admirable advantage every curve and hollow of her young, lithe figure and would surely, Anemone thought without enthusiasm, help her to make a dazzling impression upon Jean-Pierre De Vauban. And that was her goal, she reminded herself as she stood alone at the wrought-iron balcony. The plan her father had devised, which was imprinted on her mind, demanded that she ingratiate herself with De Vauban beginning this very night. As she gazed out into the darkness, feeling the cool river breezes fan her cheek, she thought again of Lord Bromford and the importance of her mission. Everything between Stephen and herself must be put aside for the time being. She must forget her pain and her anger and her betrayal, and think only of what was at stake. A man's life, a country's destiny. There was no place for heartache here. She and Stephen were partners now. Nothing more. And until this was over and Lord Bromford was safe, with the band of would-be assassins rounded up and disposed of, they would have to rise above their personal feelings and work together.

She turned from the balcony and went into the bedroom, gathering up her reticule and shawl. On her way to the door, she caught a glimpse of herself in the mirror. Delicate diamond earrings winked at her ears, and a matching necklace circled her throat. Her hair was held by a comb of silver and pearls. She looked, she thought in awe, elegant and regal. She had never seen herself so resplendent, and for an instant she recalled the night she had posed before her mirror in her nightrail, wishing Stephen Burke could see her in Cecilia's finery, wondering if then he would find her appealing. Her lips twisted with bitterness. Then she whirled from the mirror and went to the door.

Stephen rose automatically when she came into the salon. He slowly took in her appearance. "I almost pity De Vauban," he muttered, his eyes as hard as agates. He looked splendidly handsome himself in his midnight blue coat and breeches, with a single sapphire pin nestled in the snowy folds of his cravat. He moved toward her with firm, lanky strides, and without another word took her arm and guided her toward the door.

They were going to the opera. Most of New Orleans society, including De Vauban, Monsieur Bergeron, and Lord Melvin Bromford, was certain to be there. It was the ideal time to begin putting their plan into effect.

The "plan," like all good schemes, was quite simple. De Vauban, as Stephen had noted, had an eye for women. Particularly, Thomas Carstairs had pointed out when he and Stephen conferred over their cognacs, for married women. He had a special fascination with other men's wives, relishing the destruction of a happy marriage the way some men relish running a fox to ground. The stakes of human lives and happiness held their own irresistible appeal for him, and the knowledge that he could easily be drawn into a duel if the woman's husband discovered or even suspected an affair seemed a vital part of the attraction. He was a noted duelist and had killed a number of men on the field of honor. He enjoyed dueling almost as much as he enjoyed the intrigue of a liaison with a married woman. This much Thomas had succeeded in learning about the Creole, and Stephen had been able to confirm it based on his observations at the Coronation ceremonies and festivities. The plan therefore called upon Anemone to capture his fancy and to gain admittance to his confidence in a way that a man could never accomplish. Stephen's accompaniment of his daughter to New Orleans seemed positively providential to Thomas Carstairs, for now she could pose as a married woman, making her even more desirable in De Vauban's eyes. He felt confident that if everyone played his part correctly, the plan would fall perfectly into place.

One of the problems Thomas had encountered while attempting to spy on De Vauban and his accomplices in the past months had been the strict secrecy surrounding the group. It was nearly impossible to penetrate the inner circle of conspirators. One of Thomas's men had already been stabbed through the heart and his body dumped in a nearby bayou when his purpose was discovered. The main hope now rested on Anemone. She had to gain De Vauban's trust and interest sufficiently in the next few days to give her an opportunity both to learn the identity of the other plotters and to foil their murder plans. It was no easy assignment, yet it was the type of mission she had always yearned for—a chance to outwit a worthy opponent, to pit herself against the enemy with tremendous stakes at risk, to operate efficiently and creatively under incredible pressure. She felt ready to tackle it, and Thomas was convinced of her prowess. Only Stephen seemed disturbed by the plan, for reasons he did not fully explain.

In the carriage, she and Stephen maintained rigid silence as the coach lurched down the rutted dirt streets. The glow from the street lamps occasionally illuminated Stephen's harsh, handsome face, and for a moment Anemone found herself taken back to that night in London when Stephen had forcibly put her into the carriage and brought her to his ship. He looked just as forbidding now.

Anemone moved away from him, to the other corner of the carriage. The fragrance of orange blossoms drifted on the June air, and the night outside the carriage was ablaze with stars, but inside the coach the atmosphere was dank and hellish, and Anemone saw none of the beauty of the night.

When they arrived at the opera house, Stephen helped her to alight with a great show of husbandly concern. With her hand upon his arm, she entered the theater and allowed him to guide her through the elegant, chattering throng to the private box he had engaged for the evening.

The opera house was a vast, glittering arena of handsomely attired men and beautiful, sophisticated women. Everywhere Anemone looked she saw evidence of the exquisite taste and finery of New Orleans society: the rich crimson curtains upon the stage, the sparkling chandeliers, the private boxes upholstered in velvet. The women in the theater fluttered fans of delicate ivory and smoothed their pale skirts of silk and satin and gauze. Gentlemen bowed and nodded, now dancing attendance upon the ladies at their side, now conversing among themselves about the races or the latest gambling wager. Anemone surveyed the crowd with apparent unconcern, wondering which among them was Lord Melvin Bromford, and which his would-be assassin, Jean-Pierre De Vauban.

"There, in the box below and to the left, there is De Vauban now," Stephen whispered in a low tone in her ear, and she waited a moment before casually allowing her gaze to wander in that direction. The box that he had described had previously been empty, but a small, gaily dressed party was now arriving to fill it. The man who escorted the others into the box was tall and elegantly thin. She could not clearly see his face for the distance between them, yet he appeared good-looking and gallant as he smiled at the lady beside him and joked with the broad-shouldered, gray-haired gentleman at his elbow. As she watched, two more ladies and another gentleman joined the group, and all seated themselves as the lights began to dim and the first strains of the orchestra were heard. Anemone leaned toward Stephen, speaking quietly in his ear.

"Did you recognize anyone else in the party?"

"From your father's description, the gray-haired man is Lord Bromford," was his swift reply. Anemone's nerves tautened.

Grétry's *Silvain* was performed that evening, though Anemone heard little of the lovely music. Her mind was full of what she must accomplish tonight. When the intermission came, she and Stephen remained in their box, making a pretense of speaking to one another with warmth and animation. She was aware of the exact moment when De Vauban's indolent gaze began to wander about the theater, and when it touched upon them.

He recognized Stephen at once. He paused, his glance arrested, focusing with sudden interest on him. There was a certain hardness in his glance which told Anemone that he held no very friendly feelings for Stephen. She wondered why. Then Anemone saw his attention shift to her. She waited a moment, then, deliberately, she met his gaze across the theater.

A jolt went through her as she met De Vauban's dark stare. The man had a magnetism that flowed across the brightly lit room. She felt it touch her and spark something deep within. Her pulse quickened, yet she sat calmly, slender and fragile in her diaphanous white gown and upswept hair, her clear crystalline eyes directly meeting those of the man who regarded her so closely. Anemone's gaze never wavered. Slowly, she allowed a glimmer of mischief to enter her eyes, and a slight lifting of her soft lips curved her delicate mouth into an enchanting smile. She allowed her gaze to linger only a moment, and then with a flourish of her fan she turned toward Stephen and appeared to immerse herself in laughing conversation with him.

"Well done. He is still staring at you," Stephen said, leaning close to her. He lifted her hand to his lips.

"Let us hope he was sufficiently impressed," she returned with a brilliant smile, though inwardly she trembled, as much from the brush of his lips across her fingers as from the possibility that soon she would be starting her duel with De Vauban. "It is essential that he come to beg an introduction after the performance has ended."

But De Vauban came sooner than that. Stephen watched him excuse himself from his party and leave his own box. Within a very short time, while the intermission was still in progress, he was entering their box, shaking hands with Stephen, and requesting an introduction to his "so lovely" companion.

"May I introduce you to my wife, Anemone?" Stephen smiled urbanely as Anemone extended her hand. "My darling, this is Jean-Pierre De Vauban. Monsieur De Vauban and I met in Paris, at the Coronation of Bonaparte. A most memorable occasion."

"But not," said De Vauban as he bent over Anemone's hand, "as memorable as this evening when I am fortunate enough to meet such a beautiful lady." His small, cool mouth pressed softly against the skin of her hand. He straightened and looked into her eyes. "*Ravissante, Madame*," he murmured. "*Ravissante*."

At close range, the magnetism she had sensed in him across the theater was a powerful and tangible thing. The man was slim and dark and handsome in a neat, aristocratic way, with crisp black hair, ice green eyes, and small, even features. An air of urbanity and very civilized charm clung to him with every movement. He was olive complected, soft-spoken, and the epitome of smooth good breeding, yet Anemone sensed a certain oily malice in the gleam of his eyes when they rested on Stephen, and indeed when he smiled that warm, dazzling smile at her.

He reminded her of a snake, all polished, handsome leather skin and shrewd, relentless eyes—and the instinct to go for a quick, merciless kill. The hackles rose on the back of her neck when he kissed her hand, yet even as she recoiled inwardly from the cold-blooded man she recognized beneath the charming facade, she felt the powerful lure of his white-teethed smile, felt herself being drawn toward his handsome sophistication and air of nobility.

"It is a pleasure to meet you, Monsieur De Vauban." She spoke in her perfect French and saw his thin brows lift.

"Ah, but can this be? You are a Frenchwoman?"

"*Oui.*" She smiled and tilted her head to one side. "You are surprised. Is it so unusual to find a Frenchwoman in the Territory of Orleans?"

"No, but to discover that you are wed to an American—ah, that is something unusual." His gaze swung to Stephen's tall form. "Monsieur Burke, may I congratulate you upon your most beautiful wife? You have certainly stolen a jewel of incomparable worth from my native land. I should not be surprised if Bonaparte himself should come after you with an army to return such a fair lady to our precious soil."

Anemone's rich, tinkling laugh followed this piece of flattery. A slight blush tinted her cheeks as he quite openly studied the finely sculpted lines of her face, the sweep of her hair, and then allowed his gaze to fall directly to the swell of white bosom above the bodice of her dress. The man was impudent. Beneath his veneer of charm, he was smug and odiously sure of his power over women. Moreover, he was practically drooling over her! And he flaunted his interest openly in front of her "husband." *I can certainly understand why he has fought in so many duels*, Anemone thought contemptuously. *If I were a man, I should challenge him myself for this piece of effrontery!* But she hid her feelings beneath a dazzling smile.

"Monsieur De Vauban, you are a Frenchman then, also?" She allowed a trace of pleasure and surprise to creep into her voice. "I had thought you were a citizen of America. Do you not live here in New Orleans? Or are you visiting, as Stephen and I are doing?"

He shook his head. "No, Madame. New Orleans is of a certainty my home. I was born here upon my family's plantation—but my heart and soul have always belonged to France. My family never accepted the Spanish sovereignty after Louis XV ceded the colony to Spain. We have always considered ourselves French citizens—loyal servants of our homeland. The news three years ago that Bonaparte had sold the territory to America was a staggering blow. Now we are all part of America," he said with a laugh and a shrug of his shoulders, "but in our hearts, ah, that is something else."

"How delightful it is to find a countryman, then!" she exclaimed, and turned impulsively to Stephen. "Is it not wonderful, *cheri*? Monsieur De Vauban, perhaps you could join us for dinner some night during our stay? How I would love to talk further of the land that is so dear to our hearts!"

He smiled into her sparkling eyes. "I have an even better idea, Madame. Tomorrow night I am giving a ball at my plantation house in honor of a special guest in New Orleans—Lord Melvin Bromford of England. I would be delighted if you would do me the honor of joining our festivities."

"Thank you, De Vauban, that's quite decent of you, but we have other plans." Stephen answered the invitation curtly.

"Oh, *cheri*, could we not change our plans?" Anemone put a pleading hand upon his arm. Her lovely young face radiated hope and a touching appeal. "A ball at the home of Monsieur De Vauban sounds particularly enchanting! It would be so wonderful if we could go!"

A quick, challenging look passed between the two men.

De Vauban's brows rose as if daring the American to accept his invitation. Stephen appeared hesitant, but trapped into acquiescence. "Well, if it is so important to you, Anemone, certainly we shall go. We are obliged to you, De Vauban," he added with a slight note of sarcasm in his tone, which the Creole didn't miss. His smile widened.

"No, Monsieur Burke, I am obliged to you. My ball will be graced by the presence of your most beautiful wife."

The lights began to dim. "Ah, I must return to my guests," De Vauban said smoothly. "I will send a servant tomorrow morning to your hotel with an invitation for the ball, informing you of all the details. Your hotel, Monsieur?"

"The Hotel Bergeron."

"*Eh bien. Bonsoir, Madame, Monsieur.* Until tomorrow."

They sat through the remainder of the performance in silent excitement. Anemone couldn't help but be pleased by the turn of events. Stephen, too, seemed relieved that things were underway. The atmosphere in the carriage during the ride home was far more congenial than the drive to the opera house.

"That went better than we could have expected," Stephen exulted, stretching his legs out in the cramped coach. "The bastard fairly disrobed you before my eyes."

"He was quite obvious, wasn't he?" Anemone shook her head in wonderment. She, too, felt the elation of this initial success. "Why does he do it? Why does he pursue women who are married, directly beneath their husbands' noses?"

"Some men live for the chase and the challenge. The danger of discovery makes it all the more exciting."

"I find it difficult to believe he is not shunned by society if he is as transparent with all the others as he was tonight," she remarked.

"I doubt that he is. His particular enmity toward me

induced him, I believe, to flaunt his overtures in my face."

She regarded him questioningly. "What is the cause of his particular enmity toward you? I could not help but notice it. Something that happened at the Coronation festivities?"

Stephen nodded, loosening his cravat as the carriage rumbled along the misty, starlit street toward the hotel. "I prevented his seduction of a very young and wholly innocent young woman. A girl who had only just emerged from a convent school and was no match for De Vauban's advances."

"How did you prevent it?"

"I kept her so occupied with my attentions that she had no time to be alone with him." He smiled grimly, and his dark blue eyes glittered in the darkened coach. "I foiled him at every turn. Each time he sought her company he found her already engaged. It was a source of great frustration to him."

"And great delight to you, no doubt. How gallant of you to save her." Anemone could not keep the mockery out of her voice. Her hands had begun to tremble as he had related the story. "Instead of De Vauban, you were the one to break her heart."

"Not at all." Stephen folded his arms across his chest as he reclined against the squabs. "I never led her to believe that I was anything other than a friend—it was a matter of simple liking between us, nothing more. In fact, before I left Paris I introduced her to the son of an old friend. They have since married and have a young daughter."

Silence fell. Anemone twisted the strings of her reticule. "So De Vauban feels he has a score to settle with you where women are concerned," she said at last, slowly. "So much the better for us."

"Yes. Though I doubt that this past grievance was the sole reason he could not tear his eyes from you."

"Oh?" Anemone bit her lip. "Do you mean he found

me not unworthy of his attentions? How gratifying—
despite the fact that I am 'hardly a raving beauty,' to quote
your own words."

Stephen studied her in the glow of the side lamps. "I
explained that remark a long time ago."

"Yes. I remember." She gave a tight, bitter little smile,
thinking of that night in his cabin when he had said that
he must have been blind. That was when he had been
trying to seduce her, to woo her into his bed so that he
might learn more about the New Orleans plot. "But it
was all a lie, everything you said to me that night," she
said quietly, her gaze fixed upon the window of the coach.
"We both know that now, don't we?"

Stephen didn't reply. For an instant, as her gaze swung
to his face, she thought she saw an expression of pain
cross his features, then it was gone and only the cold
planes of his rugged countenance remained. She must
have imagined it, Anemone decided. There could be no
pain for him in bringing up the past, because his feelings
had never been engaged. Only his ego had been hurt,
and that was something from which he would soon recover. Her own heart, on the other hand, was breaking
more with each moment spent in his company, knowing
that the love she had thought he felt for her had all been
a fraud, that she was unimportant to him, except as a
tool. She was relieved when the carriage at last pulled
up before the hotel, for it was unbearable to sit so close
to him and not be able to touch him, to remember how
silky his hair felt beneath her fingers and how his lips
had set her afire.

They descended the carriage steps in silence and went
inside. In the salon, Stephen opened a decanter of brandy
and offered her a glass.

Anemone stood near the settee and shook her head.
"No, I think I'd better get to sleep. Tomorrow will be a
trying day."

He saw her looking doubtfully at the settee and knew

she was wondering if she would be able to get any sleep at all upon it.

"I have as little desire as you to share a bed," he announced suddenly, tossing down the brandy and then setting his glass upon the mantel with a clatter. "Therefore, I will put down a blanket and sleep in here upon the floor. You will need your rest for what awaits you tomorrow. The bed is all yours, my pet."

"Thank you." This was an unexpected courtesy, and she threw him a grateful glance, but his features hardened into a sardonic smile.

"You needn't thank me. I am thinking only of the mission. You are far more likely to make a blunder if you have not had a proper rest."

"Of course." Dully, Anemone turned and went into the bedroom alone. She stripped off her gloves, put aside her shawl and reticule and closed the French doors. Outside the room, she heard Stephen pouring himself another drink. She felt very weary. Her earlier elation over the success with De Vauban had faded, and now she was faced with the danger of tomorrow and the loneliness of tonight. She rubbed her temples and closed her eyes. Last night, she and Stephen had made love on the *Sea Lion*. Tonight they slept apart, divided by lies and deceptions. She knew that never again would he brush his lips tenderly across her throat, or cradle her in his arms like a precious doll. But, heaven help her, she wanted him to, and that only deepened the agony in her heart.

She readied herself for bed, and for another day without Stephen's love. She told herself that she had lived for twenty-one years without it and she would simply continue in the same way. But the empty feeling did not lessen, and the misery did not go away. And despite the comfort of the huge, canopied bed, Anemone slept little that night, and her slumber was fitful and marred by dark dreams.

In the salon, Stephen slept on the floor and dreamed

of a pale-haired beauty in a silver gown who lured him to her with an entrancing smile and soft promises of love, then drew forth a dagger when he reached to embrace her. He awoke sweating and paced the room until dawn, cursing her betrayal and his own damnably misplaced love.

TWENTY-ONE

ANEMONE SAW little of Stephen the next day. He was off conferring with her father, with Johnny Tucker, and with a man called Ned Boodle, who she later discovered was the same messenger who had delivered the note from her father that long-ago night in London telling her that he was indeed alive. Boodle had sailed back to America that same night and had been aiding Thomas Carstairs in his investigation ever since. While Stephen conferred with him, Thomas took the opportunity of visiting Anemone in her suite at midafternoon.

He was worried. True, between them he and Stephen had several men following Lord Bromford about New Orleans and watching Governor Claiborne's house all through the night. Yet Thomas felt the danger in his bones and cursed himself because he knew not when or how it would come. Though Anemone, from what both she and Stephen had told him, had made a good beginning with De Vauban last night, Thomas feared that something would happen before she had an opportunity to gain De

Vauban's confidence. A clock ticked relentlessly in his head. Each second that elapsed brought them closer to disaster, but when or how it would strike he did not know.

"Papa, I can see that you're uneasy." Anemone kicked off her slippers and curled up beside him on the settee, glad to have this chance to talk to him. She had come in only a short while ago from a walk along the public square, where she had hoped in vain to meet De Vauban. She had strolled past the *Cabildo*, the city hall, where the documents for the Louisiana Purchase had been signed, and had gazed in rapt admiration at the beautiful colonnade of arches marching along both the ground floor entrance and the magnificent second story where fanlights and Spanish ironwork complemented the building's symmetrical splendor. She had lingered outside the cathedral that stood alongside the *Cabildo*, marveling at its bell-shaped towers and handsome stucco-over-brick facade. Then she had taken her time returning to the hotel, stopping at various shops and browsing through the market at the levee, hoping to come across Jean-Pierre De Vauban at some point and to have an opportunity to further her acquaintance with him. But luck had not been with her. Many people had flowed through the square and bustled across the streets of the city, but De Vauban had not been among them. Now, as she sat beside her father in the gold and white salon, she sensed his tension and knew that he, too, was anxious about the wisdom of their plan.

She leaned forward impulsively and took his hand. "Why do we not go to Lord Bromford immediately and tell him of his danger? Papa, we can have him out of New Orleans before De Vauban's ball tonight."

A heavy sigh escaped her father. "No, Emmy, we've been all through that before. Let's see what tonight brings. If we learn nothing more, then perhaps tomorrow we will have no other choice than to do as you say."

"But, Papa, what if De Vauban makes his move to murder Lord Bromford tonight? Then tomorrow would be too late."

"It would be foolish of De Vauban to attempt any such thing while Bromford is under his roof. Chances are he will want the murder to occur where there is no hint of his attachment to it."

Anemone thought this over. "Perhaps you are right," she said slowly. "But De Vauban is a man who relishes taking risks. I would not put it past him to have the murder committed during his very own ball in honor of the man!"

Thomas looked at her, his face unaccustomedly grave. "Then it will be up to you, and to all of us, to be on our guard every moment. I will keep watch this evening on a man called One Eye. He is a smuggler who used to be an artilleryman in Bonaparte's army. I saw him meet on two occasions with Monsieur Bergeron at a gambling den on Tchoupitoulas Street, and once in Scar-Footed Mattie's place on Girod. I would wager my life that he's mixed up in this filthy business. When it's time for the murder to occur, no doubt he'll have a hand in it."

"Be careful, Papa." Anemone put her fingers on his arm. Her expression was troubled. "I have heard so much about this Tchoupitoulas Street. And Girod Street, as well, in the section called the Swamp. Such places are where the flatboat men brawl and gamble and drink, and a man's life is worth no more than a shilling. I don't think you ought to go there alone."

Thomas Carstairs burst into laughter that rang through the expansive suite like clear clanging bells. "Emmy, Emmy," he finally gasped when he could draw breath again. "This is me you're talking to, girl. Your old papa. I've seen far worse places than Tchoupitoulas Street, you know."

Even Anemone was drawn into smiling at her own words of caution. "Yes, I know you have, Papa, but this is different somehow. I have a feeling about New Orleans, and about these people we're dealing with." Her eyes clouded. "I'll be happy when all this is over," she said, almost to herself.

Thomas Carstairs studied her. He had never known his daughter to be "missish," to succumb to superstitious fears or anxieties. She was as drawn to danger and excitement as a bird to the open sky. Her attitude today surprised him. He took this mission as seriously as anyone and knew better than all the rest how dangerous and grim were the stakes. Yet through it all, the lure of the challenge filled him with a kind of exuberance that made his heart sing in the midst of death and danger. Anemone had always felt this way, too, from the time she was a small girl and he had first taught her to pick pockets and lie disarmingly on a moment's notice. She was good at her work, damn good, and much of that came from the joy she brought to spying. Today there was no sign of that joy. Before him sat a slender young woman in a cream muslin walking dress whose gamine face reflected worry, sober thoughtfulness, and ... sorrow. *Why sorrow?* Thomas wondered, as he leaned back upon the settee.

"What's all this between you and Stephen Burke, my girl?"

Aha. He noted the way she jumped when he spoke Stephen's name. It was unlike Anemone to give anything away, and he knew she must be badly shaken to react so visibly, even with him. "Come now." He answered the dismay written across her face with an encouraging smile. "You didn't think you could hide anything from me, did you, Emmy? Tell me, are you in love with the fellow?"

Anemone's cheeks flooded with color. A haunted look entered her eyes. "Oh, Papa..." she began, ready to pour out the whole story, and then abruptly she broke off. She clasped her hands in her lap like a schoolgirl and stared down at them. "I don't want to talk about it," she said.

Thomas moved closer and settled his arm about her shoulders. He was thinking of that fellow, Boynton, years ago, when Emmy had been little more than a coltish child. He had known more about that little affair than she had guessed, though she had never confided in him. Yet he had heard her sobbing on her bed after she had shoved the damned fellow into the horse trough. Between that, and the rumors, and what he had seen with his own eyes, Thomas had pieced the story together. He had hurt for her then, but there had been nothing he could do. He suspected the same was true now. "Shall I push Stephen Burke into a horse trough for you, my girl?" he asked softly, and there was a gentle smile on his face. "Or better yet, a muddy Mississippi bayou. Would that ease your pain, Emmy dear?"

She stared at him in numb shock, and then gave a cry that was something between a giggle and a sob. She threw her arms around his neck and buried her face in his jacket. "Oh, Papa, you knew! About Andrew ... all these years! How ... how ... oh, never mind." She began to laugh, even as the tears continued to course down her face, but after a moment, she sat up and groped for the handkerchief he offered her. "Papa, you mustn't think that Stephen and I will let ... our feelings for one another interfere with our duty. He loathes me every bit as much as I loathe him, and yet last night we worked quite smoothly together. We are united in our desire to foil De Vauban and the Spider."

"That may be, but too much hinges on this assignment to allow even the slightest distraction to interfere." Though his tone was gentle, she heard the crisp precision of the master spy in his words. "What we need now, Emmy, is clear thinking and total concentration on the job at hand. Can you manage that, despite this difficulty—whatever it might be—with Stephen?"

"You know I can," she responded, meeting his steady gaze with an equally direct look. "Or you wouldn't have maneuvered me into this situation to begin with."

Thomas threw back his head and laughed. He lifted her hand in his and cradled it between his fingers for a moment before releasing her. "That's my girl," he approved, and she felt a warming inside her at the pride in his eyes. "You've never let me down before, Emmy, and I'm damned certain you won't do it now."

He took his leave of her feeling far better than when he'd arrived. The idea of his Emmy paired with Stephen Burke sat well with him. She would have to look far to find a better man. Stephen could match Emmy's keenness and mental agility in every way, he shared her hunger for danger and intrigue, and he was strong enough to handle her stubborn temperament. They were ideally suited, Thomas realized, but they would have to find their own way to each other—after this job was finished. Until the band of conspirators was exposed and rendered harmless, he couldn't tolerate any personal distractions. By the time he left Emmy alone in her suite, he was convinced that she would put Lord Bromford's safety above all else and focus all her attention on ensnaring De Vauban. He knew his Emmy. When it came to her duty, she would not falter.

Thomas headed toward the river front and Tchoupitoulas Street. Monsieur Lamore would be furious if he knew that his hard-working accountant had deserted his office for the day, but Thomas was unconcerned about that. His role as DuBois was nearly finished anyway; once this business was settled his identity would no longer matter. He could return to England again as Thomas Carstairs, for the departmental leak that had endangered him in Spain would be plugged once the Spider was exposed and captured. And that was a pleasure Thomas was reserving for himself. He had his own suspicions about the identity of the Spider. He had a very good notion who had betrayed him and ordered his death in Spain, all because Thomas had accidentally uncovered information about this long-brewing New Orleans conspiracy. He meant to bring the Spider to justice himself—one way or the other.

As he crossed Chartres, a thought occurred to him. He had not yet voiced his suspicions to Anemone—or to Stephen, for that matter, regarding the identity of the Spider. Perhaps it was something he ought to do. Though the man who was responsible for so many deaths and such devastating betrayal of the British government was an ocean away, his reach, Thomas knew from grim experience, was vast and encompassing. He almost turned back at that moment to seek out Anemone once again. But just then, a carriage careened down the rutted road, nearly swerving into him. He jumped nimbly aside. From an alleyway behind him, he heard a low, clipped voice that was chillingly familiar, even after all these months.

"Don't move, Thomas. Not a muscle."

He was still. Shock stopped his heart for a moment, and when it began to beat again, he felt a pulsing tension through his shoulders and chest. Inwardly, he cursed his own laxity in failing to have anticipated this. And in failing to have warned Anemone. Every sinew in his body tautened as the voice continued, striking cold fury into his breast.

"That's right, Thomas. Very wise. I should hate to have to put a bullet in you and spoil all the fun."

Slowly, Thomas began to turn about to face that brisk, mockingly pleasant voice. But before he had moved an inch, he felt the barrel of a pistol jabbed between his shoulder blades. The voice spoke just beyond his ear.

"No, don't do that, my good man. No need. We're going for a short walk. Someplace where we can talk at leisure."

All about Thomas the bustle of Chartres Street continued. Men and women walked arm in arm, carriages rolled and bounced, and the moist, heavy air promised a shower before dusk. The sky was darkening already, with clouds rolling in from the swamps below the city. Thomas felt as if he were a mile separated from the carefree passers-by. He knew that if he shouted, or ran, or made the slightest untoward move, the man behind him would squeeze the trigger.

"Lead the way, Oliver, old boy," Thomas said. "As ever, I am entirely at your disposal."

"Yes," returned the voice behind him as the squat little man with the neat mustache and coal black eyes stepped closer and nudged the gun into Thomas's spine. Anyone passing would have thought they were merely two friends walking together. The gun could not be seen, but Thomas felt it and knew his own helplessness as he was guided into the busy thoroughfare. Beside him, Oliver Fenwicke gave a soft chuckle. "You always were at my disposal, old boy. And now, more than ever. Come, come, we have much to say to one another. And very little time."

These last words held an unmistakably ominous ring. Thomas felt his nerves jump, then he steadied them deliberately. Years of experience enabled him to keep his countenance blank and cold.

"I'm glad it has come to this," he remarked almost conversationally as the two crossed the road. "I've never understood the nature of a traitor. Perhaps you can enlighten me."

"Soon enough," his companion fairly purred.

Suddenly, a carriage rumbled to a stop beside them. It was the same carriage that had caused Thomas to leap aside at the alleyway. The driver grinned down at them, doffed his cap, and waited while someone inside the carriage swung wide the door. Thomas gazed up into the scarred and swarthy face of One Eye Jones, seated with his shoulders against the cushioned squabs.

"After you," Oliver murmured with a soft laugh. The gun prodded Thomas again, viciously, in the small of his back. "My good man."

TWENTY-TWO

STEPHEN STRETCHED his long legs beneath the wooden table at the Exchange Coffee House. The place was a popular meeting spot for the men of New Orleans, be they sailor or merchant or master of a grand plantation. It was a comfortable setting in which they could gossip and refresh themselves, whiling away an hour or two of the day. This afternoon the coffee house was even more crowded than usual. Stephen and Johnny Tucker had had to wait for their coffee. When it came, Stephen took a quick sip of the steaming, potent black brew and then regarded Johnny Tucker over the rim of his cup.

"You saw no signs of anything suspicious during your watch on the Governor's house?" he asked. "Nothing that would indicate treachery on the part of a servant or a member of the Governor's staff?"

Johnny shook his head. "Nothing." He shot a quick glance at his friend. "Stephen, have you thought of alerting the Governor to the situation? Surely Claiborne can be trusted."

"Yes, but any member of his staff could be in league with the conspirators. We don't know how far-reaching this is." Stephen set down his cup and allowed his gaze to rove with apparent casualness over the other customers in the coffee house. "Claiborne might inadvertently make a slip that would alert someone in his household. That could force the conspirators' hands, pushing them into hasty action—action we might be helpless to prevent."

"Any word yet on your message to the President?" Johnny asked as his fingers drummed restlessly on the little table. "I feel as if we're operating all on our own— with no orders from anyone. Damn it, if we make a mistake here..."

"I'll take full responsibility for any mistakes." Stephen spoke with quiet authority. His eyes rested briefly on Johnny's face. "You've been acting as a messenger between diplomatic embassies for too long, Tuck." A slow grin crossed his features. "You're getting too dependent on orders from up high. Remember when we first started in this business? Working on our own, catching the devil every time we finished an assignment? I still operate that way, my friend. When you're alone out there, every decision is a rough one. Are you forgetting that, Tuck—or running scared on me?"

Johnny sat up straighter in his chair, his brown eyes lighting with an answering challenge. "Running scared? Just don't forget who plucked you from a Tripoli prison at the risk of life and limb. And who tipped you off about that Aaron Burr mess—while you took the main part of the credit when he was apprehended in the Mississippi Territory? I was scarcely operating on orders then. But maybe I should have left you dangling after that serving wench—what was her name...."

"Molly."

"... right, instead of collecting fame and glory for what was essentially *my* information..."

"Enough, enough." Stephen chuckled, and his blue eyes gleamed with warmth as he shook his head at his friend. "We do go back a ways, don't we, Tuck? I thought you'd forgotten that for a while."

Johnny knew he was referring to the strain between them on the *Sea Lion* after leaving Saint John. "That had nothing to do with you." He signaled to the serving girl to bring more coffee. "But I couldn't abide seeing you make a fool of yourself over that English schemer."

Stephen tensed, and his face hardened as he started to speak. Then he caught himself and relaxed with visible effort, forcing himself to lean back in his chair. "I did make a fool of myself over her. A damned fool. But that's all over now."

Johnny waited. Despite the tumult of the coffee room, where hearty discussions of topics ranging from politics to sporting events swirled all about them, he focused on Stephen. Through the smoke and the noise and the tantalizing aroma of freshly ground coffee beans, he studied the man opposite him, knowing his expressions and gestures as well as he knew his own, and recognizing the true feelings they masked. Johnny saw the bitter pain that ran beneath Stephen's words and knew that under the self-assured facade, Stephen was hurting.

"She's not worth it, my friend." Johnny tried to ignore the uncomfortable prickings of his conscience. "She ran out on you, didn't she? She never cared a shilling about you."

Something raw and wounded flickered behind Stephen's eyes before he lowered his gaze and stared into his empty coffee cup. "I know that."

"So forget her. When this assignment is over, we'll find ourselves a couple of women, quadroons maybe, and hole up somewhere for days with them. They'll make you forget that little bitch. It will be just like the old times when we wooed the fair ladies of Spain together—remember Madrid? Remember that delightful senorita who lured us into the mountains? You'll see. It will be exactly like the old days."

Like the old days. Stephen tried to imagine going back to that wild life. He and Johnny had gone through women like wine. They had lived and loved with a rough, thirsty recklessness, as if cramming a lifetime of excitement into each short hour. The women, Stephen remembered, had been varied and numerous. None of them had mattered, but he had enjoyed himself tremendously. Strange, it seemed like a long time ago. As recently as London, he had entertained himself with Cecilia Pelham, who had pursued him with a brazenness uncommon in most gently bred young women. He had indulged her, even though his mind was on other things. He had never even given a thought to her dowdy little abigail, Letty Thane....

"Damn her!" Stephen suddenly leaned forward and dropped his head into his hands. His elbows rested on the table. "I should have thrown her overboard the first night as I threatened."

"Forget her, Stephen. Don't you see..."

"Forget her!" He gave a short bark of laughter. "Don't you think I'd like to forget her? The woman is back there in my hotel room, pretending to be my wife! I'm spending hours in her company. And even in my sleep..." He broke off, raking his fingers through his hair in frustration. "I think Anemone Carstairs is my punishment for years of living a rogue's life," he muttered.

Johnny had been watching him in growing alarm. "She's only a woman. Hell, you've had a lion's share of them, and you'll have more."

This time when Stephen looked at him, Johnny couldn't ignore the bitterness in his friend's lean face. "I don't want any others, Tuck. That's the damnable part of it. I only want Anemone."

"Then you're a fool." Johnny Tucker stood up suddenly and threw a pile of coins on the table. "I've got to get back to the Governor's house. William, Ned Boodle, and I will follow your instructions at the plantation tonight. We'll keep the carriage and horses ready to get out on a moment's notice."

Stephen too rose to his feet. Amid the smoke and din of the coffee room, he met Johnny's angry gaze. "What's the matter, Tuck?" he asked slowly. "Something is eating at you."

Johnny didn't know what to say. He couldn't tell Stephen that the anger he felt was directed at himself. He had never expected that losing Anemone Carstairs would affect Stephen this way. He had figured Stephen would shrug it off and turn his attention elsewhere without more than a passing moment of regret. Johnny cursed to himself, but didn't answer Stephen's inquiry. He strode through the crowded coffee house into the New Orleans dusk. A soft gray drizzle fell from the leaden sky.

"Keep your eyes about you tonight," Johnny said brusquely as Stephen followed him out and paused at his side. He avoided Stephen's glance. "Though I doubt that De Vauban will make his move tonight. My bet is on the official ball in Bromford's honor Saturday."

"That's my guess, too, but I won't overlook any possibility." Stephen bent his head against the rain. "Look, Tuck, I'm sorry if I disillusioned you with my lamentations of a broken heart." His smile was strained, but he tried for a light tone. "One day maybe you'll meet a woman who will wreak havoc on your good sense. The devil knows, I never thought it would happen to me."

"Stephen..." Johnny heard the word wrenched from his own throat, then caught himself before he could say more.

"What?" Stephen's penetrating gaze searched his face.

"N...nothing." Johnny took a deep breath and then jammed his hands into the pockets of his jacket. "I'll meet you here tomorrow to compare our reports—if this whole business doesn't explode in our faces before then."

"Right." Stephen dropped a hand on his shoulder. "Thanks, Tuck. You're . . . a good friend."

Johnny mumbled something indistinguishable and turned away, dodging across the path of an oncoming carriage with reckless haste as he headed toward the Governor's house. Stephen watched him for a moment, then turned toward the hotel.

He had to brace himself for the evening with Anemone. If he wasn't careful, she'd get him killed yet. He couldn't afford to be thinking about her when there was the shadow of danger all about him. *Danger.* He could feel it holding him in its web, catching them all in its evil, ever-tightening threads. For some reason, thoughts of the Spider kept returning, and he couldn't shake the feeling that the unknown genius with loyalties only to himself was a force yet to be reckoned with in all of this. He had no idea if the Spider was in New Orleans or waiting from afar to learn how well his cunning machinations had succeeded. He knew only that he had to be on his toes tonight, sharp, alert, quick. The situation was precarious enough. One mistake here, an oversight there—and disaster would result. His entire being tensed, coiling and readying itself for a battle of wits and nerves against his enemies, those who were known and those unknown whom he might encounter in Jean-Pierre De Vauban's ballroom tonight. If he was to defeat them, he had first to defeat the weakness within himself, and that meant steeling himself against Anemone. By the time he reached the door opening onto the salon, he had done so.

Anemone was dressed and waiting when he arrived. At the sight of her he forgot his resolutions, but only for a moment. In her ball gown of dull gold satin, with the sequined bodice and lacy, flounced hem, she looked as gorgeous as he had ever seen her. Her pale hair was caught up by a diamond-studded gold comb and fell in sophisticated ringlets about her face. Around her white throat she wore a necklace of gold and diamonds, with matching drops at her ears. On her feet were dainty satin slippers which exactly matched the gold of her dress. She looked utterly magnificent. Her perfume drifted to his nostrils and stirred something deep within him. Camellias, he thought. Delicate and soft, like the slender, heartbreakingly beautiful woman before him. He wanted to go to her and take her in his arms. He wanted to kiss those soft, enchanting rose-peach lips, to trace his thumb along the slender column of her throat, to stare at and cup the nearly indecent amount of creamy white bosom which rose temptingly above the sequined bodice of that shimmering gown. Instead he nodded curtly and strode past her toward the bedroom.

"I'll change and join you shortly. I was delayed in my meeting with Johnny at the coffee house."

The bedroom door slammed behind him.

Anemone heard it with a sinking of the heart. *What did you expect?* she mocked herself as she paced to the mantel and stared unseeingly at the gilt-framed seascape above it. *Did you think he would drop to his knees and declare his undying love for you merely because you happen to look rather pretty tonight?* Bitterness filled her heart. She had vowed this afternoon to put her wounds aside until this job was finished. Yet the moment Stephen had come through the door, all her intentions had been forgotten, and she had been consumed by the hope that he would smile at her, take her in his arms, and kiss her until she was dizzy. *Stop this*, she chided herself, and spun away from the mantel, hands clenched. *Think about Lord Bromford and England. And Papa. He is counting on you tonight.*

Nevertheless, she was shaken when Stephen emerged from the bedroom a short time later. He looked so compellingly handsome, so devastatingly splendid in his superb black evening clothes, that she had to fight the urge to fling herself into his arms.

"This came while you were gone." She recovered her

poise, and went to the marble table beside the settee.
There she took up a small engraved invitation, handing
it to Stephen in silence. He flicked a glance at the polite,
gold-engraved words which formally requested their
presence at the ball tonight, then turned the sheet over
almost absently. On the back, De Vauban had written in
a thin, elegant scrawl:

> *So delighted you will be joining us. Madame Burke,
> my eagerness to see you again is exceeded only by my
> admiration for your charm. Until tonight.*
> > —*Jean-Pierre De Vauban.*

"Audacious bastard, isn't he?" Stephen glanced at
Anemone beside him. "I think we ought to let him see
that I am not pleased by his admiration of you. It would
not hurt our cause if he should suspect that his attentions
are the cause of a rift between us."

A rift between them? "That shouldn't prove difficult
to enact," Anemone remarked with an attempt at light-
ness, but Stephen heard the irony in her tone. She started
to move away from him, to gather up her gold reticule
and shawl, but he caught her arm and turned her to face
him. As his fingers held her arm, he could feel her stiffen.

"Are you certain you're ready for this?" he asked, staring down into the luminous silvery depths of her eyes.
They appeared even larger and more brilliant tonight than
he remembered. "If you're going to flirt openly with the
man and set up a private rendezvous with him, he will
expect you to behave like an infatuated woman when
you are indeed alone together."

"I know that."

"Do you know what that means?" Unconsciously, his
grip on her arm tightened. He couldn't stop himself from
asking the next question. "Are you prepared to go to bed
with him to find out what we need to know?"

Fury surged through her. The question was insulting

beyond belief. How could he even imagine that she would trade herself to that filthy, womanizing murderer in exchange for his secrets? Did it never occur to him that she would have the finesse to manage De Vauban without capitulating to his sexual advances? *But then,* she reflected with a stab of pain, *Stephen already believed that she had bartered herself when she had gone to bed with him. What was De Vauban but another pawn?* This only added fuel to her white-hot rage, and for a moment her eyes glittered with wrath, but then she quickly quelled her emotions in the way she was trained to do, and cool, airy hauteur swept across her features. "Would I go to bed with him to learn his information?" she repeated musingly, a slow, taunting smile curving her lips as she leaned back and regarded Stephen from beneath her lashes. She pretended to consider the question. Then she shrugged. "Why not, my pet? I did it with you, didn't I? And it worked beautifully."

She heard his sharp intake of breath, felt the whipcord tension that ran through him in a split second of reaction. Then he let go her arm as abruptly as if she were infested with vermin. Pure cold fury sparked in his eyes, giving them a chilling, satanic quality. His face had the look of a murderer.

"So you did." His soft voice flayed her like a velvet lash. "But I was a gentle conquest, Anemone. You may find De Vauban's lovemaking a bit rougher and more unpleasant."

"Really? And how would you know?"

"In addition to being a devious murderer, the man is also a braggart. I heard things in Paris at the Coronation."

"Did you now?" Anemone shrugged. "Well. Whatever he may require of me, I'm certain it will not be as unpleasant as what I endured in your company, trying to pretend that I was actually enjoying myself, forced to endure your pathetic gropings and..."

But this time she had gone too far. Stephen grabbed hold of her so suddenly that she gasped in fright, then

winced as his fingers dug into the flesh of her arms. She
was dragged against him with a violence that robbed her
of breath, and she could do nothing but stare into the icy
blue depths of his narrowed eyes. He bit down on his
next words with a violent fury, his lips only inches from
her terrified face.

"Lies again, Anemone—when will you learn not to lie
to me? Whether you cared for me or not, I know damn
well you enjoyed every minute of our lovemaking those
months at sea!" He shook her, his mouth a thin, hard
line. "Do you deny it? Do you have the rare gall to stand
there and tell me you didn't feel anything but revulsion
when I held you?"

"Yes! It's true! I was as repulsed as I am right now!"

"Shut up!" Scorn lit his harshly contoured features. He
gave a contemptuous laugh. "You can't convince me of
that. Do you know why?" Apprehension slid over her.
Being so close to him, pressed against his huge, hard-
muscled body, she felt an increasing sense of alarm. Heat
sprang up every place their bodies touched. His strong
hands seemed to scorch the flesh of her arms, and his
breath on her cheek stirred unwanted flames in her.

"Let me go!"

Deep terror shone in her face, terror not of him, but
of her own weakness as she read his intentions. Stephen
laughed again and pulled her even tighter against his
chest. One arm circled her waist like a steel band.

"I know when a woman feels the need and want of a
man, Anemone—as you did on the *Sea Lion*—as you
would right now if I should but kiss you the way you
liked so well, the way that made your eyes go all smoke
and silver...."

"No!" Panic made her voice break as she struggled to
escape him. His proximity, his strength, his tightening
arms all rose up to engulf her in a wave of memory which
shook her to the core of her being, bringing back all those
glorious nights at sea. The passion and sweetness of their

lovemaking, the shattering beauty they had known in each other's arms all came back to her, mocking her, wounding her anew. Tears stung her eyes. "Stephen, let me go!"

But he ignored her as he lowered his mouth to hers. He captured her lips savagely, holding her in an iron embrace which threatened to crush her limbs. Anemone fought against him, but Stephen forced her lips apart, invaded the soft recesses of her mouth with his tongue, and kissed her with a thoroughness and rough ferocity that she could not escape. She couldn't breathe, couldn't move. His hard mouth pressed hers, and his body over-powered her. Though she tried to twist free she could not. Against her will, despite every effort to fight her own passion, the heat of his searing mouth and the im-pact of his hard body clamped against hers began to fuel her reaction. She tried to resist him, but her will power drained with each passing second, and she felt herself swirling, dissolving into a whirlwind of heady desire. Of its own accord, her traitorous body sprang into response, straining against Stephen with shameless yearning. Her soft mouth gave way, welcoming him, as she whispered a moan of pleasure. She felt her good sense fleeing like sunlight before a storm, and her body melted against him as if the golden gown were consumed in molten heat. She was clinging to him, kissing him, running her fingers through his thick raven hair, and abandoning herself to her need for him. Suddenly as abruptly as he had seized her, he thrust her away.

"I think I've proved my point," he said, and gave her a contemptuous smile. He, too, was breathing heavily, but unlike the dazed Anemone, he appeared completely in control. She had fallen upon the settee at his sudden, violent release, and now lifted her head to stare at him in stunned horror.

"No...no," she whispered. Shame filled her as she beheld the harsh triumph in his countenance. He straightened his cravat, shook out his sleeves, and flicked an imaginary speck of dust from the lapel of his black coat. The smile he turned on her was grim.

"Yes, Anemone. Now we both know how you felt about my lovemaking. Remember it when you lie in De Vauban's arms tonight."

She gave a cry and jumped to her feet, shaking with her fury. Stephen was reminded of the morning she had accused him of molesting her while she was drugged by the laudanum. She was magnificent in her outrage, a fierce waif with fire in her eyes and murderous venom twisting the deceptively innocent features of her face.

"You are despicable!" she cried. She drew a deep, rasping breath through the sick nausea that swelled in her throat. "You are worse than De Vauban!"

"We'll see if you feel that way after tonight."

Anemone wanted to strike him, to scream and vent her shame and frustration. Her own body had betrayed her, had shown him her weakness. She felt degraded that he knew his power over her. A thousand agonized thoughts crashed in her head, and she thought she would die of humiliation, but she held herself in check with desperate self-control. *Tonight*, she reminded herself frantically. *The ball. Lord Bromford.* She had to pull herself together.

"We have to go." She spoke through dry lips.

Stephen pulled out his pocket watch and nodded. "I suggest you remedy your appearance a bit, Anemone. Your disheveled state is charmingly suggestive, but I think it would provoke undesirable comments from Creole society."

She threw him a venomous glance, then swept past him toward the mirror in the bedroom. It took only a few moments to pin up the wayward curls which had come down during his ardorous kisses and to smooth and straighten her gown. It took longer to gain control of her emotions. Stephen had destroyed her once again. She felt ill. There was a pallor to her cheeks as she managed to compose her features and return to the salon. Stephen was on the balcony staring out at the square. He turned without a word when she reappeared and offered her his arm.

Stephen, too, had needed a few moments to recover his equanimity. He damned Anemone as he stood on that balcony, seeing not the public square below, but her face, her lips, her eyes. The woman was in his blood. Their passionate kiss had shaken him, had made him want her all over again. Her wanton response to him was small comfort for the pain she had caused, for though he had proved his ability to excite her body, the fact remained that he had never touched her heart.

They both lapsed into silence during the lengthy carriage ride to De Vauban's plantation above the city proper. The fragrance of magnolias and oleander and blue iris drifted in the open carriage window as they drove through clusters of live oaks and past meandering streams. The rain that had come at dusk had dissipated, leaving a dark, somewhat misty night, with the pungent freshness of ripe, damp earth filling the air. Anemone breathed deeply of the cool, moist breeze and thought about a little band of killers bent on murdering an unsuspecting man. She had it in her power to stop them. She vowed to do just that.

Her years at her father's elbow, listening, watching, and learning asserted themselves during that carriage ride. Through the jolting and the creaking of wheels, while listening to the din of crickets in the woods through which they passed, and the occasional call of a heron, she managed not to think about Stephen Burke at all. She deliberately ignored his tall, handsome figure as he sat opposite her in equally thoughtful silence, and she concentrated on the man she must captivate and disarm tonight, the man who was the key to this entire sordid business. Johnny Tucker, William Tuttle, and Ned Boodle, who was driving this carriage Stephen had hired, would ring the plantation as best they could, ready to advance if they were needed. Her father would keep watch on the man called One Eye, and Stephen would circulate through the ballroom and plantation house, keeping his eyes and ears open. She would target De Vauban, snare him, and dissect him, all without his knowledge. She mentally reviewed everything she knew about him and had observed in their meeting last night, then as the carriage pulled into the long, oak-lined drive leading up to the plantation house, she drew several deep breaths. It was time. Now or never at all. She mustn't fail.

Stephen helped her to alight, glancing at her small face, which appeared pale in the faint moonlight. "Be careful tonight." He spoke the words quietly, stirred by her aura of slender fragility, speaking from some uncontrollable protective instinct which he had not anticipated. A feeling flickered in him, a premonition. But before he could explore it or say anything further, Anemone gave him a cool nod, gathered up her skirts, and began to walk toward the music and the lights and the soft laughter within the great house. He shook off his unease, took her arm, and together they climbed the steps of the porch and entered the white, pillared mansion.

TWENTY-THREE

THE DE VAUBAN plantation house was a scene of unrivaled grandeur and merriment. From the moment Anemone and Stephen entered the ballroom they were caught up in the tumult of gaiety and elegance that swirled throughout the crowded room. Two thousand candles blazed and flickered. Musicians played liltingly upon their raised dais at the eastern end of the room. There were flowers everywhere, brilliant, fresh-cut blue irises and camellias and yellow jasmines filling the air with their heady perfume and exotic color. Ladies in pale, shimmering gowns seemed to flow and shift in endless pastel patterns, while gentlemen in evening dress bowed over their ladies' gloved hands, raised goblets in toast, and laughed heartily among one another. The house itself was typical of the Creole landowners. Built upon brick pillars, with turned-wood colonnettes and wide, graceful galleries, it was furnished in exquisite elegance, with Oriental rugs and Turkey carpets, magnificent paintings, sculpture, and tapestries. Anemone had had a quick, breathtaking view of all this dazzling magnificence as she and Stephen were swept through the entry hall and into the ballroom and found themselves at once borne along toward their host.

De Vauban stood at the head of a line to receive his guests. Nearby was a long, linen-draped table upon which sat a huge silver bowl of champagne. A servant filled crystal glasses for each guest who approached. There was also an array of cut glass decanters containing sherry, Madeira, and liqueurs and rosewood boxes brimming with fine cigars. Beyond the ballroom, the doors to the dining room had been thrown wide, and Anemone could see long tables beautifully laid with gold plate and cutlery, lace napkins and fine linen, with silver bowls overflowing with flowers at each end and in the center. There were fragile Dresden candelabra on each table, and wax candles flamed to life in each delicate holder. Jean-Pierre De Vauban certainly knew how to entertain on a lavish scale, Anemone thought as she edged forward in the line, a smile pasted on her face. She wondered if he plotted on the same immense scale, with each detail designed and shaped to order, then masterfully arranged. For Lord Bromford's sake, for all of their sakes, she hoped there would be some flaw in his grand plan, some tiny tear in the magnificent embroidery that either she or Stephen or her father would somehow detect.

At that moment, De Vauban's glance skimmed along the line of guests waiting to be greeted and fell upon her. The ice green eyes then gleamed with some inner brilliance. He smiled, and Anemone felt again that rush of magnetism which had assailed her at the opera house. She smiled in return, her soft mouth curving enticingly. *So it begins*, she thought, and the pressure of Stephen's fingers upon her arm signaled her that he, too, had noticed the subtle interplay. As she and Stephen moved toward De Vauban, following the crowd, Anemone's heartbeat quickened. Without vanity, she suspected that he had been watching for her, and shrewdly deduced that for him, the challenge of the evening would lie in seducing Stephen Burke's coquettish young bride. Did that mean nothing else was planned for tonight—that the murder of Lord Bromford was scheduled for another time? She couldn't be sure. She only knew that De Vauban's eyes were unnaturally bright as she and Stephen reached him and she held out her gloved hand. There was an air about him of barely restrained excitement and restlessness, but whether that was due to the prospect of her seduction or the anticipated murder of his guest of honor, Anemone could not be certain.

"Ah, Madame and Monsieur Burke! How splendid to see you in my home! Allow me to make you welcome!"

His lips pressed to her hand. The flashing smile illuminated his olive-skinned face once again. "You are beautiful tonight, Madame," he said in a low, throbbing tone. "Utterly beautiful."

"You are too kind, Monsieur." Anemone's voice had a husky quality as she looked up at De Vauban from beneath her eyelashes. A provocative smile curved her lips. "I am so happy to see your lovely home. What a delightful party!"

Stephen greeted De Vauban coolly. "My wife has an unnatural fondness for all things French," he said, with a narrow-eyed glance at the top of Anemone's head. "I believe she feels much at home in New Orleans society."

"Ah, yes, she is far too refined to enjoy the *Kaintock* way of life." Their host wrinkled his nose in distaste. "A French jewel has no place among the brawling, roisterous riffraff that make up so much of American society—if one can call it that."

"Odd that you consider yourself separate from American society, De Vauban. New Orleans is now part of American territory—that makes you as much of an American as the flatboatmen and merchants and frontiersmen who have settled across Canal Street in the Faubourg Ste. Marie—the *Kaintocks*, as you so deprecatingly call them."

"Stephen!" Anemone spoke chidingly over her shoulder. "How can you even compare Monsieur De Vauban to those dreadful *Kaintocks*? He and these others here— all of them of European heritage—are of an entirely different class than those barbarians who infest this lovely city."

"I thank you, Madame, for your spirited defense," De Vauban laughed. He had been observing the discourse between the couple with great interest. Yes, there was friction here. Stephen Burke seemed irritated with his wife and her eagerness to attend this ball. That was good— most promising for what he had in mind. He wondered with a glimmer of malice if his little note upon the invitation had triggered some disagreement. Burke could not have helped noticing the attentions he had paid his wife at the opera, and she, in the manner of a Frenchwoman, seemed only too delighted to enter into a flirtation. Whether or not she intended to let things get beyond that point was something he did not concern himself with. She would have little choice in the matter. He would have her—one way or another. He had supreme confidence in his persuasive powers over women—especially gay, spoiled, impressionable young women with an appetite for mischief. Anemone Burke was ideal prey. She was attracted by his wealth and breeding and no doubt resented her American husband's cool, possessive attitude. De Vauban knew how to exploit her resentment to advantage, how to woo her and charm her and take harmless liberties which soon would enmesh her in a liaison from which there was no turning back. Ah, yes, he would have her—and soon. How fitting a revenge upon Stephen Burke, who had foiled his plans for the innocent Jolie. His blood stirred just at the thought of it. But he had to admit that even if he did not wish to harm Stephen Burke, to drive a wedge into his marriage and provoke the American into a possibly fatal duel, he would still wish to seduce this young woman, for she was enchanting and it would give him great pleasure to take her to his bed. The fact that she was Stephen Burke's wife simply made it all the more delightful. All of this ran through his mind in the few seconds that they stood before him in the receiving line. Then he was introducing them to Lord Bromford—and a great satisfaction filled him. Yes, to complete his plans for Lord Bromford and seduce Burke's wife all in one night—it would be a challenge even for him. Yet, De Vauban loved nothing more than a challenge. Even *L'Araignée* could hardly deny him this.

"Monsieur and Madame Burke—may I present Lord Melvin Bromford? Lord Bromford has been visiting our city and partaking of the many charming entertainments available to us here. He was my guest at the opera last evening and, I believe, enjoyed it immensely."

Anemone smiled at the broad-shouldered, distinguished Englishman who bowed over her hand. He was the same man she had seen in De Vauban's box last night. "Good evening, my lord. It is my pleasure to meet you. Was it not a lovely performance last evening? *Silvain* is certainly my favorite!"

"It is a favorite of my wife's, too." Lord Bromford's eyes twinkled down at her. He was a kindly faced man, with thinning gray hair meticulously brushed, somewhat jowly cheeks, and an air of bemused wisdom which sat well upon his large frame. Anemone could imagine him in Parliament speaking eloquently on behalf of his cause, yet with the same calm good humor he directed toward her this evening. "My wife was unable to accompany me on this journey to America, unfortunately, for her health does not permit her to travel very much, but I am certain she would have vastly enjoyed the performance, as I did." He turned to Stephen and they shook hands. "How do you do, Mr. Burke? Are you visiting New Orleans for very long?"

Stephen replied smoothly, something about returning shortly to Philadelphia, while Anemone could only think:

so this is the man they plan to butcher like an animal. This is the man whose vicious murder they plan to use to propel America and England into war—and Bonaparte to victory. *No!* she thought to herself as Stephen took her arm and they joined the main crush of guests in the ballroom. *No.*

"De Vauban was quick to note the discord between us," Stephen said as he guided her toward a curtained alcove at one side of the room. "I think he'll seek you out privately soon."

"Yes."

"The dancing is about to begin." Stephen glanced down at her, noting against his will how lovely and sweet was her delicate face, how graceful the long, slender column of her neck. He would not allow his gaze to dip lower, to rest upon the creamy swell of bosom above her low-cut gown. He reminded himself with an effort that this enticing creature with her silver blond tendrils and huge diamond-clear eyes was a practiced temptress who had already made a fool of him once. He wouldn't be drawn under her spell again. "We'll dance the quadrille," he continued, his tone harshening as he steeled himself against her, "and then separate. I'll go off to get you some refreshment, and linger over it, so that he'll have an opportunity to approach you alone."

"Very well." She lifted her head to meet his eyes, uneasy without knowing why.

"What is it?" He spoke curtly.

Anemone gave her head a tiny shake. "I'm worried. I can't explain it, but . . . stay close to his lordship tonight. I have the strongest feeling that something is going to happen."

She was half afraid he would scorn her instinct and dismiss it as feminine superstition, but he didn't. He nodded, his face grim, and there was a dark glint in his eyes.

"I'll watch him, never fear. And don't forget, Johnny

and William are lurking about outside, ready to jump in if anything untoward happens. Ned Boodle has the carriage ready to leave at a moment's notice."

"I know that." She also knew that they had done all they could to guard against any action tonight. Her father was following the man called One Eye, and Monsieur Bergeron, the other suspected conspirator, was no doubt somewhere here at the ball. She scanned the faces of the people all around her in the magnificent, flower-bedecked ballroom. Which of these men or women was allied with De Vauban and the Spider in their deadly plot? Which person here harbored murder in his heart?

The reception line had dissipated. The dancing began. Stephen offered her his arm. "Shall we join the quadrille? Or will you find it too unpleasant to be in my company for the length of the dance?"

"I can bear it if you can," Anemone returned.

She went through the movements with the light grace that was natural to her. Stephen danced admirably, she noted, and could not help the little thrill that went through her whenever in the course of the dance they touched. Yet she kept track of Lord Bromford throughout the complicated steps of the quadrille, keeping him in sight whenever possible. By the time the dance had come to an end, Lord Bromford had joined a little knot of guests near the linen-draped table where champagne was being served. De Vauban was at his side.

Stephen escorted Anemone to a grouping of daintily carved rosewood chairs set near French doors leading out onto the wide gallery which ran around the house. "I'll engage Bromford in conversation while procuring you a glass of champagne. Perhaps we'll walk out on the terrace together—that will give De Vauban time to find you and take advantage of the moment."

She seated herself, with a polite smile to the plump matron on her left, and watched him go, observing the wistful glances his tall, muscular figure drew from the

women in the ballroom as he made his way toward the
champagne. There was no denying it: Stephen Burke was
a man who commanded female attention. His height, his
stride, his dangerous good looks never failed to flutter
feminine hearts, and she realized anew how accurate
Johnny Tucker's words to her had been. Stephen could
indeed have his pick of any woman. Why should he ever
have wanted her?

A stout, bespectacled gentleman with snow-white hair
came up to claim the matron beside her, and Anemone
found herself alone near the French doors. From the corner of her eye, she became aware of a slim dark figure
bearing down on her. Her pulse jumped. Stephen had
been right. De Vauban had not wasted any time in making
his way to her side. Totally at ease, he glided through
the chattering throng, smiling and nodding as he passed
guests who greeted him eagerly, but stopping for no one
until he reached her chair.

"I fear I have been remiss, Madame Burke—not having
introduced you to my other guests. You are all alone."

She glanced up at him, feigning surprise. Then a dazzling smile dawned across her features. "Alone? Not anymore, Monsieur," she replied softly.

"No, *cherie*, not anymore." He took her hand and raised
her to stand beside him, taking the opportunity to study
her appearance with great admiration and interest. Anemone railed inwardly at the unspeakable gall of the man,
for he seemed to mentally strip her as she stood beside
him. Yet she merely smiled and waited while his glance
caressed the swell of her breasts above the gold-sequined
bodice of her gown and roved with sensuous pleasure
upon every curve of her womanly form. At last his gaze
returned to rest upon her face.

"You steal my breath away, Madame Burke," he sighed
dramatically, and stepped closer to her. He still held her
hand tightly in his. "You put the other ladies in this room
all to shame. They primp and fuss and work, oh, so

diligently to make themselves lovely, while you outshine them quite effortlessly."

"Monsieur De Vauban!" Anemone shook her head reproachfully at him, though her crystalline eyes sparkled with laughter. "I am certain you say the very same thing to each woman in this room." She regarded him in playful challenge. "Admit it! You are a flatterer. A charming man, a gallant man, but a flatterer all the same!"

His eyes warmed, and Anemone sensed that he enjoyed her teasing raillery. For him it is all part of the challenge, she thought, and was determined more than ever to see him defeated.

"No, *cherie*. I do not flatter you. I admire you," he protested, with such a creditable air of sincerity that Anemone guessed this ploy had succeeded for him many times in the past.

"Well, do not let my husband know of your admiration," she responded with a laugh, "for he is already cross with me, and such a thing would only make him more angry."

"Cross with you, *cherie*?"

She shrugged, staring into his gleaming eyes with every appearance of artlessness. "Oh, I think it was your note on the invitation—and your kindness to me last night. Stephen is so quick to become jealous. He is sometimes, I think, a silly, demanding tyrant."

"Where is he now, *cherie*?" De Vauban gazed about him in surprise. "I find it astonishing that he should leave such a fair prize alone for so much as a moment."

"Oh," she waved her arm vaguely, "he went off to find me some champagne, but I suspect he fell to talking with someone or other—really, he can be most inattentive, considering that he doesn't care for me to even *speak* to another man if he is not present...."

"Doesn't he?" De Vauban clucked in sympathy. "I fear you are ill used, *cherie*."

"Monsieur, do you think it is quite proper for you to

call me *cherie?*" she said thoughtfully, peeping up at him with a slow smile. "I do not think Stephen would like it at all."

"Then we mustn't tell him." De Vauban stepped closer to her. "Come, *cherie*, let us go out to the gallery, where the air is cool and refreshing and we can talk to one another more privately."

Now they were getting somewhere. But before Anemone had a chance to accept this offer, a thin, sallow-faced man hurried up to them. He was breathing hard, as if he had just made a quick tour of the entire ballroom. With a quick apology to Anemone, he addressed De Vauban.

"Jean-Pierre, forgive the intrusion, but there is a matter of some urgency which I must discuss with you at once."

De Vauban's brows rose in faint surprise. "Oh? Very well. First, may I present Madame Burke? Madame, my good friend, Paul Bergeron."

She greeted the owner of the Hotel Bergeron cordially, yet noted that his face, as he learned her name, grew pale. Or was that her imagination? Did his eyes really glitter coldly as he bowed over her hand, or was she reading far too much into a simple introduction?

"Madame, it is a very great honor." She thought his voice tinged with mockery. "Jean-Pierre? We really must speak privately, my friend."

"Then let us retire to my library where we will not disturb the festivities." De Vauban turned his white-teethed smile full upon her. "*Cherie*, what can I say? A thousand pardons, I beg of you. Soon, we shall go in to partake of supper. I shall look for you then. *Adieu.*"

"*Adieu*—Jean-Pierre." She saw his lips lift in a pleased smile as she used his given name, then Paul Bergeron took his arm and practically dragged him off. So great was his haste that he stumbled directly into the path of a waiter carrying a tray of discarded champagne goblets. The tray toppled over, the glasses and leftover champagne spilling onto Paul Bergeron's ruffled shirt front. There was a clatter of broken glass, and then De Vauban called sharply for a towel. Nearby guests turned and murmured sympathetically as they saw the effects of the accident.

Anemone wasted not a moment of the seemingly providential diversion. She skimmed through the crowd like a pebble skirting nimbly across waves, and made her way toward the huge doors off the ballroom, the doors opening onto the other rooms of the house. She had to get to the library before De Vauban and Bergeron. She had to hide herself and discover the topic of this urgently demanded conversation.

She caught a quick glimpse of Stephen stepping out onto the gallery with Lord Bromford and a little party of two ladies and a third gentleman. There was no opportunity to apprise him of what had occurred. They were too far away, and she had precious little time. She glanced over her shoulder and saw De Vauban and Bergeron handing a towel back to a waiter, saw the debris upon the floor being swept up, and then she hurtled out into the hallway and looked frantically up and down the corridor at the succession of doorways, wondering which led to the library.

Fortunately, the hallway was temporarily deserted as she flew down the parquet and peered through door after door. Candles blazed in every room, permitting the guests to wander, if they wished, throughout the house at leisure and make themselves comfortable in the various parlors which De Vauban's father and mother had so elegantly appointed, and to which he, upon becoming master of the plantation, had added his own tasteful touches. She came upon a small salon, a music room, a huge parlor, and then finally a dark-paneled room lined with books. There were leather-bound volumes from floor to ceiling of two entire walls, and the windows opening onto the gallery were draped in pale blue and ivory damask festooned with blue silk tassels. A bronze chandelier swung above, its candles all ablaze, sending smoky light through the room. Anemone darted inside, casting a swift, appraising glance about her. There were a collection of hunting trophies, a glass cabinet containing a display of ornate and unusual guns, and a half dozen upholstered wing chairs flanked by one or two occasional tables at various places in the room. Where to hide? The murmur of De Vauban's voice in the hall sent a spasm of fear down her spine. Footsteps approached and she realized in dismay there was no time to reach the draperies. Panic assailed her as she spun about in desperation. There was only the closet, five feet away. She lunged toward the door, praying it was not locked.

It wasn't. She was inside and closing it behind her in the space of two seconds. Just as she heard the soft click of the latch, the footsteps reached the library and she heard the scraping of boots on the parquet. De Vauban and Bergeron were in the library.

Anemone shut her eyes tightly and gulped air. The walls of the closet seemed to be crushing in on her. Smothering darkness stamped down, giving her the horrible feeling that she had been buried alive in freshly turned earth. She dared not move for fear of disturbing some item stored in the closet, and this added to her sensation of suffocating confinement. Horrible fear pounded through her that she would faint or get sick and thereby give herself away. *Then De Vauban would lock me up in this awful place forever.* Perspiration began to form in little beads at her forehead. She stood frozen, her head thrown back, trying to take in enough air to keep from retching. *Fight it,* a determined little voice shrieked inside her brain, but her body was ruled by a demon of panic. *Fight it!* Little quivers shook her knees, and she struggled to keep from sinking to the floor in a huddle of shuddering bones.

The men began to talk. De Vauban's voice came first.

Anemone, still frantically gulping at the thick, heavy air, tried to listen.

"What is this about, Bergeron?" His tone was sharp, far different from the silky, sensuously persuasive tone he had used with her. "My guests are soon going into supper and I must be there to escort Bromford. If I am not, it will seem most odd. And tonight, of all nights, everything must appear totally normal in every respect."

"There is trouble, Jean-Pierre. One Eye is here. We came together from Girod Street. He entered through the servants' door in the rear of the house so that no one would see him, but he will join us in a moment."

De Vauban snapped at him in obvious anger. "He is not supposed to come here until well into the early hours of morning. What is going on? And what were you doing at Girod Street?"

"*L'Araignée* sent for me. He ... ah, One Eye. Quick, let him in."

This came after a sudden rap on the door, after which Anemone heard a slight commotion and then the sounds of the door being shut once again.

"Well, what is all this?" Impatience at having to deal with underlings, incompetent ones at that, edged De Vauban's voice. There was more than a tinge of distaste as he addressed the pair before him.

"Disaster," came the snarling response, and through her sickening breathlessness, Anemone shuddered, receiving a vivid mental picture of the smuggler known as One Eye. He spoke in a guttural tone, and cruelty flicked through the single word like a whip. But De Vauban sounded unintimidated.

"Don't play games with me, you witless fool! Tell me why you've disturbed my ball in this way! You were not supposed to arrive until four in the morning to spirit Bromford's body away for the butchering."

"Keep quiet and I'll tell you why I'm here, you pompous idiot!" One Eye rasped. Suddenly, there was a silence. "What was that? Did you hear a sound, a clicking?"

In her hiding place, Anemone froze. She had made no sound, no movement. "I hear nothing!" De Vauban waited a moment, as all three men seemed to be listening. She held her breath, counting each second, her heart beating wildly.

"There is nothing to fear here. We are alone. I think your imagination is running mad, One Eye. Now, damn you, tell me why you are here!"

"*L'Araignée* sent me to warn you. Our entire plan is at risk!"

"Impossible." De Vauban snorted contemptuously. "It is planned down to the last detail. Everything has been arranged. I have already slipped the potion into Bromford's champagne. He should be starting to feel the ill effects now."

"Jean-Pierre, there are enemy spies in our midst!" Bergeron cried in a tone of pure panic. "And you—you may have already allowed them to spoil all our meticulous work!"

Anemone went ice-cold at these words. A tense silence followed, then she heard De Vauban's voice again, dangerous as a rapier. "Enemy spies? What are you talking about, Paul?"

It was the man called One Eye who answered. "*L'Araignée* captured one today. His name, my friend, is Thomas Carstairs. Do you know who that is? Do you know what this means?"

"Thomas Carstairs? But he is dead! *L'Araignée* had him killed in Spain when he began to uncover our plans!"

"He is alive. We've been questioning him in Scar-Footed Mattie's place in the Swamp these last several hours."

Anemone felt the darkness sway all around her. She put a shaking hand to the closet wall to steady herself. *Papa! How were you captured? What have they done to you?*

"Thomas Carstairs." De Vauban sounded dazed. "What did he tell you?"

"Nothing!" One Eye was furious. Paul Bergeron broke in.

"*L'Araignée* spotted him this morning in my hotel. I swear to you, Jean-Pierre, I knew nothing of his identity, nothing of who he really was. It was my concierge who hired him, who dealt with him from day to day! He has been working under my nose for months, using the name of DuBois!"

"Working for you, Bergeron?" Anemone guessed it was De Vauban's fist which crashed onto the hard surface of a table. She heard something splinter. "Working for you in what capacity?"

"Doing the accounts. Jean-Pierre, don't look at me that way, damn you! I had no idea who the man was! He appeared harmless! How was I to know..."

"Idiot! Spare me your pitiful excuses!"

In her tiny closet, Anemone was very still, listening with every nerve ending stretched taut. Through the crying need to reach her father, to rescue him, she knew she must hear everything and prayed they would stop arguing and tell her more that she needed to know. De Vauban's words about Lord Bromford repeated themselves over and over in her head. His lordship had already drunk a potion of some sort; was he already poisoned? Was there still a hope of saving him? The moment these men left the room, she must run out and find Stephen. Together, they could spirit his lordship away and then find her father in Scar-Footed Mattie's place. Girod Street—the Swamp. She shuddered merely thinking of her father in that evil thieves' and smugglers' den. Damn it, she thought, the bile of rage rising in her throat. Who was the Spider, this man who had recognized and exposed Papa? *Whoever he is, he is mine*, she thought wrathfully. *I will see that he suffers his due.*

"We must be thankful then that the arrival of *L'Araignée* in New Orleans only last week was in time to expose this spy," De Vauban continued after a moment of pacing the room, while the others waited in silence. "Carstairs's presence here, it is very bad, but not, as you say, disastrous. The plan is already under way. This spy is our prisoner. Even if he has allies working with him to thwart us, it is too late for them. No doubt they are off somewhere wondering where their superior has disappeared to."

"They are here, Jean-Pierre! Under this very roof!" Paul Bergeron's voice quavered. "That woman you introduced me to in the ballroom—Madame Burke! She and her supposed husband arrived at my hotel only yesterday claiming kinship with DuBois—Carstairs! I have already questioned my concierge about this. There is no doubt. From the description, *L'Araignée* says that the woman is Carstairs's daughter. Her name is Anemone, and she is an agent in the employ of British intelligence—a spy!"

Anemone's heart stopped for a long, breathless moment. The Spider was someone close to her—to her and her father. Someone who recognized both of them, knew them, and had betrayed them.

"You can now stop blaming everyone else for this catastrophe, Monsieur De Vauban." One Eye spoke in a hissing growl. "You have invited this pair into your home—invited them to destroy us. You, who accuses everyone else of bungling stupidity, you are the fool!"

"Silence!" The shaking fury in De Vauban's voice sent goose bumps up and down Anemone's spine. "I must have a moment of utter quiet in which to think—something foreign to the two of you!" His words slashed the air as she huddled in the darkness of her hiding place, suddenly grateful for the four small walls which boxed her in, sealing her away from his wrath. She could almost picture that smooth, aristocratically handsome face twisted into a mask of fury. Not only had his plans been endangered, but his vanity crushed by the knowledge that he had been tricked, used. That would make him doubly dangerous. A man of De Vauban's arrogance and pride would become utterly ruthless if humiliated before his peers. She knew she would have to stay out of his way while she looked for Stephen. There was no telling what he would do if he saw her, now that he knew the truth.

"So Stephen Burke and his supposed wife are in league with Carstairs." Each word was like the thrust of a sword. His footsteps paced the parquet of the library, moving unnervingly near the closet door. Anemone tensed, drawing in another lungful of air. "I will take care of those two. Don't you fear, they will pay for their part in this. The important thing is—we must finish the job with Bromford this evening, before anything else can go wrong."

"Yes, yes," Bergeron put in. "I think you're right, Jean-Pierre. We must be done with it. You say he has already drunk the potion?"

"I slipped it into his champagne myself and watched him drain the glass. The effects should begin any time. He will feel a trifle headachy, perhaps a bit nauseous. I suspect he will force himself to endure throughout supper, and then he will need to lie down. I will of course offer him a guest bedroom, and arrange with Claiborne that his lordship must spend the night. When everyone has gone and the servants have all retired, we will take him as he lies in his drugged sleep and bring him to Scar-Footed Mattie's house. In the cellar, One Eye, you may amuse yourself with the butchering of his body." Smug satisfaction sounded in the Creole's voice. "We must all be there for the occasion—*L'Araignée*, Bergeron, One Eye, myself, and the DuFour brothers, whose ship will carry his lordship's maimed limbs in a barrel back to His Majesty in England." Thin laughter came from De Vauban's throat. "This Thomas Carstairs may watch the mutilation. Yes, I think that would be a fitting touch. If, indeed, he is still alive. One Eye?"

"He is unconscious, but living. He will be weak, I think, from loss of blood. *L'Araignée* instructed me to cut him, hoping to force from him some clue as to how much the others know about us."

"And?"

Anemone, faint with horror, heard the disappointment in his voice. "The Englishman is stubborn—he would not say a word about his daughter or Stephen Burke, or how many are working with them to undo our cause."

"No matter." De Vauban spoke briskly now. "We must get on with everything as quickly as possible. Let us go back to the festivities, and find the girl and Burke at once. No, One Eye, you wait here. I don't want my guests to see you—you hardly fit in among this company. Besides, when Paul and I bring those two here, we may need your help in subduing them."

"Why are we bringing them to your library, Jean-Pierre?" Bergeron asked anxiously. "One can hardly leave them trussed and gagged in the middle of the floor. Suppose someone wanders in . . ."

De Vauban chuckled. "Allow me to demonstrate something of interest, Paul." Anemone stiffened as she heard his footsteps moving closer—then closer still. To her horror, she heard him grasp the closet doorknob in his hand. "This is no mere closet, you see. It contains . . ."

The door opened. Light spilled into the room, nearly blinding Anemone as she crouched back against the far wall. Her eyes stared like those of a wild, cornered animal into the startled face of Jean-Pierre De Vauban.

For a moment, there was terrible silence. She felt that her chest would burst with the mad clamor of her heart. Her hands had turned into blocks of ice, and her face felt frozen, as if her skin would crack and splinter if she so much as moved an eyelash. De Vauban was the first to speak. "Well, well. *Ma cherie.* How fortunate." De Vauban's laughter swirled around her like a foul mist. Paul Bergeron and the man called One Eye crowded around him, gazing at her in open-mouthed amazement. "We

now have only to apprehend Stephen Burke, it seems."
De Vauban cast a pleased look at them over his shoulder.
"That should not prove at all difficult, since he is not
aware that we have identified him as an enemy to our
cause." He turned back to Anemone with a wide smile.

"*Cherie*, you look so uncomfortable in there. My heart
is sorry for you."

"Is it, Jean-Pierre?" Anemone straightened up from the
wall against which she had been cowering, hoping against
all reason that she would not in the end be discovered
after all. Now she blinked against the comparative bright
light of the library as it poured into the tiny closet and
stared from face to face of the three men before her.

"I am glad of your sympathy," she went on, struggling
to remain calm and poised beneath the leering scrutiny
of her captors. "If you and your friends will kindly step
aside, I think I would like a glass of sherry."

She had abandoned her French accent and now started
to move past him, needing to get out of that closet, to
breathe fresh air and have some room to think. But De
Vauban caught her arm. He chuckled and shook his head.
"Ah, but no, *cherie*. You are not going anywhere."

"Only into the library. Surely you can spare me a glass
of sherry, Jean-Pierre." She fought the rising panic within
her. The closet seemed to be closing in on her even more
powerfully than before. She eyed the three men blocking
the doorway with rising despair and tried to keep her
voice from quavering. Once again, she tried to push past
De Vauban, and once again, he jerked her back.

"Let me show you something, *cherie*," he said almost
pleasantly. "I was about to demonstrate something quite
remarkable to my associates." He reached his arm past
her then and grasped an ornamental brass hook on the
closet's side wall. He twisted it. Anemone gasped as the
wall swung backwards to reveal a tiny hidden stairway
on the other side, a stairway leading down into darkness.

The passageway was narrow enough for only one to walk at a time, and where it led Anemone could not see. She was less then two feet from the top step.

"One Eye, bring some tinder. There are wall brackets set with candles alongside the stairway. We don't want this beautiful lady to stumble as she descends."

"I . . . I'm not going down there," Anemone said, moistening her dry lips with her tongue. Terror gripped her. The closet had been bad enough; this staircase leading heaven knew where, to some hidden cellar or dungeon below the ground, was like a passage into a tomb. She began to talk quickly. "Jean-Pierre, you are making a mistake. Your plan with Lord Bromford is doomed to failure. . . ."

"Do you think so, *cherie?* You will soon see that you are wrong. Ah, One Eye, thank you. Now we may proceed." Squeezing past Anemone, De Vauban quickly lit the candles inside the concealed passage. Flickering light revealed stucco walls and the narrow stairs made of plastered brick. Dank air filtered up from the unseen chamber below.

"Go ahead, *cherie.*" De Vauban stepped back and gestured for her to precede him. "We will all accompany you. We must make certain that you are most comfortable in your new quarters. I will not be able to stay long, unfortunately, for I must find your supposed husband and bring him to join you—and also, *naturellement*, I must attend to my guests. It is too bad you will miss the excellent supper I have ordered. There are to be capons, oysters, soft-shell crabs, pompano and redfish, turkeys plump and juicy—as well as a vast assortment of fruits from my own orchards, iced cakes, jellies, and custards. In short, all manner of delicacies have been prepared, but you will not be present to enjoy them." Again, that silky laugh. "One Eye will wait in the library until Monsieur Burke is brought down to join you. Then, *petite*, you and he will tell us all that we need to know." He leaned closer and cupped her face in his soft, yet surprisingly strong hand. "When Lord Bromford is safely asleep upstairs, prior to his journey to Girod Street, I will join you below and perhaps have an opportunity to personally thank you for your unwanted interference in this affair. Won't that be pleasant? You and I—we have something to settle between us, I think."

Her skin crawled at the touch of his hand. She shrank back and slapped his arm aside. "I'd rather have you kill me than touch me, De Vauban. Do your worst, but don't subject me to your loathsome presence any more than necessary or I will die of revulsion."

De Vauban went stiff as a ramrod. His ice green eyes lit with unholy rage. "So, the little kitten has fangs," he murmured between clenched teeth, and suddenly drew back his arm and struck her across the face. Behind him, One Eye leered at her and Paul Bergeron bit his lips. Anemone fell against the back wall, raising her hand to her stinging cheek.

Stunned from the blow, she blinked and peered from one man to the next as they crowded about her. One Eye, the smuggler, wore a black patch across one side of his face. He was tall and massive, a huge, ugly, scarred man with a gaping, evil smile and foul breath. Paul Bergeron appeared nervous and grim, perhaps unhappy with the course of events, but too timid to voice any objections. She knew she wouldn't get any help from either of them. That left De Vauban. She met his stare, and she knew utter hopelessness. The candlelight sent dancing shadows across his cheeks, and illuminated the sinister gleam in his pale, icy eyes. His voice, his whole demeanor had an undercurrent of cruelty that filled her with a chilling dread. She thought of Stephen, of Lord Bromford, of her father, and knew despair, for if she could only get to them, to one of them, they might all be saved, and yet she was hopelessly cut off from them all.

"I hope you die like a beetle, De Vauban. Squashed,

obliterated, so that nothing is left of your evil soul but a smear of blood upon the earth." Anemone spoke in a whisper. She stared him down, her own face blazing with hatred.

De Vauban grabbed her arm and pushed her toward the steps. "Go on, you little bitch. I don't have all night to tarry over you."

The step felt cold to her slippered foot. She hesitated.

"Hurry up! Or I'll throw you down the length of them and let you break your lovely neck."

She had no choice. She moved forward and down into the unknown gloom of the passageway.

TWENTY-FOUR

JOHNNY TUCKER edged away from the windows outside the library, cursing softly to himself. He took a quick glance about him, then let himself over the gallery railing and eased his tall frame down into the cover of the azalea bushes. Moonlight illuminated his path as he kept low and moved with all the haste that caution would allow, rounding the house until he reached the part of the gallery facing off the ballroom. His sinewy, assured movement belied the jumbled alarm he felt within. He had to get to Stephen, and fast.

As he reached the wing of the house where the ballroom guests had spilled out onto the spacious gallery, he slowed and lowered himself still further into the bushes, leaving only his eyes to peep over the branches. Strung lanterns added their candescent glow to the frosted light of moon and stars, bathing the gallery in silvery luminosity. The earlier mist had lifted, and the air was fresh and soft and remarkably clear, carrying the delicate scent of forest wildflowers. Johnny had no trouble distinguish-

321

ing Stephen's strong figure among the satin-skirted ladies and elegantly clad gentlemen who strolled along the gallery, chatting and laughing and admiring the fine clear night. Stephen was part of a small group about to return to the music and gaiety of the ballroom.

Stephen and Johnny had arranged two signals between them. The call of a woodcock repeated twice meant a conference was necessary to share information. Three times warned of disaster and signaled that Bromford should be escorted from the house immediately.

The latter was the one that Johnny used now, calling out three times in the manner of a woodcock. Stephen, just about to enter the French doors, froze, and put a hand upon his nearest companion's arm.

"Your lordship, stay with me a moment. There is something of a private nature I need discuss with you."

Lord Bromford looked surprised but excused himself to the rest of the party, who nodded and passed on into the ballroom, where a country dance had just ended. The guests were being assembled for the grand supper De Vauban had arranged for them. Stephen drew his lordship toward the gallery rail.

"Sir, this is urgent. I must ask you to come with me," he said in a low tone, casting a quick glance over his shoulder to be certain that no one was observing them.

Lord Bromford, his kindly face a little drawn, glanced at him in surprise.

"What is this about, Mr. Burke? It seems rather odd. I believe we ought to return to the ballroom."

"That is the one thing we should not do."

Stephen took hold of the other man's arm. He drew him toward the broad steps of the gallery. "You must trust me, sir, and come without delay. Lives are at stake."

Lord Bromford was not feeling at all well. He had refrained from mentioning the dismal headache that had come upon him in the last few minutes, not wishing to disturb the festivities or the lighthearted spirits of his companions. But the dull ache between his temples was worsening—and he now felt a queasiness in his stomach that made the prospect of the feast awaiting him in De Vauban's dining room distinctly unappetizing. Still, it was unthinkable to wander away from a ball which was being held in his honor. His host would be searching for him at any moment to join him at table, Governor Claiborne would wonder where he had gotten to, and if he did not make his appearance soon, the entire party would begin to buzz.

"Really, Mr. Burke, I must insist that we go back." Lord Bromford halted at the foot of the gallery steps. "I don't know what you refer to when you say lives are at stake, but..."

"It is your own life I refer to, Lord Bromford." Stephen's fingers tightened on the Englishman's arm. His handsome face was grim, yet alert, his eyes piercing the darkness of the plantation grounds all about him. He paused a moment and stared intently at his lordship. He didn't like the odd pallor the man now wore or the way he passed his hand across his eyes as though dizzy. "We must find cover, your lordship. We're going to meet a friend of mine within the shelter of these oaks, then we can talk."

It was all very strange, but his lordship felt too ill to argue. The tall young man beside him had begun drawing him firmly forward, over the drive, past the waiting carriages, then through the web of gnarled oak trees draped by Spanish moss. Twigs rustled underfoot, and a marsh wren fluttered by their heads, disturbed from its tree branch by their passing. Lord Bromford, peering ahead with difficulty, saw that he had been led into a little stand of hickory trees. A man, tall and huskily built, with moonlight touching his fair hair, stood beneath a spreading tree.

"Stephen." Johnny sprang toward them at once. "We've got to get his lordship away immediately. He's been poisoned."

Stephen wheeled to face the man at his side, staring into his features. His earlier, unexpressed fears had suddenly taken on a terrible reality. "Do you feel ill, sir?" he demanded, knowing the answer even as he spoke.

"Y . . . yes. I . . . I am a bit weak, and my head aches like the blazes, but . . . what is this you said, young man, about poison?"

"I'm sorry, sir. Don't be alarmed." Johnny spoke with quick reassurance. "It's not fatal. Merely something to put you under the weather, so that you'll stay here at the plantation tonight. The real danger is to come later."

"How did you learn all this?" Stephen demanded. In the pale light that threaded its way through the tree branches, his lean face was grim.

Johnny launched into a swift explanation. "I saw a carriage draw up a while ago, and two men alighted. Only one headed toward the main entrance; the other rather furtively headed toward the rear of the house. I was hidden nearby and heard the first man, who was attired as if to attend the party, tell the other to meet him in the library in a few moments' time. He said something about it taking a bit of time to locate De Vauban in the crush of the ball. I was suspicious. I worked my way around the house, wondering where the devil was the library. I prowled around, peeking in windows as best I could, until I found them. It took a bit of doing, but I managed to unlatch the window. They heard me working with it, but didn't realize what had caused the sound. Anyway, they were too involved in their own discussion to heed it. They went on with their talk, and I listened to every word."

"Tell me the whole . . . quickly." Suddenly, Stephen's attention became riveted on Lord Bromford. The man was pale and appeared to be in a daze. He was beginning to rub his temples as if trying to alleviate some intolerable pain. "Wait," he told Johnny. "Is the carriage ready to take his lordship away? Good. Now where's William?"

"He heard my signal and reached me just a few moments before you did. He's gone to alert Boodle that we're going to depart."

"Then you go to the carriage with his lordship—I don't think we ought to delay any longer in putting him under a physician's care. I'll go back to the house, find Anemone, and tell her what's happened. You can explain all the details to us back at the ship...."

"Stephen, wait—there's more you need to know." Johnny grabbed his arm as Stephen started turning back toward the plantation house. "It's ... about Anemone."

"What about her?" Something in Johnny's voice tindered flickers of alarm beneath his flesh, and he rounded on his friend sharply.

"She's been discovered by De Vauban and two of his men. They've got her in a closet in the library and the last I saw, through a small opening in the draperies, they were forcing her down some kind of hidden staircase."

Stephen felt every muscle in his body go rigid. His heart was gripped by a terrible fear, and he spoke, white-lipped. "What the hell happened, Tuck? Tell me quickly! Did they hurt her?" Never before had he felt such overwhelming dread as he waited for an answer.

Swiftly and with the articulateness that had earned him laurels as a diplomatic aide, Johnny Tucker outlined what he had overhead outside the library, concluding with the brief glimpse he had had of Anemone inside the closet, being forced into the hidden passageway. Stephen's brain worked with lightning speed as he evaluated all the repercussions of what he had heard. When Johnny had finished, he nodded and spoke with curt decision.

"The first thing we have to do is get his lordship out of danger. Sir, can you walk?"

"Of course." The Englishman spoke through clenched

teeth. There was perspiration on his upper lip. "Am I... mistaken in understanding that you young men believe Jean-Pierre De Vauban is plotting to... to murder me? That this... indisposition is the cause of some potion he put into my champagne?"

"Yes, but there's no time to explain it all to you now." Stephen began to guide his lordship away from the plantation, leading him as quickly as possible up the long oak-lined avenue to where the carriage was hidden within the woods. They kept under cover of the trees as they walked, and Johnny took the Englishman's other arm, guiding him with firm gentleness. "Johnny will take you to our ship in the harbor and he'll send for a physician to attend you there."

Johnny added his endorsement of this plan, then addressed Stephen. "What do you want me to do about Carstairs?"

"After you and William have sent for the doctor, take a small force of men to Girod Street. Do whatever is necessary to get Carstairs out of Scar-Footed Mattie's place."

By now they had come to the head of the main drive leading to the house. Johnny gave his woodcock call once again, and immediately, a carriage pulled out, ghostlike, from the stand of trees opposite the road. The horses drew abreast of them, and William Tuttle leaped out from inside the coach. Ned Boodle peered down from the driver's perch, waiting for his orders.

"Where's Miss Anemone?" William demanded after one quick scan of the little group.

"She's in trouble," Stephen replied shortly. "I'm going back for her."

"I'm going with you." The red-haired giant strode forward.

"No." With his customary tone of cool, quiet command, Stephen checked him in his tracks. "Our first priority is his lordship's safety. William, you and Johnny must accompany him to the ship—and then rescue Anemone's father from his captors in the Swamp."

"But Stephen..."

"I'll get her out, William." Stephen faced him, his hard, handsome face resolute as he stood before them, hands clenched. "Don't doubt that for a minute. I will get her out."

There was a moment of silence. Only the rustle of underbrush as a gray squirrel burrowed past a clump of hibiscus disturbed the hushed quality of the night. William Tuttle nodded slowly.

"All right. But if anything happens to her..."

"Nothing will." Stephen's eyes glittered with determination.

Satisfied, William turned and held the carriage door for Lord Bromford.

The Englishman climbed with difficulty into the coach. William clambered up after him, but Johnny hesitated. Ned Boodle held the reins in readiness to depart.

"Good work, Tuck," Stephen said with a thump on Johnny's back. "You've saved all our necks tonight."

"Stephen..."

"Hurry. His lordship needs medical attention, and I've got to reach Anemone before those bastards do her any harm."

"There's something I've got to tell you."

Stephen's patience thinned as Johnny made no move either to enter the coach or speak his mind. "Damn it, Tuck, say it and be done. The night's work is hardly over, you know!"

Suddenly, Johnny began to talk in a rush. "I lied to her—I lied to Anemone. I should have told you before. We talked on the ship the day we docked in New Orleans and I told her..."

"Yes?" A sudden stillness had come over Stephen. Every

muscle had tensed, and even his pulse slowed to long, steady beats. "Go on," he instructed with an oddly quiet calm.

"I told her that you had never loved her—that you were using her to gain information about De Vauban's plot. I . . . I convinced her that she was nothing but your pawn. That's why she left the ship without a word. She was devastated. I don't even think she knew what she was doing, but she had to get away." He swallowed. "I drove her away."

Night loomed over them like a huge, engulfing specter. Crickets sang. A deer crashed through the hickories beyond the road, stared at them, and bolted back into the wood from which it had come. Silence fell between the two men, a silence so intense and unbearable that they could each hear the breathing of the forest, the thousands of tiny woodland sounds and creature-stirrings which made up the night all about them. Stephen drew a breath which sounded like a loud echoing hiss to his own ears. The implications of Johnny's confession stunned him. For a moment, he couldn't move, couldn't speak, couldn't shatter that deafening silence. Then, as if released from some mesmerizing spell, he acted. His arm drew back, then swung forward, hitting Johnny a punishing blow which knocked him backward onto the muddy earth.

Johnny lay unmoving at first, dazed by the raw power of the blow. Then he put a hand to his jaw. Pain seared his face and exploded in his ears. With an effort, he raised himself to a sitting position and tilted his head up toward Stephen, who towered above him, fists clenched and a storm of fury on his face.

William Tuttle leaned out the carriage window in astonishment. Ned Boodle swore. Stephen never took his eyes off Johnny. Cold, terrifying rage molded all of his features into a deadly mask.

"I deserved that—I know." Johnny's words sounded odd as he spoke through the crunching pain in his jaw.

"But Stephen..." He winced as Stephen started to reach out to grab him. "Don't you think... we can settle this later? Anemone..."

"What do you care about her?" Stephen snapped, but he paused without laying hands on Johnny. Abruptly, he spun on his heel and started back toward the plantation house. Johnny's voice stopped him unexpectedly, but he didn't turn, didn't glance back.

"I do care..." Johnny called. He staggered to his feet, sounding weary. "She has wit and... style... and... courage. I hope one day she'll forgive me... and you will, too."

Stephen didn't answer. Johnny Tucker no longer mattered. There was only one thing that he cared about now.

He sprinted through the woods without looking back to see Johnny enter the carriage, but he heard the door slam shut and the horses set to. Then there was only the nighttime murmur of the forest and the distant din of laughter and commotion from the white house ahead. Thoughts tumbled through his mind as he raced through the live oaks, his gaze fixed upon the brilliantly lighted scene before him. What Johnny had just said explained so much. He saw everything now, and he wondered at his own blindness in not seeing it before. He realized with a rush of joy that Anemone did love him, that she had loved him all along. Johnny had driven a wedge between them, a wedge which had grown sharper and deeper when Stephen himself had started to doubt Anemone's love. It was damned confusing, and damned sad, but somehow they had compounded the confusion and mistrust until neither one of them had believed in the other, each thinking that he was the one who had been used. A sadness and an inexplicable ache came over him as he recalled all the terrible things they had said to each other. He knew that this pain would only be relieved by folding her in his arms again. And that was something he would do very shortly.

First he had to get into the library. And get her out of that damned secret passageway. His lips tightened when he thought of her fear at being confined. What private hell was she enduring now, locked up, probably below ground? Stephen swore to himself that when he found her, he would make up to her for every moment of horror she had suffered.

He reached the courtyard of the house and could see to his right and left the clusters of carriages, whose horses had all been led to temporary pasture and whose drivers had been provided with their own refreshment in the kitchen house behind the main building. In two long strides Stephen reached the gallery and ran up the broad steps, re-entering the plantation hallway. He strode past the servants without a word and began to make his way along the corridor, but suddenly, from the doorway of the ballroom, he heard a voice that stopped him cold.

"One moment, Monsieur, if you will," said Jean-Pierre De Vauban. Stephen wheeled about.

"Are you in need of something, Monsieur? Perhaps I can be of assistance." The Creole looked him up and down with an air of smug disdain.

"I'm looking for my wife, De Vauban," he answered coolly. "Have you seen her?"

"Ah, no, I have not had the pleasure." The Creole spread his hands regretfully. Stephen stifled an impulse to knock him cold. "But then," De Vauban went on slowly, "I have not seen Lord Bromford either—a circumstance of great concern to me. Do you, by any chance, know where he may be? My guests have already begun going into dinner, and it is most unseemly that he is not present."

Stephen suppressed a grin. De Vauban and his cohorts must be growing uneasy. Their prey had vanished from beneath their noses. He noted the tension in De Vauban's slim shoulders, and saw the slight crease between the Creole's brows. If he had not been so worried about

Anemone, Stephen might have enjoyed watching De Vauban go to pieces as his plans collapsed in ruin. But at the moment his only concern was getting to Anemone as quickly as possible.

"Lord Bromford mentioned earlier that he was not feeling well." Stephen met the other's watchful gaze and shrugged. "Perhaps he found a quiet parlor in which to sit and compose himself."

"Perhaps."

Stephen saw the exact moment when suspicion entered De Vauban's cold eyes. Then a thin, pallid-complexioned man came quickly down the curving staircase in the center of the hall and joined them. Stephen saw him give his head a tiny shake in answer to De Vauban's look of inquiry.

"There was no sign of his lordship in any of the rooms upstairs," he said somewhat breathlessly, with a harried stare in Stephen's direction.

"Monsieur Burke, allow me to introduce you to Paul Bergeron, my very good friend. Paul is helping me, you see, since it seems I have somehow misplaced the guest of honor."

"Damned careless of you, De Vauban." Stephen's smile was tinged with mockery. "But don't let me keep you. I will certainly understand if you wish to continue the search. I think I'll join the other guests and see if I can locate my wife in the dining room."

"Not so quickly!" De Vauban snarled, and stepped suddenly into Stephen's path. "Perhaps you know a bit more about this matter than you profess. Paul..."

Bergeron suddenly produced a small pistol. He held it close to his body and pointed it at Stephen. "It is a tiny gun, Monsieur, but at this range, most deadly." Nervously, Bergeron licked his lips, but his grip on the pistol was surprisingly steady.

"Come into the library, Monsieur Burke, and we shall discuss this matter at length." De Vauban gestured him along the hall, and Stephen, after a moment's hesitation, began to walk in that direction.

His senses were keenly attuned to everything around him. The smell of candle wax and perfume mingled faintly with the drifting aromas of succulent meats and steamed oysters from the dining room. Brilliant candlelight flickered upon the pale blue and cream floral wallpaper and reflected off the burnished surface of a gold-lacquered table as he passed it in the hall. He heard laughter from within the dining room and was aware of the clink and clatter of cutlery and goblets, of the roaring murmur of guests enjoying their meal. His body coiled itself for the moment when he would spring into action and wrest control from Bergeron by seizing the pistol. His reflexes bunched and gathered for the coming fray. As they reached the library, and De Vauban ordered him to go in, Stephen spun suddenly about and lunged for Bergeron's gun hand.

He was far stronger than the other man and wrenched the pistol from Bergeron's grasp before the latter even knew what had happened. Then he rammed Bergeron in the stomach with his elbow, shoved him across the hall, and sprang about to confront De Vauban. But Jean-Pierre's reflexes were quicker than Bergeron's. Before Stephen quite turned to face him, De Vauban charged in like a bull and knocked him backward into the library with the full force of his body. Stephen tumbled back onto the parquet. De Vauban aimed a vicious kick at his head, but Stephen rolled aside just in time and came to his knees with the gun clenched in his hand, pointed straight at De Vauban's heart. The Creole froze, along with Bergeron, white-faced and trembling at his side. Then De Vauban gave an ugly little laugh and regarded Stephen mockingly.

"Well done, my friend, but not quite clever enough," he rasped.

Stephen's eyes narrowed. He was breathing rapidly.

"Where is Anemone?" he demanded, and started to get to his feet. "You're going to take me to her at once."

"I don't think so," De Vauban retorted, and the next moment, Stephen felt a blinding pain crash through the back of his neck, and the world went dark. One Eye, behind him in the library, brandished the brass candlestick in his hand, grinning evilly.

De Vauban hurried forward, perspiration beading on his brow. "Don't just stand there, you idiot. Get him in the closet and down those stairs before someone comes in here. We've got to find out what he's done with Bromford. . . ."

"Yes, indeed." A new voice sliced through the air, startling all three men. They turned and stared at the squat, mustachioed figure who had slipped into the library unnoticed. With smooth alacrity, this person now shut the door and then turned back to stare with biting contempt at the little group.

"L'Araignée! What are you doing here? You were going to wait at Scar-Footed Mattie's until we brought his lordship!"

"Wait? How could I wait?" The newcomer's black eyes snapped at De Vauban with ill-concealed scorn. "You've botched this whole affair, De Vauban—you've all but destroyed us. You have allowed a gaggle of spies to enter our midst this very night, when we were ready to strike. And from what I gather now, the devil knows what has become of our so carefully selected victim—Lord Bromford."

L'Araignée, otherwise known as the Spider, glared with undisguised contempt at the men before him. All their carefully laid plans, their preparations and anticipations, and all the riches they would reap when Napoleon had conquered Europe dangled before them on the verge of obliteration. Oliver Fenwicke could barely suppress his wrath.

De Vauban paled under his steely scrutiny and began

to stammer. He was not afraid of many men, but this one had a ruthlessness and cunning which inspired even his anxiety. "We'll question them, Oliver—we'll find out all we need to know. We can still carry on with our plan. . . ."

"For your sake, I hope so." Then Oliver's gaze fell upon Stephen's unconscious form. "You have the girl safe?"

"Below—in the dungeon. She's tied up. We can question her—she'll break far more easily than her father—she is only a woman, after all."

"You forget—I know this particular woman," the mustachioed man retorted. His brows drew together in a frown. "She will not be easy to break, but perhaps . . . yes. If we hurt her, and question the man, *he* may be induced to talk. That might serve better."

"You heard *L'Araignée!*" De Vauban turned to One Eye furiously, taking out his own frustration on his subordinate, but unlike Bergeron, who appeared on the verge of a nervous collapse, One Eye held his ground with a faint sneer on his lips. "Bring him below at once!"

One Eye stuck the pistol into the waistband of his breeches and bent over Stephen. "We should have butchered Bromford the moment he set foot in New Orleans, as I wanted from the first!" he growled. With an effort, he managed to drag Stephen upright. "Quickly—a gang of men could have rushed him, slit his throat, cut him apart before anyone had time to move—and then it would have been done. Look where all your clever planning has brought us—to the edge of failure!"

"We have not failed yet," De Vauban said between clenched teeth. Paul Bergeron groaned.

Oliver glanced from one to the other with grim purpose. "If we have failed tonight, we still have not lost. We will make this pair tell us what they've done with his lordship and we will form another plan. And we will make them pay, both Anemone Carstairs and Stephen Burke—and my friend, Thomas, as well. They will suffer for having wandered into the Spider's web."

De Vauban nodded. "Yes. It is now a matter of pride, of honor. In particular, I have a score to settle with the woman."

Oliver's hard gaze rested briefly on him. "Anemone Carstairs seems to have a talent for succeeding at whatever role she chooses to play."

"She will regret this one," De Vauban vowed, and turned on his heel so that the others could not see his face. He brushed past One Eye, who was laboriously dragging Stephen's unconscious form toward the closet. Reaching it first, he yanked at the brass ornament which unlocked the hidden stairway. With his lips set tightly together, he led the way down the narrow passage.

"She will regret it very much," he thought, and the words were a promise to himself.

TWENTY-FIVE

IT WAS a vile place, the dungeon to which they had brought her. Slime oozed upon the plastered brick walls and a wet, foul odor clung to the dank air. Rats and water beetles scurried over the plank flooring. Anemone watched them in the flickering light cast by the branch of candles which De Vauban had lit upon the small table three feet from her chair. That table and two other crude chairs, plus an assortment of empty crates and barrels, were all the furnishings of the small, bleak cell in which she found herself. With her hands tightly bound behind her back and the rope knotted to the chair upon which she sat, Anemone tried to keep her rising panic at bay, but little by little, as the candle wax dripped and melted and the shadows of the room wavered eerily, she felt her last shreds of hope slipping away.

The closet had been bad enough, but this underground dungeon held a ghastly horror all its own. Her flesh crawled as she gazed bleakly at the narrow, enclosing walls. As the minutes dragged by, she felt her breath growing shorter, and the bile of nausea rose in her throat. Desperately, she shut her eyes, trying to escape the terrifying closeness of her prison. She tried to imagine that she was on the *Sea Lion* once again, standing at the rail and gazing out at the jewel-blue ocean. She strove with all her might to recall the sensation of bitingly fresh sea air, of salt spray upon her face, of dizzying blue sky that stretched forever and foaming waves that rolled and dipped into eternity.

The ropes were cutting into her flesh. She twisted her wrists, trying in vain to free them. Though the rope that bound her was thin, it had been cruelly knotted. She could not loosen it at all. Slowly, her eyes came open. She stared at the floor. There was no escaping this hellish place. At least not through her imagination. She had to face it. She had to defeat it. With something of her old stubbornness, Anemone reminded herself that there was far more at stake here than her own fate.

She wondered if Stephen was searching the ballroom for her yet. He would wonder where she had gone— *maybe*, she reflected dismally, *he would think she was upstairs in De Vauban's bed.* Perhaps he would even grow suspicious and alert Johnny and William that she was missing. But none of them would ever find her here. She pictured Lord Bromford seated beside De Vauban at the dinner, forcing himself to nibble at the grand feast set before him while the insidious poison ate away at his system, making him ill, weak, and vulnerable for the kill. He would be murdered tonight, carved up like an animal while he slept off the effects of the potion. And her father, she thought with a tiny, choked sob. They intended to make him watch the butchering of Bromford's body— and then? What would happen? Would Papa, too, be slaughtered like a pig?

A ragged weeping shook her. She struggled frantically

at her bonds, but only succeeded in scraping her flesh with the rough rope until her wrists bled. A feeling of faintness washed over her.

Anemone sucked in air and forced herself to peer about the dungeon. There must be something here she could use. Something...

There was. Her gaze fastened upon a pile of crates several feet from her chair. They were roughly made of pine, with splinters and jagged edges. At the corner of the crate that was uppermost in the pile, a nail jutted out. It was a long nail, with a sharp tip. *It might do*, she thought with a sudden surge of hope, *if only I can position myself in the proper way.*

At least her feet were free. She managed, by half jumping, half dragging, to slide her chair over to the crates. The light was dimmer here in the corner. She saw that the crate with the protruding nail was too high for her bound wrists to reach. She turned her chair with some difficulty and kicked at the bottom crate with all her might. It skimmed backward, and the ones on top of it fell forward. She tried to dodge out of the way, but the edge of the highest one scraped her face as it toppled past. Anemone cried out. The blow stunned her briefly, but she blinked back tears of pain and instead focused on the fallen crates. The one she sought lay on its side. The nail protruded from its topmost corner. Eagerly, Anemone edged her chair closer.

It was necessary for her to lie upon the floor in order to be level with the nail. She bunched her muscles for the effort and then threw herself forward onto her knees, dragging the chair with her. Quickly, she rolled sideways. Her breath came in short, hard gasps. A beetle crawled across her nose as she lay panting upon the damp wood floor. She ignored it, squirming backward until she was even with the crate and her wrists were level with the jutting nail. Straining with the discomfort of her position, she clenched her teeth and lifted her wrists behind her.

She painstakingly began to rub the rope against the nail. Back and forth, again and again, she made the chafing motion, concentrating all her efforts on fraying her bonds. Her side ached as she lay on it. A searing pain burned her arms. The chair was cutting into her skin, and she felt moisture from the damp floor of the cell soaking the skirt of her gold dress. Back and forth. Again. And again. She was biting her lips so hard they bled. The comb had come loose in her hair, and pale silvery strands now tumbled in her scratched, bruised face as she lay upon the dungeon floor, moving her wrists back and forth behind her, wearing away ever so slowly, ever so steadily at the twined bonds. It seemed like hours passed, but suddenly, she felt something giving way. She rubbed more furiously. The rope frayed, broke. Her arms dragged forward, and she fell face down in exhaustion upon the floor. Through her weariness, a glorious sensation burst through. She was *free*.

The next moment, she heard something from above. The hidden panel swinging open? Was that a footstep on the stair? She dragged herself to her knees in heart-pounding alarm.

Her next movements were swift and purely instinctive. Despite the fiery ache in all her muscles, she sprang to her feet and piled the crates one upon another as they had been. An instant later she carried the chair back to its original spot. She stripped off her encumbering silk gloves, seized the shredded rope, and sat down, thrusting the gloves beneath her billowing skirt. As the heavy thud of footsteps descended the passageway, she positioned her hands behind her, still tightly gripping the rope. No sooner had she done this than a pair of booted feet came into view, followed by another. Within a few seconds, the cell was full of men. She saw De Vauban, Bergeron, and One Eye—then her gaze widened and a cry was wrenched from her throat. One Eye dumped Stephen's unmoving form at her feet.

"Stephen!" She couldn't help the agonized word that tore from her throat. "He isn't ... he isn't *dead?*" she gasped in horror, unable to tear her gaze from his face.

"No, Anemone, my dear, he isn't dead."

Stunned, she withdrew her gaze from Stephen, now sprawled upon the ground. She stared instead at the last man to reach the bottom of the staircase, the man who had spoken to her, the short, squat, dapper man with the neat mustache and the familiar deep-set black eyes. Oliver Fenwicke, her superior at the office of British intelligence, the man who had hired her, instructed her, supported her—the man who had first recruited her father, now gazed at her with a faint, amused smile curling his moist lips.

"*Oliver.*" It was a croak, barely audible. Anemone could only gape at him in numb disbelief.

"Allow me to introduce you to the Spider," De Vauban said mockingly, with an expansive wave of his hand. "Though I believe you know him by another name, *cherie.*"

"You ... are the Spider, Oliver?" She felt as though in a dream, a strange and grotesque dream, peering through an evil wizard's looking glass at a distorted reality, where nothing was as it seemed and everything was wrong, disjointed, and vaguely threatening. "But ... how? Why? Why would you betray England—betray us all?"

"It is England who betrayed me, Anemone, dear. Years ago." Oliver strolled closer, terrifyingly casual as he surveyed her seemingly hopeless predicament. In his dove gray breeches and waistcoat, with a shirt of exquisite linen, he looked every inch the respected commander she had admired over the years. Even as he spoke to her, telling her of his treachery, she could scarcely believe that it was true, for Oliver Fenwicke had been her father's friend, and her own, especially after Papa's alleged death in Spain. She listened to him in sick amazement, wondering how he could have fallen so low, shuddering at the notion that he had been the one to capture and torment her father and to mastermind this entire grisly plan.

"I gave my heart and soul in the service of our fair land, Anemone, and what did I receive in return? Riches? Glory? The esteem of our notable citizens? Hardly." Oliver's lips twitched. He tugged at his mustache in the gesture she remembered so well. "I served magnificently my entire career, and then, four years ago, the opportunity came along which rightfully belonged to me, and England, in her infinite stupidity and arrogance, passed me by."

"A promotion?" From the corner of her eye, Anemone saw Stephen's arm move ever so slightly. How she wanted to go to him, to cradle him in her arms and kiss away his wounds, his hurts but more than that she wanted to get them both out of here alive. She had to keep the others' attention away from him long enough for him to regain consciousness. One Eye, Bergeron, and De Vauban were all watching Oliver, absorbed in his story. She wanted to keep it that way.

"What promotion was that?" she inquired steadily.

Oliver snorted in contempt and waved his hand at her. "Not merely a promotion, my dear. Something far more desirable than that. I had an opportunity to be knighted— to be recognized for all I had done for England. A high honor, indeed. I would have been Sir Fenwicke. Do you know what that would have meant to me—the youngest son of a career infantryman? Do you have any idea how very badly I wanted that distinctive and peculiarly British honor?"

"Quite badly, I would guess. You betrayed your country for lack of it." Anemone spoke dryly.

"Yes." Oliver's round, nearly black eyes shone in the eerie darkness of the underground cell. "Because my country betrayed me! They chose not to bestow that honor upon me, all because of a chance discovery. An indiscretion in my youth came to light, a trifling offense whereby a small sum of money was taken, but later returned. . . . It

doesn't signify! Not anymore! They used that single occasion as an excuse to deny me the honor that was my
due, and I have made them pay dearly for that omission.
I decided to punish them for their pomposity and ingrat-
itude! And, Anemone, I have done so most effectively!"

Contempt welled within her. "My father has never
been knighted for all of his years of service, Oliver. Odd
that it never seemed to occur to him to expect such a
thing."

"Your father! The largest fool of them all! For all the
years I have known him, he has never thought of anything but England—and his damnable, noble love of
country!" A muscle quivered in Oliver's jaw. He strode
forward, nudging Stephen aside with his boot, until he
stood directly before her. "You are of the same ilk, my
dear!" He spat out these words with venom. "Patriots!
Fools! I was content merely to laugh behind your backs
at your foolish efforts—to know all along that I was un-
dermining those who labored beneath my command. I
grew rich beyond your wildest dreams, my dear. Information is more valuable than gold or rubies, and I had
information in abundance. It was an easy matter to sell
it to the highest bidder. And the rest, the scheming, the
plotting, the betrayals, they were merely part of the game,
part of my very sweet revenge."

"And the killings? A dozen men? Fifteen? Or more than
that?" She shook her head, her gray eyes alight with fury.
"How do you sleep at night, Oliver?"

"Quite peacefully. My dear, you are looking at a very
contented man."

Her face blazed at him in the candlelight. "I am looking
at a particularly ugly specimen of vermin."

Oliver shrugged. "Your opinion is of no importance to
me. I have other things with which to concern myself
tonight. You, my dear, and your father, and this damned
American, have gotten in my way. This conspiracy has
been my dearest goal! To propel America into a war which

will almost certainly aid Bonaparte in the defeat of England—ah, what a sweet revenge! You must know, Anemone, that if Napoleon wins the war, my prize will be inestimable. And my fellows here will share equally in that reward."

De Vauban came forward and shook him by the arm, interrupting the impassioned tirade. "Enough of this! Have you forgotten our purpose? We will have failed in our endeavor if we cannot get our hands on Lord Bromford this very night! Let us find out what they have done with him."

The news that Lord Bromford was missing caught Anemone by surprise, but it filled her with a sudden hope. She didn't know how Stephen had known to spirit his lordship away, but she felt wonderful relief and a sudden belief that her own escape, and Stephen's, was possible, too. She had to keep them talking a bit longer to give Stephen time to regain his senses. His head moved ever so slightly. One Eye glanced down at him. As if for good measure, he gave Stephen's limp form a vicious kick. Stephen made no sound, but Anemone cried out quickly.

"And you, Jean-Pierre! What has become of your ball? No guest of honor, no host! I imagine all of New Orleans will be gossiping about it for weeks!"

"My guests will scarcely miss me, *petite*. I shall return to them quite soon."

"Tell me something," she invited coolly, and stared at him with a challenge in her eyes. "Do you truly believe that this motley group of conspirators can bring ruin to England?" Cold laughter rang from her lips. "Your ego is even more monstrous than I guessed! But of course, I knew you were impossibly arrogant the moment you first spoke to me. Though how you could imagine I would betray a man like Stephen Burke for you, I can hardly guess!"

A crimson flush coursed through De Vauban's olive

cheeks. One Eye snickered behind him. De Vauban strode toward her and jabbed an elegant finger in the air. "You will regret your mockery, *cherie*," he said softly. "When we have finished questioning you, you will be mine to dispose of. And I will do it slowly, lingeringly. You will suffer a long and agonizing death."

"Better than to suffer your foolish cajolery," Anemone retorted, throwing her head back to stare scornfully at him. "I admit I grew quite ill at the thought of having to endure a single kiss. But as Oliver has said, I am nothing if not devoted to the service of my country."

"One Eye! Come here. Take out your knife. I think a slash or two across her face will end this slut's impudence."

"Burke is not even awake yet." Oliver glanced back at Paul Bergeron, who stood silent near the table with the candles. "Bergeron, bring him around. We want him to witness what we do to the woman."

Anemone braced herself. One Eye's hand dipped downward to his waistband and emerged with a sheathed knife. He slipped the sheath off with one fluid motion and a razor-edged dagger glinted in the candlelight. He grinned and lumbered forward. Then everything happened at once.

Stephen's arm shot out across the floor and grabbed One Eye's boot. He yanked at it viciously and the smuggler crashed to the floor. At the same instant, Stephen rolled over and sprang to his feet, knocking Paul Bergeron sideways. Anemone leaped off her chair.

She shoved De Vauban away from her and darted with agile grace from beneath Oliver's reach. The cell suddenly exploded with fighting, sending the candle flames dancing precariously in their tarnished sconces. Stephen fought One Eye and Bergeron. Anemone had a swift glimpse of his face as he leveled a hard right fist into the smuggler's belly. For a moment she marveled at how cool he looked, how calm, despite the intensity of the fray. But she had no time to watch his pugilistic skill, for De Vauban had recovered his balance and, cursing, he spun toward her. Oliver lunged from the opposite side. She reached the pile of crates and grabbed one, then hurled it at Oliver's head. De Vauban held her shoulder, but she wrenched free, then, to his surprise, whirled to confront him, raised her arm, and slashed the rope she held hard across his face. He screamed and clutched at his skin, ribbons of white showing across his olive flesh. Anemone ran past him and reached the three men struggling near the stairs. She was in time to see Paul Bergeron collapse to his knees after Stephen's blow to his chin. Bergeron's eyes seemed to roll in his head for a split second, then they closed and he toppled forward to lie unmoving upon the floor. One Eye had gone after the knife he had dropped when Stephen tripped him, but Anemone saw Stephen kick it aside before the smuggler could lay his hands on it. She dove after it. Behind her, she heard a sickening thud and saw that One Eye had dealt a sledgehammer blow to Stephen's stomach. He was doubled over, pain etched in his lean face. Her fingers closed on the cold handle of the knife, but as she got to her feet, De Vauban jumped at her, and they fell together upon the floor. He was far stronger than she, but she held on to the weapon tenaciously, fighting with all of her strength, refusing to slacken her hold even as he half-pinned her with his body and began to twist her wrist viciously. Gasping in pain, Anemone brought her knee up hard into his groin. De Vauban screamed and fell back. Like quicksilver she was up, the knife lifted ominously in her hand. She jumped out of his reach. De Vauban hadn't yet risen from the floor, but lay groaning, his eyes closed. Oliver, who had been watching both ongoing battles in disbelief, started toward her, but she made a quick upward motion with the knife.

"Don't try it. Stay where you are!"

His eyes narrowed. "You little bitch."

"Don't move, Oliver. Another step and I'll drive this

through your heart." Her voice sounded strangely cool. But she was watching Stephen's fight with One Eye, and her flesh was damp and clammy with fear for him. Her temples throbbed as she kept Oliver and De Vauban at bay with the knife and watched the furious battle between the two massively powerful men. The smuggler had tremendous strength and he fought with the ferocity of a rhinoceros. Stephen had only a few moments ago regained consciousness, and she knew he had to be hurt, yet he faced the smuggler with astonishing dexterity, parrying many of the powerful blows his opponent swung at him and wielding his own fists with a rugged, sinewy strength that showed no signs of flagging.

Anemone caught her breath as he hit One Eye in the nose and the smuggler fell back against the wall, blood pouring from his nostrils. With the candlelight weaving and dancing, throwing pale beams of light across his blue-black hair and sweat-glistening jaw, Stephen wasted no time in following up his advantage. He sprang forward and struck One Eye again, this time in the stomach. The man doubled over. Stephen brought his fist down hard on the back of his neck. With a groan, One Eye dropped to the floor as if weighted by a sack of bricks. He lay there, unmoving, a scarred and vicious giant felled at last.

The spitting of the candles and the sounds of labored breathing were the only noises now in the suddenly hushed room.

Stephen turned from his fallen adversary and saw Anemone brandishing her knife. He chuckled suddenly, taking in the two men she had bested and subdued. Oliver Fenwicke appeared to have been changed into stone. He stood like a statue, white and still, gaping at the overturned chairs, crates, and bodies all about him. Jean-Pierre De Vauban had pulled himself to his knees, and now stared in shock at the chaotic scene. He started to stagger to his feet, reaching toward the hem of Anemone's skirt. Stephen strode toward him and grabbed him by the lace of his elegant shirt. He hauled him to his feet.

"Since I won't have the pleasure of meeting you for a formal duel in St. Anthony's garden, I shall have to content myself with this," Stephen said quite calmly, and hit the Creole a punishing blow to the chin.

De Vauban screamed, and Stephen hit him once more before letting him drop to the floor. Oliver Fenwicke, his face the color of ashes, backed away.

Anemone gave a shaky laugh. "Well done, Stephen. I dared not hope it should turn out so well. Are you... are you hurt?"

"Nothing to complain of," he returned with what she thought was an amazing cheerfulness. His glance pierced her, going over her bedraggled, filthy gown and tangled hair. His tone changed, softening. "What about you, my love?"

She was so dazed by all that had happened that she hardly caught the endearment. "I...I am all right." She pushed a stray tendril of hair from her eyes and surveyed the men before her. "What shall we do with them?"

Stephen had no trouble answering this question. He began to move about the cell, searching for rope. "I think we ought to leave them down here 'til tomorrow. Why interrupt the Governor's enjoyment of the ball? Though I expect he'll find it rather odd that his host has completely disappeared. Still," he added with a derisive glance at De Vauban, "that's hardly our concern. In the morning will be time enough to notify Claiborne, and we'll let the officials handle it after that."

The next few moments were spent in tying up the prisoners. Anemone stored the crate with the protruding nail safely out of reach and turned to survey their handiwork.

"Excellent," she said with satisfaction as Stephen pulled the final knot taut about De Vauban's bound wrists. They had tied their feet, as well, and removed all sharp objects and weapons. Only Bergeron, who had come to at last, bothered to plead with them, but they turned deaf ears to him and mounted the staircase, taking the branch of candles with them.

When they reached the head of the narrow flight, Stephen guided her through the passageway and into the closet. "For someone who was terrified of a ship's hold, you've managed to stay fairly calm through all this business," he commented.

"I had no choice. I wanted to survive." Suddenly, as she passed into the library, the panic she had so valiantly fought overcame her. She felt her knees tremble, and she flung herself forward, grasping the arms of a wing chair for support.

Stephen quickly shut the false panel and then the closet door behind him. He came into the library and took Anemone's arm. Gently, he settled her into the wing chair. For the first time in all the excitement, he noticed the bruises on her face.

"You're bleeding." With surprise she heard the anger in his voice. "Who did this to you? Did it happen during the fight?"

"No. A crate fell on me and scratched my face." She put a fingertip to the bruise on her cheek. "And De Vauban hit me before I was brought below."

She heard Stephen suck in his breath, and then he swung around. "I'm going back down there and untie the bastard so I can teach him a thing or two about bruised faces—and broken bones. It won't take long...."

"Stephen, no!" Somehow, she found herself giggling. "It's nothing. Don't be so foolish."

He paused at the doorway, glanced back at her, and then came back to her side. He shook out his handkerchief and gently bent down to wipe a smear of blood from her cheek. As she raised her hand to take the handkerchief from him, he saw the raw bruises on her wrists.

He caught her arm and stared at them. Again, that quiet fury came over his face, but this time it quickly changed to concern. "We've got to get you back to the ship and have these tended," he said abruptly. "You must hurt like hell."

She shook her head. "No, I . . . I had forgotten all about it." Suddenly, her head cleared. What had she been thinking of to forget all this while? How could she be so stupid, so selfish. . . .

"Stephen, we've got to get to Girod Street. My father . . ."

"Has probably already been rescued."

He smiled down at her, and her heart did a strange somersault in her chest. He was acting so strangely. So kind, so tender. She had never thought to see him look at her with that gentleness in his eyes again.

"I sent William and Johnny with some of the crew to get him out of Scar-Footed Mattie's house as soon as they had Lord Bromford safe on board the *Sea Lion*."

"But how . . . how did you know?"

"Johnny overheard what was said in the library—including De Vauban's discovery of you in the closet. I knew your penchant for eavesdropping would get you in trouble one day, my love."

She stared up at him blankly. *My love?*

"Anemone." His voice was like a caress. "I have something to tell you."

She was about to inquire what it was, but he suddenly reached down and pulled her from the chair, drawing her gently into his arms.

"Johnny told me tonight what he said to you on the *Sea Lion*."

She felt herself paling and tried to jerk away from his grasp, but he held her tightly. Though his arms encircled her waist with sufficient strength that she could not escape, his hold on her was oddly gentle.

"It was a lie, Anemone. Every word he spoke. I never misled you or lied to you about my love. Johnny betrayed us both."

"I don't understand."

"He told you that I used you as a pawn—that wasn't true. He only wanted to cause a rift between us, an end to it all—and he damn well succeeded." Stephen's eyes were grim. His hand reached up and caressed her hair, causing warm, tingling sensations as he stroked the tousled curls. "My love for you was genuine, Anemone. It always was. And I swear to you, my brave, darling girl, it always will be."

She felt that she was dreaming, caught between fantasy and nightmare. "But Johnny said you even told William that I wasn't important, that you were only after information." She searched his face. "Was that a lie, Stephen? I could have sworn he spoke the truth when he told me that. I saw it in his eyes."

"That was the truth. I did tell William that." He cupped her face in his hand as she started to turn away from him. His fingers on her chin, he forced her to look at him. "I started out with the intention of seducing you for my own purposes, it's true. But those plans quickly fell by the wayside, Anemone. I fell in love with you. That first dinner in my cabin was my undoing. From that moment on, I realized how much I needed you."

Her heart had begun to beat so frantically that she was certain he could feel it against his own chest. She gazed up at him, studying his face, that strong, rugged face that was so dear to her. Was this some cruel, horrible jest he was practicing on her—or part of some new plan he had concocted with Johnny? But his gaze was warm and tender, and there was love in his eyes. He was watching her, his arms tight around her waist, holding her close against him. "Anemone, I love you," he said, with that husky yearning in his voice that turned her knees to taffy.

Suddenly, the bubble of pain around her burst and she

was free—free of misery, of the terrible despair that had gripped her since that morning of arrival in New Orleans.

"I'm going to strangle Johnny Tucker!" she cried fiercely, and then Stephen laughed, and gathered her to him. He kissed her, a deep, dizzying kiss that banished the last traces of doubt from her mind and left her clinging to him, pressing her mouth to his, exulting in the hot, flowing passion that enveloped them like the rush of a desert wind.

Then the kiss slowly changed. It softened into a delectably beautiful kiss, full of the need they both had denied for so long. It filled them with joy and a burning warmth that went beyond mere passion, touching the depth of their souls and twining them together with ribbons of love.

"Stephen, Stephen, how could we have hurt each other so?" she murmured when she could speak again. Cradled in his arms, she wanted never to move, never to break this lovely enchanted feeling of warmth and belonging.

"Pride, my darling. That most dangerous and self-defeating emotion."

"It is my fault for doubting you. No, it is Johnny's fault for deceiving me." She shook her head suddenly. "I'm too happy to think about it now." She snuggled her cheek against his chest contentedly. "But your friend had better stay out of my path come morning."

"My friend will still be nursing a swollen jaw come morning," Stephen growled. Suddenly, he started. "Anemone, let's get out of here. I want you all to myself— and not in De Vauban's damned house, either."

"That would please me immensely, but let us leave by the window. I don't wish to run into any guests looking like this." She gestured at her stained and dirty ball gown. Stephen grinned. He, too, had a bruise on his cheek, and his shirt was torn and spattered with One Eye's blood.

"You look wonderful to me," he assured her. "More wonderful than ever."

"That is not much of a compliment," she retorted. Hand in hand they went to the window and parted the draperies. It didn't take long before they were outside, crossing the gallery, and Stephen was helping her to climb the railing in her gown.

The air was sweet and fresh with the odor of ripe earth and wild azaleas. They kept to the woods, running together under cover of the moss-shrouded oaks, their path lit by thin patches of moonlight coming through the leaves. William Tuttle and Johnny had left their horses tethered in the same stand of trees that had hidden the carriage. Anemone hitched up her gold skirts and allowed Stephen to toss her up onto the handsome gray gelding with white markings. He vaulted into the saddle of a muscular bay.

"Ready?"

She cast a quick glance down the winding drive and glimpsed the house still ablaze with lights. The faint strains of music drifted to her ears. "Ready," she replied, and lifted the reins.

All her tiredness had fled. She felt a magical flow of energy caused by Stephen's love and the victory they had wrested tonight from their enemies' hands. She cast a glance at Stephen as they rode through the forest path, surrounded on all sides by underbrush teeming with creatures of the night, by rustling wildflowers and ancient trees. *I love you*, she thought, and at that moment he turned his head and their gazes met.

"I love you," he called above the patter of the hooves, and the expression on his face sent a surge of joy through her heart.

They rode in silence to the city, and then through the rutted, lantern-lit streets of New Orleans until they reached the harbor. Thomas Carstairs was waiting on the *Sea Lion*'s deck.

"Papa!" She threw her reins to Stephen, slid from the gray's saddle, and flung herself into her father's arms. She cradled his bruised and bandaged face between her hands. "Those monstrous bastards," she whispered, but with so much gentleness in her small-boned face as she looked at him that Thomas's chest heaved with laughter.

"Don't fret about me, Emmy. I've been through worse. Not that I wasn't glad to see William and Johnny and their crew who came and got me."

"His lordship?" Stephen had turned the horses over to Tom Ruggins for stabling in Canal Street. He strode up the gangplank behind Anemone. "Is he well, Thomas?"

"He's recovering. The physician claims all ill effects should be gone by morning."

"That's welcome news," Stephen said with relief, then glanced at his companions. The three looked around at each other and grinned. Stephen's arm settled across Anemone's shoulders.

"It looks as if you two have had a very successful night," Thomas remarked, and Anemone gave her rich, clear laugh.

"Very successful, Papa."

"If you'll excuse us, sir, your daughter needs tending," Stephen broke in. "Is the physician still on board?"

"Yes." Thomas frowned as he became aware of Anemone's various injuries, and he noted the bruise on Stephen's face. "I'll come with you two. You obviously need looking after," he added sternly.

Some time later, Anemone found herself cuddled warmly in Stephen's arms in his familiar cabin on the *Sea Lion*. Her chafed wrists were bandaged, as was the scratch on her cheek. A cold compress had helped to stop the swelling of her bruise. She had bathed and changed into one of Stephen's silk shirts, and she now felt as delightfully safe and at peace as she had ever felt in her life. Drifting on a cloud of contentment, she sighed as Stephen gathered her against him and held her tightly for a moment before releasing her to the delicious softness of her pillow.

"Sleep, my love." He kissed her brow.

"Only if you promise not to go away."

"I promise."

She opened her eyes and gazed at his superb form beside her. Suddenly, the need for slumber ebbed away. She reached out a pair of slim arms and drew him languidly down to her. "There is something I must do before I sleep," she whispered. His eyebrows lifted. Blue eyes gleamed at her beneath the shock of thick raven hair. His mouth nuzzled enticingly at the corners of her lips.

"What's that, my love?"

"This," she said softly, and wrapped herself about him, drawing him into her arms, into her dreams, and showing him the love that flamed so strong and sure and bright in her heart.

TWENTY-SIX

IT WAS quiet on the river levee. A pink dawn had only moments before broken through the blue shadows of night, and a single young woman with a shawl about her shoulders walked slowly along the embankment. She paused a moment and took in the scene. There was a flatboat making its sluggish way up the Mississippi, and further downstream she saw a keelboat and several sailing ships gliding through the muddy waters. The *Sea Lion* was docked a long way down the harbor. She could see it, its tall sails billowing in the early morning breeze. Warmth spread through her at the sight of it. The *Sea Lion* was home to her now. It was familiar, comfortable, and safe. And its tall, recklessly handsome captain was the man she loved.

A slight morning mist still clung to the atmosphere over the river and the gradually awakening city, but it was lifting as the opalescent light of day drifted over flat slate roofs and ships' sails alike, bathing all in a pearly, ever-glowing sheen.

It had been two days since De Vauban's ball. In that time, Stephen and her father had accomplished a great deal. They had met with Governor Claiborne and other officials of the government and explained all that had been going on. De Vauban and Oliver Fenwicke, along with their accomplices, including the DuFour brothers, were in custody, and a full-scale investigation was underway to be certain that all the conspirators had been found and arrested. Lord Bromford had recovered fully. After returning to the Governor's home the following day, he had sent for Thomas Carstairs, Anemone, and Stephen and had listened to their entire explanation of the events that had passed. His lordship, though paling somewhat at learning the gruesome fate the conspirators had planned for him, took the brunt of the story with remarkable composure, then expressed his sincere and heartfelt gratitude to them all. Now, most of the official explanations and procedures had been completed. The *Sea Lion* was due to depart this morning, and Anemone had felt the need for one last stroll along this magnificent riverfront, one last glimpse of the rich, lively city that thrived on the banks of the Mississippi.

"Emmy, I see you had the same thought as I."

She turned at the sound of her father's voice and smiled.

"Papa, isn't it lovely here? I am going to miss New Orleans."

"I hear that Philadelphia is a fine city, too." He studied her a moment, noting the fleeting hesitation in her eyes. Then he put a hand to her chin. "You're not nervous about meeting Stephen's relatives, are you, my girl?"

"No, of course not." But her voice lacked its customary assurance.

Thomas Carstairs chuckled and took her arm. Together they walked along the levee as the Mississippi churned beside them. "You know, I have never been more proud of you than I was the other night. I know how difficult it must have been for you—being locked up in that hidden cell below the library. Yet you carried it off as I always knew you could. You did a good job, Emmy. If not for you and Stephen and that Johnny Tucker, I'd be a dead man by now, and so would his lordship."

"Yes, we owe Johnny our lives, don't we?" Her tone was subdued. It was difficult to be beholden to Johnny Tucker. She hated him still.

Thomas turned his head to stare at her. The rising sun glimmered on her ash blond curls, fetchingly swept off her face with a peach ribbon. She looked quite sophisticated, elegant really, in her peach cambric gown and matching gloves and shoes. Stephen Burke had purchased all this finery for her at his own expense when they had first found it necessary to enter New Orleans society, but now, though she had suggested they sell all the jewels and expensive ornaments, he had insisted that she keep everything. It was all startlingly becoming to her, these fine gowns and necklaces, the silk stockings and ivory combs. Thomas realized in rueful amazement that she was no longer the eager child who had soaked up his teachings word for word, nor the daring young girl who had rushed to spy for England in his place after his supposed death. Anemone was a woman now, still with those charming waiflike features and that beguiling smile, yet with a woman's joy and dignity and need to be loved. He felt a swell of pride at all she had accomplished, at all that she had become. And he was happier than he could say that she and Stephen Burke had settled their differences.

"Did you see Oliver yesterday?" Anemone asked, changing the subject from Johnny Tucker. Thomas nodded.

"I did. I wanted to get my hands around his throat, Emmy. Traitors don't sit well with me, especially ones who try to kill me and my girl. But the guards at the jail wouldn't let me near him."

She laughed, and then sobered. "When did you first

suspect him, Papa? I swear, I was never more shocked in my life than when he appeared in that dungeon and I learned he was the Spider."

"I began to wonder when I was in Spain, Emmy. That's when I first got wind of this whole nasty conspiracy, when I first heard of De Vauban and his dreams of aiding Bonaparte. I reported to Oliver, naturally, and then the next thing I knew, someone tried to kill me. I didn't know for certain that Oliver was involved, but I began to suspect some things. I figured I'd best let everyone think I was dead until I had the answers I needed."

"It is still difficult to believe. But we're fortunate to have uncovered his betrayal at all."

"And as for De Vauban," Thomas added, shaking his head, "he is a broken man. He talked to me a bit yesterday. He boasted about how he intended to complete the night's work, if all had gone as planned. As you know, he meant to make a great show of putting his lordship up for the night after Bromford suffered the effects of the potion. In the morning, my dear, the theatrics would have begun. His servants would have ventured into the main wing of the house to discover him bound and beaten (though not too severely, I imagine) by the supposed blackguards, who De Vauban would claim had descended upon the house in the dead of night to spirit his lordship away. Oh yes, Emmy, he had it well thought out. The scene would have matched his story perfectly, with broken vases and overturned chairs, everything necessary to support De Vauban's story that he had heard his lordship's cries for help and gone to his aid, but that he had been overpowered and brutalized by the masked assailants."

"Diabolical."

"Yes, but his spirit is now destroyed. His only sign of vitality appeared when he told me of these plans, of when he spoke about his dream for the Napoleonic empire.

When he recalled himself to his surroundings, and the fact of his defeat, all the life went out of his eyes. He sat in his cell, a beaten man. I almost pitied him."

"It is difficult to imagine him like that," Anemone mused. "He was such an intense, ruthlessly determined man. I thought I'd have to kill him in that horrid dungeon once I'd gotten hold of the knife. Oliver, too. Fortunately, it did not come to that."

Thomas chuckled suddenly. "I'd give a lot to have seen you fending off those two with One Eye Jones's knife. I'm surprised you didn't help Stephen battle One Eye, as well."

"He didn't need my help," she answered with a mischievous smile. "He fought like a Viking. You would have enjoyed the spectacle immensely had you only been there to see."

"Too bad you children had to do all the work," Thomas grumbled, scanning the river which was gradually becoming crowded with skiffs and pirogues and all manner of vessels. "Though I did manage to inflict a little damage on the DuFour brothers before One Eye helped them to restrain me at Scar-Footed Mattie's place. And after William and Johnny arrived with the rescue party, I personally broke Louis DuFour's nose."

They walked in silence for a little while, and then Thomas spoke again. "It does my heart good, Emmy, every time I see you with Stephen." He squeezed her arm. "There is a love between you two that reminds me of what I had with your mother."

"Really, Papa?" She stopped and hugged him impulsively. His words touched her more than she could say. "Thank you for saying that. And for understanding about..."

She broke off, blushing. But Thomas read her thoughts and laughed.

"For understanding why you choose to share a cabin

with the man you're going to wed? Come, come, Emmy, there's nothing remarkable in that. Your mother and I did the same thing." She regarded him in wonder, and he smiled and shook his head.

"Ah, yes, you young people think you invented passion. Well, it isn't true, my girl. And I'll tell you another thing. I'm damned glad Susannah and I did as we did, because we had too little time to spend together as it was." He bowed his head suddenly. "Far too little time," he muttered.

Anemone stared at him, moved by his words, as well as by the husky sadness in his voice.

"Thank you, Papa, for telling me that," she said softly. Thomas cleared his throat, blinked rapidly, then resumed his walk at a brisk pace. Smiling to herself, Anemone matched his strides.

"Stephen thinks we ought to have a large wedding," she said suddenly. A cloud descended over her face, and she bit her lip in silent agitation.

Thomas's shrewd eyes missed none of this. "And that troubles you, child?" he inquired.

She stopped and half turned to face him. She gripped his hand. "Papa, I am thinking of all that Johnny Tucker told me the morning we docked in New Orleans. Oh, I know it was a lie about Stephen merely pretending to love me, but ... he said other things as well. Things which make me wonder how Stephen's parents will receive me. They are important people in Philadelphia society and in American politics! I don't know if they will accept an English daughter-in-law. For all I know they might be as intolerant as Johnny Tucker!"

"Emmy, it is not like you to worry in this way. Stephen's mother and father will be delighted to have such a brave and beautiful girl wed their son."

"That's true, Anemone."

Johnny Tucker's voice behind them startled them both,

and they turned as one to face him. He had come up silently upon them and was now standing with his feet apart, his thumbs hooked in the pockets of his buff breeches. "Elizabeth and Alexander Burke are two of the finest people I know. And they'll be pleased and proud to welcome you into their family."

Thomas felt Anemone stiffen beside him as she stared at the fair-haired young man. He glanced between them, and then made a decision. "My girl, I think I'd better get back to the ship and say goodbye to Stephen. I have an appointment with Claiborne in less than an hour." He smiled warmly down at her. "As soon as all this business is finished here, I'll be on the next sailing ship for Philadelphia, so don't despair. And no matter what happens, don't have the wedding without me!"

"Don't be silly." She put her arms about his shoulders and gazed at him a long moment, ignoring Johnny Tucker's presence. "Papa, don't be long. I shall miss you."

"I'll be less than a week behind you, Emmy. And I can't wait to meet this family of Stephen's." He laughed suddenly and kissed her on the cheek. "It should be quite a wedding."

He shook hands with Johnny, then sauntered off toward the harbor. Anemone found herself alone with Johnny Tucker.

She turned and resumed her walk along the levee, a slight, angry flush in her cheeks. Johnny fell into step beside her. "We haven't had a chance to talk," he began. "There is something I have to say to you."

"I have nothing to say to you."

He accepted this remark in silence. All about them, the river had come alive with activity. More boats appeared, and men shouted and worked in the streaming sunlight.

"I was wrong about you, Anemone." Johnny shoved his hands deep into his pockets. "I was wrong to condemn all the English because some damned British officer impressed me on board his ship. I had no right to dislike you for that."

"Is that all? Will you go away and leave me alone now?" Anemone asked, gritting her teeth.

But Johnny shook his head. "I'm not finished. Do you know what really bothered me about you, Anemone— beyond the fact that you were English?"

She stopped and looked at him, her curiosity aroused despite herself.

"I hated that you were so close to Stephen." He gave a short laugh, and then shrugged. "It sounds strange, I know, but . . . there was a time when Stephen and I were inseparable. We did everything together: we worked, we drank, we bedded women. We were friends who had fought for each other, even killed on behalf of each other. We'd have given up our lives for one another. Never had anyone else come first." Johnny met her gaze, speaking with an urgent need to express himself that Anemone couldn't ignore. "We were adventurers, Anemone, skilled agents, yes—but also hell-raising partners. Even when we went our separate ways, and I became a diplomatic courier, we still had that camaraderie, that special loyalty to each other. Nothing had ever threatened it before. No woman had ever come close to interfering with our own rough and rascally brand of friendship. Then, the night I was rescued in New Brunswick, I saw you with Stephen and I knew that everything was different."

Anemone was watching his face. From his expression, she could tell this was spoken from the heart and that it was not easy for Johnny to tell her all this.

"Stephen cared for you. Not in the way he had cared about other women he's been with in the past—but in a way that I had never seen before. I think I viewed you as an enemy—an enemy to our days of wild drinking and whoring, to our freedom—or at least to Stephen's freedom to join me in the rogues' life to which we both had grown so accustomed." He grinned suddenly. "I guess I realized when I saw him with you that Stephen was getting ready to settle down. I sure as hell wasn't ready to do that, and I couldn't accept the idea that Stephen was."

"So you lied to me." Anemone's gray eyes pierced his. "You tried to ruin my life and his—to make me believe that I meant nothing to him. Surely you cannot expect me to forgive that."

"No. It was unforgivable." Johnny's head dropped. "But I had to explain. I had to ... try." He lifted his head suddenly, and the look he gave her was direct and honest. "Stephen needs you, Anemone. He was damned miserable when he thought you didn't love him. He didn't want any part of the kinds of antics we engaged in in the past. And I finally started to realize that I hadn't been a true friend. Believe it or not, my conscience finally got the better of my resentment." She didn't answer him, and he cleared his throat. "Anyway, I wanted to tell you— I think you're every bit as brave and as ... noble as Elizabeth and Alexander Burke. They've wanted Stephen to fall in love—parents always feel that way, I guess, especially when they're as much in love as the Burkes are themselves. And there's no doubt about it—they'll take to you like honey to molasses. I know you'll be happy."

He stopped walking suddenly and ran a hand through his fair hair. "Well, I guess that's all I had to say. I'll let you get on with your walk, and I'll wish you a good voyage. Maybe I'll see you and Stephen some time in Philadelphia."

"But ... aren't you sailing back with us this morning?" Anemone watched him in puzzlement.

Johnny drew a pattern in the earth with the toe of his boot. "Stephen prefers that I find my own way home." He smiled somewhat ruefully. "He said that my presence on the ship was offensive to you—and to him, too. You see, you're not the only one who can't forgive me."

He gave her a small, lopsided grin that only partially hid his pain, then with a salute, he started to turn back. Anemone struggled with herself.

"Johnny, wait." She grimaced as he spun quickly toward her, an eager look on his face. In two quick steps, she was before him, her hands clenched into fists which she shook under his nose. "I ought to strike you—as Stephen did! But..." A slow, irrepressible smile touched her lips. "I was never very good at doing what I 'ought' to do. And that includes holding a grudge."

He caught her hands in his large ones. "Anemone—do you mean it? May we try to be friends?"

She shrugged, but a dancing light sparkled in her eyes. "I learned the other night when you saved us all that a girl cannot have too many friends," she said softly. "Come, Johnny, let's tell Stephen that we're going to have one more passenger on our voyage."

Stephen was waiting on the quarterdeck when they reached the ship. From the expression on his face as she and Johnny mounted the companionway, Anemone knew she was in trouble. *What now?* she wondered, richly amused. Of course, they had gone two days without a disagreement, so she shouldn't be surprised that her volatile betrothed had found something to argue about, but at the moment she couldn't imagine what it could be. He said nothing to her as they reached the quarterdeck, and she regarded him with mock gravity.

"Good morning," she offered, trying not to laugh. He glowered at her. Then his gaze shifted to Johnny.

"What the hell are you doing here?"

"I invited him. We've called a truce," Anemone put in.

Stephen glanced from one to the other of them. "Have you now?" There was restrained anger in his voice that Anemone guessed had nothing to do with Johnny Tucker, but she was without a clue as to what had triggered it.

Johnny grinned. "It seems Anemone is far more understanding than you, old friend. She's not as thickheaded, either. And she's a helluva lot prettier—even when she's mad."

"She may be pretty, but she's damned unreliable," Stephen growled in response to this. He eyed Anemone with quiet fury.

"Do you have any idea how worried I was when I woke up this morning and didn't know where in hell you'd gone?"

So that was it. She opened her mouth to reply but he cut her off.

"Your father was kind enough to tell me a few moments ago that you were walking on the levee, but that's not the point. It isn't exactly the first time you've left this ship without a word to anyone, my pet."

"You were sleeping so soundly I didn't want to wake you," Anemone protested. She lifted her hand to his cheek. "Stephen, do stop being so foolish and..."

"Foolish?" Midnight blue eyes flamed dangerously in his bronzed face. "It was barely dawn, and you were strolling down the levee just as carefree as you please. The riverfront can be a dangerous place, Anemone. Do you think I want my future wife attacked by Tschoupitoulas Street ruffians?"

"From the account I heard of what happened in that underground dungeon the other night, my sympathies would go to the ruffians," Johnny put in, and Anemone giggled. Stephen glared at both of them.

"Stay out of this, Tuck. This is between my wife and me."

"Future wife," Anemone corrected. "Although if you're going to behave in such a tyrannical fashion after we're married, I may have to reconsider my acceptance of your proposal."

"Oh, you may?" An ominous quality entered Stephen's voice, but Anemone deliberately ignored it.

"Yes, for if we're going to continue to work together on assignments of joint interest to England and America, we're going to have to have a real partnership. How will I ever get to do anything truly intriguing and dangerous if you're going to worry about me all the time?"

"Not all the time," Stephen retorted. "Only when I wake up in the morning and you've vanished."

"Did you want me for something in particular?" Anemone teased, tilting her head back and regarding him provocatively from beneath her silky lashes. Johnny Tucker burst out laughing.

"Yes, and as a matter of fact, I still do." Stephen reached out in one swift motion and took hold of her, then before she realized what was happening, he tossed her over his shoulder as though she were a sack of potatoes. Anemone, hanging upside down, gave a screech.

"Stephen! Let me down! This is outrageous! Johnny, do something!"

Johnny Tucker lifted his hands, palms out in a gesture of helplessness. "I've interfered in your affairs once too often, Miss Carstairs." Merriment shone in his brown eyes.

She fumed and struggled as Stephen bore her down the companionway to the main deck, and then below to their cabin. As they passed the staring crew members, she felt her cheeks go scarlet and her rage mount. She *had* been teasing Stephen mercilessly but—he had no right to treat her this way! When he strode into the cabin and kicked the door shut behind him, she braced herself for battle. He plunked her down none too gently on his bunk.

Anemone sprang to her feet, shaking with indignation. Stephen crossed his arms before her.

"How dare you!" she cried, tossing her shawl into his face. "I have never been so humiliated in my life!"

"Next time, don't run out on me without a word." Oddly enough, his bad humor seemed to have dissipated. Calmly, he deposited the shawl over the back of a chair, then turned to her once more. "Now, let's see. Where had we left off? Before you departed so rudely, we were..."

"Asleep," she reminded him, backing away at the purposeful glint in his eyes.

"Yes, but asleep *together*," he commented, and seized her once more. "I think," he drawled, "the scene was something like this."

Anemone felt herself lifted in iron arms and carried again to the bunk. She stiffened, but this time, to her surprise, he set her down smoothly, her head upon the pillow. He held her still with his body, ignoring her protests. Ever so slowly, his fingers touched the peach ribbon in her hair and tugged it free. Silvery curls cascaded about her shoulders.

"Stephen," she began, fighting to retain her righteous indignation, but it was fast deserting her. As the pressure of his hard-muscled body molded to her soft curves, as his hand smoothed her hair across the pillow with aching gentleness, she felt a warmth springing within, ready to break free.

"What, my love?" Now his eyes caressed her face, and she saw tenderness and desire burning in their inky depths. A warm flush traveled up her throat and tinged her cheeks. Her breathing quickened as he rubbed his thumb along her lips and then followed the same path with his tongue. The weight and feel of him, along with his tantalizing scent and provocative touches, sent hot tingling shivers through her.

"You don't really want to fight me, do you, Anemone?"

His voice, that deep, gritty voice, caressed her so softly she moaned. She felt drugged, helpless to resist the emotions he set burning inside her. Stephen Burke—if you only knew your power over me, she thought sinkingly. Against her will, she responded to his gentle murmuring tone and seductive words. She tried to answer him tartly, but her own voice was a mere breathless whisper.

"You started it." She felt his muscles tauten as her lithe body moved beneath him. He was staring into her eyes, his own darkened with obvious desire. His firmly chiseled lips hovered only an inch above hers.

"Then I suppose it's up to me to finish it," he said huskily, and with exquisite slowness he brought his mouth down to capture hers.

It was a gentle kiss, deep and intoxicating. Anemone was gasping for breath by the time it was finished, but she was also clinging to him, wanting more. Her arms came tightly about his neck, holding him close to her as she reached up and pulled his head down to hers. She kissed him, cradling both hands to the sides of his face and holding him still as their mouths met and locked together, finding a fiery ecstasy that shot through them both. Anemone never knew how they managed to undress, for she didn't think their lips parted at all, but eventually she found herself lying naked with Stephen upon the bunk. The silk coverlet of midnight blue felt smooth and cool beneath her burning skin. Stephen's bronzed frame was poised above her, and she gazed at him through half-closed smoldering eyes.

"You're so splendid." She slid her fingertips across the crisp black hair of his chest. Bulging muscles rippled as he bent over her and touched his lips to hers very gently. "If only you weren't so arrogant and autocratic, my love."

"If only you weren't so stubborn and quick to doubt me, *my* love!" Laughter glinted in his eyes and touched his hard, sensual mouth. He surveyed her glistening, pearl-white body with slow intensity. His eyes seemed to scorch her upward-straining breasts and the lush curves of her hips. Anemone's already racing pulse skittered madly as she felt the heat of him intensify with his leisurely appraisal. Then his hands, those strong, skilled hands, touched her and she trembled. They wandered up her silken thighs and across her abdomen and roamed purposefully to her breasts, cupping them. Her nipples hardened in his palms. "I love you, my impudent, enchanting Anemone. I love your temptress body, your gamine's face, your lovely little dusting of freckles across that adorable nose, your eyes the color of smoke, and your brave, indomitable soul." He kissed her quickly, his tongue slipping inside her mouth. Then he drew back and frowned. "But I do not love waking up and finding you gone!"

An ache was growing deep inside her. She drew him down, tangling her hands in the thick silk of his hair. "Never again, my love. I promise."

His need was as urgent as hers. Desire's flames engulfed them, and they gave themselves up to the inferno. It sucked them into a searing, wild world, consumed them, and left them entwined exhausted in each other's arms.

Later, Anemone rested with her head against Stephen's shoulder. He inhaled the sweet scent of her hair. Suddenly, they felt the ship rock and sway. A steady rolling motion took over, and Anemone sat up, glancing at Stephen in surprise.

"We're sailing?"

"I left orders with William to set sail an hour before noon. We are now on our way to Philadelphia."

"Oh." She bit her lip, then asked the question that had been troubling her mind. "Will they like me, do you think? Your family? I've heard so much about the Burkes."

"Yes, I suppose you have." He grinned. "They're pretty formidable, all right, but don't worry. I won't let them eat you alive." Then he saw the worried look in her eyes, and his chest shook with laughter. Reaching out an arm, he pulled her down beside him once more.

"My sisters will adore you. My Aunt Jenny and Uncle Adam will spoil you, and my mother and father will be in awe of the woman who finally brought their rakish son to heel. Does that answer your question?"

"Yes." She laughed softly, feeling infinitely better all of a sudden. She pressed her lips against his shoulder. "*Have* I brought you to heel, Stephen?"

"Unquestionably."

"Good. Now you may kiss me again."

His lazy grin made her heart hammer as he suddenly yanked her up and across his chest, so that she was lying full upon his muscled body. "That, my love, will be a great pleasure," he drawled, and that was the last thing either of them said for a very long time.

They had smooth sailing all the way to Philadelphia. Anemone felt wedded to him already, for he was her partner in every way, her friend, her lover, her strength and her delight. Yet on the day that she and Stephen took their solemn vow before a grand assemblage of Philadelphia society, the beauty and grandeur of the occasion filled her with awe. The momentous importance of the moment filled her mind and heart. In her dress of shimmering white satin, crowned by a veil of handmade lace adorned with pearls, she moved forward to meet her love. There was a wreath of jasmine in her hair, and her eyes sparkled as they met Stephen's loving gaze. The ceremony brought tears of happiness to both their eyes as it united them through vows and prayer.

With her own father beaming at them from the front pew, and Elizabeth and Alexander Burke kissing her cheek and welcoming her with dazzling warmth to the folds of their family, and Stephen's sisters exclaiming over her gown and her hair and her flowers and her jewels, Anemone felt that her heart would burst with joy. Later, when she danced with Stephen at the ball in his parents' home, whirling and whirling in his arms through the candlelit hall, she knew that happiness had come to her like a moonbeam in the night, touching her with that luminous glow that imparts its own special magic. And she knew that the love between them would last as long as the stars shone in the evening skies, and as long as the moon sailed on its endless journey through velvet nights.